Strange Forces

"The stranger," the High Priest said in a lowered voice, "was a schell with a name. He called himself Sportus, and claimed to have been sent by your aunt. He asked to be alone with the King, and the King agreed. Some minutes later, the King emerged alone, very much agitated."

"What did the schell want?" Careev asked.

"I'm afraid your father refused to tell me. He did say, however, that the schell transformed himself from a man into a woman in front of his eyes as a kind of demonstration."

"Is that possible?"

"It's possible this schell was able to impose a powerful delusion upon the King. Which is why I wanted to speak to you now. When you left with your sister, Lady, did she give any sign that *she* might know anything about the stranger?"

Books by Mike Conner

GROUPMIND
EYE OF THE SUN

MIKE CONNER

EYE OF THE SUN

ACE BOOKS, NEW YORK

This book is an Ace original edition,
and has never been previously published.

EYE OF THE SUN

An Ace Book/published by arrangement with
the author

PRINTING HISTORY
Ace edition/April 1988

ISBN: 0-441-22388-5

Ace Books are published by The Berkley Publishing Group,
200 Madison Avenue, New York, New York 10016.
The name "Ace" and the "A" logo
are trademarks belonging to
Charter Communications, Inc.
PRINTED IN THE UNITED STATES OF AMERICA

10 9 8 7 6 5 4 3 2 1

This book is for Patricia Spiglanin

ONE

THE GIRL LEANED BACK against a cushion in the bow of the skiff with her arm draped over the gunwale. She held her hand flat in the water like a rudder as her father rowed against the river current, turning her wrist to the rhythm of his strokes and comparing the eddies she made with those the oars made as the skiff left them behind. It was midsummer, and though it was still early, the day was already hot and muggy, and the girl could hear cicadas buzzing in the cottonwood trees shading the banks close to the weir. Once or twice the girl, whose name was Maud, lifted the brim of her woven-straw hat to blow strands of her fine hair away from her forehead. Other than that, she made no sound until her father skulled the oars to bring the skiff around so that the current could gently back it against the weir.

"Grab that post," her father said. Maud shook water from her fingers and did as he asked.

"I don't see the other boat, Poppa."

Her father stood up, spreading his legs to keep the flat-bottomed skiff steady. He wore cut-off trousers and no shoes, and the muscles of his heavy calves tensed and relaxed as river waves gently rocked the boat. In spite of the fierce sun he was hatless, and the skin of his bald head was the color of a ripe peach. Scowling, he peered over the weir across the backwater where he had intended to fish and saw that his daughter was correct.

"You couldn't see that from where you're sitting," he said. "How did you know it was gone?"

"Poachers have it," Maud replied absently.

"Really."

"They painted it green, Poppa, and they keep it in the harbor with the other boats."

Her father cursed loudly. "You'll show me where!"

Maud said nothing. Her father knew that sometimes she dressed in old clothes and went down to Wharvesunder to play with children who lived in the hutches that were suspended from the bottoms of the harbor piers. She was observant, and would not have missed the boat if she had seen it hauled in. More than likely, she knew who the culprits were. The King felt his anger rising.

"Look. That boat had my mark on it. The people who stole it should be punished."

"Would you kill them, Poppa?"

"I would make an example of them. People in the city would see the results of the crime. They have to see that. In the end they feel much better when they know what's going to happen to them. You understand, don't you? If you were Queen, and it was your boat that was stolen by poachers, you'd have to do the same thing."

"You said we were going fishing," Maud said. "You said we were going to forget about Kings and Queens for the whole morning." She looped some line around the post, pulled it into a half-hitch and climbed out onto the top of the weir. Maud was seven years old, already tall, with slender legs that were long and tanned where they showed beneath the hem of her tunic. She looked down at her father, staring at him with sea-green eyes that had the lustre of pearls.

"Well?" she demanded.

"I'm thinking."

"Why don't you pull the boat up and over this thing?"

The King laughed and shook his head. "Twenty years ago, maybe. Not now." The sun was getting to his head a little, and it was hard to look up at her. He knew she wanted him to prove something, but he could not haul the boat over the weir, and that was that.

"We could try our luck from shore," he said. "There's a nice snag near that point that I would have tried with the boat anyway. The fish won't care whether we're casting from shore or not."

Maud shrugged her shoulders, then stepped back into the skiff to gather the long bamboo poles and their tackle box. She hoisted the poles on her shoulder and started off, leaving her father to take the creel and the net, and the hamper with their lunch. She walked quickly, leaving footprints in the mud that half-filled with water by the time the King reached them.

If I had any guts at all, her father thought, *I'd strangle her now.*

The point they walked to was a boot-shaped hump of crumbling green stone screened by clumps of pampas grass and shaded by a pair of ash trees whose leaves had curled over in the heat. The King cleared away driftwood and some broken glass from a wide ledge just above the water, then went to work setting up the lines with sinkers and cork bobbers from the tackle box, baiting the hooks with strips of pork rind from a jar. He also dipped a towel into the water, wrung it out, and put it over his head with a billed cap on top to hold it in place. When he was finished, he gave Maud her pole.

"The snag's right there," he said, pointing to a spot where the waves were broken up. "Try a little to the left or to the right."

They cast their lines. The King found a wide crack in the serpentine behind the ledge and jammed the butt of his pole into it. Maud did the same; then, while she opened the hamper and rooted through the food, the King got out his gold cigarette case and his lighter.

Maud looked up.

"Here." He handed over the lighter, a clever device made up of a gas-filled metal lozenge sparked by a flintwheel. To make it work, she had to press the lever that turned the flintwheel with both thumbs. After several attempts, she got it going and lifted the flame toward her father. She smiled. Among the things she had inherited from her father was his love of gadgets.

"Watch the beard, kiddo," he said. Around the bend of the river, back toward Almheraz, a steam barge blasted its horn three times. He said, "You want to eat something?"

"I'm not very hungry, Poppa."

"No?" He bit into his sandwich.

After a moment's silence, Maud said, "Will it be a boy?"

"Who knows?" The king pulled his pole out of the rock, checked his hook and recast his line.

"Auntie did a test. She strung a silver ring on a thread and held it up over Momma's tummy. It went round in a circle. She said that meant it was a girl."

Maud had been working the lighter while she spoke, and now held it so she had to look through the flame to see him.

"Well. Your auntie's been wrong a few times."

"First you had Careev," she said, meaning her younger sister, who had stayed at the palace. "Now you want another girl. What was wrong with me? I want to be Queen. Now Careev's gonna be Queen, except now you're having another baby. What's wrong with us?"

"We've had this talk before," the King said. "Your mother and I don't decide who's Queen. Fate does. What we do think about is the good of the Realm. What if something happened to Careev? What if you fell off that rock and hit your head and drowned? We'd have no heir. Having another child is insurance. We had the same thing in mind when we had your sister."

"I think this one is going to be a boy." Maud's eyes were vacant, cold. "He had a girl's soul for a while, but I chased it off."

"Oh? And how do you chase off souls?"

"I used to sneak into Momma's room while she was napping, and put my head down on her tummy and close my eyes so tight that I could almost see inside her. I could feel its little soul there, wrapped tight around its heart. It knew I was there. It knew I was supposed to be Queen. It didn't want to go, but I made it go.''

The King looked at her and blew smoke over her head. "You've been talking too much to that damned aunt of yours."

Maud flicked the lighter, blew out the flame, and did it again. Then she looked up.

"I want it to die."

Now, the King thought, *she's certainly given me provocation.* He wished this could be done quickly, and without pain for her, but he was conscious of how much force a killing blow would take—of having to set his feet and follow through with his shoulders. It made him hesitate. When he swung, she was ready for it, looking deep into his eyes.

Cyre pulled his punch and struck her hand instead of her neck, sending his lighter skipping across the water. Maud gasped. Muffled explosions echoed across the water.

"Rockets," she said coolly. "Three rockets. It's a boy."

The King felt old and tired. "That's my son," he whispered. "Don't you ever forget that. *My* son."

"Your bobber's down," Maud said after a moment. "You'd better take your line, if you don't want to lose your tackle."

Trembling with anger and frustration at his loss of nerve, her father yanked his pole out of the rock.

The line came back empty.

TWO

THE CITY OF ALMHERAZ was built on a spade-shaped gouge cut
into the bluffs along the north bank of the Tumulos River. In
ancient times, this spade had marked the confluence of the
Tumulos with another river, the Kir, which flowed south
from its icy source in the mountain ranges to the north. Legend
had it that a great earthquake had swallowed up the Kir and
that it now took an underground course to the sea. Whether
that was true or not, its former mouth remained, and made a
perfect site for farms and scattered villages that would later be
consolidated into the capital of the realm.

To the east, the city was bounded by point Draco, where
the bluffs reached the water again. To the west, rose a
flat-topped promontory, which served as a site for a succession of ancient fortresses, the last of which was the Citadel
with its walls of blue tile. These walls were not in good
repair; huge patches of the tiles had spalled off, littering the
slopes below with shards that glittered on the scrubby cliffside
between the palace and the houses of the Old Town.

It was toward this promontory that the King and his daughter traveled just after noon. The sun was almost directly overhead, and though shrouded as usual by the almond-shaped veil of streaming gases that kept its face hidden ten months of the year, it could be felt and seen as a faint disk, pulsing like a brass gong. Because of the heat, the streets of the city were mainly deserted. Later, when the sun grew more moderate, celebrating would begin. Even though the baby was only a boy, surely the King would declare a holiday!

In truth, King Cyre did not feel much like declaring a holiday. Maud had maintained an accusatory silence the whole way home, and Cyre found himself feeling guilty about what he had planned to do. He watched her as she finished paring an apple with the little knife she carried. Their eyes met, and it was the King who looked away.

They passed among the end of the wharves, and suddenly Maud was moving, grabbing one of the fishing poles and the towel that Cyre had used to cool his head, jabbing it onto the hook and waving it back and forth in the air like a flag. This signal prompted loud cheers, pot-banging, and a fusillade of firecrackers from under the wharves. There, in the deep-green shadows, net catwalks sagged with dozens of wide-eyed Wharvesunder folk, waving their pale arms to greet the Princess. *They know her too well*, the King thought, making a note to himself to pursue the matter of the stolen boat as soon as the commotion about the baby died down.

Cyre brought the skiff into the quay. Four schells dressed in the King's livery—gold tunics crossed with the red bar of the Panault family—waited on the dock. They wore no hats against the sun, and though the air shimmered with heat, they looked as cool as if they were standing on the porch of the Winter Palace in February. One of them tied up the skiff; one attended the Princess, extending a gloved hand to help her out of the boat, while the other two stepped up to the King to await his orders.

"What's the word?" Cyre asked.

The schell to whom he had directed the question closed his eyes and spoke in an eerie imitation of the Queen's voice: eerie because it was as tired and drained-sounding as a woman might be after a hard labor and delivery.

"He's a beautiful child, husband. He's well, and I will be well too with a little rest. Midwife wants me to sleep, but please come see us as soon as you've returned. We—"

Cyre waved his hand. Instantly, the schell became silent.

"That's enough. I'm going over to my barque to clean up. Escort the Princess into the palace and get this gear stowed away."

"Yes, Majesty."

"Maud? Come here."

Maud looked back.

"I'm sorry for what happened."

"Yes, Poppa."

"I didn't want to . . . do that. But I thought the child would be a girl. You'll understand someday."

She made no reply, and after a moment or two of waiting, the King motioned for the schell to take her to the quayside elevator and up to the palace.

Maud kept hold of the schell's hand, and they walked together through a tall arched doorway carved into the rock at the base of the cliff. Vestals guarding the entrance bowed as Maud walked between them. She paid no attention. The Vestals who served her mother were as silent and beautiful as the King's schells, but they made Maud uncomfortable. They were always looking at her. She always wondered why they looked at her so intently, when there was so much to see and do in the world!

It was cool inside the rock. Maud took off her sun-hat, wincing as the schell pulled open the grate, whose slides needed oiling and screeched loudly. They stepped inside; Maud pulled the lever that started the car, smiling to herself because the schell put his hand against the side of the car to keep his balance.

"You didn't want to fall, did you?" she said.

The schell said nothing. Schells could respond to questions, but they were like machines and had to be prepared to do so.

"Answer me," Maud said. "Were you afraid of hurting yourself?"

"No," came the flat-voiced reply.

"I think you were. Otherwise you would have let yourself fall."

"The King ordered me to escort you into the palace. Injury would have prevented me from doing that."

Maud got out her pocket knife, opened the blade, rubbing it across the front of her jacket. "This is really sharp," she said. "I have a stone and I whet the blade every morning as soon as I get up." The knife blade glinted in the light from the lamp in the car. "Suppose I told you to stand still and put your arms over your head."

The schell said nothing. He was a particularly handsome one, with curly, straw-colored hair, straight teeth, a strong jaw.

"Go on. Do what I said."

Slowly, the schell lifted his arms. He was tall, and his fingertips touched the ceiling of the car.

"You know what a knife can do?"

"Yes."

"And you can feel me doing this—" Maud touched the knife-point gently against his tunic. "If I pushed it in, what would you do? Aren't you just a little bit afraid that I might gut you?"

Just then the elevator stopped. Someone outside yanked the door open, too quickly for Maud to react and put the knife away.

"How charming it is to see children at play," came the pleasant voice of the woman who had opened the door.

"Auntie!" Maud squeaked. Auntie was Sheeme, the Queen's elder sister and Warden of the Queen's Preserve. She was a tall, rangy woman with a broad, sensuous face, coppery skin, and deep brown eyes. She dressed in soft boots, dusty quilted trousers decorated at her thighs and ankles with bundles of feathers taken from the hawks she raised, yellow leather gauntlets, and a blue tunic with padded shoulders and a high collar. Maud ran from the car and hugged her.

"You were saying?"

"N-nothing, Auntie. I was only—"

"Curious? Well, I am too. Let's see."

Maud folded the blade of the knife back into its hasp with her palm and hurriedly put it into her pocket. The schell stayed where it was. Sheeme smiled and pulled a dagger from a beaded sheath on her hip. "This is a much better blade for that kind of work. You'll find it's not difficult to do, once your mind is made up."

Maud looked back at the cruel-looking blade, and the bone hilt, worn white and smooth from many years' use. She swallowed. Killing the schell had fascinated her when it was her idea, but not now.

"Poppa would be furious."

"Ah, Poppa. We wouldn't want that, would we?" Sheeme said, snapping the dagger back into its sheath. "Some other time. I've really been waiting here for you because there's something I want to talk to you about. Where were you going?"

"To have a bath, and change, and go up to see Mummy and the baby."

"Good. Please come to my rooms now? I promise I won't keep you long."

"All right."

Sheeme touched her hair, started off with her, then stopped. The schell was still in the elevator with its hands in the air.

"I suppose you may go," she said to the schell. "But first thank the Princess for sparing your life."

"Thank you, Lady," the schell droned.

"You see what that's worth," Scheeme laughed, as the elevator door closed.

Since Sheeme was the Queen's sister, and Warden of the coastal forest lands of the Queen's Preserve, apartments were maintained for her in the palace. Maud could not remember her aunt having ever used them before, and in spite of the fact that the Princess had thoroughly explored most of the galleries, ramps and chambers that honeycombed the rock beneath the Citadel, Sheeme quickly led her into a passageway she had never seen. Phosphor-torches cast ghastly light across the worn floor and smoke-stained walls; there were frescoes on the ceiling, faded and also smudged with smoke. The paintings were divided into panels bordered by chains of stylized mushrooms and intertwined leaves. One of them showed three wild-eyed women in flowing gowns, graceful and lithe in spite of the archaic rendering, dancing before the horns of a stout bull.

The passage descended a little, and the air grew musty and cold. Here and there water dripped from needle-sharp stalactites where wall and ceiling met. Finally, at what seemed to be a cul-de-sac, Sheeme pressed against the wall and a doorpanel swung open with a faint squeaking sound.

Inside, Maud smelled pine, a hint of jasmine or lavender and a sour smell, like ammonia. The sills of the narrow windows high on one wall were crowded with pots of evergreen branches, garlands of flowers. Pine needles littered the floor. In the far corner of the room a young man with a wispy beard worked on the trigger mechanism of a crossbow with a screwdriver. He looked up briefly from his work when aunt and niece entered the room.

"As you can see, I've brought some of the Preserve with me," Sheeme said. "It's too hot and stifling in Almheraz. I've never liked it, and when business forces me to come here I leave the instant I can. Come into my room. I've got some sweets I think you'll be very fond of."

Sheeme's room was dark, but something made Maud tense, just before a loud screech sounded next to her ear. She jumped back. Then her aunt got a torch going, and Maud saw a tiny, hooded hawk on a perch next to the door. It was no bigger than a robin, and whipped its stingerlike tail angrily back and forth. With its bone-colored barb, hooked like the claws of a cat and unsheathed, the hawk was menacing in spite of its size.

"Shhhh!" Sheeme said, chuckling. "You're both afraid. Shhhh now!"

She reached over, unclipped a toggle from the perch, hooked it onto a metal ring at the end of her left gauntlet. All the while she continued to speak softly to the bird, stroking its brown and yellow feathers with the back of her free hand.

"There, my girl. This is a real Princess you're screaming at. Someday you'll know her, Princess to Princess." To Maud she said, "Will you pet her a little?"

Maud eyed the tail.

"She was frightened, and because she is young she gave her venom when there was no certainty of striking either prey

or an enemy. Soon she will know when and how to strike, but
for now her sac is empty. She can't hurt you.'' Sheeme held
her up on the gauntlet. Tentatively, Maud reached out and
touched the bird's soft chamois hood. The hawk tensed, then
suddenly pecked at one of the tiny silver bells dangling from
Sheeme's ears.

"Isn't she fine! This is Yundai, one of Fantil's daughters,
the first fledgling to be born alive from her in twenty-three
years. You remember Fantil, don't you?''

Maud nodded. When she was four, the Queen had taken
her to the preserve for a visit. She could still recall how the
deep stillness of the forest had frightened her, and how Fantil
had appeared, soaring along the red bluffs, her twenty-foot
wings stretched against the fading violet of the Veil. Fantil
had harvested many souls with her barb and venom. She was
an ancient bird, bred for war, according to legend, in the time
before the Fall.

"She's young yet, and so I had to bring her," Sheeme
said, returning the bird to its perch. "The young need training. The young need to know their place in the world." She
pulled over a chair. "Sit down, please.''

"Yes, Auntie.''

"Here's that sweet I promised. Let it dissolve on your
tongue. What I have to say won't take any longer than that.''

The candy was wrapped in a twist of waxed paper. Maud
peeled it off, and put it into her mouth. The taste was resiny,
bitter at first, but as it began to melt a warm, sweet flavor
spread through her mouth and into her throat. It was faintly
numbing, and it took her breath away a little.

"You went fishing with the King this morning," she began, sitting on the edge of the cot, leaning forward so that her
face was close to Maud's. "I knew that it was on his mind to
kill you.''

"That's not true!" What her aunt said frightened her and
made her angry.

"Don't forget, child, that I'm an older sister too, and
before your mother was born, your grandfather took me out
on the river with the very same thing in mind. But he was
afraid, like Poppa was. He was a much weaker man than your
poppa, but it was the same fear.''

"What fear?" Maud asked.

"What everyone properly fears, Maud. Death." She pulled her gauntlets off slowly. "A King gets to be a desperate creature when his wife gets old. He reigns only as long as she lives. He might be healthy and strong, like Poppa, and an excellent ruler, like Poppa. But the source of his power is the Queen, and when she's gone, his power is gone. How does that candy taste, Maud? Do you like it?"

Maud nodded. The taste and perfume of the candy blossomed, filling the inside of her head with a pleasant warmth. She watched the bells of her aunt's ears jingle as she spoke.

"Now what Poppa always hopes, when a Queen bears a daughter, is that the daughter will be weak. Weak enough to marry him and allow him to rule again. If a Queen bears a strong daughter who is quick and strong-souled, Poppa will press her to bear another child. That is why I am not Queen now. And that is why you have a younger sister who will be Queen instead of you.

"That is nothing new. Many older sisters have been killed since the time of the Fall. What is new is that your poppa wants more than a weak Queen. Poppa wants his son to rule after he is gone."

Sheeme leaned forward. "Your poppa is very strong. When I saw you go out on the river this morning I wondered to myself whether I would ever see you again." Maud's head suddenly felt very heavy. She felt her aunt's fingers combing through her hair. Her mouth was dry, and a bit of undissolved candy was stuck to the middle of her tongue. Sheeme's voice hardened.

"The King wants a revolution, and that little baby is his greatest weapon. But you can stop him."

"He said. . . ."

"Said what?" The fingers tightened in Maud's hair.

"That the baby was his son. That I better remember it, too."

"If he were strong enough to kill you he would have done it this morning. You are the only person in Almheraz greater than he is! Even I, with all my arts and the power of all the mothers in our family behind me, am only his match. He has formidable soul and immense will, but he is weak where you are concerned because you have been formed in his image and he loves you!

"Don't let love make you weak, Maud. be loyal to your kind! There never can be peace between women and men. One must serve the other, and in our age it is the men who serve, and the men who always shall serve! Poppa would kill you if he could, but he failed. You must punish him. You must do worse than kill him. You must destroy his plans and put him in his place! Say you will, child!"

"Yes . . . Auntie" Her voice sounded far away to her.

"Good." Sheeme opened her fist, smoothing Maud's hair before getting up and fetching a cloth bag from the other side of the room. She sat down on the bed again, opened the bag, pulled out a narrow glass tube that was stoppered with a cork. Inside it was a twig that had a daub of gray mud stuck to it. Sheeme flicked the glass with her finger, and a pair of yellow wasps appeared, beating their wings and falling to the bottom of the tube. The insects cocked their heads from side to side, trying to get their bearings. After Sheeme held the tube steady a moment, the wasps climbed back inside the mud-daub.

"The Queen's child is my kin," Sheeme said softly, "and so I made these. Their venom gives a soul power to liberate itself. Sweetly. You must believe that I honor your brother by choosing such a death for him. You know that I could have chosen a hundred others ways to do this! Be stronger than your poppa, Maud. Do what must be done!"

"How . . ."

"Take the cork out and shake the tube into the baby's swaddling. Then be sure to take the tube and cork away with you. The insects know what they must do, and they will sting the baby where no one will see the mark. Then he will go to sleep, and you will have acted like a Queen. Now take this, put it into your pocket."

"Yes, Auntie."

Sheeme helped her to put the tube in her pocket. Then she kissed the side of Maud's mouth.

"Good, beautiful girl. I am going to teach you what I know. Someday, you and I will be one soul, one mind. Now go. Bathe and put on your best dress. Your mother has just given birth, and it is your duty to honor her for that. Don't worry about Poppa. He can't touch you. No one can!''

As Sheeme helped guide Maud toward the door, the bird slid across her perch, and gave an inquisitive whistle. Sheeme clucked her tongue gently. Then she took Maud into the other room and spoke to the forester.

"Take her back upstairs. Then come see me in my room."

"Yes, Mother," the forester said without much enthusiasm.

Stupid boy, Sheeme thought as they left her. There had to be a better way than relying on flesh and blood. If only schells could be relied upon to use brains, and will. Well, someday, if she had the time, she would make such a creature to do what she needed to have done. Until then . . .

Well, one made do with what one had.

THREE

"GOODNESS, LADY, where have you been?"

Nana Mara stood at the door to Maud's room with her hands on her hips. She tried to sound stern, but she was more worried. "They told me your father brought you back more than a half-hour ago."

"I was sleepy, Nana," Maud said. "I took a nap. Sorry."

"And I'm sorry to see you looking this way, on such a happy day." Nana pulled her into the bathroom. "Strip off those rags while I draw your bath! Your sister's been ready an hour."

Maud sat down on a chair while Nana Mara opened the faucets, and stared at the steam that filled the room.

"It was really hot on the river today," Maud said, above the sound of the tub filling. "Then we got to the weir, and Poppa's other boat was gone."

"That put his ears back, I'll bet!"

"I told him I knew who took it."

Nana helped Maud get up, and out of her tunic. "Ach

16

you're a willful child, Lady!'' She took a wooden box of bath-beads from a shelf, spooned some into the tub and stirred it with her hand until bubbles began to mound up under the spigot. ''There. Soak that silly head of yours!''

Maud tested the water with her toe, grimaced, then stepped in. Nana closed the taps.

''He said he wanted to kill me,'' Maud said.

''Glory! You're full of stories today! I suppose you think your poor poppa's ready to draw and quarter you to keep you from smothering the babe. Who told you such nonsense? Tell me, so they can feel the back of my hand!''

''Nobody told me,'' Maud said desolately. Her brows knit together, as though she was trying to remember something. ''It wasn't anyone.''

Nana brought in a fresh towel, then knelt by the tub. ''Baby, if anyone had to worry, it was Careev, and she hasn't given it a thought.''

''She's only four years old. She can't think.''

''You've just never got used to being older sister, have you? Lady Maud, you've just got to realize what an important job you've got, Lord willing. You might still be Queen one day, in the event of a catastrophe. I know about that right enough! Why, I lost my youngest the very year you were born. She had the grippe, but the physician was treating it with tea he brewed from the mold on bread, and . . .''

Nana dabbed at the corner of her eye with the towel. ''Adon took her soul, just like that. It was Fate, so I accepted it, and thought of the good. I still had one daughter. And soon, your family brought me into this house to take care of you and your sister. That wouldn't have happened if I'd let the sadness take hold of me. Now I'm happy for the way things turned out. And, though it's hard for you, Lady, one day soon you'll see how right I am!''

Mara stood up, reaching for Maud's jacket.

''Leave that alone!'' Maud snapped.

''It needs washing, Lady,'' Nana said, voice hurt.

''Just let it—and let me—alone for a while.'' In spite of the warm water, she was shivering under the suds. ''Please. I want to be by myself for a little while. I'll be all right. I promise.''

"You don't look so right to me now, young Lady—"

"Just do as I say!"

"Yes, Lady," Nana replied coldly. "But remember that it's your mother waiting for you upstairs." With that she left, closing the door behind her.

Maud cupped her hands, molding shapes in the bubbles. Not so long ago she had loved to make bubble-boats, blowing them down channels she cleared with her knees, imagining she was the captain of a barge plying the coastal towns along the Crescent Sea. She was surrounded by pearls, and mounds of iridescent opals. Now, however, the game did not interest her. She got out of the tub, wrapped herself in the towel, and took Sheeme's tube out of the pocket of her jacket.

She shook it; one of the wasps crawled out of its nest, looking at her curiously. *I should take out the cork,* she thought. *Let it sting me, put my soul to sleep. Nana could find me dead in the bath, and she'd scream, but then she'd tell herself it was meant to be. At least Poppa would be happy, and Mamma, and Carry. . . .*

She touched the cork, and remembered the flash of silver earrings, and the sound of her aunt's beautiful voice, the taste of candy on her tongue. The wasp went back inside the daub of mud. Maud let the towel drop to the floor and put on her robe. The tube was inside her pocket as she went to get dressed.

"Act like a Queen," her aunt had said.

"Act like a Queen. . . ."

FOUR

THE KING STOOD in the shade of the pomegranate tree on the terrace outside the Queen's apartment. He took a cigarette out of his case, stuck it into the corner of his mouth, and then remembered that he had slapped his lighter into the river. He went back inside to the sitting room, and walked up to the Vestal who stood at stiff attention to the left of the cracked floor-to-ceiling mirror on the west wall.

"Got a light?" Cyre asked.

The Vestal did not reply. Vestals attached to the Queen's service in the palace were not pledged to silence, however, and the King frowned.

"Move that thing around little," he said, eyeing the plume-topped staff she held. "It's hotter than hell in here."

Just then his youngest daughter, Careev, pushed the toy train she had been playing with off its circular track. "Wham!" she cried timidly, looking at Cyre with big, expectant eyes.

"Hey, what did I tell you. You can't push 'em that hard or

they break." He knelt to put the train back together. "Listen to me now."

Careev giggled, and slapped at the car so it rushed three-quarters of the way around the track and derailed again. Cyre swore under his breath.

"Oh, Poppa, I don't know why you bother. She does it on purpose." Maud had come in, and had been watching from across the room. She wore a yellow gown—yellow being the color of a second Princess—sandals, and a black pillbox headdress hung with beads that covered her hair and made her look much older than she was.

"Maud!" Careev cried, running to her. Maud slipped out of her embrace.

"Sorry I'm so late, Poppa," Maud said.

"Well, she's been asking."

"Okay, so I'm here now."

"Csreev, leave your sister alone. You've got to promise to be quiet or you can't go in to see the baby. Mummy's very tired."

Careev nodded, and the King took her hand. Maud came with them, looking serious and pale.

"Who put all that stuff on your eyes?" the King added.

"I did."

"That's not how a little girl ought to look. At least, not in this part of the house. Nana let you upstairs looking this way?"

"She didn't see me. She was upset about something. I'll wash it off if you want."

"Later. Let's go see your mother."

Vestals opened the door and let the family through. It was stuffy inside the bedroom and so dark that Maud could hardly see her mother's bed. The mural she had always been fond of, porpoises dancing on iridescent waves that glowed and moved, had been switched off. Her mother's bed looked like a slab of black marble in the twilight filtering through the heavy curtains.

Midwife came out of the bathroom. She had recently given birth to a daughter of her own, and looked tired.

"Princess," she whispered, curtseying to Maud and Careev. "Your Majesty. Congratulations."

"Thank you." Cyre remembered the unlighted cigarette dangling from his lip and hastily jammed it into his shirt pocket.

"The birth went beautifully. I've given her something to help her relax, though, and she may be a little groggy. Now, if you don't mind, I'm going to see if I can squeeze a cup of tea and a biscuit or two from the kitchen. I'll be back in a few minutes."

Smiling, Midwife left the room. The King and his children stayed where they were; finally it was Careev who ran to the Queen's bedside.

Queen Gormayne lifted her head a little and smiled at her daughter. She was broad-faced, like her sister Sheeme, though finer-boned and not so tall. Her features were pleasant and interesting, and her clear blue eyes sparkled as she lifted her head from her pillows. Her arms were clasped gently around a tiny bundle snuggled to her side. The King went over to her and quickly kissed her on the forehead.

"Hello, dear," he said. "I understand you've done very well. Oh! Look at you." Cyre touched the bundle with one of his thick, stubby fingers. "Look at all that hair! Hello, there. Do you know your poppa? Yes! I'm your poppa."

Careev ran around to the other side of the bed. There, she stared at her baby brother as if she'd discovered him alive in a pile of toys in the playroom.

"Maud?" the Queen asked.

"Yes, Mummy. I'm here." It seemed she had never seen her mother look so beautiful. She felt sick to her stomach suddenly, and wanted to run away.

"Come see me."

Maud hesitated at the edge of the bed, until the Queen reached out and gently pulled her close.

"Shhh," she said. "Don't say anything." Maud could feel her mother's heart beating, hear the baby's gentle breathing next to her ear. Sudden tears burned in her eyes. Why did things have to be so hard?

Her mother said, "Two nights ago, before all this started, I couldn't sleep, so I went out walking in the gardens by the wall. I've always gone there when I wasn't feeling right, even at your age, darling.

"Well, there I was, strolling as best I could on the part of the path where the cycads grow. I was carrying the child very low, it was hard for me to breathe, so I sat down. Just as I did, the most amazing swarm of fireflies rose from the bushes right in front of my face.

"They danced for me! All the colors: blue and red and gold, just like little jewels. I thought to myself, these are the souls of unborn children, and here I was, with a child of my own about to be born, watching them dance in my own garden.

"Then I thought about how most of them had been here before, and how hard life is, how full of sadness, and yet here they were, wanting to come back, rejoicing in their chance!"

The Queen sighed. "Do you know, when Midwife wrapped him up and put him on my stomach, he opened his eyes! Oh, Maud, how I wish you could have seen. How I want you to love your baby brother!"

The Queen's eyelids fluttered. She sighed again, and seemed to drift off to sleep.

"You should listen to her," Cyre said. He reached over Maud's shoulders and gently picked up the baby, holding it straight-armed. "Here. I'm not much good at this."

Maud saw how his face was flushed with pride. *He looks as if he's won a race*, she thought. *Maybe Auntie was right about what he wanted. . . .*

She took the baby from him. He had a red face and a tiny, perfect nose.

"We'd better go," Cyre said. "We can come back later when your mother's had some rest."

"I'd like to rock him for a while," Maud said. "I'll stay until Midwife comes back."

The King gave her a hard look.

"If you don't trust me, Poppa, then stay. I just want to rock him."

"All right. Come on, Careev." The King took Careev's hand and left the room. Maud sat down in the Queen's big bentwood rocker. She put her feet together and pushed off easily, trying not to think. The baby in her arms wasn't moving, and, bundled up as it was, didn't even feel warm. Maud didn't look at it. Suddenly she felt contempt for her

father and what he wanted to do, and contempt for her
mother, for going along with him. Do your duty, was what
Auntie had told her. All right, then!

She took off the beaded headdress, turned it over on her
lap. The tube with the wasps in it was inside. Both insects
buzzed against the glass, as though they knew how close they
were to their intended victim. Maud started to pull the cork
away, then became aware of someone watching her. She
looked up and saw Careev's fair, wide-eyed face.

"Get out of here!"

"Uh-uh."

"You see these? One of them's for you, unless you leave
me alone!"

Careev grabbed at the tube. Maud snatched it back, jostling the baby as she did. He stirred; Maud was looking right
at him when he opened his eyes.

It took her breath away. His eyes were blue and calm and
innocent, but there was something about them. *He knows me!*
Maud thought in horror. *He knows what I want to do!*

"Here," she said to Careev, sliding over on the chair so
that the baby half-rolled onto the seat cushion. "Watch him."

"Where are you going?"

"Never mind." She ran to the window, pulled the curtain
aside, intending to throw the tube over the terrace wall. But
suddenly Careev came up from behind, jostling her hand. The
tube fell to the floor and shattered.

"Idiot!" Maud hissed, clouting her head. One of the wasps
flew past her out the window. The other circled around the
room. Maud watched in horror as it lighted on the bundle in
the rocker.

"Let's get out of here."

The baby gave a faint, strangled cry. Then it was still.

"Not that way," Warden Sheeme snapped. "How many
times do I have to tell you?"

The forester rolled up on one arm. His face showed neither
apprehension at her displeasure, nor, if Sheeme cared to
admit it to herself, interest in her nude, flushed body.

"This is how you said to do it last time."

"I didn't mean you should do it that way *every* time."

"You said it pleased you."

"Pleased me *then*!"

The boy sighed softly. "I'm sorry." He started to get out of the bed, but Sheeme grabbed his arm, sinking her nails into the skin of his arm.

"You're dull, boy, do you know that?"

She was angry now, but even that failed to get a response out of him. Here she was with a murder going, which never failed to heighten her excitement, and yet Fate had given her a dolt on whom such dark passions were completely wasted!

"But what should I expect? Your father was a bootmaker, and so was his father, and doubtless all the rest of you since the beginning of boots! Get out of my bed!" She pushed him away and he padded off into the other room, swathed in the peculiar dignity ignorance sometimes provides. A moment later, Sheeme heard his chair scrape across the floor. He was back at his work table, fletching his crossbow bolts.

She had just stretched and was punching the ends of her pillow when the yellow wasp flew in. It hovered, and she could see it was alert and full of energy. Sheeme drew in a breath, sat up. On the other side of the room, her hawk whistled softly, sensing the abrupt swing of her mistress' mood.

"You're alive," Sheeme whispered incredulously. The wasps could only live a short while after stinging something. They would never have had the strength to return here if they had killed the baby. Something had gone wrong. Somehow the girl had lost her nerve, but that was impossible; it had not been a question of nerve. Sheeme had given her a drug that sapped the will, and her instructions had been clear. Maud was her instrument, just like the dagger she carried in her belt!

"Come here, little one," Sheeme said, holding out her hand. The wasp lighted on it. She brought her hand close to her face, watching the insect tilt its head and groom its wings with its hind legs.

"We underestimated her, didn't we? My spell was strong, and she still broke free." A strange elation filled her as she considered what to do next. She could try to corrupt one of the Vestals or a schell, or commit the murder herself, but either way, Maud would know. That gave Maud power over her.

But it was useless to speculate, and besides, only one wasp had returned. She needed to know what had happened! There was a way, she realized suddenly. The means were in her hand, in the soul-liberating venom of this wasp.

Sheeme closed her hand lightly. She got out of the bed and went into the other room. There sat her forester with his broad back to her, brushing glue into a notch he'd cut into the shaft of a crossbow bolt. Sheeme put her free hand onto his shoulder.

"There you are," she said. "Fixing things." She rubbed the hand with the wasp in it into the top of his thick, curly hair, pressing down, feeling wings beating against her palm for an instant before she snatched it away. The forester grunted, slapped at his head. He started to turn, caught the look in her eyes and then the glue brush clattered onto the table as his body stiffened and trembled and the chair legs tapped against the floor. Sheeme grabbed the back of the chair, swiveling it around so she could look at his face. It was slack, the lips drawn back from the teeth. His breath released slowly into a faint mist that was acrid-smelling and clouded the air between their faces.

Her heart beat faster. She lifted her hands, touching the mist with her finger as though it were a bubble she was trying to hold in place without breaking. The mist was very cold. She had to fight to stay with it, but she knew her own soul was much stronger than this one.

"Stay." she said. "Stay and speak to me."

The mist seemed to press outward.

"I have his body. I'll cut it up, burn each piece, scatter each ash so that when the day comes for you to return from Heaven, Lord Adon himself could not help you find your substance. You'll be lost!"

The pressure lessened, and the mist stabilized.

"Show me the baby," Sheeme said.

The mist clarified into a vision of a room with a bed in it, and a mural of fish above the bed. A woman was bent over the bed, pushing at the body of an infant, trying to breathe life into it. Finally she stood up, and shook her head. The other woman lying in bed moaned wearily.

There, sister, Sheeme thought. *It's only a baby!*

She pulled her hand back to release the mist, but it stayed, rolling into itself. In a moment another room, small, with a high table in the middle of it, showed itself. A small man Sheeme recognized as the chief embalmer of Almheraz was busy opening a barrel with a knife. A small bundle lay on the table.

He turned suddenly, as though someone had called him from another room, then left. As soon as he had gone, someone else entered. Wearing a sun-cloak with its cowl pulled up, the figure could have been a man or a woman; whoever it was, the person snatched the bundle off the table and ran out just as the mist dissolved and the body of the forester slumped in the chair.

Someone would steal the baby's body from the embalmer! That meant the child was dead, that her work was done. But why would someone steal the body? She put her hands on the forester's face.

"Who took the body of the child?"

"I . . . do not know. . . ."

Yes, Sheeme thought, *Of course his soul would be as dull as he was.*

"I liberated you! You're outside of time now, and there are things I need to know. A baby died in the palace today."

"The Arcopatrinas of the Vestal Order," the voice said.

"Arcopatrinas? What are you talking about? This was the Queen's child. A boy!"

"Soulless. And then reborn."

"It can't be reborn!"

"It will be by the power of the Gatherer of Souls."

"By God," Sheeme exclaimed, "can't you speak plainly?"

"I *am* speaking plainly."

"What about the girl, then? The Princess Maud? How do I control her without destroying her will? Tell me how to do it!"

"Shape-changer. Soul-stealer. One not born of woman will control. . . ." Felex's body stiffened. It rose, straight-legged and tottering, turned, clamping its hands onto Sheeme's shoulders.

"You hold me here against my will!" the body said, pushing her back. "Take care to preserve your own soul!" The hands moved from her shoulders to her neck, closing. Sheeme clutched at the wrists, but she was caught in an ever-tightening vice. Bright pinpoints of light pricked her vision. . . .

"Go . . ." she managed to croak. "I release you!" As soon as she said this, the body collapsed. Sheeme gasped and let it drop. As it fell there was a sound like dry beans clattering onto the floor.

The dead wasp had come out of Felex's hair. Sheeme looked at it for a while. Then, slowly, a smile came to her face.

Not born of woman. Shape-changer. That's what the soul had told her. And that's just what she had been working on at home in the Preserve.

It would take time, but she would be patient. She would have Maud, and through Maud, the Realm!

FIVE

THE ROAD WAS HARD-BAKED and deeply rutted, and the bow-topped wagon bucked and rattled as its draught wolf, assisted by a little steam engine in the wagon, strained to get over the top of the last rise overlooking the town of Panault. It had been a hard morning's work to make the journey, for the road had cut through rolling country that was dotted with cone-shaped hills marking the sites of ancient volcanic vents. Now, at the top of the rise, the driver of the wagon could see Panault nestled against a gritty slope. The town looked as though it had been spewed out of the same vent as the volcanic ash, its buildings scattered around the base of the cone.

The old man driving the wagon tugged on the traces and set the brake before the wagon had stopped completely. His wolf looked back, twitching his tail and releasing puffs of cinder-colored dust that powdered his coat, but his annoyance was lost on the old man, who had already disappeared inside the wagon. When he came back, he had a tattered notebook that he began riffling through, while his wolf stared at him. Finally, he looked up.

"Sorry, Muff. Did I stop too fast? And you making such time on that terrible terrible track."

The wolf yawned, showing ivory fangs that were long as the old man's thumb. The man patted the wolf's haunches, and went back to flipping pages until he found what he wanted.

"Here's my dad's own entry for this town. Seat of the Duchy of Panault, about two thousand souls . . . mmm. Says the King lived here for a time as a boy. They mine cinders here. What else? Mercury, sulphur, lead, and tin. That accounts for the wonderful scenery, eh, boy!"

Well, the old man thought, *at least it isn't farming or herding here.* Weather had been very bad for farming in the Cordillera foothills this year and there really hadn't been agreeable weather and a good harvest for the past five. That made things difficult for travelers like the old man. Gentry— the traveler's term for town-folk—had little to trade in exchange for his services. Empty purses also, unfortunately, increased their natural suspicion toward strangers riding wolf-and-steam-drawn wagons.

"Well, boy, what do you say? Do we give it a try?"

The alternative was bringing the wagon back up that road. The wolf shook himself violently.

The old man laughed and he took up the traces again, working the throttle and the brake until the road leveled out closer to town. Then he stood up on the buckboard and got his pitch ready. He always made up the first few lines to match the spot he was in, and now, yanking the cord of the brass bell bolted above the wagon door, the little man puffed out his chest and sang, lustily rolling his *r's*:

> Kettles for soap-making,
> Bottles of lye,
> Boarrrr's-hair tooth brrrrushes
> Brrright Purrrple dye!

> I'm Marten the Trrrraveler!
> Bring something to trrrade!

If it's not in my wagon
It hasn't been made!

As the wagon approached the town square, Marten sang the song again. Usually, his arrival in a village caused a stir: Doors and windows opened. Dogs barked. Children streamed from the houses like bees from an overturned hive. Today, everything was still.

Marten scratched his head. The houses were shut up, and in the market square, most of the half-dozen or so stalls were unattended. Near one that held a small box of shriveled apples, a scrawny man smoked a cigarette, concentrating on blowing clouds of smoke into the air. Marten hopped off the wagon and came over.

"G'day to you sir!" Marten said.

The man ignored him. Marten pressed his tongue against the inside of his cheek. Then he smiled brightly and picked up an apple.

"If you'll pardon my saying so, I haven't seen a specimen of fruit like this in all my life. I've been on the road all morning now, and I'm thinking one of these apples would be a fine thing."

"Five coppers each," the young man said.

"Yes, there's a price to pay, I'm sure. But would you consider something else? These perhaps?"

With a turn of his wrist, Marten produced a card with buttons sewn to it.

"These are pearly buttons from the port of Baraqu. Buttons just like these fastened the Queen's gown during the marriage night last Adon's Feast. What man wouldn't do himself proud, bringing buttons like these home to his wife?"

The vendor said nothing. Marten noticed a second man, older and much larger than the apple vendor, staring at him from a stand on the opposite side of the square.

"No wife? What about your sister, then?"

"Keep 'em," the man snarled.

"Well now, I see you enjoy a smoke. How about some cigarettes? I've several boxes with me of a fine blend, half black tobacco, half hemp."

"I've got plenty." Just then the bigger man walked over.

He was a head taller than the first, but otherwise had the same dark eyes and prominent cheekbones, a common type in the north. *Brothers*, Marten thought.

"Look, pilgrim," the vendor was saying, glancing at the taller man, "If you can't pay, get your paws off the stock."

Marten sighed. He opened his purse, pinched out a copper, handed it over. It was the same corroded green color as the apple. Marten took a bite, wincing at the sour taste.

"Something wrong?"

"No, no, it's delicious. I'm thinking, though, how surprised I am that Penault seems such a quiet place. It does have some small fame, after all, as the birthplace of our King."

Now the big man finally spoke. "We don't care what you're thinking, old man."

"Ah, but that's where you're wrong m'friend! Tell me, have either of you gents ever been outside this valley? Seen other towns? Follow the lay of the land with your own eyes? No, I'll wager you haven't, because you're too busy scraping and working to earn your bread. That's why you need the likes of me, as you put it, because I can tell a story or two. I can also fix your tools, birth a baby, tin your pots, even trade a sour apple for pearl buttons from Baraqu—"

"You son of a bitch!" the smaller man growled. He was around the table in a flash and pushed Marten hard. The traveler staggered, caught himself, heard his wolf growl. Muff lunged for the vendor with bared fangs, dragging the wagon, even with its brake set, over the dust and cinders. The vendor retreated, disappearing behind his stand for an instant. When he popped up he had a pistol.

"Muff!" Marten yelled. "Stay!"

"No, let him come." The pistol trembled in the vendor's hand. "He'd feed my sister's family for a month. Him, and what you've got in that wagon."

Muff growled again. Marten felt the rumble of it all through its huge, taut body, but he knew the wolf would stay so long as he held on to his harness.

"So your sister likes the taste of wolf," Marten said calmly. "What do you think she will do when she bites the bullet you put into the wolf? What do you think she'd say if she knew you had a proscribed weapon here?"

"She ain't around."

"No other of the women around, either?"

The vendor grimaced. "They're all out on the hill, having a trial."

"Trial. You mean a Vestal trial?"

"Yes!"

"I've seen those. Maybe you will, too, if you shoot me or my wolf. There'll be no way of concealing it, short of burning our bodies or burying them somewhere. And I'll pledge something else, gents, while I'm at it. I was born on the road. I'm a traveler, I've got the traveler's soul and it's not a timid one. You have my word, both of you, that you'll be haunted by my ghost until you drop."

The two men looked at each other.

"On the other hand, you might just let me go on my way. I see right enough how bad things are here. They're bad all over these Steppes. I'll pass the word and say my prayers and be sorry for that and sorry for you. Now, gents. What'll you have?"

"He's right," the bigger man said, unfolding his arms. "Too much trouble, with the Matron here."

"But—"

"Gimme the gun!" he snapped, yanking it away by the barrel. The vendor half spun; his brother kicked him in the seat and sent him sprawling over a pile of empty crates.

"You've got a good tongue, old man, I'll give you that. But you'd best hit the road."

Marten nodded, starting for the wagon seat, holding the wolf harness as he did.

"One thing more." The man said. "The way things are, maybe you'd best think of another line of work."

Marten smiled. "Well, now, I appreciate that, but it's not likely. I'm a traveler. Born that way and probably die that way, too."

"Suit yourself, old man. Jerris, let's close up and go home!"

Marten unrolled a packet of parchment paper from around a

dozen brown slabs of dried, filleted fish, dropping them into a pot of boiling water. He had already sliced carrots, an onion, and added a little barley to it. When the fish softened, he lifted it out with a slotted spoon, put it into a tin pie pan for the wolf to eat. It was, he knew, more of a courtesy than a meal. Later, when it was dark, the wolf would leave him and spend most of the night hunting in the scrub pine forest between the cindercones.

The wolf took his time eating the fish, watching the old man sipping the broth, carefully licking his own pan when the last of the fillets was gone. They finished at the same time. Marten took out a long-stemmed corncob pipe, filled it with some of the black tobacco and hemp he carried in a pouch, then pulled a stick from the fire and lighted it. The wolf yawned. His long, pointed ears made a flapping noise when he shook his head.

"You know, Muff? This is truly a depressed area."

He puffed on the pipe, and stared out through the shrubbery that shielded the wagon from the banks of the pond. The overgrowth was thick, with faint ruts marking the old road leading into what had once been a quarry. From the look of it, and the rotted rope-tackle on the top of the hill over the cuts, this place had not been used for a long time.

"Still, Muffy, we've seen bad times before," he mused. "Been rousted before, too. But I can't recall gentry acting quite the way those two did. Pistols! And all the women gone to trial. Something more than hard times here, old Muff."

The wolf padded over, dropping its head to let Marten scratch its ears. He made a low growl of pleasure, backing away, stiff-legged and playful; then, when he saw the old man was not in a playful mood, he snorted, and crawled underneath the wagon to sleep.

After a time, Marten tapped out his pipe against a rock, stretched, walked out of the thicket and down the short path that lead to the side of the quarry pond. He tested the water with his fingers. It wasn't too cold, and it was very clear: he could see rocks, and silvery fish swimming along the bottom, fifteen or twenty feet below. He decided to take a swim. On impulse, he kept his knife-belt on. There might be a fat, slow carp along that bottom, or a snapping turtle that would make a fine pot of soup.

Marten slipped into the water, liking the way the chill tightened his muscles. He stroked easily halfway across, turned onto his back, frog-kicking with arms at his side the rest of the way. Touching bottom along the far shore, he cut several reeds, and rubbed his arms and stomach with the abrasive stems. Then he dove to look for clams.

As he came up he heard a commotion coming through the trees above him: snapping branches, a murmur of voices, beating wing, birdcalls. Doves flew low over the reeds. Feeling excitement, Marten back-paddled to where the reeds were thickest and waited.

A crowd of women appeared out of the woods, lead by a dozen or so who were dressed in dust-streaked white cloaks with sun-hoods, white gloves, no boots. *Vestals*, Marten thought sourly. Behind them walked townswomen, following the Vestals to the edge of the water. When the crowd reached the shore, it parted like a cell dividing itself, revealing a nucleus of two Vestals, each holding an arm of a thin, serious-faced boy.

The boy looked about fifteen years old, and was dressed in a torn shirt and short pants. There were fresh scratches on his neck and bruises on his arms and legs. In his arms he held a large black stone that had a metal ring in it; chains ran from the ring to shackles on his ankles. He walked erect, with great dignity even though the stone was very heavy. Marten could see his eyes. They were soft green, almost gray, and they stared ahead in a detached way.

Two Vestals escorted the boy to the edge of the water. There, the woman who had headed the party drew back her cowl and slowly surveyed the crowd. She had a forceful bearing and a hard stare, enough to quell the noise. Even the woods grew strangely silent, until the boy dropped the black stone into the mud with a thud that echoed dully across the water and the smile disappeared from the Vestal's face.

"This boy has been found guilty!" the Vestal said. "We are here to witness his punishment. Examine your hearts, all of you, and chase all pity from them. We are here to witness punishment! Mercy is not possible for us. To think of mercy now is unwomanly, weak. I, Rarei, Matron of the Order of Vestals, declare this is so!''

Murmurs of agreement came from the crowd. Some of the women bowed their heads, others held hands over their faces. They were chasing pity from their hearts, Marten thought, and making it look harder than carrying stones wearing leg shackles.

The Vestal turned to the boy. ''Will you still not speak?''

The boy said nothing.

''Very well. We won't linger here. Accept the fact that you are going to die. It will be easier that way.''

From the way she talks, Marten thought, *she's done it before*. He watched the boy pick up the black stone. He shifted its weight in his arms, and stepped into the water, then pushed off, arching his back as though he were a racer diving into a pool. Gradually, the water smoothed itself over the spot, then a gout of bubbles burst the smoothness.

''Poor thing!'' someone wailed.

''Silence! Another word and you'll join him!''

Marten took his knife and cut a thick reed. Working as quickly as he dared without stirring the water, he trimmed off a long section between the tiny side leaves, blew into it to clear it out. He put his knife back into its sheath, took a breath, then dove, following the drop-off to a place where the boy had pushed off. Mud clouded the water here; Marten held himself just below the surface and used the reed to take another deep breath before swimming down the slope of the ledge. Where it flattened out the water was clouded with more mud. Marten waved at it with his hands, trying to clear it away. His heart pounded in his chest.

Then he saw the boy, floating calmly at the end of the chain, making slow circle around the stone at the bottom, he was holding his shirt over his head and taking breaths from the big bubble of air trapped inside. His eyes were open and seemingly unconcerned. He could have worn the same expression if he were sitting under a tree somewhere chewing on a stalk of grass.

Marten swam up, took a breath, surfaced inside the rushes. Back at the shore, several of the Vestals were peering anxiously into the water.

"I'm telling you, Matron Rarei, I saw something move down there!" one was saying.

"I see nothing," Rarei replied impatiently.

"We should at least post a watch."

"That's right," someone in the crowd said. "He was always a strange boy. There and gone in the time it took to turn around!"

"Sisters, how long can *you* hold your breath? The boy is chained to the bottom of this pool. What you saw is a fish, perhaps, or maybe even his soul."

"But—"

"We have carried out the judgment. There's nothing else left except for legal details, which require my attention right now." Rarei raised her voice. "You have done a hard thing today, all of you, and done it well. Go home. The boy's soul may well choose to haunt she who tarries longest!"

Marten waited until some of the crowd dispersed. When he dove again, he found the boy more quickly. The bubble in the shirt was almost collapsed, and Marten soon discovered the reason. The boy was reaching for the shackle bracelets, bending his knees to bring his ankles closer to his arms. There was no way to avoid extending his arms in doing so, however, and when he did the back of the shirt came up and released part of the bubble.

Marten swam close to him. He drew his knife, and quickly cut the shirt away from the boy's arms and neck, taking it back to the surface near the rushes again. When he popped up it was all he could do to keep from gasping. This swimming underwater was not as easy as it used to be.

Most of the women had gone now. Only the Vestal guards remained.

"There!" one of them said, pointing.

"It's just a turtle. Come on. Let's get some wine into us!"

They turned away. Marten held the four corners of the shirt, filled it quickly with air and swam down again. The pull against him was considerable, but he managed.

Somehow, the boy had slipped out of one of the ankle irons; his cheeks were puffed, and his hands floated over his head. Marten could see his stomach move in and out, trying to breathe. He pulled the shirt with its bubble of air over the boy's head, floated up a little, and breathed some of it himself. The boy reached for the ankle iron again, pointing his toes. He was biting his lip, trying to block the pain; then the joint seemed to snap, and he could work the iron around and off his heel. Marten grabbed him, swimming underwater toward the opposite shore until his chest pounded. He opened his mouth, and swallowed some water, then suddenly it was the boy who was supporting him, pulling him to the surface and treading water until Marten could catch a breath.

"You're strong as hell!" Marten gasped. "Might as well tow me the rest of the way in."

The boy said nothing. He looked at Marten without really seeming to see him.

"All right, boy, have it your way. But we can't stay here."

He tugged at the waistband of the boy's pants. The boy began swimming with him, and in a moment they had reached the bank below the traveler's wagon.

SIX

THE BOY WAS SILENT as Marten helped him out of the water. He kept his fists clenched and his face showed the same calm detachment Marten had seen when the Vestals had him.

"Can you walk?" Marten asked.

The boy bit his lip, limped up to the top of the slope. When they entered the thicket, Muff crawled out from under the wagon and loped over with his tail straight, stopping right in front of the boy and standing there nose to nose. The wolf sniffed then slowly moved his tail back and forth.

"Appears he's willing to tolerate you."

As Marten spoke, the boy shuddered and began to cry. Muff made a whine, and cocked his head.

"Careful, boy! Wolves don't like to see people lose confidence. Makes 'em wonder whether they'd be better off alone. Anyway, his name's Muff, and I'm Marten. You come inside with me. We'll get some clothes on you and some food in your stomach and see if that makes a difference!"

The sun had set, and though its Veil still cast a soft pink

light over the countryside, the wagon was deep inside the shadow of the quarry hill. Marten lit a lantern before he opened the wagon door.

Inside the wagon things were packed tight: There was a platform bed in the back, with built-in shelves and cabinets below. The left front was taken up by a small gas stove, with wire racks of dishes and cooking supplies above; a fold-down cutting board, and a short-handled broom with a dustpan pushed onto the end of the handle. On the other side of the narrow aisle was a workbench with vise, and the steam engine that powered the rear wheels and also helped run a lathe. There were cases of wrenches and hammers, soldering irons and welding torches; saws; a grindstone; screwdrivers, chisels and awls; crucibles for melting tin, a brazier Marten used as a forge; bellows, planes, files, and rasps, drills and augers; then, closer to the bed, more metal bins filled with old clocks, gears, wood stock and sheet metal, soft goods. The walls surrounding the bed were completely covered with books, held in place on their shelves with lengths of elastic cord. Straight back over the pillow hung a hand-numbered calendar decorated by a watercolor view of Almheraz, seen from the riverbank opposite Point Draco.

The boy looked around, taking everything in. Some of the disinterest had vanished from his face. Eventually he sighed, wiping the tears away with his fist.

"Sit on the bed, if you please. There's not much room to work here. You'll find a robe in that upper right drawer."

The boy found it, then hopped up on the bed while Marten removed his knife belt and pulled his own trousers on.

"What's your name?"

No answer.

"Are you hungry?" When the boy didn't answer, Marten said, "Or did they stop your trial for a nice bite of lunch?" Marten put a pan on the stove. He sliced an onion and a stalk of celery, put them into the pan with a lump of butter. When the butter melted and the vegetables had softened, he added enough flour to make a paste, pepper, and a can of tinned milk. He stirred the mixture until it just began to bubble, moved it back off the burner, then opened another can, this one of chicken meat. He used a fork to flake the chicken into the sauce, stirred it in, and tasted it.

"More pepper," he said. "Do you know how to cook?"

The boy stared at the food.

"You should learn. Cookin's has saved my skin more than once." Marten put some flour in a bowl, along with baking powder he'd concocted himself, and a little salt. He put in another lump of butter and mashed it into the flour with a fork. Then he broke an egg into the bowl, added the rest of the tinned milk to make a batter. The little stove had a griddle on it. Marten wiped it with the parchment paper the butter had been wrapped in, then poured four circles of batter onto it.

"These are emergency rations, m'boy. Stuff in cans is hard to come by, and the people tend to like to hold onto it. I had to make a dozen tin spoons to trade for this one can of chicken."

The bubbles set in the center of the griddle cakes. Marten used the knife he'd cut the vegetables with to turn them over. They were done a moment later. Marten arranged them on a tin plate, poured on the creamed chicken, and handed the plate and a fork to the boy. As the boy began to eat, the old man poured more batter onto the griddle. When the cakes were done he spread what was left of the butter on top, rolled them with his fingers and ate them one by one. The boy ate quickly, holding the plate between his thumb and his fist.

"Good. Now drink some of this."

Marten gave him a wine-bag that was full of new cider, not very strong. The boy was very thirsty for someone who had swallowed so much water.

"There, now, not too much," Marten said, taking the bag away. "You just rest a moment while I take these outside to wash. Then we'll talk."

He went out to the fire with the dishes, and put the pan upside down over the coals to burn clean. As he did, he noticed the wolf staring at him balefully.

"I know what you're thinking. Marten gave good food to strangers while you pull hard all day for soaked fish. Maybe you've got a point, but in my opinion it's a sad day in the life of a wolf, eating chicken from a can."

The wolf snorted loudly, and closed his eyes.

"Sulk then," Marten said.

When the old man came back inside, the boy was at his workbench running his hands over a box-shaped machine that was half-embedded in a slab of sandstone. The box had switches on it, and a disk on top held in place by a metal spindle. In his free moments, Marten had been chipping the machine free from the rock.

"It's from the old time," Marten said. "Some places, there's mounds alongside the road. Usually, that's where our roads were laid right on top of the roads from the old time. The mounds are full of stuff that used to be on the side of the old roads. Sometimes, when I get the energy and I'm sure nobody's around, I'll do a little digging. Don't know what it's for—and I doubt if I'll ever be able to make it work, but I want to see it looking the way it did once."

The boy grunted. He moved on to examine the rest of Marten's things. He spun the governor on the steam engine, rooted through the parts bins, found a box of washers, and stuck several onto the ends of his fingers. Marten took the box away, gently, selected a brass washer that was the size of a twenty-copper piece. He pinched it between two fingers and turned his wrist back and forth so that it flashed in the lamplight and got the boy's attention. Then he started rolling the washer from finger to finger, palming it so it seemed to disappear, snapping his wrist and producing it again between thumb and forefinger. The boy stared as Marten repeated the sleight.

"Like that, do you?"

The boy slipped all the washers off his fingertips but one. Slowly, and awkwardly at first, he imitated Marten's finger roll. He passed it back and forth several times, but when he tried to flick his wrist as Marten had done, the washer dropped to the floor. Marten stepped on it before he could retrieve it.

"Talk to me, boy! Tell me your name."

The boy shrugged his shoulders, hopped onto Marten's bed and stretched out on his back. Suddenly he sat upright, pulling down a picture that Marten had tacked to the ceiling.

"Hmmm!"

"By the sun's fiery Eye, what are you doing—"

"Hmmm! Hmmm!" the boy repeated, waving the picture. Marten sighed, came over to the bed, and took it from him.

"What's caught your fancy?"

"Hmmm!"

"Hmmm? You mean who?"

"*Who*," the boy mimicked.

"By Adon, so you do have a tongue! You'd think you were a boy-schell, or—all right! This is the Queen's family. Queen Gormayne and her husband, King Cyre, and those are the two daughters. Princess Royal, who's twenty or so, and the Queen Apparent, Careev. Look at those sad eyes, eh? And look what a beauty the sister is. Maud's her name. I've spent many a night pondering that face, the pride in it, the way she dominates the whole thing with just her eyes! The eyes tell the story all right. The King's lost some of his fierceness since I saw him last five or six years ago. And the mother, meanwhile, seems dull. She'd have to be dull, to be content with the way things are now: no weather, Baraqu rising in the south, and these Vestals making village after village their private estate, and here in the King's own home-land as well!"

"The King," the boy said softly, staring at the picture.

"That's right. The King." Marten reached for the tintype, but the boy hissed at him and hugged it to his chest.

"So you fancy it, do you? Well, boy, you're forgetting I'm a traveler. If you want it, you'll have to give me something in return."

The boy eyed him warily. Marten laughed.

"You've got wit enough to want to make sure I won't be fleecing you! Very well, all I want you to do, boy, is show me the same sleight you did before." Marten held up the washer and demonstrated the finger roll, this time adding a pass and a quick misdirected exchange of hands good enough to fool most people. The boy's eyes, however, were riveted to the hand where Marten had palmed the washer, and when Marten finally produced it from underneath his tongue, he had the feeling that the boy had been waiting for him to do just that.

"Very well, then, your turn." This time, the boy dupli-cated the finger roll and hand pass perfectly, and followed the trick even to the point of sticking out his tongue. There was no coin underneath, though, when he did. Marten blinked, and scratched his head. When he did, he found the washer in his hair.

The boy was a natural mimic, all right, but he had taken the trick one step farther. Still, he did not look pleased with himself, the way a normal boy would having fooled an old man so well. He had come to life for a moment and then let go. His eyes, Marten noticed, were very much like the eyes of the Queen: disky, and focused on some other world. *Well*, Marten thought, *if he's to stay with me, we'll have to bring him out of that.*

"Boy, that's a rare talent you've got, and you've earned your picture. I'm thinking now that you could be very useful, given the right training. It's hard times for travelers, and the old business is changing, and since Fate's more or less put me in your hands—me saving your life and all—what say you throw in with me and the wolf? It's your decision; you can leave here now if you want, though they're bound to burn you for a vampire, not knowing that you got yourself loose, if they catch you anywhere in this Duchy."

The boy gave no indication that he understood.

"Well, I'll tell you what. I'm going to take that as a yes. Now look at me and pay attention. We're going to teach you to speak. We're going to teach you to conduct yourself as a normal human being, and the first thing any normal human being has to call his own in this world is a name. Now, I learned sleights from an uncle of mine in the caravan. Komaso was his name: a fine, tall man with an unfortunate taste for the grape. Fought with another man, gentry, over the price of a young wolf when he was in no condition to fight and took a dagger in the heart. Oh, but what a funeral his was! They embalmed him and waited six weeks so every caravan in the whole of the northern provinces could gather, and then we raised him up with a howl loud enough to shatter the gates of Heaven. He waltzed in, my uncle said. And now he lives with Adon in the real world, if you're inclined to believe such things. You don't know until you die, my boy, and then it's my opinion that you could care less about coming back to tell the tale. That would be like giving your own hard-earned money away to strangers. Anyway, there he is, watching us poor puppets, helping pull on those strings that Fate has us tied to. Maybe he's got a hand in all this. Whatever the truth is, I've never seen anybody make a pass like you did having just seen it once, so in honor of my old, dead uncle, we'll call you Komaso. You are Komaso. Can you say it? Komaso.''

"Komaso,'' the boy repeated, eyes flickering.

"I am Komaso.''

"Eye yam Komaso.''

"Good. And my name's Marten. The wolf you met before's called Muff.''

"Muff,'' the boy said.

"Exactly. And now we ought to turn in. We've got a long pull tomorrow, and you're going to earn your keep while we turn you into a proper young man. You're going to work, and you're going to learn. I expect, before too long, you'll be able to tell us just why those Vestals were so interested in putting you down for good!''

The boy seemed to understand and nodded his head. Marten pulled the coverlet back and helped tuck him in. Seconds later, the boy was asleep, arms around the tintype like an old and tattered stuffed toy.

SEVEN

"I TRIED TWICE to get him over that jump, Poppa," the Princess Royal was saying. "The first time, he dropped his head and dumped me, so, when I'd got back on and brought him around again, I reined him back really hard. So he stopped and tried to bite me!"

The royal family was having lunch around an oval table beneath an arbor of kiwi vines, with the King at one end and Maud at the other. It was cool in the shade, and a breeze that smelled of river and rustled the leaves of the vines as the King smoked one cigarette after another and looked through the morning's dispatches. Occasionally, he reached for a slice of melon, or handful of almonds from bowls resting on his papers.

"Poppa, you're not listening! Careev was there. Tell Poppa what happened, Carry."

"He did show his teeth," Careev admitted. She did not like to disturb her father when he was working, and wished that Maud had not brought her into it.

"*And* bit me," Maud prompted sharply.

"Well. . . ."

"Oh, she's just too nice! I've just got to have a new wolf. The old one's bad tempered, he can't run nearly fast enough, and his coat's a disgrace. Mother, surely you don't want me riding next to you at the Festival on that mangy old dog!"

The King picked a stray bit of tobacco from the end of a fresh cigarette, and lighted it. "Your mother's contemplating Heaven," he said, blowing smoke through his nose. "Don't ruin it for her."

Indeed, Queen Gormayne glanced up from the prayer-scroll she had been reading, peering over her glasses at Maud. "I'm sure you'll look fine," she said, smiling.

"I will *not* look fine! How come Carry's got a nice mount? She doesn't even like to ride!"

Careev winced to hear her name again. She tried to concentrate on eating her salad, spearing a long strip of cheese on her fork. Holding it up, she tore off tiny pieces, which she put into her mouth and chewed one at a time. Maud watched the procedure with growing incredulity, until at last she snatched what was left of the cheese from the fork and shoved it into her sister's mouth.

"And why can't you eat like a normal person?"

"*Girrrllls*," the King growled without looking up.

Just then, a schell in white-and-red livery came onto the terrace carrying a sealed pouch, which he handed to the King. Still engrossed in his reading, Cyre broke the seal, unfolded the dispatch and smoothed it several times with the flat of his hand before he turned his attention to it. When he did, his face grew very red.

"Uh-oh," Maud said under her breath.

"Gormayne, what is this about?" he sputtered, shoving the dispatch across the table to her.

The Queen looked at it. "Some property of mine was annexed, I believe." she said.

"Annexed? Seized! By Vestals! That's my property. It's the place I grew up in!"

"Perhaps it's a mistake, Cyre."

"No. No, it's no mistake. I've told you time and time again that they've grown far too bold."

"They were given a charter to consolidate some of their estates—"

The King leapt up in a fury, slamming both hands on the table so hard the dishes jumped. "This is not a *consolidation*! This is a personal affront to me!" He glowered down at her while she carefully rolled up her scroll and slid into its embroidered case.

"The property didn't belong to you," the Queen said. "It's always been leased to your family. I shouldn't take it as an affront when your landlady fails to renew a lease on one tract, and offers a larger, better one in exchange."

"What about my house?" the King roared. "My *birthplace*."

"When was the last time you were back there, Cyre? Not since we were married, certainly."

"You don't understand. It's not just the house."

"Well?" the Queen demanded. "What is it, then?"

"I shouldn't have to explain it to you. I *won't* explain it. What can you be thinking of, allowing those witches to seize my house? Even if you felt no need to consult me, Gods, woman, can't you see their incomparable arrogance?"

"Cyre, if you would just calm down a moment—"

"You're raising those Vestals up at my expense!" Cyre shouted.

"I am supporting a religious order whose good works are vital to the Realm and my throne. They are no threat to me, and certainly no threat to you, in spite of what you think."

"You'll live to regret feeding them when they could have been starved so easily."

"*How* will I regret it, Cyre? If you know something about the order that I do not, tell me now! Otherwise, pray curb your temper and leave me in peace."

The King gathered up his papers, motioned to his schell, who had been silently standing by, and dropped everything into its arms. "Stay peaceful. Good day, daughters."

"Poppa? What about my wolf?" Maud called after him.

"Maud, that will be quite enough," Gormayne said. "Have you girls finished eating?"

"Yes," Careev said.

"*Yes*," Maud repeated, mimicking her.

"Then go downstairs and get ready. We'll be leaving to visit the hospice in an hour."

Maud groaned. "Another hospice visit? We just did that."

"A month ago. You know very well we go on the first Wednesday of every month. Now make yourself presentable —or would you rather spend the day with your father?"

"Oh, all right!" Maud sighed, getting up from the table and grabbing Careev's wrist. "Come on, Careev!"

Maud was in a hurry, and Careev had to run to catch up with her. As usual, her sister did not bother holding the door open for her, it slammed shut right in Careev's face. The door was carved with a relief of Adon sitting cross-legged on a cushion between his sisters Perse and Psyche, who, gazed lovingly at him. Adon had two faces, so he could look at both of them at once. Someone had scratched a big smile into the wood on the face that looked toward Perse. Careev knocked timidly on the door, which was too heavy for her to manage alone.

"Ooff!" Nana Mara said, as she opened it. "Here, now, Lady Maud, is that any way to be treating your sister? Come in, Princess, I've got your clothes all laid out—and I suppose we ought to do something about your hair." Nana ran her fingers through it. Careev's hair was light brown, and very fine and straight; how she envied her sister's hair, which was full and wavy, and shone like bronze in the sunlight!

Careev went into her room and sat down on the bed, Nana following her in. "You be sure to wear what I put out for you!" she called to Maud in the other room. "You'll be out with your mother, and she'll want you looking chaste and modest, as befits a Princess!"

"Yes, Nana," Maud called back.

"Yes, Nana!" Nana repeated, chuckling. "And what about you, looking so sad on that bed? Did you have a nice lunch today?"

"Not very. Momma and Poppa were fighting."

Nana unbuttoned Careev's tunic, helped her slip into a fresh cotton gown. She went to the dressing table, got a brush and some bobby pins and started brushing out the Princess's hair.

"Fighting?" Nana asked through the pins.

"Poppa found out that the Vestals took some land in his home town."

Nana stopped brushing. "In Panault?"

"That's right." Maud said, coming into Careev's room. "Poppa was absolutely livid. He said it wasn't just the land that made him angry, but when Momma asked him to explain, he just stomped out."

"Oww!" Careev cried out. "Be careful, Nana!"

"Sorry, Lady. Are you sure it was Panault?"

"Yes. Why?"

"That's no concern of yours, begging your pardon, Lady!" Nana jammed a last bobby pin into the chignon she had twisted in the back of Careev's head. "When we're meant by the Lord to know something, we know it and that's that!"

"Think of poor Careev, Nana," Maud said, plucking two bobby pins from Nana's mouth and jabbing one into Careev's hair. "One day soon, she'll have to be Queen, and she's absolutely ignorant."

"I am not!"

"And of course, Nana, it's all your fault. You know everything that goes on here, everything that's whispered in the corners, things that would break her heart, or even mine, but do you tell? You do not. You stand strong and silent, Nana, a rock, a living statue, keeping these things to yourself to spare us the terror of knowing what the real world is like. No one can make you speak of these things!"

Nana flushed, and she grimaced so tightly that she couldn't pull the last bobby pin from her mouth.

"Look at her, Careev! Have you ever seen such courage?"

"—Nana! Ow! No!"

"I'll bet that if Psyche appeared in this room now, floating right here over the bed. . . . There she is, all radiant, eyes flashing, clutching sheaves of moonbeams in her hands. To her right, sitting on a cloud, is the ghost of Nana's mother, and to her left, staring fiercely, is the soul of her father's mother, and they're all imploring her to speak—I'll bet even then, our Nana would fold her arms and shake her head no, and maybe even spit in the Goddess's eye for good measure!"

"Lady, taking the Goddess's name in vain will bring nothing good."

Maud cupped her hand to her ear. "I don't hear any thunder." She stomped down to the floor, and shook her head in amazement. "No cracks opening up, either. Maybe it's all right to talk!"

"By the Eye of the angry sun himself, Lady Maud, you know how to vex me! Now, where's that last pin? Heaven knows you've made me swallow it!"

"It's right here, Nana," Maud said, flourishing it. "Here you go, sister!"

Careev winced as Maud fastened the last pin.

"There, you've hurt her," Nana said.

"It's all right, Nana."

"And she won't even blame you. Oh, Lady, why can't you be more like your sister?"

"But that's just the point, Nana. If Carry's to rule properly, we will have to be more alike. But she's got to be like *me*!"

"Eh? And what do you say to that, Lady Careev?" Careev looked at herself in the mirror. She looked older with her hair up, and, with her long, slender neck exposed, taller too.

"Well, Nana. Spreading gossip is certainly wrong."

"See? She's sensible!"

"And I'm sure Poppa was just upset about losing the house he was born in."

"The person who lived there, more likely," Nana blurted out.

Maud sensed the opening and she did not let it pass.

"So you *do* know something. Tell!"

"No. There's nothing—"

"Too late, you've already started. What person lived in Poppa's house?"

Nana went pale, and sat down heavily, staring into the mirror. Alarmed, Careev said, "Leave her alone! Can't you see she's upset?"

"Yes, and I want to know why!"

"No one lived in that house," Nana said in a whisper.

"You heard her. No one—"

'Oh, shut up!" Maud pulled on the cloak Nana had laid out on the bed, struggling fiercely with the heavy folds of material as though she were wrestling with a ghost. When she finally did get it on, her hair, which Nana had spent so much time fixing, crackled with electricity, standing up like the stubble left in a newly cut hayfield. Instinctively, Nana reached for the brush on the dressing table.

"You won't touch me, Nana! Don't expect me to kneel down purring like a kitten after you won't say what you know." Glancing at Careev and ignoring the nanny's confusion, she snapped, "I'm riding today. If you want to ride with me, you'd better come along now!"

She was out the door as Careev looked back at Nana, unsure of whether she should stay and comfort her, and risk Maud's wrath, or leave the poor woman alone with her wretched feelings. Quickly, Nana made the decision for her, waving her off.

"Nana, I'm sorry. . . ."

Nana managed a smile. "You've got nothing to be sorry for. I ought to know better than to trade secrets with a girl. Go with her, Lady—it'll do more good than staying here watching your old Nana blubber. Go now! And give some of that sweetness to people who can use it, to those poor patients in that hospice!"

EIGHT

THE ROAD DOWN from the palace to Almheraz was cut into the face of Citadel Rock. It was wide, paved with cobblestones, protected by a wooden guardrail, and even though it switched back three times, was fairly steep. Careev had never liked traveling it, even in the confines of a sedan, and she liked the descent on the back of a wolf even less.

She rode her wolf, a gangly roan named Mint, gingerly, knees pinched against the saddle. Maud rode a little in front of the rest of the procession, which included the Queen's green-and-black sedan drawn by three matched, sable-coated wolves, and four Vestal guards, whose mounts were dusty white. Because the day was a mild one, the Queen rode with the sedan's top down. Sunlight glinted off her breastplate, a lapis and silver representation of the crescent moon, whose horns touched her shoulders.

As the sedan bumped over the rough pavement, she remained erect and perpendicular, as though mounted on gimbals, and moved her finger across the text of her prayer-scroll.

Maud had been waiting in the switchback. Careev joined her, and the two Princesses let their mother's carriage pass.

"Look at her," Maud said. "Off in the clouds again. It could be raining toads, and she wouldn't know it."

She started off. Careev had to snap Mint's reins to catch up with her.

"You shouldn't talk that way," she said, a little breathlessly when she had.

"Why not? It's true."

"She was all right when she told Poppa to stop bothering her about the Vestals."

"Automatic," Maud said. "Just like a schell."

Careev clutched at her saddle horn as Mint moved closer to the rail to give Maud's mount some room. "So what about that? Do you think the Vestals really are trying to move against Poppa?"

"Who cares?"

Careev's face felt hot all of sudden.

"I just wonder what Nana knows about all this, that's all."

"Yes, and I guess you're pretty sorry that Poppa worries more about an old empty house than he does about you! But that's all right. You won't have to worry about anything. By the time you're Queen, I'll be nothing but a dried-up Warden, like Auntie, out there on the Preserve!"

Surprised at the bitter words about their aunt, Careev fell silent. She did not know Sheeme very well, but knew Maud loved her. Sheeme had come to Almheraz once eight years ago for Festival week, occupying rooms in the palace catacombs, and had doted on Maud. She brought her presents, took her on shopping expeditions into the city, and even brought along her finest young hawk—so she could begin teaching Maud to hunt. There had never been another visit—Poppa absolutely loathed her!—and yet, Careev reflected as the procession swung through the last hairpin turn, it was Sheeme who bred the King's schells in barns on the Preserve. Without his schells, a King had no power at all in Almheraz. Careev had always wondered why, if Sheeme hated Poppa so much, she continued to supply him with hundreds of new schells each year. It was a family thing, beyond understanding.

Now the road widened beneath the shade of palm trees and

led to bronze gates that were opened by Vestals as the Queen's sedan approached. Usually, there were people waiting outside them hoping for a glimpse of the Queen, but this morning the area around the gates was deserted. Gormayne glanced up from her prayer scroll, ready to acknowledge her people; her face registered no surprise, however, when she saw no one. She merely waved for her driver to go on. It was then that a mounted party overtook the procession from the rear: a dozen schells in Panault livery armed with crossbows and swords, led by the chief priest of the Sun-temple, Magister Eccles.

The priest cut a dashing figure as he pulled his black wolf to a stop. He was olive-complected and broad-shouldered, with short hair curling in moist ringlets above his high fore-head, setting off deep-set eyes that were an incongruous pale brown and kept his face, with its sharp nose and forked beard, from seeming demonic.

"Look at him!" Careev whispered excitedly, as Eccles trotted his horse alongside Gormayne's sedan.

"My Queen! A word with you, if you please."

Gormayne ordered her driver to stop and regarded the Sun-priest coolly. She had never made a secret of the fact that she did not care much for Eccles, who was a longtime protege of the King's. He was a southerner, from Baraqu, a distant cousin of the Vestal Arcopatrinas, and though he was the King's man completely and had been unstinting in his devo-tion to the Temple and the throne since he had arrived in Almheraz, Gormayne had never quite trusted him.

"What is it?" Gormayne said with a glance toward the schells.

"My Ladies, the King has reason to believe that it would be better for you not to travel through the city today."

"Really? And where is my husband now?"

"Attending to his devotions in the Temple sanctuary."

"Did he mention that he and I had lunch not an hour ago? He said nothing to me then about any danger."

"The King asked me to come," Eccles replied evenly.

"Well, then?" the Queen snapped.

"My Queen, Almheraz is hungry, as you well know. We have word that agitators are about, seeking to turn that hunger into hatred for you. These people say that a new Queen would

please Heaven, and that Heaven will withhold the rain until a
new Queen reigns. The King fears for your safety because of
this, and therefore, he humbly requests that you return to the
Citadel until these traitors can be identified and eliminated.
Or, if you will not, out of consideration for obligations that
cannot be severed on such short notice, he asks that you will
at least permit an escort of Temple Guards.''

Gormayne tapped her scroll against her lap. Then she said,
''Your eloquence does you credit, Magister. But I already
have an adequate escort.''

''It is your husband's opinion that, in the present circumstances, these ladies of the Vestal Order create more peril
than they prevent.''

As soon as he said this, all four Vestals tensed and brought
their lances down.

''Stay!'' The Queen snapped.

Eccles smiled. ''Thank you, my Queen. A battle among
those charged to protect you would not be seemly.''

''He accuses us of treason,'' the Vestal captain cried.

''Silence!''

Maud began to laugh, until her mother turned and silenced
her with a single hard look.

''It's raining toads,'' Careev whispered to her.

''Girls! All of you!'' She waited for the Vestals to raise
their lances. Then she said to Eccles, ''What the Fates have
ordained cannot be undone. Our lot is in Psyche's hands, and
you may tell my husband so. And you may also tell him that
the day I require an escort of schells in order to travel through
this city is the day I give up my throne. I decline your
escort.''

''That, of course, is your privilege,'' Eccles said. ''Troops.''
The schells reined their wolves back and moved into forma-
tion behind the priest, leaving the way clear for the Queen's
party to continue. She gave the order to do so, and it passed
through the empty plaza, then down a slight embankment and
underneath a red stone portal that guarded the dusty jumble of
the Agora, the city's marketplace.

Soon they were riding along an avenue of sagging tents,
sun-blasted marquees, stalls patched together out of lodge
poles and nailed-on sheet metal, kiosks with awnings whose

frayed edges flapped listlessly in the midafternoon breeze.
Occasionally, these structures gave way to dirt embankments
with doors on them, leading down to the subterranean stalls
of merchants who preferred doing business away from the
injurious rays of the sun. Everywhere there was merchandise
for sale: birds in matchstick cages, stalls where you could buy
a kiss, or have your fortune told out of the patterns made by
mud worms inside glass boxes. There were wolf traders and
smithies, marriage brokers, and storytellers who could give
you a glimpse of the world before the Fall for a copper or
two. There were elephants and steam engines, scrawny cats
roasting on scewers over charcoal, glass blowers and jug-
glers, barbers with jars of leeches for those with minor ail-
ments. There were artisans hammering on sheets of copper;
shoemakers, cloakmakers, poets who sold verses written inside folded cards; others more prosaic who would construct
family trees from a town and the name of a relative or two.
Anything that could be sold was for sale here. The Agora
smelled of sweat and onions and meldewed cloth and dust and
old coppers and it was the heart of Almheraz.

It was usually crowded even when the Eye was at its
zenith. Today, mild as it was, the market should have been
packed, but it was not. Some stalls were empty, and much of
the food that was for sale looked withered and dull, as did the
people walking dispiritedly from tent to tent.

The appearance of the Queen's entourage caused some
commotion, but it was grudging. Careev, riding on Mint and
passing closer to the crowds, felt a curious depression. It was
as though the people wanted her to do something, but did not
know what, and what's more, resented her for failing to
inspire them. After a while Careev stopped trying to look at
anyone, concentrating instead on sights that had nothing to do
with people, or glancing at Maud, who seemed to enjoy the
sour atmosphere. Careev began to wish that her mother had
indeed allowed the Sun-priest and his schells to escort them.

At the Avenue of the Laurels, the party turned and headed
north toward another arch leading into the Old Town. A
good-sized crowd had gathered at the base of this arch, but
the people in it had not come to see the Queen. Instead they
gave their full attention to a wicker cage that twisted slowly at

the end of a rope. Some men were busy building a fire beneath it.

"Somebody's inside!" Careev gasped, standing in the stirrups for a better look.

"Not somebody. Some *thing*. It's a seer!"

As they rode closer to the edges of the crowd, one of the men held up a flaming brand and whatever was inside bawled loudly. The cage rocked, prompting another big cheer from the onlookers. One of them stepped forward and wrested the torch away.

"Not yet! The one that fires this cage pays for the privilege. A gold ducat's what I'm charging. Just five hundred coppers! Who'll pungle up that sum for the privilege of freeing our Realm from this blasted drought?" The man raised the torch again, and the thing in the cage yelped.

"Come on, now! You've seen the bands on this thing's cursed tongue. A Seer this old must have captured a hundred souls by now. It's a cursed thing, I tell you, an abomination! It's one of the reasons why Adon's punishing us now, why you wake with growling stomachs every morning, why our fields are dry and blasted, why our rivers are empty of fish. Five hundred coppers! Why, you've got three times that among you right now. What good's money, eh, when there's nothing to buy? I'm asking again, who'll pay a ducat to see this soul-stealer burn?"

"I will!" Maud cried, reaching into her purse and holding up a gleaming coin. People turned, annoyed at having their sport interrupted. This quickly turned to amazement.

"It's Princess Maud—"

"—the Queen—"

"—whole bloody pack!"

"—What's the matter with you? Take your fucking hoods off to the Ladies!"

"Maud! You can't!" Careev cried.

"Just watch me. I knew there'd be some fun today!"

"Mother!" Careev began, but the Queen gazed out at the scene dispassionately, apparently content to let events sort themselves out. Maud, meanwhile, had thrust the reins of her mount into the hands of a bystander and leapt down, pushing through the crowd until she reached the man who held the torch.

"L-lady—" he stammered.

"It's clear this seer wouldn't get away with much if he tried to take *your* soul," Maud cried. "Maybe he got your tongue instead!" She waited for the laughter to die down. "Let's get this over with! Who'll pay more than a ducat for the privilege of torching the cage? You, my good man?"

"L-lady, it's *my* cage."

"Your cage? Tell me if I'm wrong, people, but isn't this a man here? Properly speaking, this cage belongs to his wife! Where is she?"

"My wife is dead, L-lady!"

"Not burned to death, I hope!" The crowd hooted again. How quickly she commanded them, Careev thought. How easily she redirected their anger. Why, she could do anything with them!

"Well, a man without a wife can't hold property, and all property without an owner belongs to the Throne, and, if my mother gives me leave to do so, I can take this cage and do what I please with it, including selling what's inside for a ducat. Come on now, what the man said before is quite true. This creature, hideous and malformed, is the cause of all our present misery. Who'll make a martyr of his or her purse for the sake of our sun-blasted Realm? Think of my poor sister there! She doesn't want to rule over a graveyard."

Careev smiled weakly. A soft moan issued from inside the basket.

"Even the seer is getting impatient. Give me a bid!" Maud waited a moment, and, when none was forthcoming, put the ducat back into her purse. "Very well! It seems I've purchased the honors myself. Ladies, gentlemen—"

Careev watched in horror as her sister raised the torch to the bottom of the cage. The seer screamed, and that got the crowd moving: Heads bobbed up and down like bubbles on the surface of a pot of boiling water. People in the crowd bounced off each other, milling around Maud until all Careev could see of her was the hand holding the torch, and flashes of her golden hair.

Suddenly, Careev snapped the reins and spurred her wolf

into the throng. Mint hesitated an instant, a low growl in his throat, until Careev slapped his neck.

"Go on!"

Lowering his huge head, the wolf plowed people aside, or stepped over them, rising once on his hind legs over screaming onlookers who clawed at each other trying to scramble away. Careev slid to the ground, drawing her dagger as she did. She caught a glimpse of the Vestal guards; they were doing nothing. Then the part of the crowd trying to get away from the wolf—Mint was whirling around, snapping his jaws as if he'd stumbled into a cloud of gnats—surged toward the gate, pushing Careev close to the post where the rope that held the cage had been tied. She grabbed the rope with one hand, sawed at it with the other until it parted with a loud snap and the cage came crashing down, sending smoldering splinters and the torch Maud had been holding cartwheeling away.

The Queen's carriage was gone.

"Maud! Maud—" Careev cried, but the uproar was general and there were too many arms legs and heads to pick anyone out. Some of these parts clutched at her, yanking her back. Careev gasped, tried desperately to keep her balance, but she couldn't move her feet. She was going over, thinking that the crowd had wanted a sacrifice and was going to get one. She felt their need as a kind of hunger, hot and acrid-smelling, covering her, smothering her. . . .

Then the seer rose to its feet. Careev didn't realize it at first; she was down, and what she felt was a rush of cool, fresh air, and silence. She shook herself and looked up, and saw the creature standing over her. It was tall, and draped with a tattered cloak; dark-skinned, with angry red patches on its ankles and calves where the torches had burned it. Though it had no eyes or ears, it bent its long, bullet-shaped head and seemed to look at her with a kind of curiosity, flicking its tufted tongue as a lizard might, tasting the air for a scent that would tell what eyes or ears could not. It made a soft, murmuring sound, then held out its hand. The fingers were long and delicate-looking, with large, fleshy pads at the tips.

"Don't touch it, Lady!" somebody yelled. "It's your soul it wants!"

This started the yelling again. *What did* they *want?* Careev felt a cold anger inside, freezing everything so that it was solid and she could look at things as they were.

She took the seer's hand.

Her heart pounded as she did; she remembered what she had heard about seers, how they were the reborn bodies of people who had died unshriven; that their souls were dead; that in order to gain rebirth they must steal new souls belonging to some unfortunate living person. In that way, they were like the hawks Auntie raised in the preserve, though more tragic. The souls a seer took gave it no sustenance. Instead it was said a seer was required to *nourish* the soul it took. If it succeeded, it became a person; if it failed, the soul died, and the seer must search out another victim.

The seer's hand was dry and cool, like the skin of a snake. The crowd gasped, but as the seer pulled her to her feet, she felt nothing except how strong it was.

So, she thought. *The legends are wrong. . . .*

But there was another legend as well. If a seer touched you and you held onto your soul, somehow, you could wish for something. Careev closed her eyes and thought, *I want my family to be whole again. . . .*

And then she felt the pain. Her eyes clouded, and the people around her, the wolves standing a little away, the red arch and the rest of the Agora retreated, as though flattened into a painting against a wall. She cried out, the nerves in her legs and feet suddenly aflame. Her throat was dry. She felt terrible thirst, and realized that the creature had probably spent three or four days inside the cage without anything to drink.

She felt something else, too. An awareness, not like intelligence she could comprehend, but one that knew her, and knew what she had wished for. She realized she was still angry. The crowd that gaped at her now had wanted this creature tortured for its amusement, and even now was waiting for her to slump down, soulless. She could see the man who had tried to conduct the auction licking his lips. How much could he burn the seer for now, when it held the soul of the Queen Apparent!

She pointed to him with her free hand. "You!"

"Lady! You can still speak!"

"Of course she can, you idiot!" Maud snapped. She had struggled forward to join Careev. Her cloak was torn and her hair hung down over her face, but excitement shone in her eyes. "Wonder of wonders," she shouted. "My sister speaks!"

"Shut up, Maud!"

Maud opened her mouth in amazement, It was the first time Careev had ever spoken to her that way. There was force behind it, too, and it stuck.

"Auctioneer! Bring something to drink!" Careev said.

"I'll fetch water—"

Careev felt a surge of fear and revulsion from the seer. "No! Something else. Beer."

"Yes!" The auctioneer cuffed someone on the head, and that man scurried away, returning a moment later with a stoppered bottle that the auctioneer took from him and timorously handed to the Princess, pulling the cork out with his teeth as he did. Careev gently put it into the seer's hand. It snatched the beer up, put the bottle to its lips. Careev's hand tingled where the seer had touched her; otherwise, the pain in her legs and feet had disappeared. She watched the seer drink. Then there was a commotion, and a party of wolf-riders rode into the edge of the crowd.

It was Eccles, and his escort of mounted schells. She heard the seer growl.

"Ladies! Are you safe? We saw the crowd from the top of the Rock, and hurried back here as quickly as we could—"

"You missed the seer," Maud said. "Careev touched it."

Eccles drew his sword. But there was the sound of breaking glass, and what was left of the bottle lay on the ground.

The seer was gone.

NINE

"YOU LEFT THEM there! In the middle of a damn riot!"

Cyre paced back and forth in front of his wife, who was reclining on her chaise and looking perfectly composed.

"You know what I've been asking myself all night long? Why the hell you didn't just drown both of them when they were babies. Get it over with." He whirled, stopped in front of her. "Remember when you were pregnant? Can you remember that far back? You were sick every damn morning with all three of them. A day and a half on the birthing bed with Maud! Just about that long with Careev. I remember hearing you scream all the way down on the deck of my boat when she was born, and your life was hanging by a thread when it was over. This—" snapping his fingers "—would have killed you! So why the hell did you go through that? Why put yourself through that when your damn scrolls told you you were gonna leave 'em in the middle of a human garbage heap to get their heads pulled off. Tell me!"

Gormayne said calmly, "Are you finished?"

"You're answering one question with another goddamned question!"

"I told you what happened. The sedan moved through the gates. I didn't give any order, it just moved."

"Bullshit."

"I then asked the captain of my guard to see about the girls. She respectfully refused because it was her sworn duty to protect me. The only way I could have got them to move was to go into that crowd myself, on foot."

"Like any woman with a dram of mother-love would have done."

"Your daughter Maud went into that crowd of her own free will. Her sister followed her."

"*My* daughter? *Her* sister? Gods, are you nuts? These are the heirs to your throne!"

"I got them to turn the sedan around, Cyre," Gormayne said. "It was all over by the time we got back. The girls were safe. And there was no sign of a seer, either."

"What? You think because you didn't see anything, it wasn't there in the first place? Why don't you try talking to Careev. She keeps rubbing her hands together like some sun-struck fool. Oh, and beer! She's been asking for it ever since she came back. And Maud was getting it for her, too. They were both half in the bag before I came down and put a stop to it. Careev told me she had a sudden craving. And there's a riot still going on down in the marketplace, and it's spreading! What are you going to do about that?"

"The Vestals will keep order."

"The Vestals are the cause of the damn problems, Gormayne! They're hijacking the food barges, blocking the roads, blowing rail lines! I know for a fact they are. They're putting the screws on us until we do what they want."

"Which is?"

"They want you to divorce me. Disinherit the girls. Adopt someone suitable to them. It's not to stop! Gods, woman, you let them run wild in Panault, take my land—*my land*—dishonor my house. There wasn't anything I could do about it, what's done is done, but by Adon's Eye, I will not sit still and let them take over this city. Not while I'm King!"

"It's in the hands of Fate."

Cyre groaned, clapping his hands over his ears. His eyes were red and his beard was specked with bits of tobacco, because he had been chewing the ends off every cigarette he put into his mouth.

"Take some responsibility. Arrest that Arcopatrinas and tell her you'll pickle her alive unless she calls her Vestals off. Or, if you won't do it, let me. I don't have any religious scruples when it comes to Vestals!"

Gormayne sighed. "I'm sorry."

"Okay. Okay, if you won't help me, I know somebody who will."

She looked at him gravely, as though she knew what he was talking about. Then she started to fade again.

"I'll pray for you," she said softly.

"Yeah, you do that. Say hello for me."

Walking across the Red Courtyard toward the Temple of the Sun, the King felt calmer. The break had been made. What he had been dreading—the going it alone—was already underway. It wasn't so bad, once you accepted what was going on. It hurt, but you could deal with it because the uncertainty wasn't there to sap your will.

He walked into the shade under the collonaded portico of the temple, making a big shadow as he crossed the beam of the heliostat that projected an image of the veiled sun on the wall above the altar. The harvest, such as it was, was underway in the Realm, and Adon's altar was loaded with corn husks and bundles of wheat and rice stalks, and gourds and shriveled melons.

The God was getting old, getting ready to die so he could be reborn. Cyre always thought that it was a lousy deal for a God. Maybe that was what you got for being in love with your sisters. Especially when both of them would rather have you dead than not have you at all.

The Vestal temples were to the west of this one—Psyche's House, the shrine most venerated by the Order, was a cube draped in huge white linen panels that hid doors through which no man could pass. Meanwhile, the Dark Sister, Perse, had a much simpler shrine atop a platform between them. On it was a mynhir of black stone, drilled out at the top. For a long time, this had been the only shrine on the Rock, in the days when Queens were old Believers, venerating Perse and seeking ecstasy in dances held in secret at the sacred grove just north of the Rock. Back then the Citadel had been a real fortress, commanding the river and keeping the tablelands safe from bands of subhuman survivors of the Fall.

It was right that Adon's Temple should have been built beside them. Adon spent half the year with Psyche, and half with Perse, by arrangement made by the great Mother of Darkness, Rho, from whose womb all things had been born. Nobody ever asked Adon what he wanted to do. Probably all he wanted to do was go fishing.

The King entered the Temple sacristy, found an acolyte, asked for Eccles, and was told the Sun-priest had gone to the palace, but would return presently. In the meantime, would his Majesty like a cup of wine, or some fruit?

"Got any sausage, that kind of thing?"

"Only the bounty of the fields, your Majesty."

Cyre declined. He lighted a cigarette, watching the young man glance back in disapproval. So he wasn't very devout. But who could get excited about the bounty of the fields, when the meat-eaters were all in the other temple next door? He smoked and paced, his sandals slapping against the polished tile floor, and was down to his last few puffs when Magister Eccles finally arrived.

"Where the hell have you been?" the King asked, stubbing the cigarette out on a silver dish atop a side table.

"Majesty," Eccles said, raising his eyebrows. Eccles was highly rational, and, when he needed to be, as ruthless as anyone at court, but he took his office seriously. He believed in Adon. If you believed in Adon, you talked to him sometimes, too, and that had an effect on a man.

"Sorry," Cyre said. "Now where the hell have you been?"

"I was attending the Princess Careev," Eccles went on. "She was most upset by what happened this morning."

"And you were most anxious to provide some measure of comfort," Cyre said. Eccles pursed his lips, which was about as much emotion as he ever showed. The King cut the air with the flat of his hand.

"Never mind. She's almost ripe. You two together would

not be a bad thing, but we've got other problems. Right now I need your full attention." Eccles put his fingertips together and bent his head. Like everything he did, the movement was fluid, graceful.

"Majesty?"

"My wife's gotten very religious lately," Cyre said, picking up some grapes from the bowl the acolyte had left in the sacristy. "She's convinced that what's happening now is the will of Heaven. You know the way I am, Eccles. I might be against the system, but I've never been against her. Everything I've ever done has been to help us, but now it's no good. She's short-circuited. Leaving those girls in a riot!" He stopped and looked at Eccles. "You've got that look on your face."

"What expression is that, Majesty?"

"That, 'so you've finally seen it' look. I know it. It makes my stomach twist into knots."

"The Queen's religious development has been of some interest to me, I admit."

"Well, she's not like you. You want to join Adon when you die, but you've got a job to do here first. She doesn't think so anymore. That leaves a vacuum, and the Vestals are rushing in to fill it. She can be as religious as she wants, so long as she does her job. If she doesn't do it, you and I aren't covered. We can't afford that now. We've got to make the Vestals think about their own survival, and for that we need help. God, these grapes are sour!"

Eccles nodded. "Sour indeed. What do you want me to do?"

"We're going to pay my sister-in-law a visit. Convince her I'm in a forgiving mood."

"When?"

"Today."

"The Preserve is a day's journey by train—if the train is running."

"That's why I want to take that machine you're so proud of—the one your people uncovered and figured out. The one that flies."

Eccles put his fingertips together, spread his hands.

"That would not be possible," he said, finally.

"Why not?"

"The machine is a museum piece, your Majesty."

"Really? Then why do I hear you've been flying it yourself?"

The Magister smiled. "There are not many secrets in Almheraz."

"No," Cyre laughed. "There are not." He clapped Eccles heartily on the back. "Let's go. Fly her around. Impress her to death. I'm anxious as hell to see her!"

TEN

NANA MARA SAT DOWN on the edge of the porch of her cabin and sipped a glass of lemonade. She had been on a long walk through the grove of gum trees that shaded her property, and now she was hot, and her eyes watered from the menthol scent of gum-berries she had stepped on along the path. She sipped her drink, then dabbed at her eyes and at her forehead with the back of her sleeve.

She felt better now, knowing what she had to do.

She'd only half realized it before, on her way out of the city, where half the Agora was burning. Riding down with an escort of Vestal guards, Nana had seen the results of her meeting with the Arcopatrinas in close, horrifying detail.

The Arcopatrinas had seemed so calm, so reassuringly kind when they had met here for the first time last month. The questions she'd asked about the Gormayne family were inno-cent enough, the kind of thing anyone curious about the royals would have wanted to know! She was such a nice old woman, and had taken Nana into her confidence, told her there was reason to believe that the King had committed a high crime against the Goddess. That was the reason for the ill favor that now clung to the Realm and threatened the people of Almheraz.

They had sat together on this very porch, a nanny and the spiritual head of the Vestals, who was dressed in fine silks, looking like she had just worshipped in Psyche's House. There was terrible power and authority in the way the Arcopatrinas held herself. She had mahogany skin and deep blue eyes, and when she was still, she resembled an ancient statue, carrying a calm born ages ago, when the Goddess had first chosen a soul to represent her on earth. When an Arcopatrinas died, her soul did not rest in Limbo; instead, it immediately sought out the body of a newborn babe, returning to life with full awareness. It was said that the present Arcopatrinas had called out her mother's name the moment she was born, then, when the shock had sent her mother into a faint, instructed the midwife how to revive her.

"This wrong must be set straight," the Arcopatrinas had said to her. "It would help if you could tell us what you know about the crime."

Such a reasonable request, so gently put! The Human Incarnation of Psyche's Love pulled back her cowl and smiled at Nana. Her eyes twinkled as if the whole thing were an amusing trifle, as if they were planning a joke together. She ruffed her close-cropped white hair, put her hand gently on the nanny's leg, waiting while Nana's panic grew.

"What's the matter?" She had said kindly. "Surely you want to tell us."

"Lady, I don't know what crime you mean."

The Arcopatrinas's eyebrows lifted. "Are there so many? I said high crimes against the Goddess. These are not ordinary transgressions committed by common people, Nana."

"No, of course not. But—"

"Calm yourself. Have some wine." The Arcopatrinas unslung a wine-bag from her shoulder and gave it to Nana, who took a long drink. "It's better, of course, if I don't color your mind with what I know myself, but in this case, I'm sure your confusion is genuine and heartfelt."

"Thank you, Lady," Nana said gratefully, wiping a dribble of wine from her chin with the hem of her cloak.

"There. I want you to stop being afraid. What I'm talking about happened fifteen years ago, when the Queen gave birth to a son. The King had us barred from the birthing-room. Do you remember? Yes?"

"Yes."

"Good. We were told the babe was stillborn. Who can forget that tragic funeral, how the whole city lined the streets and wept when they brought that precious, tiny mummy out on a tumbrel, all loaded with flowers! And the King riding behind shaking with grief, barely able to stay atop his wolf! Do you know, Nana, that he embraced me that day?"

"No," Nana said with some astonishment, knowing how Cyre felt about Vestals.

"I had a feeling, when he touched me, that something was horribly wrong, but I put it down to sadness. Who can explain why fathers are so attached to their sons, when the birth of a boy is such a misfortune to any family?"

"Who knows?" Nana said, swallowing more wine.

The Arcopatrinas chuckled. "But you were there, Nana. And so were some schells, and the Princesses. You witnessed the birth."

Nana could only nod her head.

"Good. I've seen visions, Nana Mara! I've seen a babe rising from the dead. Someone who breathed slowly enough to fool the embalmer."

"But that's not what happened!" Nana blurted.

"Are you telling me my vision was wrong?"

"It looked dead enough, Lady. See, I was to wash the baby and get it ready for shriving—his parents didn't have the heart to do it. The little thing lying there, with its eyes looking like glass beads! I took the poor thing to my room, and was standing with the body in my arms in front of the mirror in my bathroom. It was so sweet, and I was rocking it back and forth, singing to it a little, because my heart was breaking! The King . . . well, he has not been the same since that day, nor the Queen either, and my heart was breaking for them, too. So I was looking at the child in the mirror, and I was praying to the Goddess. 'Let this soul come back!' I said, 'and let it be born a girl!'

"That's when I felt it, Matron! Something touched my arm, something cold, and I turned, and Gods, there it was, the anima of old Queen Cleilla, standing right next to me, and there not being any sign of her in that mirror! I know who it was because I was there at the funeral when I was just a little girl. Well, maybe not so little, but I knew who it was all the same. Oh, she was a horrible sight: Dry as shoe leather, wearing tatters of the gown she was buried in. And she didn't have eyes, exactly, either. The eyes had rotted away long ago, you see, but inside the sockets there was something burning like the last coals of a fire.

"I tried to pull away, but it held onto my arm, moving its feet a little with a sort of scratching sound. Then I was too frightened to do anything but watch as it reached out with its other hand and touched that poor child. And the baby moved again when it did! Then the anima spoke to me.

" 'Care for this child,' it says, shaking all over like the leaves on a tree in November—'' Nana's voice caught.

"Go on!" the Arcopatrinas ordered.

"Well, I wanted to fall down on my knees, but I was holding the baby, so I said, 'Praise to you, Lady, let me go and I'll tell this poor child's parents!' But the anima looks at me with those coal-socket eyes and says, 'His soul is sleeping until one comes who can wake it. You must protect him until that day.'

" 'But how?' I ask. She says, 'Go to the barge of the embalmer in Wharvesunder. Tonight an infant that was born dead will be brought to him. You must wait until he and his apprentices are asleep. When they are, go aboard, and bring the dead baby here for shriving in place of this one.' ''

" 'And what will I do with this baby?' I asked, because by now he had started smacking his lips as though he was hungry-like, though he didn't cry, and kept staring out ahead, never blinking, looking right at me without seeing, any more than I could see the anima of the old Queen in that mirror!'''

"The anima touched my breast. It got cold, and then hot, and then I felt it getting heavy. 'You may feed it,' the old Queen says. 'It will suck from you tonight, but tomorrow you

must take the child to Panault, to the woman who is caretaker
of the King's birthplace there. She will know what to do.' "

"And did you do all that, Nana Mara?" the Arcopatrinas
had asked.

"Yes!" Nana wailed. "Yes, and one thing more. The
anima said I must never tell a soul. And I never have! Never,
even when I looked at the King's face and saw the sadness in
his eyes because he'd lost his son! Gods, Matron, what have
you done to me! What have you done . . ."

*Then the Arcopatrinas touched me and told me to sleep
. . .* Nana Mara remembered, finishing her lemonade. *And I
woke up here.* Something in the wine made me talk, made me
forget. . . .

*And they went to Panault and destroyed the King's house
. . . Destroyed what was in the King's house! Why didn't I
tell him? He could have done something to protect his son, if
only he had known. The old Queen wanted to save the boy's
life, and now it's lost because of me. All because of me!*

She sighed, then yawned, getting up slowly, going inside
the house. On the kitchen wall, over the sink, was a tintype
of the Princesses, taken last spring. Maud had a flower
behind her ear, and grimaced at the camera; Careev sat
demurely at her side wearing a beaded headdress, holding
flowers in her lap. Careev would be getting married soon,
Nana thought, to the Sun-priest if the King had his way. But
it would all be for nothing, because that boy in Panault, who
could not speak except to repeat word-for-word anything that
was said to him, who did nothing except eat what was put in
front of him, that boy was the key to the King and Queen
surviving. It must be, or the anima would never have appeared to her. Why should it swear her to secrecy, hint at dire
consequences should Nana fail?

And fail she had . . .

Nana's vision blurred. Warmth spread through her chest,
almost the way it had when the anima had touched her
breast. It was almost enough to cover up the desolation she
felt. Almost . . .

There were cut and squeezed-out lemons on the counter, a
wooden box of sugar, and a tiny dark bottle, stoppered with a
plug of blood-red wax, whose contents she had poured into

the pitcher of lemonade. Wharvesunder was the place to go for bottles like that. Wharvesunder, her old home, the place the sun never touched, where it was always cool, where Adon never came. It was Perse's world, dark and cold . . . where light was an invader. . . .

Nana sat down in a chair. The Eye was just beginning to set, and she had failed. Her soul was for the Dark Sister to take now. Let her do with it what she would, as she deserved. . . .

She closed her eyes and went to her.

ELEVEN

THE FLYING MACHINE looked like a dragonfly with a fan mounted at the end of a long, narrow tail and a pair of cylinders, each with its own fan, mounted on either side of the egg-shaped passenger compartment. Except for a few dents, the machine was cleaned up and gleaming.

"We had three of these," Eccles explained, rolling the machine on its three rubber tires through the large doorway to the shop. "I'm the only one left who knows how to fly it."

"I thought you said you were incapable." Cyre said.

Eccles lifted the top of the riding compartment, helped the King climb inside, and got in himself.

"At the time, I was not lying. This machine was still being restored. That rendered me incapable of operating it—"

"Oh, can it," the King said disgustedly. "You wanted to put me off."

"True," Eccles replied matter-of-factly.

"I don't like you hiding things from me."

"Perhaps you should look at it as managing information."

Eccles busied himself throwing switches on the console between the two seats. A whine started that rattled Cyre's teeth, and when the Sun-priest pulled a T-handle on the floor, the machine rolled up a ramp that led to a platform in the rear of the Temple. The fans on the side pads began to spin; Eccles pulled on some knobs, listened to the sounds the machine was making, and then, when they seemed to stabilize, grabbed a tiller and eased it back toward his body.

Immediately the machine lifted into the air, banked slightly, and soared up and away from the Rock and over the river. Soon Almheraz became a scattering of white dots against the great scoop taken out of the Tablelands, while the Tumulos River resembled flat steel strapping coiling this way and that as it headed toward the hazy expanse of the Crescent Sea. The Veil was thin today; the Eye also looked like steel, cutting through the violet haze that normally shrouded it.

After several minutes, as the land passed steadily beneath them, Cyre realized that flying was not entirely to his liking. For one thing, he did not understand what kept the machine in the air; for another, he wasn't sure they were going where they were supposed to be going. The river seemed too tiny, the familiar landmarks unrecognizable. As the river separated into crisscrossed fingerlets spreading from the main channel, Eccles pointed out a button of dark green in the middle of it.

"That is Queen's Island, Majesty,"

The King did not want to believe him. He jabbed a cigarette into his mouth, and groped through his pockets for a light. Eccles let him grope for a while, before glancing over at him.

"Are you going to insist on fouling our limited supply of air?"

"Come on, Magister. I've got a lot on my mind. I don't think I feel so good, either."

"Then by all means." The Magister pulled one of the knobs out of the console, revealing a cylinder that glowed at one end. After hesitating, Cyre touched his cigarette to it and got it going.

"Gee, that's great," the King said, admiring the device, smiling for the first time since they'd left the Citadel.

"Yes. Apparently, the ancients were as fond of smoking as

you are. We found the remains of several cigarettes underneath the seats when we were refurbishing this flyer.''

"Maybe they weren't all bad."

"They fell," Eccles replied, as if that was all the refutation he needed.

"What's that supposed to mean?"

"They used powers that did not rightfully belong to them.''

"So what did that make them? Blasphemers? Tell me something, Magister. If you really believed that, why did you put this thing back together? How come you learned to fly it?"

Eccles shrugged. "It was Fate."

"Convenient."

"And we prayed for guidance."

"Well, maybe that's the difference between them and us. They didn't sit around waiting to find out what God wanted them to do. They wanted to fly, and they went out and did something about it."

"As I pointed out, their world no longer exists."

"Okay. Say they were punished. Say that God and his two sisters were up there getting tired of people trying to be something they're not. So they lower the boom. Instead of flying around, now we're looking under rocks for grubs to eat. Doesn't that seem like a warning to you? So how come you're willing to risk it happening all over again? Don't you think Adon's getting a little twist in his stomach, watching us now?"

"No."

"Why not?"

"Because we would not be able to do it, if he did not will it to be so. That is the price of resurrection after the Fall."

"I can't believe it," the King said. "The Gods we have now had to be around then, too. The same rules that apply to us should have applied to them."

"They did," the Magister replied. "That is why the sky is presently not filled with these." He nudged the control stick to the left. "I'm turning," he said. "Please be ready."

The horizon tilted; the sea swung behind them. Now the King could make out a thin red line of cliffs to the northeast: the Red Cliffs, where hawks nested and launched themselves to soar above the densely forested valleys of the Queen's Preserve.

"Think if you were a father, Eccles. What would be the point in having children if you made them do and think the same things you did? Nobody grows that way. Nothing gets done, and the world gets cheated, because it's already had a dose of you to begin with."

"When one is a child, one has the *illusion* of being free, because there is not yet an understanding of the world as it is. A child believes he is invulnerable, yet he would not be able to survive without the support of his parents. In the same way now, you travel to see your sister-in-law under the illusion that you choose to do so by your own free will, and further, that you can change the course of events if you are successful in gaining her assistance and avoiding the high price she will surely wish you to pay for the privilege of having it."

"That's a swell line of reasoning," the King said, looking around for a place to stub out his cigarette. Eccles opened a small ashtray in the front of the control console for him. "Why bother to do anything at all then?"

"Because we are meant to act," Eccles replied. "The very fact that we do act proves we are meant to. The illusion I just spoke of is what protects us, prevents us from becoming unhappy about it. Just as the Veil keeps us from the harm of the direct rays of the Eye; just as the curtain protects the audience from the actions of the puppeteer, so the illusion of freedom protects us from the intolerable tension of wanting to be free and knowing we are not."

Cyre stared out toward the Preserve. Brilliant white thunderheads, poised in billowy procession above the foothills of the Northern Cordillera, had gathered at the edge of the plateau country, tantalizing it, as they did every afternoon this time of year, with the thought of an outward march and a barrage of hailstones and blessed rain. He stared at the clouds wistfully, wishing he could snap his fingers and get them started.

The flyer veered down and sharply right with such violence the King banged his head against the bubble. Half stunned, he looked to his left, saw an immense shadow come between him and the sun. The shadow drew back, and the King saw that it had been cast by outstretched wings, whose fingerlike tips spread and pointed toward the sun. Eccles whispered softly.

"That, I believe, was the hawk called Fantil," the priest said. "It came directly for us. If I hadn't taken evasive action, the rotors would have cut it to pieces."

Cyre rubbed his head ruefully. "I think," he said, "that was the *illusion* of taking evasive action."

Eccles did not reply, and Cyre allowed himself a smile. Sometimes, it was a great wonder and immensely satisfying to shut off that fountain of rationality.

Flying just above the treetops now, slow enough for the prop wash to stir the branches of the taller trees, the machine passed the rail depot where schells grown on the Preserve were loaded for shipment, and broken-down schells disembarked to be reborn. The depot was guarded by an elite troop of Templemen who also patrolled the western perimeter of the Preserve with checkpoints in all the canyons and passes through the coastal mountains cradling the Preserve. Their orders were to prevent the Warden from leaving. With one exception, they had been successful for fifteen years.

Some of these troops saluted as the flyer passed overhead. Eccles had telegraphed his plans before leaving the temple. He had also given orders that, if the flyer should not pass over the station again within three hours, a squad was to enter the Preserve prepared to fight.

A tarmacked road wound down through the forest from the railhead, and Eccles followed this. Soon trees gave way to fields of corn and wheat—apparently there had been plenty of rain in these mountains—silvery ponds stocked with fish, barns and silos and farm machinery moving slowly between the plots. This was all for the raising of schells, and tended by schell labor, supervised by Sheeme's foresters, who were human males initiated into the cult of Old Believers. Several of these were walking along the road, schells in two ragged lines trailing behind. Glancing at Eccles, Cyre thought he caught a flicker of resentment on the Magister's face.

"Don't care much for Old Believers, do you?"

"They seek ecstasy, which comes from within. It is not right that anyone should worship what comes from within."

The King sighed. "That's what I like about you, Magister. You're never confused." Suddenly he pointed. "There's the house, I think."

A fence overgrown with vines and ivy separated the house from the well-ordered reaches of the compound. There was a gate guarded by foresters; Eccles hopped the machine over this, settling the machine into a litter of dead leaves beside an arbor that grew over sagging cables and shaded some rough-hewn tables. A flurry of leaves flew thickly about and blocked the two men's vision. Eccles stopped the motor, and, as the whine died, opened the top of the bubble. Cyre started to get out.

"Please, Majesty. If you will wait a moment." He nodded in the direction of the foresters who ran around the ivy-covered corner of the house armed with drawn crossbows. Eccles reached under the seat and pulled out a weapon of his own.

"An automatic pistol," Cyre said. "God want you to have that thing, too?"

"Would you prefer that I put it away, Majesty?"

"I'll leave that up to you."

The Magister nodded, swung himself out of the flyer, and pointed the weapon at the foresters.

"Old Believers!" he cried, addressing them, "I have brought Cyre of Panault. He has business with the Mistress Warden Sheeme, if one of you will so inform her!"

Two of the foresters dropped to their knees, sighting their crossbows on the priest. The King could not help admiring the way the Magister stood there. A willingness to offer yourself up for martyrdom was an excellent quality for a religious leader to have.

"You messed up the yard," the King said. "Maybe you'd better apologize."

"Please tell the Warden we are here!" Eccles repeated. "We will defend ourselves. Do not send your souls to the Dark Lady so lightly, I beg you!"

The door on the porch opened. The King saw someone

come out into the shadows, yawning and rubbing her eyes, and he felt his pulse jump.

"What is all this?" the woman said in a soft, dry-sounding voice. She moved her hands into the sunlight, and he could see that they looked dry, too. The confinement here on the Preserve had not agreed with her, the King thought.

He put another cigarette into his mouth, climbed out of the flying machine and stood with his legs slightly apart and his fists on his hips. Either of the bowmen could have killed him easily, but he had a presence: the way he held his head with his chin tilted in toward his chest, intensifying his gaze; the way the muscles worked across his neck and back. The presence made pulling the trigger difficult.

"Is that you, Sheeme?" the King asked. "Come out of the shade, so I can see you."

The figure on the porch let go of the tattered screen door; Cyre watched with a mix of horror and fascination as she reached up for her cowl and slowly drew it back. Her mouth had tightened, held prisoner in a rigid grid of lines anchored between her nose and the point of her chin. The rich brown hair was now dull and streaked with gray. And the eyes! Once they had been like opalescent windows screening a quick and formidable soul. Now they too were dull and milky, and they stared without showing any emotion at all.

"I knew you would come here one day," Sheeme finally said.

The King spread his arms, acknowledging that he was, indeed, there.

"Only, in my vision your cloak was torn. You were bruised and scratched, and caked with your own blood, the price paid for fighting your way through this forest to me." She looked at the flying machine. "I didn't dream of your arriving in a machine."

"More godlike," the King said. "And quicker."

"Yes."

"So why don't you call off your boys? We can go inside and compare how disappointed we are."

Sheeme turned, and walked back into the house. Cyre shrugged, following, watching how the foresters tracked him with their bows. Either they didn't know or care that Eccles

could have mowed all of them down with a single burst from
his machine pistol.

How nice it would be, the King thought, *to have some
fanatics working for me for a change.*

The inside of Sheeme's house stank of sour milk, and
ammonia and rotting wool. Inside the front room were a
couch and a desk, both piled with books and papers; beyond
was a kitchen whose windows were plastered with vines that
gave everything inside a greenish cast. Near the back door, a
black cast-iron stove stood on ball-and-claw feet. The oven
door was open; inside, a tiny dog was curled up asleep atop a
filthy towel. Flies were everywhere, making a low, constant
hum, though most of them devoted their attention to an
enamelled pan filled with clotted cream on the floor beside
the stove. Cyre glanced at Eccles, thinking the fastidious
Magister must have been horrified, but he showed no sign of it.

"I was just fixing my supper," Sheeme said, nodding
toward a cutting board piled with cubes of red meat. The flies
were leaving the meat alone. "Would you like to stay?"

"I think our business won't take long," Cyre said.

"I see." Sheeme gathered the meat up with her hands,
walked it over to the stove and dumped it into a pot. Wiping
her hands clean on the front of her cloak, she looked at
Eccles. "You can start by telling me who this man is."

Cyre stroked his beard.

"Is that an impertinent question? I'm sorry if it is, but as
you can see, I haven't had much chance to practice my court
manners of late." Sheeme's gaze was open, and Cyre felt
compelled to answer.

"It's just than I have trouble believing that you don't know
exactly who he is, how much he weighs, how much money
he has in his pockets, and who he's kissed since he was old
enough to want to."

"There used to be a custom called an introduction."

"All right. This man is Eccles. He's the Magister of the
Sun-temple."

"That was once the King's office."

"He's better at it."

"And does he perform all your offices for you?"

"He's great at setting things on fire. Also believes that

everything that happens is supposed to happen, which makes him a valuable commodity.''

"I see." Sheeme went to the pantry, slid the lid part way off a stone crock, and dipped a mug inside, holding it over the crock a moment as foam dripped down the sides. She gave the mug to Eccles. "This is some beer the schells brew for me. Enjoy it while I walk a little with your King."

Eccles took the mug. Cyre nodded that he would be all right, then Sheeme pulled on her cowl and they went out to the yard. There, goats and a few chickens nosed the dust around. Sheeme strolled past a twisted oak, nearby stood a tank house and a stone tub that the farm animals used for drinking. A dark-haired schell put a plate of something that looked like liver in a tin pan. The schell looked up at Cyre, and the King was surprised to see something like curiosity in its dark eyes. A scrawny wolf chained to the tree started eating from the pan. Bones were scattered all over. Some of them were tiny skulls.

"He eats what doesn't live," Sheeme said, walking over one. Cyre expected to hear the sound of it being crushed, but she was wearing soft boots.

"Don't we all."

"I mean from the schell-barns."

"Yes. But I was thinking about something else. My son."

Sheeme glanced back without saying anything, and went into the vine-arbor to sit down on a bench in the shade.

"He would have been almost old enough now," Cyre went on, pressing. "He could have married Careev, started my line."

"Yes," Sheeme said.

"But you wouldn't let it happen." Bitterness welled in the back of Cyre's throat. "What difference would it have made to you? We would have left you alone."

"As long as I stayed away."

"What else would you have done? You made your choice a long time before I even met your sister. You could have killed her a dozen times over. You could have been Queen. But then, there'd be no time to dabble with darkness. Too many responsibilities, too many people looking at you. Too much light. You knew you couldn't live that way, and so you made your choice. You wanted to be here. What I did or what Gormayne did would have made no difference.''

"I wanted your child.''

"You had your chance. Passing it up didn't give you the right to kill that baby.''

"It wasn't just a killing. I had a way to bottle that soul, and by paralyzing it first, I could have taken it. Your daughter was to have helped me, but something went wrong. Only half the venom I needed to make it work got to the baby. The soul escaped. The baby died.''

"I should have killed you.''

Sheeme sighed. "That was a long time ago. What I did then doesn't seem so urgent any more. I'm telling you what mattered to me then.''

Cyre got another cigarette going.

"It still matters.''

"Why? You've got the Magister. He's as good to you as a son.''

"He's not my blood!''

"And it's angry blood, isn't it? It rises up and washes through you and gives you wonderful power. But when it stops bubbling and drains back, you look around and don't quite know what you've done, or why. You've locked me here for seventeen years, Cyre. Didn't you every think of me all that time? Didn't you ever wake up in the middle of the night wondering where I was, whether I way lying awake thinking of you? Didn't you ever wish you had my help?''

Cyre was silent. The Warden shook her head.

"Yes, there's your blood, and your blood rules you and you rule by anger and not by will, and if your son had that blood in him, he would rule the same way and it would not be good enough. Change requires will and reconciliation, my great and glorious King. Your youngest daughter's full of that. Be content. She and the Magister can have a son. You know that. Otherwise, you wouldn't have come here, wouldn't have swallowed all that anger.''

"Damn,'' the King said, rubbing his eyes. "You're still the same. Still twisting everything until it comes out your way.''

"Still telling the truth.''

The schell that had fed the wolf was still standing nearby, watching them intently. Cyre pointed to him with his thumb. "What's with that schell?"

"He's a project of mine."

"Well get him the hell away from me. He's giving me the creeps, the way he stares."

Sheeme smiled. "Very well. Sportus! Go tend to the hawks."

The schell moved off. Cyre wiped his forehead with his hand.

"This damned weather!" Cyre's eyes narrowed. "Can't you do something about it?"

"In these times, men fly about the countryside in machines. They feed wood to the boilers of trains. What do they need magic for?"

"I notice you've had plenty of rain here."

"The Goddess we worship is a lonely and neglected one. Perse rewards those who are devoted to her."

"Bullshit," Cyre said.

"You want my cooperation. You expect that, because you think there's a debt remaining between us."

"I must be nuts to want to make a deal with you," Cyre said. "I don't know what you want from me."

Sheeme got up. "You came here to see me. You were sure you were over me and so you came to tell me about it. You and your deals! I saw how you were when I came out. Pleased at yourself that I was looking so horrible. Oh, she's been sitting here biting the ends of her hair! She's scrawny and gray and dried-up, and I don't have a thing to worry about. Well, come here, stupid, pig-brained man!" She caught his sleeve, twisting it in her surprisingly strong hands, so that he had to turn and face her. The breeze stirred then, pushing the hood of her cloak back a little. Cyre swallowed. Her eyes had come to life.

"Remember the night my mother announced your and Gormayne's betrothal? I slipped away from the banquet, that awful party! And I went into the garden, and you were there, smoking. You wouldn't look at me or talk to me; you were acting just like you are now. So I put my hands on your shoulders, just like this. And I tilted your chin up and I said that you really weren't much of a man at all. You scowled

back. Oh, but you were a man, so you said! You were doing
what you had to do. That's what real men did. What they
were supposed to. Now tell me, my big, strong, invulnerable
man. Do you remember what I said to all that?''

"No," Cyre lied.

"I said," Sheeme said, touching his beard with her fingers, "that if you were a man you would stand up for what
you wanted. That was what you had to do. You still tried to
get away, telling me you had what you really wanted—as if
my sister had anything to offer you! She had nothing except
that crown, and that would have been yours for the taking
without her! But what you really wanted was me, wasn't it?

"Do you remember how it felt to touch me, Cyre? You
reached inside my cloak, and unfastened the pin of my gown.
Do you remember how I trembled when you did that? How
all the breath seemed to come out of me, and how you put
your fingers into my hair and closed them just enough to
bring my head up, and then backed me two steps—funny how
I remember taking those steps, your Majesty!—against the
trunk of a tree and kissed me? And then you lifted my gown
up and pushed inside me? Remember how that felt, Cyre!
Remember how I spread my legs and leaned back against that
tree and you took me, moving your hips so that every time
you pushed deeper into me you lifted me up off the ground! I
would have done anything for you then. Anything.''

Her voice lowered to a whisper, and she kissed him. *All
right,* he thought, *I'm letting her kiss me.* But that changed. It
was she letting him kiss her, and him not caring about
anything but the taste of her and the soft strength of her body
against his. They kissed for a long time, until she pushed him
back.

"Now will you admit it?" she whispered. "You didn't
imprison me here. I was waiting! Hoping you'd break free of
the fences you put up.''

"I don't know," Cyre said huskily, rubbing his eyes.
Sheeme kissed his cheek. "I don't—"

"Shhh! Now we've made a start. Now you can tell me who
you want killed.''

Cyre blinked.

"I know you've got troops, and plenty of schells, but civil

war makes you hesitate. You don't know what the people would do. The men might complain about their status, but when the fight came, they would be out there with pitchforks dying for the right to live in their wife's house.''

"They would."

"So. Who is it to be?"

Cyre said, "The Arcopatrinas."

"You don't need me for that."

"I want her soul. I want you to do what you were going to do to my son. I want her soul so there'll be no more infants speaking Psyche's name in the birthing room. No more miracles. I want the soul, so I can hold it for ransom. They'll have to pull back, then. When they proclaim a successor, we'll unmask it, show it's a fake. No rebirth. No direct line from Psyche. No more Vestals."

"I see. And what will I get in return?" Sheeme seemed amused.

"Your freedom. You can leave here without worrying about your birds."

Sheeme winced. Eight years ago, when she had gone to Almheraz, Cyre's men had entered the Preserve and captured the hawkhouse. After that, one hawk was killed each day until the Warden returned.

"I've already got my freedom," Sheeme said. "I don't need to leave this place ever again." She was silent for a moment, pulling a grape leaf from one of the vines in the arbor, twirling its stem. "You're as shameless as you accuse me of being. And as faithless. However, you've come here, you've asked, and I'll admit there's a certain challenge in it."

"Will you do it?"

"Ah. Now that is a touching question. Will I do it? After seventeen years, after the murder of five of my best young birds. After watching you go to someone you thought you could use, instead of the woman who loved you. Will I do it." She turned to him. "What would someone whose past was stolen need, except the future?"

Cyre's eyes narrowed. "What are you talking about?"

"Did you imagine that I'd keep the Preserve for you until the day I died, when you could swallow it up along with the rest of the Queen's possessions? No, I intend to pass on my knowledge. I fully intend to train a young woman in the ecstatic arts I practice. You'll have a new Warden in your grandson's time, I promise you."

"Who?"

"Maud."

"No."

Sheeme laughed. "Who would you give. Careev? I'm sure she'd be useful to me as she would be to you! No, I want Maud. That way, both sides share the risk. You wager your grandson will be strong enough to hold the Realm, and I wager that magic will survive. That souls will always come when they are called!"

"I'll want proof," Cyre said. "I want to see the Arcopatrinas's soul in a bottle!"

"Very well. And when you see it you'll send Maud here to me."

"All right."

"Then we have a deal." The Warden pulled on her hood and walked out of the arbor. The King jogged after her.

"I want you to know something."

"Yes?"

"I meant that kiss. I just wish things could have been different. That we could have been together."

"Are you trying to be sweet?"

"I'm trying to be honest."

"Yes. Yes, I suppose you are. But Cyre, you know how its always been. As soon as you go away from here, you say to yourself how muddled-up I make you. You feel that real, true self coming back, wanting to take back everything you said, all the arrangements you made when you were foggy. And you'll fly out of here wondering how you can get me to do this thing without paying what you owe."

"And I'm sure you took that into account when you set your price."

"I can always come get her," Sheeme said. "I'll send word when the Arcopatrinas is gone."

"When?"

Sheeme turned. "You had seventeen years to do this, and now you're impatient. What a man you are! Would tonight be soon enough? I have to find out where she is and I have to get ready. Capturing a soul is not easy. You can capture a thousand hearts with what it takes to capture a soul.''

She walked off toward the hawkhouse and the King went back inside to fetch Eccles. He found the Magister still in the kitchen, sitting in a chair and petting the little dog that had been in the oven and which was now on his lap.

"I gather you were successful,'' the Magister said.

"Charm still counts for something in this world. What have you been doing?''

"Getting to know this excellent little creature,'' Eccles said, stroking the dog's long, silky ears. "It is sweet-tempered, intelligent—and I think you will agree, very handsome-looking for a dog.'' Eccles picked the dog up, turning it around for Cyre to see.

With the exception of the long ears, its face was a miniature copy of the King's.

"Put it back in the oven,'' the King said, feeling queasy.

"I will,'' Eccles said, doing it. "There's my girl. Back you go.''

"Gods, that's disgusting.''

"Yes, and I pray you will keep it in mind when you deal with her.''

"Let's get out of here,'' the King said. "You can tell me how I did.''

TWELVE

IN ANCIENT TIMES, the Queen of Almheraz also served as Arcopatrinas, as well as Priestess of both Psyche and Perse. In those days she reigned at Queen's Island in the Tumulos delta during the summer when the sun was in Psyche's house. The other six months of the year she spent in the forests of the Preserve, practicing Perse's dark mysteries with the Old Believers. The King, meanwhile, stayed in Almheraz, administering as an agent of the land-holding Families of the Realm. He was High Priest of the Sun, visited by the Queen during the Death of Adon Festival in the fall, and at the Vernal sacrifices each spring.

Thus a King sat in the Citadel until the sun passed through the twelve Houses. Then the King floated down the river aboard a golden barque, presented himself to the Queen at her Island, and, after suitable ceremony, was gutted and cut up alive, some pieces burned, some buried, the head thrown into the river.

A hearty and energetic Queen might go through three or

four Kings during her reign. But crops were always good, and the Realm was happy.

Later, as religion became more formal and less mysterious, Kings started to live longer. They invented something called politics, and appointed somebody to be cut up and scattered in their place. The sky didn't cave in when this happened. Changing the rules only opened the door for other things, such as when Queen Dulshe, Materfamilias of the Gormayne branch, gave birth to twins who emerged from her womb tangled together, thereby giving dual heirs to the Realm. When neither disease nor assassination carried the extra Princess back to Adon's loving arms, Dulshe ordered the family split. One daughter would be Queen of the Realm; the other Arcopatrinas, commanding the loyalty of the Order of Vestals, and holding title to all the lands belonging to it. The Arcopatrinas would not marry, since she was considered the co-wife of the King; and to keep the King down and balance maintained within the Realm, his office and the office of High Priest were also split—although in practice, some Kings took the priesthood for themselves, or priests became King when they married the Queen.

The present Arcopatrinas, however, never thought of it that way. She considered herself rightful ruler of the Realm—and Queens, all of them, temporary custodians of the throne.

But today, these questions were far from the old woman's mind as she sat sipping iced wine from the veranda of her house on the bluffs above the Tumulos, across the water from the capital. Rarei was back. She had just returned from the Steppes, and what the Arcopatrinas had heard about the trial in Panault made her feel secure in a cautious, contented way. The King's plans were dashed. His son—whose existence had been a nagging rumor for fifteen years—was dead at last. The Order was now in a position to triumph once and for all over the other powers in the Realm. It was a good feeling. Let the King send his schells!

She had eaten a big dinner of chicken and boiled asparagus, washing it down with a sharp white wine from one of the Order's southern vineyards. She was a little drunk, but felt the urge to be active that comes when plans have been set into motion. The Tumulos was blocked. The roads were closed, and so were the rail lines. The city was hot and starving and ready to riot. It was only a matter of time before the Queen would have to give up her husband.

The Arcopatrinas finished the wine in her cup, lay down on a chaise—waving away the Vestal who stepped forward to fan her—and closed her eyes, listening to the sound of the river.

After a while, she opened them. Moonlit clouds scudded across the sky. Someone was saying how sorry they were to wake her up.

Matron Rarei had come. The Arcopatrinas was not sure she liked the way Rarei was looking down at her, as though she was examining a mummy inside a glass case.

"They should have announced you," she said.

"I asked them not to. I wanted to pray here awhile, before I go back to the Temple."

That was like Rarei, the Arcopatrinas thought. She was a strong girl, with a firm jaw and steely, constantly shifting eyes; when she spoke of spiritual things, she used terms like *running,* and *lifting,* and *pushing* down. The Matron was very sure of herself, and ambitious, knowing that when the present Arcopatrinas finally retreated to Adon's arms, she would run the Order for the successor, until the reincarnation reached the Age of Reason as determined by a series of tests that was part of ancient Vestal lore. The Arcopatrinas had no great love for Rarei, but had to admit that she had been very good for the Order, very good indeed.

"So," the Arcopatrinas said, feeling eager now that she was waking up. "Tell me everything! Was the old nanny telling the truth?"

"Yes. There was a boy living in the King's house there. He was the right age, fifteen or so. He lived with a caretaker woman who was deaf or dumb. He couldn't really speak himself. We examined some of the townsfolk, and everyone knew him, but didn't really know who he was or what he was doing there. They just accepted him, like some sort of idiot mascot."

"But he would have been just about the right age for the King's son."

"Yes."

"And what happened when you examined him?"

"Well, as I said, he was an idiot. He'd speak, but only to repeat things, like a schell. I had things from the palace with me, including some of the Queen's prayer-beads. They didn't make much of an impression on him. He tried to put the beads into his mouth."

"That was a sign."

"I wouldn't call it that. I wanted to make sure, so I called out the townswomen and we had a trial. Circle and candle. It was an excellent one; the chanting just seemed to swell after a while, and people fainted. I think—in fact I know—we could have called out any soul we wanted, and gotten it dancing over the candle. But the *particular* soul—"

The Arcopatrinas reached for the wine. "Nothing?"

"Nothing. If the boy had a soul, it would have taken Adon's ten wolves to yank it free. He just laid on the ground, still as a stone. Hot wax dripping onto his hands and he didn't even flinch. I started wondering after a while whether it was some kind of gross, perverted act. I admit, Mother, that I became angry. I wanted that proof, and it wasn't coming! But then I began to think, there's got to be a reason somewhere, that this boy's like this, faking or not, because of something else. Deaf and dumb caretaker, the nurse sneaking up there every couple of months, spending time with the boy, talking to him, rocking him like a baby, telling him someday he'd know who he was, someday he'd make his father proud."

"But he was a half-wit."

"I pushed the candle into his stomach and looked into his eyes. Nothing! They were like buttons, like the eyes of fish you catch in deep water and pull into the boat. He couldn't feed or dress himself, from what we got out of the caretaker."

"Hm. You know, the nanny swore to me the King didn't dream his boy was still alive."

"I think she was telling the truth. Everyone I examined said that Cyre had not been home in at least twenty years. And the boy never left Panault. If the King had known about him, I can't help but think he'd have brought him to Almheraz."

"Which was what the nanny was hoping for. Is there more wine?"

"A little."

The Acropatrinas held out her cup. *Just like her*, Rarei thought, *not offering me any, not because she's rude, but because the thought never occurred to her.*

"Right, then," the Arcopatrinas said. "Tell me what you did."

"We drowned him," Rarei answered, feeling a warm spot at the top of her stomach, remembering how it was. "He carried the weight himself, right up to the edge of a pond outside of town. Some of the women got a little frightened about it—as I said, the boy was a mascot. I took him by the shoulders and pushed him in. I was looking for a little bit of tension, some sign of fright. After all, this is the end of the King, his plans for a dynasty. But there was nothing. Just a splash and a few bubbles, and, somewhere out there, his unshriven soul." This last was said in a faraway voice.

"Where's the body?" the Acropatrinas asked.

"Well. . . ."

The Acropatrinas stiffened, as if all the wine in her had suddenly evaporated.

"We went back the next day with a diver, one of the men from the village. He spent two hours looking, but this pond was in a quarry, and there'd been some kind of rockslide after we were there, so the bottom was all stirred up and murky. There were big piles of rubble right over the place we'd dropped him in. I mean, I'd rather have the body, too, Mother, but where else could it be? He was chained to a chunk of granite the size of that pillow. And he was just like a schell! I could have told him to walk in the water himself, and he would have done it."

The Arcopatrinas relaxed.

"Well. I just found out a couple hours before you got here that the nanny's dead, too. She drank poison, out at a little house she owned."

"She must have found out about the boy."

"I think she remembered that little talk I had with her. That drug we gave her to make her forget didn't work, or maybe it wore off."

"I don't think it matters, Mother."

"No. She couldn't help the boy, and she couldn't help his

father. It's over for him. We've got the Queen, and we'll soon have that dull little daughter of hers. He knows it's over, too. He left the city. They tell me he flew out.''

"Flew?"

"Oh, yes. He flapped his stubby little arms and lifted right off the ground!'' The women laughed, the Arcopatrinas because of the wine, Rarei because of how laughing broke the Arcopatrinas's face into pieces that were like the curled plates of sun-baked mud on the bottom of a dried-up lake. Rarei knew all about the King's flying. Vestals had seen him and the Magister taking off, and reported it to her. Let him fly! He'd be punished for his presumptuousness and his pride soon enough.

The laughing died down. The Arcopatrinas stared into her cup. Bell sounds from the prayer-wheel mounted on the roof came faster all of a sudden, and then died. Rarei looked up, saw something moving—a flash of something green.

I'm tired, she thought. *Maybe it's time I got out of here, before I have to listen to her snoring.* Her escort was out in the kitchen getting something to eat. Rarei decided to check on how they were doing. She sent a Vestal, who came back with the news. Nobody was in the kitchen.

"Tell the Bachelor Sergeant I want to see him right away.''

"Mind of his own?'' the Arcopatrinas mumbled, face in one of the cushions.

Rarei did not answer. They waited. Rarei's impatience turned to anger as the Vestal did not return. The house was very still. Then a single clean whistle-note shot through the silence. Rarei stood up, feeling the tension in her neck and shoulders, letting it ease until she felt strong and sharp.

"Mother, you've got to get up.''

"Not ready yet—''

"Come on.'' She draped the Arcopatrinas's arm over her shoulder, yanking her to her feet. "We'll go down to the pier.''

"Whafor?''

"So you can sleep in my boat.'' *So you don't get killed.* She gave the Arcopatrinas a little shove to get her started, stood back against the cool rock wall, and looked for people moving around up at the top of the ramp.

The prayer-bells started ringing again.

She heard the Arcopatrinas bumping against the rail, saw the enormous silhouette of a bird with wings stretched out against the silvery clouds, saw the wings pull in and a dark shape, pointed and streamlined, fall in from the clouds with a piercing whistle, just as the skin seemed to tighten at the top of her right thigh. She looked down and saw blood rolling down her gown, looked over and saw the bird hit the Arcopatrinas from behind, sending her stumbling forward and down onto her stomach, looked around and saw a man in a green cloak holding a crossbow, and a full-faced, brown-skinned woman in a dusty quilted suit walking toward her.

Just like that, one, two, three, with the leg starting to throb being the fourth thing, the thing that made Rarei want to sit down. It was hard to breathe, all of a sudden; her leg felt like a piece of wood. She sat down, tried to figure out why the woman looked so familiar.

The woman and the bowman stood right over her. "The bolt's poisoned," the woman said. "Sorry, but we ran out of the plain."

The bird climbed onto the Arcopatrinas's back, shifted her tail feathers the way a chicken does getting on a nest, and covered the Arcopatrinas's body by pointing her wings forward and spreading the feathers.

"Bellflower makes a good antidote, though," the woman was saying. "It grows all over this bluff—in fact, I noticed a nice clump right beside the back porch. Four or five leaves should do the trick. And you've got three hours. Well, maybe just two. You'll be unconscious at least an hour before your heart stops."

The hawk brought its stinger out. It looked like a black leather whip, and the hawk slapped it twice on the floor before arcing up, white barb gleaming just for an instant, and then she whipped it hard into the soft, thick shoulder of her victim. The Arcopatrinas shuddered, sighed, as if she had just seen the ending of a sad play.

"You're . . . the Warden . . ." Rarei said. The whole lower part of her body was numb now.

"Thank you, yes, I am. And now, you'd really better start. I calculated this very carefully before I let him shoot you.

How far to crawl, how your speed will decrease, getting off the porch. Now, if you'll pardon me, my good Lady, I've got something to do that will take a lot of concentration."

She told the forester to stay where he was, and walked slowly down the ramp, coming close to the hawk. Fantil shifted nervously on the Arcopatrinas's shoulder. She was jealous of her kill, and if disturbed too much would leave it before she took the soul. But Fantil had also done this for Sheeme a dozen times and would stay so long as the Warden remained courteous. The Hawk's tongue flicked out. If was swollen bright red, the end beginning to separate into fibrils. Sheeme licked her lips. Fantil was going to do it!

She grabbed the Arcopatrinas's headdress with her talons, pulled it away. Then she put her beak against the back of the Arcopatrinas's head and started drilling. The ends of a Hawk's beak were like a rasp. By working them side to side, Fantil could penetrate the bones of the skull. She stood on her toes, still covering the Arcopatrinas with her wings, making tiny clicking sounds like a woodpecker. After a while, the clicking stopped and she slowly, almost lovingly fed her tongue into the hole. There was very little blood. Hawk saliva made it clot very quickly. Enough of it made an excellent poison that would turn all the blood in a person's body to brown sludge in about ten minutes.

Fantil's feathers ruffled in pulses as she fed. By now the tendrils had come out and gone all through the Arcopatrinas's brain, and through her body. The dose of venom that preceded the drilling had stunned the soul and made it want to leave her body; the tendrils made a path that a soul could follow. The ruffled back and wing feathers made Fantil seem to grow before Sheeme's eyes. At the same time, the Arcopatrinas began to look like a pile of clothes. Sheeme held her breath. The great bird lifted her head, turned—because, like all hawks she could not step backwards—and hopped groggily to the floor.

She looks stupid with her tongue hanging out that way, Sheeme thought. Truth, she was stupid now, gorged on a soul. In the wild, a hawk had to be careful to find a victim in a spot where there was some cover. Fantil would not be able to fly for fifteen or twenty minutes, until the trapped soul stopped fighting her, accepted fate, gave up. Then she could soar higher than anyone could see without a glass.

"Look at you," Sheeme said to the hawk. "You're the only one who could do this. You're the only one who could swallow that and live!"

She unslung the bag she had been carrying from her shoulder, knelt on the floor, and took out a bottle, a black lacquer box, and a jar whose screw-on top was fitted with a metal shaft that ended in two strips of gold foil. She opened the jar and filled it with a pale, faint-gold oil from the bottle. Then she opened the lacquered box, took a pinch from the lump of waxy, black-red material inside. She kneaded this between her fingers to soften it, so that when she dropped it into the oil in the jar, it dissolved into twisted curls, spreading out and thinning like smoke.

The oil started to glow a faint, steady blue. Sheeme twisted the top on; as soon as the foil strips touched the oil, they stood straight apart from each other. Sheeme felt a touch of pride, seeing that happen. The waxy substance was Dragon's Egg she had made herself almost ten years ago. It was one of the ingredients for the aqua vitae, the Elixir of Life. A bit of it would nourish the soul, make it want to stay, as it had wanted to stay in the body the bird had taken it from.

All right then. Now comes the hard part. Sheeme took another bottle out of her bag, opened it, and drank. It was new malt whiskey that burned her throat like lye. She took another sip, feeling it hit her stomach.

What she was about to do she hadn't tried for a long time. Fantil had to give up the soul she had just taken. It was Sheeme's job to dominate her, convince her that holding on was not in her best interest. Then the bird had to expel the soul without hurting it or herself.

"All right," Sheeme said, thinking of the time she had tried this with the tiny wasps, how she had failed because of Maud losing her nerve, and because she herself had wanted to coax a free soul into entering a jar long after it had been separated from its body. Things were different now. Now love wasn't affecting her thinking.

Jar in hand, Sheeme crawled over to the hawk. Fantil's head was tucked down, her eyes hooded. Next to her, the

Arcopatrinas lay still. Sheeme reached out, touched the bird's shoulders, felt her tense suddenly, talons balling up underneath her on the wooden floor.

"All right. You look at me."

Press in, so that she can't use her wings, then turn her, both thumbs under her beak, pushing her head up a little so that she has to look at me. Lock in those eyes, the way she locked into mine once, when my aunt brought me into the hawkhouse and turned me over to you. Let her know I can strangle her, just by pushing a little harder. Convince her she's got to give it up. That if she doesn't she's not going to live.

Pushing harder, the hawk's eyes coming to life as though waking up at the end of a bad dream and realizing that the dream was deadly, and real. Both hawk and handler had to believe that, if this was going to work. Let the anger build. All that time spent feeding, imping feathers, keeping eggs warm. All those days sitting behind the house with a belly full of this whiskey, seeing that little speck in the sky, knowing it was Fantil, that she was free, and that the person who had to take care of her could not leave, because if she did, the King's men would kill her birds, the birds more important than she was. All those times she'd felt like setting fire to the hawkhouse. All those times she'd been stung, felt the venom creeping up her arm or her leg, cold spreading, reaching for her heart, how she had to beat that cold back with her will, how she had to fight for her life—fight for it!—because of a careless flick of a tail. Did it amuse them when it happened? She'd always wondered, telling herself that it wasn't true, but if she really thought about it, it *was* true, they were using her, keeping her instead of the other way around, and they had nothing to do with men or women, or even other animals, they were something else, like a schell or a seer, something that had been made in the times before the Fall, something that had no right to be, and knew it, and hated what had made them in the first place.

Her fingers tightened, Fantil trying to reach her with the beak, tail whipping but no threat now, venom spent for the next five or six hours.

"*Give it up!*" Sheeme gasped, feeling her heart pound. "Give . . . it . . . ."

The tongue came out of the beak, only it wasn't a tongue, but a bundle of fibers red as fresh blood, blossoming and swirling like strands of coral in warm, clear seawater. She was doing it! But you couldn't think about it that way, putting all that effort toward the point where she would give it up. You had to focus *beyond* that point, to where the bird would be dead in your hands, and do that while you were reaching for the glowing jar that ought to be by your knee somewhere. Take your hand off, squeezing even harder with the other, feeling the tongue fibers brushing cooly against the back of the hand, then taking the jar, putting it up against the tongue, the bird shuddering now, spitting out something that smelled like raw fear.

And then the jar lighting up like an electric torch. Sheeme could feel it warming up in her hand. Fantil shrieked, pulled away, spreading her wings. She was smaller suddenly, and alert, and angry. She lashed her tail at her keeper, hit her with the barb on her arm, but the suit was quilted with a mesh of tough fibers, pure protein grown in the schell-barns, and the barb glanced harmlessly off. She shrieked again; glaring at Sheeme, but Sheeme was staring into her capture jar, and didn't notice. The great bird flew off, circling the ramp and riding the current of warm air that shot out of the top of the open vent. Sheeme stared at the jar until the light didn't hurt her eyes anymore.

The soul of the Arcopatrinas, in the form of a tiny anima, floated in the oil. It moved its arms, bumped against the glass, turned, swam, bumped into the glass again. Sheeme held the jar up and flicked it with her finger. The anima swirled through the oil like a frightened goldfish.

"There you are!" Sheeme whispered. *Is that what a piece of the Goddess looks like?* She'd done it!

She stood up over the body of the Arcopatrinas and laughed again loudly. Getting ready for the raid hadn't given her much time to think. She had one soul, and she could get another the same way. How would the King know the difference?

This jar was about to change the meaning of the word patience. It turned the fullness of time into right now. It occurred to her that there was more than a King's ransom in that jar. The Dark Goddess had suffered at the hands of her sister for too long. Here was a way to help Perse, a way to make Psyche helpless!

The anima floated still, arms outstretched. Sheeme held the jar over her head.

"Yes!" Sheeme called to it. "This is one day you'll never forget, Psyche! The day the door to your house got kicked open. This soul's been taking care of your business on earth, but not anymore! It's mine now—mine to do with as I please! Do you hear that? My—"

Something clutched at her ankles, pushed hard at the back of her legs. Sheeme grabbed at the porch rail as she went down, but she was twisting as she fell, and missed. Her other hand, the one holding the jar, cracked against wood. Sheeme heard the sound of glass shattering from the bottom of steps. She turned over, kicked hard, freed her legs.

Rarei, looked up at her, red-faced and gasping.

"You fool!" Sheeme hissed, trying to prop herself up, screaming as pain shot up her arm. Out of the corner of her eye she saw her forester lying still further up the ramp. Rarei had put a dagger into him somehow.

Blue light, pale and cool, like a firefly's, flitted up, hovered for an instant above the porch, then shot up and out of the vent toward the moon. More foresters ran around the house.

"Get my bag" Sheeme ordered, voice shaky.

"What about her?"

"She's dying. Let her enjoy it."

"I'll live to see you rot!" Rarei hissed, trying to move. The forester motioned with his crossbow, but Sheeme shook her head again.

"Get . . . me . . . out of here!"

The foresters helped her to her feet. Sheeme cradled her broken wrist and looked up at the sky, wishing she could pull the vanished soul back, trample it until it looked like a piece of dented tin, something a traveler would pull off the side of a road and beat into a cooking pan.

Someday she would. *Someday.* . . .

THIRTEEN

ALMHERAZ WAS A CLUSTER of milky lights, filtered through the smoke of fires that still burned in the Agora, at blackened piles of trash piled up in intersections. Closer to the river, the haze cleared. Wharvesunder was busy, as it was every night. The people who lived beneath the piers there spread out their nets, and got to work patching them as though nothing was wrong. They rubbed their eyes as they worked, cursing clumsy fingers. The tide was rising, and underneath the piers, Eye-bells—bell clappers tied to floating weights that bobbed in the water, rang out prayers behind tin shields that were painted with the image of the Eye and nailed to the pilings.

Bells had been the last sound the Arcopatrinas had heard.

Citadel Rock looming over the city, topped by a sprinkling of lights from windows on the north side of the palace. Everything dark on the river side, and the floodlights in front of the Temple of the Sun and Psyche's house had not been tended and so flickered in their braziers, casting faint splash-ings of red that made the pillars jump against the closed bronze doors. Back across the Red Courtyard, toward window light and through one that was open. Inside, the Princess Careev sitting at a dressing table in front of a mirror. She held a brush in her hand and stared at it, wiping a tear away from her eyes with her other hand.

"Why did she do it?" Careev said, hardly able to speak. Her sister Maud was on the other side of the room, leaning against the wall. She had a bottle of cherry brandy in her hand, taken from the breakfront in the Queen's private dining room. It was only half full, and Maud put it to her lips and drank from it again.

"Who knows?" Maud said. "She was acting really funny when we talked to her, just before we went down today. She looked funny at breakfast, when she heard about Poppa's house." She snorted and drank again. "Maybe she just got tired of living." Her sister slammed the brush down.

"You think it's funny? Everything's going bad! They want Poppa dead, and he can't do anything about it, and Momma won't. And now, poor Nana, and you don't even care!"

Maud wanted to say something back, but she could only wince. Careev was right: the old, safe days were gone. She found herself thinking about the Arcopatrinas, how Nana had gone death-pale when she'd mentioned that name. And she remembered something else, too: her aunt speaking to her in a strange voice, and the taste of candy, and the little amber tube, and what she had done with it.

She took another drink and told her sister to shut up.

Out the window, and up to the top of the palace, where the Queen's terraced garden was. The soul of the Arcopatrinas sensed a tiny light there, moving back and forth above the hedge. It was the King, pacing and smoking his cigarette.

Thunder rattled across the Tablelands. He took a last puff, crushing the butt against the tiles of the terrace wall, and thought about whether or not Sheeme had done the job. He wanted to see that soul in a bottle, wanted to make it do tricks! Thinking also about a fall-back plan. Vacating the Capital. Killing the Queen. Killing the daughters. Taking Almheraz by force with schells. Declaring a republic.

He felt something brush his ear, half turned, saw a blue light disappearing out over the dark city. The soul had considered entering his body, moving it over the edge of the rail, letting it fall into the Old Town. But the effort would have been too much. It circled the palace again and went through another window, this one in the Queen's chambers. She lay asleep on her back, caught in a shaft of moonlight that fell across her bed, her dark hair fluffed around her face, as though she were lying in a cushion of it. Thick clouds started moving across the face of the moon, and the shaft grew narrower, becoming an arrow of light, a string, and then darkness. The Queen dreamed of Adon, lying drunk and sluggish in Perse's dark lair, and of Psyche sneaking silently in with her lamp, pulling the covers off, letting the light shine on his adorable face. Of Perse flying at her with murderous thoughts and Psyche fleeing into the sky, watching the world burn until Perse brought the rains that extinguished that fire and flooded the world, and drowned her lover who was held by chains he could not break.

Outside, the first few drops of rain fell onto dry earth. The drops hit the ground and disappeared, like payment snatched away on a longstanding debt. More rain fell. Down on the river, slabs of mist began to condense, hugging the water, big drops punching holes through it.

Up through the Spillway, up onto the Plateau, the rain pounded the tent city that had sprung up to house refugees from the hinterlands. Men and women weaved drunkenly from one smoky fire to the next as their tents, which were much better at keeping out sun than rain, sagged lower and lower.

Beyond the tent city stretched a deserted highway leading north to the mountains. Rain ran off the paving stones and began to fill the ditches on either side. Water in them rose quickly.

Something lying in one of them started when the water covered its mouth.

Its feet and legs were burned, it was bruised and weak and half dead, but when the water rose the seer lifted its head, pushed itself up with its arms, and sat up.

It put its tongue out to taste the rain. The water burned, but it knew about rain and could control the pain until the rain stopped. It gave an inquisitive whistle, put its tongue out as far as it could, yellow tufts bristling like a bottle brush.

The Arcopatrinas's soul halted over it.

Its blue light was dull now and it flickered. The fear that fueled its flight from Almheraz was almost exhausted. Resignation—long needles of it, like frost crystals—were creeping in along the edges of the soul's awareness. It wanted rest. Soon there would be golden slumber, a cleansing time, preparation for rebirth. It could sense the gateway to that place; it had been through that gateway many times, could remember how it felt each time to pass through that gate.

It hurt. Even if you only had to do it once, passing through the Veil hurt enough to make you never want to go through it again. And she had done it more than once; twenty-six times, once for each rebirth of an Arcopatrinas, remembering how it was to go through the gate each time, remembering each life.

The gate was pulling her now. She could feel it, and was frightened. All the times before, when the body she had lived in was ready to die, she had been able to prepare herself, compose prayers to Psyche, achieve a state where the pain of passing through the gate did not matter as much as her duty to be reborn. This time there had been no preparation; the idea of dedication seemed hollow and unreal. This time, she wanted to stay! Stay in her own form, as she really was!

As a freed soul, the illusion that created a thing called an Arcopatrinas no longer existed. The mastery of time and the reach of space were both diminished. By expending energy—exercising its will—the soul could exist moment to moment at the quarry pound outside Panault, could see Rarei putting the boy into the water, could see him come to the surface again, saved by an old man!

The boy was alive! Soulless, as he had been from infancy, but alive and in someone's care. The King's son! If she could get to him somehow, but she was so weak, the pull of the gate so strong.

And then she realized that something below, something living, was aware of her presence. Knew her. A seer! Something like joy pulsed through it, and for an instant the blue light hovering over the road was dazzling as a lightning flash. Psyche was helping her! Showing her the way. All she had to do was come close to the creature, hold herself there . . .

She dropped toward the seer, fighting the pull of the gate with the last of her will.

The seer reached out its hands. Lightning ripped through the sky toward the empty horizon, reflecting off the wet road, making it into a silver ribbon that glowed in the darkness when the lightning had gone. The soul hovered above the seer's hands, started to move. The lightning had come from the center of the gate, and he could visualize it now as a satin-blue ring with lights flying into it, lights from people dying all over the world. The gate was there for these souls, but the gate wanted her, and pulled harder.

Just as the seer's tongue flicked into the soul, the tufts on it stood straight out, turned blood red. Then the light was gone.

The seer trembled a moment, sitting in the water. It tried to get up, lost its balance, tried again, this time splashing to its feet. It took a deep breath, stuck its tongue out, felt the rain. The rain did not hurt any more.

It had only one need now. Stepping onto the road, the seer started walking north.

FOURTEEN

"RIGHT, THEN. You watching me now?"

Marten the Traveler was on a roof in a village called Shiraz. The sheet tin roof was steep, and very hot because the Eye, even though it was low in the sky in the late afternoon, was very strong again after three straight days of rain.

Those three days of rain had turned everything around in the northern Steppes. Even though it had come too late in the year for a really decent crop, most everyone in Shiraz was out in the fields, or tending to their flocks. Already a hint of green showed along the verge of the brown hills to the west; there were shoots popping up in the dirt collected in the folds of the tin roof.

Marten knelt on a scrap of tin, adjusting his soaked headband, ready to nail the patch over a hole. People had found out about their roofs with the rain, and rain had made them willing to part with coppers, or to trade in exchange for Marten's labor and skill. Marten was finding this to be a profitable day indeed. And he had a partner to help him.

Up near the peak of the roof, the boy Komaso also knelt on a piece of tin. He held a hammer aloft in his left hand, as Marten did, and had a nail poised in the upper right corner of the patch, using the same grip and crooking his arm with his elbow out exactly as Marten did.

When Marten hit his nail, Komaso did too, and he got another nail and drove it home just half a beat behind the other man. Together they had patched three roofs that way: as long as Marten put the tin down in the right place, maneuvered the boy into the right place over it, and drove nails into a patch of similar size and shape, Komaso would copy him perfectly and hammer his patch down. Komaso was a puppet, perfectly willing to do anything Marten ordered him to do, just like a schell. Except that he was human! Marten had made sure of that, lifting the boy's shirt that first night. Schells, grown from lumps of tissue out in the Preserve, didn't have belly buttons. This boy did.

Marten finished pounding his last nail, saw the mistress of the house walking in from her chicken coop with an apron full of eggs. It would not be such a bad thing to get her to throw in an egg or two to pay for the work. He waved, and walked to the edge of the roof.

"My good Lady," he began speaking as he always did to gentry. "It appears we're through up here. Your roof—"

The woman yelped, jumping back with her eggs just in time to avoid being hit by Komaso. He had stepped to the edge of the roof when Marten did, but had been slightly closer to it and wound up walking out on nothing.

"Hell's bells!" the woman sputtered, opening her apron. "My eggs! He jumped at my eggs! What's the matter with him?"

"Beggin' your pardon, good Lady, but I'm wondering that myself. Would you mind kicking him, maybe, to see that his neck's not broken?"

Komaso groaned as he said this, and got up on one knee. The woman touched his back with her foot. "Oh, he's fine!" she snapped. "Every bone in his body'd be broken, though, if he'd done that last week, hard as that ground was. What can you be thinking of, boy!"

"That's just the trouble, ma'am. He don't think of too

much at all." He laid his finger on the side of his nose and nodded knowingly at the woman. "Sun-struck."

"Then a roof's the last place he should be!"

"Oh, no! A roof's the perfect place for somebody like him. You don't want to put healthy people up on the roof for the Eye to see."

"That says a lot about you, traveler!"

Marten smiled. "I've got a hard head."

"Hmph!"

She started for the house again. "Uh, ma'am, there's the matter of what you agreed to pay for us fixing your roof."

"Five coppers, wasn't it? Well, come down and join your boy, and I'll give 'em to you!"

"Five coppers and some produce, was what I believe we said. And I'll confess to you, good Lady, that I haven't seen so many eggs all in one place in, oh, three years! Five or six of those would ease our journey out of here all right."

"I'm sure they would. But I just broke one because your boy thinks he can fly like a bird, and I'm not in a mood to spend more. Come down here for your coppers. Produce would have been a bonus, and you just lost it!"

Marten sighed as she disappeared into her house, door slamming. He had learned a long time ago that gentry liked to have their way with travelers, and what you received in exchange for your labor was what they decided to pay. He gathered his tools and scrap tin, climbed down, putting everything neatly away inside the bow-topped wagon before knocking on the woman's door. Komaso had already climbed painfully onto the buckboard by the time she pushed four coins into Marten's hands, slamming the door again without so much as a thank-you, or an offer of something cold to drink.

Muff growled loudly from a patch of shade underneath the wagon. Marten pocketed the coins and brought him out, smoothing his fur and telling him to calm down as he fastened him into his harness. He wanted to be well out of town by dark. The exhilaration following the rains was starting to wear off as people began to remember how things really were.

Marten climbed up onto the buckboard, snapped the reins. "Come on, Muff!"

Shiraz wasn't much. They left it behind in a few minutes. Marten looked over at the boy and noticed that he was cradling something inside his shirt.

"What's this? You're not hurt, are you?" He reached for the boy, but Komaso turned away. "Come on now, let me see, let me see—"

The boy let go suddenly, and Marten saw that he had six eggs in his lap.

"Hey!" Marten laughed. "Don't tell me you squeezed those out of that missus back there? And she holding onto 'em like she laid 'em herself!" He laughed again at his joke, hoping for a response out of the boy, but Komaso's expression didn't change, and Marten straightened up and concentrated on the road. He was disappointed. Every time Komaso showed signs of native wit—and there was no denying he was good at stealing things—Marten's hopes rose, only to be dashed by silence. There was no reaching him. Marten had to be content, not push things. Finding the boy had already made his life better. You couldn't have everything. Thinking about it only made you careless with what you did have.

But it was hard, wanting a son, when you only just discovered that a son was what you really wanted.

They traveled east over rolling terrain, kicking up dust because the road was already dried out. Even so, by the time the Eye set behind the Cordillera, amber-tinted clouds were piling up high in the west, blocking out most of the Veil and dropping distant claps of thunder that rumble across the Steppes. The air had a sharp scent; Marten reckoned that it would rain before nightfall, and he was not happy about it. Funny, how a week ago he would never have imagined getting sick of rain. . . .

He looked around for a good place to camp, and when he found a notch in a hillside just off the road, he reined Muff over and closed the throttle on the steam engine. Here was shelter on three sides, and wood for a fire. One of his customers in Shiraz had given him a fine ham for his labor. They would eat well. It had been a long time since Marten had eaten ham and eggs. If he could get the eggs away from the boy, that is. . . .

He made camp, built a fire. When he got out the cooking-box, the boy seemed to understand and shyly presented the eggs to him. Marten sliced four thick slabs from the ham, and gave the rest to Muff. He melted a spoon of lard in his black cast-iron pan, sliced some tiny hard potatoes (also from Shiraz, and the best that harvest had to offer so far) and an onion, and browned them. He turned them once, shoved them aside, and browned the ham slices one by one, placing them atop the potatoes when each was done. The eggs came last: four with eyes, the last two scrambled because he accidentally broke the yolks. When everything was ready he divided in onto two tin plates, handing Komaso his along with half a loaf of fresh-baked bread.

"That's only right. You did half the work today," he said, wincing as Komaso picked up one of his slices of ham with two hands, ripping into it like a starved dog. The old man cut his own food into pieces, poured himself a cup of wine. He was taking his time, using more manners than he normally did, as though he could make up for the boy. But after another cup of wine he got up.

"Hey! You, boy! Why don't you watch what I'm doing here?" Marten broke a corner from his bread, dipping it into a pool of egg yolk with a flourish. Komaso did the same, but used his whole loaf.

"No, no, no, don't you see? Manners is what separates us from things with no souls. If you practiced enough, who knows? Manners might make you real."

Komaso stared back with bread sticking out of his mouth.

"Ahh, what a life this is," Marten groused, easing back against a rock. "Living by your wits, the world full of things that have no business being here."

He drained his cup, looked at it, then put it down and poured wine straight from his wineskin into his mouth. "Wasn't always that way. I'm not speaking of the old times now, boy! I'm talking about what I can remember, when I was your age. Things were slower then, everything had its place. You had a certain order that everybody accepted, from the Queen and King on down! Husbands respected their wives and wives took care of their husbands. Nobody worried about who was supposed to own what. Nobody questioned their place in the

world. You were born—luck of the draw—and that was that!
I was born a traveler, so I learned my trade, learned how I
was supposed to act and what people expected of me, and
then I behaved that way, and didn't have no trouble, either.
Because people knew what I was going to do, see, and so
they knew how they were supposed to act. Everybody had
their place, just like they tell us, and it was tranquil. Rained
every year, then it got hot, the Eye came out, harvest time,
then the rains again. Wet and dry and wet, and everybody
showing respect for tradition the whole time, all the time!''

He swigged more wine. ''You didn't have this tension
between men and women like you do now. You didn't have
Vestals dumping kids into the water, or squeezing the life out
of the country just because they're afraid of the Queen's
husband. I guess he is out to change things, having decided
that the old ways aren't any good. Who put that in his head, I
ask myself? Doesn't he have it good enough as it is, plenty to
eat and drink, nice places to live in, a beautiful family with a
couple of daughters who just happen to be Princesses, both of
'em! But he don't feel right about it, 'cause his wife's got the
say-so, and he wants it for himself. He wants to own the
property, he wants to say who's King after he's gone, he
wants the men to be back on top the way they were before the
Fall, and to hell with what the Ladies and Gods and Goddesses
say about the whole thing!''

''Hell!'' he squawked, squirting wine into his beard. ''What
d'you think makes him want to be like that? Think it's God's
will? Or maybe he doesn't care what Heaven thinks, he'll just
do as he pleases until Heaven decides to strike him down.
And if they don't strike him down, that means he's doing
right and everybody else is wrong, and how'd they get that
wrong in the first place? What made it change? Why isn't
what happened before good enough for now? Why're we the
ones to suffer because things ain't right? Who's gonna help us
put 'em right?''

Thunder rumbled strongly through the ground. Marten looked
up blearily. Both the boy and the wolf were asleep.

''Well,'' Marten said sourly. ''Deep thoughts never killed
nobody. An' you better not stay there, 'cause you'll be wet
soon enough. Pretty soon.'' He tried to sit up, but found he

was just too tired. Maybe take a little nap, he thought, before he cleaned up the pans.

Rain hitting the fire made the logs hiss. The wolf woke up first and growled. Marten turned over. Someone stood at the edge of firelight. The wolf sat up with raised hackles, and Marten could see him standing big and dark against the dying flames.

"Who's there?"

Then Marten realized that the stranger had no eyes. It was a seer!

Muff growled again, ears back, and then, before Marten could say or do anything, sprang at the creature. Both of them crashed through the brush outside the circle of firelight; Marten heard the wolf bay, the sound fading into the night, everything happening too fast to sort out.

"Muff! Hey!"

He was astonished. In all his years of traveling, he had never come across a seer this far south. In fact, it was the first time he'd ever been this close to a live one. Some of the villages in the Steppes kept seer mummies as trophies, and once, when he was a boy and his caravan was camped within sight of the Northern Cordillera, he and his uncle Komaso had used a spy glass to watch some seers move across the top of a ridge toward the mountains. His uncle told him then that the seers kept a lost city there, where they cared for records of the time before the Fall.

Marten didn't believe that, nor did he believe in soul-stealing, but as he peered into the night, rain spattering his face, he began to think there was something supernatural about anything that could outrun his wolf. Once, he thought he heard Muffin baying far to the southeast. After a while, he decided to try to get some sleep. There was no use worrying about Muffin. The wolf could take care of himself, after all, and he had run the seer off.

"He'll be back," Marten said, turning. "He knows where his dish is—"

Marten gaped. The boy was gone, too.

It had only been an instant—Marten was certain he'd seen Komaso out of the corner of his eye when he'd started after the seer—but now there wasn't a sign of him in camp. He crawled into the wagon and tore through the blankets in hopes that the boy was hiding. Finally he lighted a lantern, walked out to the road and called Komaso's name until his voice was raw and the rain coming down in sheets drove him back. Now he could think of only one thing: that the seer had come for his boy and stolen him away.

Pain and frustration welled up in him, and he picked up his frying pan and flung it out into the darkness.

"Hope it brains the damn thing," he muttered, opening one of the cabinets under the sleeping platform, pulling out a bottle of grain alcohol that had been flavored with a long sprig of anise and some juniper berries. He put the bottle to his lips and took a long drink.

"To hell with it." He drank some more. "To hell with it twice and back!" The alcohol was raw. It burned the top of his stomach and put him down to the floor, where he sat by his stove, heart hammering, out of breath and dizzy. Lightning flashes brought the hillside up, made the trees jump around. After a while it seemed as though the trees could dance, that his wagon was surrounded by trees dancing to lightning and thunderclaps.

"Blast 'em!" he yelled to the lightning. "*Blast* 'em. . . ."

He started thinking, knowing how stupid it was, about the day before yesterday. They'd got some coppers at a dog meet (Komaso having culled them from purses all day long), and had enough to spend the night at an inn. There, Marten had paid for a bath, and led the boy to a tub of fresh hot water. After some coaxing, he'd gotten Komaso in and had washed his hair. He could remember how the boy's hair felt in his hands, how it squeaked when he rinsed out the soap. Most of all, he remembered how Komaso stared at him while Marten had ruffled his hair with the ragged towel the innkeeper charged an extra copper for. The boy knew he was being cared for! He *had* to know. Hadn't he let Marten brush his tangled hair? That brush was in the wagon somewhere. Marten yanked open his drawers one by one, spilling everything out onto the floor between his legs. There were coils of wire, bolts, dirty tablets of paper. Marten stirred the mess around, but couldn't find the brush. When he tried to get up he lost

his balance and fell on top of the drawer, splintering the wood
with a sharp crack.

The rain began to let up. Some time later—he didn't
remember closing his eyes, but was painfully aware of how
hard it was to open them—Muff stuck his head through the
door. He put his ears back and whined, and Marten could
hear his tail thumping onto wet ground.

"Ohhh . . ." Marten said, thick-tongued. "Where did you
go, huh? Where did you go?"

Muffin scratched at the floor with his muddy paw.

"Didn't find him? Okay. We wait. He'll be back. He
knows where his dish is. We'll wait."

Muff backed out of the door and curled up under the
wagon. Marten pulled a jagged piece of drawer bottom out
from underneath him, threw it outside. He waited. The hour
was a long one, and at the end of it the first hazy glow of the
Veil reached the top of the western hills. Marten went outside. He was very thirsty. He drank a dipperful from the
water bucket, then noticed the plate Komaso had been eating
from when the seer had appeared. The eggs floated in rainwa-
ter, and the bread was soaked and crumbling. Marten fell to
his hands and knees and threw up until he thought he would
turn himself inside out. When he was through, he looked over
and saw the wolf looking at him.

Fate was balancing things again. Fate had given him something, and then taken it away. He was no worse off than he
had been a week ago, or a year ago. He could remember a
time when there had been no boy, when he could not have
imagined a boy existed. All he had to do was go back to that
time. It would take some effort, but he could do it. Marten
summoned the last of his strength, got up, staggered into the
wagon and made it to the sleeping platform.

His last thought was what it would be like to wake up and
see his precious, speechless boy again.

FIFTEEN

BUT THERE WAS NO BOY in the morning.

Marten tried to make the best of it at first, getting the wagon ready, filling the water tank, adding wood to the pile in the stoker. In the end he surrendered to the pain and drank another bottle of gin. It was like that for two days. Then, when the taste of the gin began to hurt worse than not having the boy, he got going again.

For three weeks, Marten followed the road east into the Cordillera foothills. With the rain having saved some of the year's crop, there was a belated harvest, and plenty of smithy work. Marten worked late by lamplight soldering canning kettles and strainers, reforging ploughshares, sharpening scythe blades and even making a few fine things like silver thimbles, a sign that people were feeling more optimistic. Soon, Marten had collected enough coppers to cash at a swap meet for five gold crowns, which he nailed over the door of his wagon for luck.

He was very deliberate about nailing those coins. Fate

owed him some luck. Even though Marten did his best not to
think about the boy, he had the idea he'd find him one day.
Everywhere he stopped, he asked people whether they'd seen
him. Skinny, dark eyes, sandy hair, won't speak? A thief? He
checked the jails of towns that had them, or looked up the
oldest Ladies of each place and questioned those who would
answer him. He found out plenty of things, but nothing about
the boy.

Gradually, the pain of not having Komaso turned into the
idea of not having him. As long as it was an idea, Marten
could function and keep busy. Then another idea started that
maybe he could get along without the boy, because he *was*
getting along. That brought him back to the gin. Yet, since he
was a practical man at heart, Marten knew that if you wanted
to manage your thoughts you couldn't do it from the outside.
He knocked off the gin and went back to having wine with his
dinner.

He was feeling much better by the time he reached Semele,
a railhead halfway between the northern edge of the Preserve
and the eastern edge of the Cordillera. Semele was packed.
There were three or four trains waiting in the rail yard and
pilgrims—whole families of pilgrims—ready to board them
for the trip to Almheraz and the Festival of Adon, which was
held every year at harvest time.

Marten liked Semele. Most of the people there this time of
year were in transit, temporary travelers who were no longer
able to rely on their gentry ways. Marten always felt magnan-
imous when he came to Semele in the fall. When he worked
for a pilgrim he sometimes did it for nothing. The good
feeling he generated that way never carried over to the rest of
the year, but Marten did it anyway. He wanted to keep the
scales of Fate tipped in his favor.

This year he was more generous than ever. He pried two of
the crowns loose and bought train tickets for three poor
families who couldn't afford the fare. He forged new tires for
the wheels of a wagon loaded with Old Believers in dark
hoods who swore to him that Perse would take him into her
bosom for it.

"I'd better take a lantern then," Marten joked. The people
in the masks just blinked at him. That was the thing about

unpopular religions. People who practiced them could be awfully grim.

It rained the first night in Semele, and then the weather turned cool. Marten was feeling as though he had nothing left to do in life but to make as many strangers feel happy as he could. He pried two more coins loose, leaving one, and wandered down to the market square to see what was happening. It was crowded, and Marten was surprised to see some Vestals ride in on wolfback.

It had been almost two weeks since Marten had encountered anyone of the Order. Before that, Vestals had been all over the road, blocking traffic and stirring up trouble. These particular Vestals were escorting a prison van into the square, stopping at a platform where stock-posts had been set up. As Bachelor troops brought out the prisoners, the crown stirred. Marten strained to see what was happening, and finally tapped the shoulder of the man next to him.

"What's this about, Pilgrim?"

"Blasphemers," the man replied without turning around. "Some of 'em claim to have seen the old Arcopatrinas. A few tried to pass their children off as the reincarnation."

"Reincarnation? You mean the old Lady's dead?"

"Of course she's dead. Can't be reincarnated without passing over, can you? They say she was done by the King himself!"

Bachelors clamped a thin, toothless woman into the stocks. She accepted her lot—and the jeers of the crowd—dispiritedly, and the Bachelors went back to the wagon for another prisoner.

They were thrown back outside. Two more rushed to help, along with one of the mounted women. What they brought out kicked and screamed and swore, biting one of the soldiers on the arm and getting clubbed back. Momentarily stunned, the prisoner was stretched across the wooden frame of the stocks and locked in, but it was only a moment before he recovered and began yelling again.

Marten stared. It was Komaso. Komaso *yelling* things.

"You!" he screamed at the woman on wolfback. "I know you, Thessia! Not only did I recite the Vow with your own mother, but I bounced you on my knee as well. Don't you remember how I let you fall to the floor just to toughen you up? I know you've got a birthmark in the back of your head that looks just like a fly. Come down here and look me in the eye. You know I'm telling the truth!''

Marten pushed his way through the crowd to the Vestal Komaso was screaming at.

"My Lady!" he called. "Lady, please!"

The Vestal looked down from her wolf.

"I know this boy, Lady Thessia," Marten said. "Please let me have a word with him."

"Can you shut him up?"

"I've never had a problem doin' it before," Marten replied truthfully.

"Show us your birthmark, Thessia!" somebody yelled out. Thessia reined her wolf around, knocking part of the throng back. There were no more gibes.

"Very well, old man," she said. "But be quick!"

Marten stepped out of the crowd. When he did, the boy stopped railing. He stared at the traveler, wide-eyed, breathing hard. His face was hollow-cheeked and streaked with dirty sweat, and his wrists hung limply out of the stocks.

"I know you," he said quizzically, when Marten came close.

Marten smiled in spite of everything, nodding his head. His prayers had been answered!

"I was in water. You saved my life, I think!"

"Yes!" Marten reached forward to brush the hair out of Komaso's eyes.

"Don't touch me!"

"I'm sorry. It's only that I'm so happy to see you, happy to hear you talk!" Komaso was looking at him hard, and Marten felt his heart sinking.

"What's happened to you, boy? Where did you go that night? Was it the seer? Tell me!"

"I was reborn." Komaso said, starting softly and raising his voice with each word. "Now I must go to Almheraz. Miracles have occurred that should be proclaimed from the Citadel. You must help me!"

Marten did not know what to say.

"The King is a murderer, the Queen a collaborator, and

they and their family must pay! You see that, don't you old
man? Don't you see that!''

Tears filled Marten's eyes.

''I'll say that you're my son.''

''Your son? *Your* son! As if that would make any difference!'' Komaso lifted his head. ''I wouldn't be your son, nor
any man's son! Thessia! Get this old fool away from me!''

The Vestal rode up beside him. ''You promised to shut him
up, traveler.''

''But he's . . . confused, Lady. If I could be alone with
him—''

''You're welcome to join him in the van. Tomorrow morning, too!''

''What's going to happen tomorrow morning?''

''What happens to all blasphemers. Tomorrow he'll be
burned.''

Marten looked back at Komaso. The boy was laughing.

''Burn him, too!'' Komaso roared. ''He drinks so much,
he'll never feel it!''

With the jeers of the crowd in his ears, Marten turned away
and left the square.

It was dark. Marten sat on the ground outside his wagon
and clutched a handful of the fur on his wolf's neck. He was
drinking again and hadn't bothered with a fire. The lamp
hanging from the side of the buckboard was starting to sputter. Marten wasn't sure he wanted to sit in the dark, or that he
wanted to do anything about it.

The thing about pain, he decided, was that your stomach
reached up and took hold of your mind. The thing to do was
to kill your stomach. Then, maybe, you just might be able to
sleep.

The sputtering got worse.

'' 'Mon, Muff,'' Marten said. ''Need some more alcohol.'' He got up. His stomach was not dying. He wanted to
laugh about the lamp needing alcohol but he needed alcohol
too because he had still not drunk enough to get rid of the boy
and he knew he could not sit alone in the dark. The wolf had
gone to sleep a long time ago.

Marten climbed the buckboard. He was going to fill the

lamp with what was left in the bottle, but suddenly noticed a gold crown gleaming above the doorway, and drew his knife and pried it out of the wood. So much for his luck. So much for playing by the rules. Just when he was getting by, just when he was starting to forget! Mocking him, that's what it was!

Marten looked at the coin in his hand. His stomach grabbed hold of his head again, and with an anguished cry that pounded in his ears Marten threw the crown out into the night. He had one more in his pocket and a big bag of coppers inside. He'd throw them away too!

Don't touch me. . . . To hear Komaso say those words . . . Marten groaned and slumped down to the buckboard. Somewhere, he heard his wolf growling. The lamp flared up. Somebody walking toward the wagon, Muffin getting up, tensing, hackles raised, ready to spring. Whoever it was got there first, moving with incredible swiftness to grab Muffin by the jaws. The wolf shuddered then sighed, dropping to the ground.

"Whoa," Marten said, holding up his hands. "What did you do? 'Smy only fren'." He picked up his knife and started waving it around. "Cutcha!" he said. "Cutcha—" lurching forward, losing his balance, feeling himself falling into arms, sickeningly and then—

He sat down, blinking his eyes. The seer stood over him and the world had stopped spinning.

"You!" he began, stopping as he realized his head was clear. He stood up. Somehow, he felt absolutely sober. It had happened in an instant. His knees hurt a little, and his eyes watered, but otherwise he felt clear, and surprisingly calm.

The seer seemed to be looking at him. The yellow tufted tongue flicked out; then it turned and walked a few steps in the direction of town, motioning as it did.

"Devil! I'm not following you anywhere! Muff! Muff! wake up and chase this thing off into the hills where it came from!"

Muff yawned, shifted his head, and continued to sleep. *All right, then,* Marten thought to himself, *consider things. If it meant harm, it had the chance to do it. It could have killed the wolf and killed me, too. Instead it put Muff to sleep and brought me back to my senses. Why, if not for some purpose?*

Marten took the lamp from its hook, filled it, put his knife back into its sheath and followed the seer along a path through a gorge that opened up near the rail line. The Vestals maintained a post somewhere north of the town, Marten remembered. When the seer slowed, he extinguished the lamp and stepped out of the bush. Sure enough, there stood the armored wagon that the Vestals had driven to the square, guarded by a squad of Bachelors. Maybe Komaso was still inside!

"All right, now what?" Marten said, turning—but the seer was gone.

Damn! Would have been decent to put those guards to sleep first. Still, he thought, *maybe this is for the best. May I never have to set eyes on such a god-forsaken monstrosity again!* He watched the Bachelors for a while. They were standing around smoking, looking bored. Marten felt a burst of joy, the first in a long time. He reached into his tunic pocket, found his last unspent crown, and smiled to himself.

He walked drunkenly across the clearing toward the soldiers. They stared. One put out his cigarette and drew a sword, jabbing the point into the dirt and leaning forward on it. *Stay away from that one,* Marten thought.

"Evening, gents," Marten called. "Wheresa train?"

The Bachelors looked at each other, and the one with the sword said, "Hold it, old man. Nobody's allowed near here. Beat it."

"I wanna train," Marten insisted.

"Wait your turn at the station yard like everybody else. Now move off."

" 'S'too bad. They wouda lemme on, 'cause I can turn coppers into crowns, see?" Marten held up an old green copper, pinched between his thumb and middle finger. He turned his wrist slightly, snapping his fingers, turned his wrist back—and revealed a gleaming gold coin.

"Hey, let me have that," said one of the Bachelors, trying to snatch it away. Marten grabbed him by the wrist, yanking him around so that his arm was pinned behind his back, sweeping the knife out of its sheath at the same time and drawing its blade ever so lightly across the stunned soldier's throat.

"Open the van," Marten ordered. The Bachelor leaning on the sword had watched the whole thing. Now he grinned.

"Say! That was pretty good for an old man. Except for one thing. We don't like him."

"What?"

The bachelor looked at his mates. "The old man's not getting it, is he? See, last week we had a little deal going to cover for each other so we could each have a break. Only he snitched to Thessia, and now we got night duty from now until the day Adon comes up for air, and, me being the one that was gone, I got a whipping besides. So go on and cut him. We'll be heroes. Refusing to surrender to terrorists, even when it cost us one of our dearest comrades—"

The words were cut off in his throat.

Somehow the seer had come around the other side of the van. It stroked the Bachelor lightly with the tips of its long fingers, and he collapsed like a bundle of rags. The two others looked at each other.

"The keys!" Marten ordered. "Quick now, or I'll have that thing suck the souls right out of your bodies!" From the center of town came the blast of a whistle, and the chuffing sound of steam pistons. The night train was pulling out of the station.

"I-I've got 'em," Marten's prisoner stammered.

"Give them to me!" He did, and Marten pushed him away toward the seer. The ground was starting to rumble as he fit the key into the lock and swung open the van door, the van casting a long shadow in the lamp beam of the approaching train.

"Komaso!" Marten whispered hoarsely. Somebody stirred in one of the bunks, though it was too dark to see. Then, suddenly, someone burst past him. Marten pulled himself up by the sides of the door, stuck his head out in time to see the boy run along the tracks. The night train rumbled by, coaches crammed with passengers, and somehow Komaso grabbed the stair rail of the last car and swung himself aboard. Marten stared in disbelief as the red light on the back of the train grew smaller, then disappeared altogether as the train rounded the bend out of town.

Marten sat down. Fate. He was exhausted, and would gladly have taken the boy's place. Let them burn him! But then the seer was tugging at his arm. It tugged sadly, as though it too were tired, dispirited. But it pulled Marten up and out of the van. Some of the prisoners followed. The seer kept hold of Marten's hand, and he felt thoughts beginning to form. *Almheraz. . . . Go to Almheraz. . . . The boy loves you. . . . Help him. . . . Help him. . . .*

"Old man, what's to become of us?" one of the prisoners said fearfully, looking at the guards on the ground, and at the seer.

"Who knows?" Marten said, starting back toward the wagon, the seer touching his shoulder lightly, pushing him on. *"Who knows?"*

SIXTEEN

THE MEDICINE BALL caught the King high in the chest, but he braced himself and the shock of it felt good running down his legs and into the heels of his bare feet. He snapped the ball back to Magister Eccles, who caught it awkwardly and staggered back toward the tiled walls of the palace training room.

"Your education's showing!" the King laughed. "Come on, put something on it!"

Grimacing, Eccles fired it back one-handed, hard enough to make Cyre grunt when he caught it.

"Wait a second," the King gasped. He got out a cigarette, lighted it, and stood there puffing like an engine.

"Really, your Majesty!"

"What are you looking at? Come on, throw the ball!"

"Of course you know you're defeating the whole purpose of exercising."

"Well, I do better this way." The King took the cigarette out of his mouth and spat stray flakes of tobacco. "Really. Throw it."

Eccles complied. They tossed the ball back and forth in silence a dozen times, while the King flared his nostrils and let the cigarette roll from side to side in his mouth. After a while, he spoke up.

"I heard you visited our friend Rarei yesterday."

Eccles let the ball drop. "My compliments, Majesty."

Cyre stubbed out his cigarette, found a towel, and buried his face in it, scrubbing as though he were polishing a marble bust. "Yeah," he said through the towel, "much as you'd love to be my sole source of information, I'm no damn good unless I find out things for myself now and then. How was she?"

"Some of the Matron's fighting spirit has returned, I'm afraid."

"I'll bet. How's the leg?"

"The surgeons did an excellent job. She's already walking a few minutes a day on crutches."

"Well. May she and her real leg be reunited in the after-life!" Eccles frowned and the King continued, "Okay, sorry. I also heard you gave her permission to sell scapulars this year." Cyre meant Black Scapulars, two patches of black cloth sewn together and worn around the neck on a ribbon. Inside each were bits of broken mirror—pieces of the sun, devout pilgrims believed.

"Under the circumstances, I felt we should be conciliatory," Eccles said.

"A month ago they were trying to burn this town to the ground," Cyre said, voice rising. "They wanted me out. They wanted me *dead*. I wouldn't be so damn nice to my *friends*, for God's sake!"

"Conciliation is more usefully applied to one's enemies. And you did reply in kind. The Arcopatrinas is dead, the Matron incapacitated, and the Vestals, in general, are dispirited and confused."

"So we should let them make money? What do they need more money for? They already own every vineyard in the Realm, except for what the Queen's got in the Preserve." Cyre started another cigarette. "Come on, let's run a few laps."

He stepped onto a banked wooden track that followed the perimeter of the steam room. Shaking his head, Eccles caught up with the King and jogged beside him.

"Maybe you're right, Magister," Cyre puffed.

"I was right to be conciliatory?"

"Right I smoke too damn much."

They went around again, Cyre lifting his knees, driving himself higher on the track. "See, you would have done the logical thing. Kill them both. That's the difference between you and me. I get inspired sometimes. I mean, what really happens if I kill Rarei too? Nothing, except things would have opened up for some new dame with lots of energy and new ideas that nobody ever listened to before. Who knows? We might have ended up worse off. Instead, we get Rarei hopping around on one leg with a taste of the afterlife fresh in her mouth, and all she can think of is getting even with me. Personally, don't you see? It makes a difference. Before, she had the big picture of what she wanted to do. Now, all she sees is me."

It was just like him, Eccles thought, to take credit for an accident. His spies among the Vestals had provided the Magister with a good account of what had happened at Queen's Island, and Eccles was certain that the Warden had given Rarei at least a chance to live. The poison had been slow-acting, shot into the leg where it took longer to reach her vital organs. Perhaps Sheeme had done so for the pleasure of watching Rarei suffer. There was no love lost between the Vestals and Old Believers, after all. But Eccles suspected something more. There had always been a reason for the things Sheeme did, no matter how pointless or cruel they seemed.

He was thinking this when the door to the training room opened and the Princesses came in. Both girls wore blue student's gowns, and Careev carried a wooden box that she eagerly brought up to the track railing. Maud walked more languidly, like a cat who had just been stretching in the middle of a hot day, and now looked for a shady spot to sleep in.

The difference between the two girls fascinated Eccles.

Careev had nearly the same body as Maud, but she was wound up tight and walked awkwardly, head bobbing as she waved at her father. One was sensuously beautiful, the other quirky. He wondered, remembering what the King had just said to him, whom he would choose if he put logic and his own plans aside. Certainly, there was something to be said for sex, and many a life had been spent in pursuit of it. But his life? Eccles preferred more refined passions. Rather, he had trained himself to prefer them, and because he had, the Princes Careev appealed to him more. He could handle her without becoming overly involved. And, for leisure moments, there was sex in her, too, well locked, but there below the surface. Tapping it might well be interesting indeed. . . .

"My Lady Careev," he said, bowing to her. She colored, and spoke a little breathlessly.

"We didn't know you'd be here, Magister."

"I try to take exercise every day."

"Well, I hope you haven't worn Poppa out."

"Wear me out!" Cyre boomed. "Hah!" Cyre came over with his arm outstretched. The Magister handed him another towel.

" 'Lo, Poppa," Maud said in a sleepy voice, slowly bending forward to lean against the track rail.

" 'Lo, Baby," Cyre replied, kissing her forehead and ruffling her hair. He got out another cigarette and stuck it into his mouth.

"That's not good for you," Maud said, pulling it out. "How many times do I have to tell you?"

"Save it," Cyre groused. "What's in the box?"

"Adon's gardens," Careev said. "We made one for your room, and for your office, and there's one for your boat, too, if you want it."

The King peered into the box and took out a bowl-shaped basket made out of woven reeds and filled with wet sand. The sand was planted with grain seeds that would sprout and grow quickly before Festival time.

"Very nice," Cyre said, putting one back and pulling out another. This one was badly shaped, with gaps in the weave through which sand and water dripped into the box. "And who made this one?"

"I tried," Maud said with a shrug. Cyre put his arm around her shoulder and gave her a squeeze.

"Thank you, daughters. I'll give them a place of honor."

"We had reeds left over," Maud said. "She'd make a broom for you if you asked her. Wouldn't you, Carry?"

"Of course," Careev stammered, suddenly unsure of herself.

"Ask her to make you one then, Poppa!"

The King grinned, stroking his beard, and Eccles saw that he would play the game as far as Maud would take it. He spoke up quickly.

"There are plenty of brooms and not enough gardens, Majesty. With the Feast so close, I'm certain there are many more profitable ways for the Princess to spend her time." He turned to Careev. "My Lady, I understand that you composed the elegy you read for Nana Mara at her interment. It was an excellent remembrance of someone who must have been very dear to you."

Careev brightened. "Really? Did you think so?"

"Yes, and not only I. Everyone who heard it was moved."

"I felt something move all right," Maud drawled.

Careev's eyes flashed. "Don't talk that way, Maud. Nana's family asked you to say something, and you refused!"

"I was busy."

"Lazy was more like it! And after everything Nana did for us, the least you could have done was say something."

"What for? You talked enough for two—"

"Why do you pretend you don't care? She was the best friend we ever had, and you didn't even cry! You—"

"That's enough!" the King shouted. His voice echoed off the tiled walls and stopped both girls with their mouths open. "I'm here to relax. If I want squabbling, I can go back upstairs. I don't need my youngest daughter bringing it down here to me."

"That's not fair," Careev said quietly.

Cyre went over to her. "What?"

"I said it's not fair. I didn't start anything. I only came down to give you the baskets I made." Her voice was trembling and she blinked her eyes, but she stood tall in the face of her father's fast-building rage. For an instant, Eccles feared the King would hit her, but then Maud said:

"Poppa, somebody's here to see you, I think. They're making a fuss at the door."

A chill shot through Eccles as a bronze-skinned, broad-shouldered man pushed through the door, Templemen guards trailing behind. The schells remained where they had been posted, standing at attention as though nothing were amiss. Halfway into the room, the intruder halted. He was dressed in a green tunic, quilted trousers and soft boots, like a forester, and his gaze shifted from the King, to the priest, to the King's daughters with precise, almost machinelike coordination. There was life and intelligence in his eyes, but only at intervals, as though life were a spark that had not yet reached full flame.

"Who the hell are you?" Cyre demanded.

"My name is Sportus. I bring greetings from the Mistress Warden Sheeme, and a message from her to the King."

"It's a schell!" Maud exclaimed. She went over and made a full circle around him, looking him up and down with a flushed, amazed expression on her face.

"Get more guards," Eccles said to the Acolytes.

"No." Cyre said. "He's not armed. Let's hear the message."

"It is for you alone, Majesty."

"Is that so? Well, I'm ordering you to give it to me now."

Sportus fell silent, eyes dull again, exactly like a schell. Maud had moved close, and touched his arm the way a child touches a statue.

"Well?"

Sportus's voice changed, becoming breathy, dry, melodic. "We have unfinished business to discuss, Cyre." It was Sheeme's voice, mimicked by the schell.

"All right," Cyre said. "Girls, out."

"Poppa—"

"I said out. You too, Magister."

"I'm not certain that's wise, Majesty."

"Don't tell me what's wise! Out!"

Eccles bowed curtly. "Princess?"

"Thank you, Magister," Careev said, taking his arm.

"Princess?"

"Gods," she said to Eccles on the way out. "What a gorgeous . . . *thing* he is!"

When they were gone, the King said, "Do you mind if I hop into the whirlpool while we talk?"

"Not at all." Cyre felt the water with his fingers, stepped over the edge, took the towel off his waist and eased himself in.

"I am here to remind you of the bargain you made with the Warden," Sportus said, speaking as though this was some thought of his own.

"Hand me another towel, will you?"

Sportus did not move. Maybe Sheeme had put some kind of voice-lock on him, so that he would only obey her commands. He sighed and used the old towel on his forehead.

"Okay. So what? She was supposed to give me the Acropatrinas."

"You don't trust her, do you?"

"What the hell do you know about it? You're a schell!"

Sportus smiled, and there was something in that smile that chilled Cyre to the bone. *Steam's fogging my eyes,* he thought, blinking at Sportus, who seemed to be changing. There was a mist around him that seemed to contract. Only the eyes remained steady, but then they too seemed to shrink and change color.

"You have to trust me."

It was Sheeme, as she had been thirty years ago: lithe, strong, rapaciously alive. Smiling, she slipped out of her cloak and entered the tub. She put her arms around him and drew him close so that he could feel her breasts against his chest. She pushed her hips forward, and he began to feel a tingling fire start at the top of his stomach.

"You remember how it felt to touch me, Cyre? You trusted me when you felt like this, didn't you?" She reached down, fingers closing gently around his cock. "How could I ever cheat you?"

"You're not real."

"Not real? Oh, I'm real enough."

The King said, "I saw you at the Preserve. You were watching us."

"And now I know you all too well. Let me show you how real I am!"

With that, she caught him by the neck and pushed his head under water.

Leverage was his first thought. Air was his second. He pushed with his legs, but couldn't budge her. It was as though he'd been sealed beneath the surface by a huge slab of granite. *Gods*, the King thought, *I'm going to drown*! He started punching, but only found water; he clamped his jaws, willing himself not to breath no matter how his lungs burned and his heart pounded, but then he knew he wanted a breath of anything, water or air, that he didn't care anymore and so opened his mouth just as he felt himself being yanked upward and held up, dripping, like a rain-soaked kitten.

Gasping, the King opened his eyes. There was the schell Sportus with his huge arm extended straight out, holding him up. The schell smiled at him. The smile faded, dark eyes turning disky. Sportus released his grip on the King's arm, and Cyre touched the bottom of the tub with rubbery legs. Then the schell put on his clothes and walked out.

Anger snapped Cyre back. He jumped out of the tub, snatched his dagger, and went after him. His own schells stopped him at the door.

"Damn you all!" Cyre bellowed. "I want that schell!" He watched helplessly as Sportus disappeared around the corner. Powered by fury, he twisted free, driving his dagger into the gut of one of the schells who held him. The schell sighed, sat down, blood trickling from the corner of his mouth. The King slashed at the other one until he was free, and ran down the corridor around the corner straight into Eccles.

"That schell! You let him go!"

"I saw no one, my King," the Magister said, frowning. "There's blood—"

"Its not mine. That damn thing took control of my own guards. I had to gut one of them to get out of the weight room!"

Now the Acolytes came running up, followed by the two uninjured schells. "You saw that schell," Cyre said. "I want the Citadel sealed off, and that thing captured and brought to me alive. And use men. Our schells can't be trusted around him!''

The Acolytes glanced at Eccles, who nodded.

''What's this?'' Cyre roared. ''They check my orders with you first? By God, I'll have you gutted and hung out in the Agora to cure!''

''Those who serve the Temple are in harmony,'' Eccles said. ''They were merely asking me to point out something that you would surely realize were you not so excited. That is: Sportus would never have released the schells if there was a chance of his being captured.''

''Oh, so he just vanished?''

''More likely, he has left the same way he entered, via a route that would afford a means of escape if an alarm were raised.''

Now Cyre came close to the Magister, peering into his eyes.

''Do you have a question, Majesty?''

''That thing's a shape-changer. It turned into my sister-in-law right before my eyes. And it could have changed into you!''

''If you think so, why not hold me? To change shape requires energy. Sooner or later, I would tire, and have to change back.''

Cyre shook his head. ''Aww, forget it!'' he said disgustedly. They went back into the training room.

Eccles said, ''Have you heard from the Warden?''

''Today was the first time since we hit the Arcopatrinas.''

''Hmmm.''

''What?''

''It occurs to me, Majesty, that sending this kind of schell is an elaborate means of conveying a message. You've been given a glimpse of great power, which implies a threat. Hardly the actions of an ally.''

''She's trying to convince me that she's still got some tricks. Fine. I've seen them. We'll make a few adjustments.''

''Perhaps, Majesty, there is more to the arrangement between you and the Warden than you have told me?''

Cyre was getting a cigarette out of his case. He stopped, and gave the Magister a hard look.

"I'm not implying any mistrust on my part. I am merely . . . concerned."

"Concern yourself with finding that schell. It shouldn't be so hard to spot."

Eccles bowed. "As you wish, Majesty."

The King drew heavily on his cigarette. "As *you* wish, you son of a bitch," he said.

SEVENTEEN

I'M HUNGRY.

It was still dark, but the Veil was rising and the train brakes made a forlorn squeal as brakemen atop each wagon cranked their brake wheels tight and brought the train to a halt.

I'm hungry, the boy thought again. He lifted his head, turned it, trying to work out the stiffness in his neck. His night had been spent shoved into a corner beneath the swaying hammocks that more experienced passengers had brought with them on the trip. These were hung three deep between the slatted walls of the car. Some held whole families of pilgrims. The floor of a third-class wagon was for the hapless, or for those who didn't know or care what might drop on them from above.

I'm hungry. What a strange thought. Not, this body is hungry. Not, food has to be taken at certain times every day. *I'm* hungry. *My soul,* the boy reflected, *has found itself a home.*

Somehow, the thought didn't frighten him now as much as it had yesterday. Yesterday, knowing that she was locked inside a male body had nearly driven her to despair. How could Psyche have permitted such an abomination! Every time she had been reborn before, the moment of awakening had been in the body of an infant girl, and the terror of rebirth had been balanced by the comfort of knowing that the Vestals would soon find her, that life would begin anew, that the infirmities of body and mind that had saddled her soul were gone. Now, there was no such comfort, no prospect of childhood spent in the loving care of the Order. Yesterday had proven that the Vestals charged with finding the rebirth would never accept the truth. He had wanted to kill himself then. That would have been the sensible thing to do. She could set her soul free and be reborn properly. But there had been the doubt: What if her rebirth produced circumstances worse than this?

Then he had seen that old man in the square, the one this boy had known as Marten, and had felt something like love invading him, giving the boy strength. He could go on, he could make the sisters realize the truth. If he was vigilant, if he stayed fit, he could return to Almheraz and help Rarei defeat the King. Whose body she inhabited wasn't important. It was soul that mattered, and her soul was still dedicated to the matriarchy, to maintaining the veneration of the Goddess of the Realm!

But he was hungry. He, Komaso!

The doors of the wagon slid open, and people stirred in their hammocks. Komaso squirmed his way outside and watched as what seemed an impossible number of pilgrims spilled out of each wagon, most of whom went to relieve themselves among the trees on either side of the track. Meanwhile, the Acolytes who operated the train filled its tank with water, and loaded the tender with wood. Both would be needed for the long, heavy pull up the spine of the Coastal Range whose peaks now caught the first brilliant violet glow of the Eye above the pre-dawn shadows.

People began queuing at the side of a white-painted wagon coupled directly behind the tender. The aroma of food—onions and eggs and baking bread—wafted toward Komaso. Soon the canvas sides of the wagon lifted, and young women in white with red sashes—Vestal Novices!—started selling breakfast.

Komaso's mouth watered. He had not eaten since awakening in this body, and knew the boy had had nothing since the seer had taken him from the traveler's camp. He had refused food while in the custody of the Vestals, thinking that to eat would have acknowledged the permanence of her unfortunate transformation. But he needed to eat. He walked over to the side of the line, watching as the Novices ladled porridge into bowls, handed out steaming hunks of bread spread with soft, fragrant cheese. Five coppers was the price, he noted with satisfaction, still considering it his duty to see that the Vestal coffers were always kept full.

Eagerly, he stuck his hands into his pockets, but found them empty. Five coppers! And to think that a month ago, she, as Arcopatrinas, would not have stooped to pick up five coppers on the floor!

He noticed there were other hungry pilgrims haunting the fringes of the line. A few of them asked for money, but people were clutching their purses tightly, the long drought having drained their impulse to be generous. *It might be wise in future*, he thought, *for the Order to distribute food to the needy. Let them depend on us for protection, look toward us for their sustenance.*

The boy's stomach growled. It was all very well to consider future policy, but that did not put breakfast in his mouth now. He edged closer to the front of the line, where steam from the cooking pots mingled with that bleeding from the valves of the train's boiler. How he wanted to order those young girls to feed him and everyone else who needed something to eat. He, the Arcopatrinas, soul of Psyche!

Then again, perhaps he could snatch something and lose himself among the rest of the passengers.

He noticed some Bachelor guards stationed at either end of the wagon eyeing him. *Traitors*, he thought, wondering where the words had come from. He had never thought of Bachelors as traitors before!

The line was moving quickly now. The train had already finished taking water, and soon everyone would be fed and reloaded into the wagons. Komaso had to make his move, guards or no guards, but then he saw someone he recognized pushing to the front of the line.

"I do *not* have to wait!" this woman whined. She was dressed in a fine brocaded sun-cloak, with a yellow sun on the back pierced with a black arrow, the emblem of the Duchy of Jelavay. The Arcopatrinas had been in convent with the matriarch of this family, and had found her to be grasping, stupid, and decidedly non-devout—qualities she could see had been passed on, along with a thatch of flame-red hair, to the daughter. The boy searched his memory and came up with a name. Tove. Yes, that was it. The Arcopatrinas had officiated at the girl's christening, at the insistence of the by-then bedridden mother, who threatened to reduce her yearly contribution to the Vestal Hearth by half if the Arcopatrinas did not undertake the journey north to her dusty, flea-infested estate. Two days on a train, coughing and scratching, only to be met at the station by a wolf cart driven by an old man with cataracts who had managed to drive into every pothole on the road. Then, at the family house, the matriarch informing her that supper had just been cleared, but there might be a plate of cold chicken for her, if she would care to look in the kitchen! The boy remembered all this, and listened to the grown-up Tove berate the Novices for neglecting to wake her before the best of the food had been served.

"There's plenty left, Lady," one of them said with a sigh.

"What, porridge? You take me for a common laborer? I own an estate that supports three hundred families!"

Komaso moved through to the left of the line. "Then maybe you could have afforded to bring your own food!"

"Who said that?" Tove demanded. "You Bachelors! Find out who said that!"

The boy knew what to do next. Marten had taught him. Slipping in from the right side, he spotted the bulge in Tove's sun-cloak where her purse would surely be, and moved his hand through the opening of the pocket. Its strings were drawn and tightly knotted, but the boy's fingers were long and nimble and he was able to slip two of them into the purse and pull out some coins while Tove continued to argue with the Bachelors. One of them, patience exhausted at last, said,

"What do you want us to do, Lady? Stop time and run it back a little so you can be first in line?"

"How dare you! What's your name?"

Komaso went up to the wagon and stood on his toes. "Excuse me, Ladies," he said, forcing himself, trying to remember what body he was in. "Could I buy some breakfast please?"

One of the Novices smiled down at him. "Where's your money?"

"Right here," he said, offering a shiny, ten-copper piece. "Some for me—and how about some for those poor people over there? They look hungry, and I've more money to pay for them." He put two more coins on the counter. "There. Five breakfasts for them, and one for me."

The recipient of this charity looked startled. "Why, that's kind of you, boy," the mother began.

"Wait!" Tove snatched up one of the coins. "You, boy! Where did you get these coins?" Komaso looked at her. Tove was taller than he was and carried herself with the full power of her sex and wealth. But the Arcopatrinas's soul knew all about Tove, and would not be cowed.

"I earned them. Patching roofs after the rains in Baraqu, three days ago."

"Don't lie to me, boy!" Tove insisted. "These were just stamped in Jelavay. None have been spent yet. You couldn't possibly have been paid with them. Arrest this boy! He's a thief, and ought to be gutted right here!"

The Bachelors moved to catch him, but before they could, Komaso hopped up onto the wagon, waved his arms and spoke to the people.

"Before you do, you should know something. I must admit, I was hungry and I did think of trying to steal her purse, but then I said to myself, why should I make it so hard? I know this woman's family, and they're famous for pinching coppers. In fact, she swallowed a coin from her necklace the day she was christened!"

A few people laughed. Most were simply astonished. No boy ever talked this way about a high-born woman.

"And I can prove it!" Komaso went on, turning toward Tove, now open-mouthed with outrage. "Watch this!" He passed his hand over her mouth, turned his wrist, and showed a coin pinched between his thumb and forefinger. While the laughter built he did it again, and then a third time, the last more out of a desire to see if he could repeat the trick rather than to heap humiliation on the noblewoman. Obviously, this body knew more—and could do more—than he had given it credit for!

"Are you going to let this go on?" Tove was finally able to sputter. "I'll have all of you gutted and hung up to dry in the middle of the Red Courtyard! These are still my coins, stolen by this miserable . . . boy!" Two Bachelors came then and took him by the arms. "Sorry, kid," one of them whispered. "We've got our duty."

"You can arrest me all right. But what about *them*?" He pointed with his foot at the family he had tried to help. "They're still hungry! Maybe this good woman will have them arrested too, for staring at her freshly minted coins."

"Yeah, what about it?" A woman called out. "He bought breakfast for these poor folks with what he took."

"Oh, very well!" Tove said. She yanked her purse out of her pocket and slammed it down on the counter. "Feed everyone who wants it, but mind you keep hold of that boy. "I'll deal with him later!"

The Eye rose looking like one of Tove's new coppers, and the day quickly turned hot as the train puffed away from the fueling station and began negotiating the switchbacks up through the passes. This time of year, with the height of summer past, the Veil began to thin and became almost transparent, and the protection it offered against the fierce gaze of the Eye disappeared. The heat made things difficult on the train, and on the Templemen who ran it. Some of the brakemen had double duty walking alongside the slow-moving train in order to inspect the hot-boxes on the axles of each of the big-wheeled cars. They carried buckets of grease and wooden spades to pack it with, should any of the bearings become overheated.

There was also a boiler to fire, and because one of the firemen had been pressed into service walking the track, Komaso was now loading wood. Sweat stung his eyes and streamed down his dirt-streaked chest as he tossed one split log after another onto the grate, or shoveled ashes and cinders onto the side of the track. Sometimes the smoke and exertion made it difficult to breathe. He was aching and thirsty, and, at times, almost sick with despair.

This was, for the soul of the Arcopatrinas, a new experience indeed. Time after time he came forward, staggering under a load of wood. The engineer, a huge man whose fat rump seemed to ooze like butter over his seat, kept shouting orders: "Too green!" and, "Get 'em in there! You're not afraid of a little fire, are you?" between great swigs of fortified wine from a skin kept slung from the throttle wheel. Eventually his eyes glazed over, and Komaso thought it safe to make a grab for the bag. But, when he reached for it, the big man instantly became alert and slapped the boy's hand with breathtaking quickness.

"Here, now! What do you think you're doing?"

"I'm thirsty!" Komaso said, almost whining and hating himself for it. A week ago, this obese Temple parasite would have paid for his blow with his life and his soul. Vestals would have fired that boiler with the fat from his body, and his unshriven soul would have wandered these woods howling more forlornly than the whistle of this train!

"Thirsty, is it? Ha! One shot of this and you'll be on your ass." He took a tin cup that hung from a wire on the sidewall of the cab, held it under one of the valves, and filled it with a spitting stream of water.

"Here. This's good enough for you."

"But it's hot!"

"And so am I and so are you, and so's the rest of this damn train. Let it cool off!" With that he gave the throttle wheel another few turns and propped his elbow against the window. Komaso felt the cup. It was too hot to hold yet, so he went back to the tender for another load of wood. As he returned with it, the train seemed to lurch, and something in the rhythm of the engine drivers changed. The engineer frowned, twisting valve-cocks with both hands as the train slowed.

"More wood!" he yelled. "We're not going to make this grade!"

"What's wrong?"

"Shut up and get me more wood!"

Komaso got more, and stuffed it into the grate. Huge clouds of black smoke mixed with brilliant white steam shot from the stack, and the open cab was pelted by a hail of cinders. The throttle was wide open now.

"I don't understand it!"

"What about that?" Komaso pointed out a plume of steam jetting with great force from the right side of the engine. The engineer cursed, blew the whistle sharply three times—the signal for the brakemen to set the brakes on each of their wagons. Some of them, still helping with the greasing, had to scramble up ladders to get it done. The engineer, meanwhile, puffed and groaned his way out of the cab with considerably less alacrity. Komaso followed him along as he inspected the drivers and radius bars, and finally stopped next to the engine's front wheel.

"Damn Adon's Eye! That's a bent valve rod."

"Is that bad?"

"Hhmp! That rod pushes the slide valve that lets live steam into the steam chest, and that's what shoves the piston back and forth. With this one bent, we're under half power. Wouldn't be so bad if we were on the flats, but up here . . . shit!''

Just then Tove and her Bachelors stumbled forward over the gravel.

"Why are we stopped?" she demanded. Instantly the engineer's attitude changed. Transformed from a cursing Pluto into a stammering butterball, he tore his hat off his head and turned bright red.

"A thousand pardons, Lady, but as I was telling the boy—er, your prisoner here, there's a piece broken. This one. It's bent, and because of that, this engine ain't goin' any further up the hill."

"Straighten it, then!"

"Well, Lady, that I could do, but you see, it's got to be reforged and tempered, or it'll just bend again in the same place. No, we'll have to send one of our crew with it back to Semele for the smith to fix."

"That might take hours!"

"Actually, a day's walk."

"But there's trains behind us. Can't we use one of those engines?"

"No siding, ma'am. No way to get around us, and no way of pushing all these wagons. "I'm sorry—"

"I can forge the rod," Komaso said.

"Quiet, boy!"

"I'm telling you, I can do it. I worked with a traveler. I've helped to do it."

"Well, that's all very nice, considering we don't got a forge here!"

"You've got a furnace for this boiler. All you need is some bellows and a good-sized hammer. It won't be difficult at all."

"You shut up," the engineer growled. "Haven't you caused the Lady enough trouble?"

"Wait," Tove said, staring thoughtfully at Komaso. "Maybe he can do what he says."

The engineer slapped his cap against his thigh. "But there's something else, and that's my vow as Acolyte of Adon's Temple. Machinery's serious business. Mess with it, and the Lord's liable to blow the whole thing right off the track. Seen it happen!"

"My dear engineer," Tove said soothingly, "The Lord has a feast coming, and all the people on this train travel to Almheraz in order to honor him. Couldn't it be that Adon placed this boy at your disposal for a reason?"

Komaso shuddered. What a depressing thought!

"That's for a Magister to decide, Lady. Not me."

"But we have no Magister here."

"Well . . ."

"Get the boy what he needs," Tove snapped to her Bachelors. "And if this swine won't assist, tie him up until the boy's through." She looked at Komaso. "Do you understand what I'm offering you? You can redeem yourself right here and now—or we'll appease the Gods with your carcass. Can you remove that part?"

"I'll need tools."

"Engineer?"

"Tool chest's under my seat in the cab."

"Good. Begin."

Komaso took a deep breath, bridling at the order. At the same time, he was eager to try fixing the train—eagerness to please seemed to be a dominant trait of whatever personality had been submerged in the witless sea of its former self.

"Will you close the steam line?" Komaso shouted to the engineer. He grunted, wrapped his hand in a rag, and turned a valve. Meanwhile Komaso found pliers and a set of wrenches in the tool chest. Everything was rusty.

If Marten were here, he'd have this thing fixed in fifteen minutes, Komaso thought as he studied the broken piston-rod assembly. The first thing to do, Komaso realized, was to take the pin out of the bearing where the valve rod was attached to the radius bar. This wasn't easy, because the bent rod put the bearing under tension, but by gripping it with the pliers, he was able to lever it back and knock the pin from the joint with a punch and small hammer. Next, he pulled the slide-valve all the way out, removing the cotter pin that held its bearing in place.

Now the rod was free. Because it was still hot, Komaso turned it over gingerly in his hands, checking for cracks that might make repair impossible. There were none.

"Now what?" Tove asked, waving a pair of paddle-shaped fans in front of her face. The valley below the tracks shimmered in the heat. *If this keeps up,* Komaso thought, *I won't need a furnace to melt this steel!*

"We heat it and hammer it straight. We'll need a bucket of water for quenching and a bellows—" He stopped. The engineer and the other Templemen were staring at him.

"Anybody know what a bellows is?"

No one volunteered an answer. Great Sun in heaven, what buffoons these Templemen were! None of them could fix a sandal strap without the direction of a priest!

"It puts a stream of air onto a fire," Komaso said, visualizing the one Marten used. Without one, he doubted he could get the boiler fire hot enough to heat the steel properly. Then he remembered a funnel he had seen in the engine cab. That, along with some leather and the fans Tove was using might just do it!

"Pardon, Lady," he said, snatching them away from her, "but I need 'em for the train." A half-hour later, using tacks, some pitch taken from cut logs in the tender, and a needle and stout thread, Komaso had made a serviceable pair of bellows.

Now both Templemen and Bachelors watched him with growing admiration, and Komaso found himself wanting to perform for them. He—or rather, his soul—was used to adulation from the sisters, but to have the respect of men as well! An Arcopatrinas who had that had the world in her hands!

He put these thoughts from his mind. There was work to do, and the soul had found the boy worked best when his mind was not burdened with thoughts about the sisterhood.

"Okay, we're ready, I think." He climbed into the cab, gripped the valve rod with the tongs, and shoved it onto a pile of hot coals in the grate.

"Give me the bellows."

One of the Bachelors handed them up. *That's another thing I must remember,* Komaso thought. *In an uncertain situation, people will obey you as long as they think you know what you're doing.*

A strange elation filled him as he pumped the fan handles and blew streams of air across the coals, whose color changed from red to almost white. He quickly found the rhythm to keep them that way, stopping once to turn the rod. After almost ten minutes, he pulled it out. It glowed bright yellow, and gave off a sharp, oily smell. He put it on the deck of the cab, wedging one end underneath the engineer's jumpseat so that the peak of the bend was up. After a few tentative taps with the hammer, he reared back and let it fly the way Komaso had seen Marten do it. "Make it sing, boy!" was what the old man had said, and Komaso did, striking blow after blow that sent sparks flying. Soon the rod was flat again, dull red now. Komaso turned it on its edges to pound them flat, reheated the rod briefly, then plunged it into the water bucket, which erupted with clouds of steam and a prolonged, gradually dying hiss. When it stopped, Komaso held up the straightened rod.

Everyone watching started to cheer. Komaso smiled. Never, in the long succession of her lives in Almheraz, had she heard such a heartfelt sound!

It took only a few minutes to reinstall the rod. When he was finished, he waited anxiously with the rest of the crew as the engineer built up pressure in the boiler and then opened the throttle.

The valve-rod moved in and out, the piston pushed the big drivers, which in turn drove the wheels. It worked!

"All right!" the engineer yelled. "Brakemen, get back where you belong. We'll try this grade again!" He looked down at Komaso. "And if I turn zombie because of this, you'll be the first I'll visit, boy!"

Komaso started for the tender.

"Wait," Tove said. "I want you to ride with me."

"What for?"

"It's hot. You've worked very hard, and saved this train. You deserve a reward."

"That's true," Komaso said, matter-of-factly. Several of the people who were still watching laughed or shook their heads at the way he spoke to this high-born woman. "But if I go, who'll help fire the boiler?"

"They will," Tove snapped back, pointing to her Bachelors. "A few hours in the tender might do them good. And you and I can get to know each other better."

Komaso shrugged. "Why not?" As he started after Tove, one of the Bachelors bumped his shoulder.

"She'll do more than feed you, kid," he whispered.

"I doubt it."

"Balls out," the Bachelor said. "Good way to lose 'em."

EIGHTEEN

ON A TRAIN so crowded that people rode on the roofs or hung onto the undercarriages of the cars, Tove and her entourage had an entire wagon to themselves. A *decorated* wagon. Rugs and pillows covered the floor, and the walls were hung with tapestries depicting hunting scenes from Jelavay. Hunting was about all there was to do in Jelavay.

There were also blocks of ice.

In each corner of the car, jagged chunks of glistening, blue-tinted ice dripped into metal pans set beneath them. There were more of the same sort of fan he had used to make the bellows scattered about, and he noticed there was room enough behind each ice block for a man to stand and fan air over it. *Well, why not?* he thought. After all, he had benefited from such luxuries through all his terms as Arcopatrinas. If you could afford to have huge blocks of ice quarried out of mountain glaciers and hauled down to Semele, melting all the way until they were small enough to fit inside a car like this, then more power to you.

Still, something about it offended Komaso now. Maybe it was because of how he felt about Tove and her family. Maybe it was the monumental waste. He suspected (and was sure Marten would have known) that fanning air over ice was not the most efficient means of keeping a rail-wagon cool. Besides, there were candles burning all over the place, throwing shadows around when Tove shut the door. Together they probably created more heat than the ice got rid of in the first place.

The wagon swayed gently as the train began to pick up speed. Tove swept her cloak over her head with a swirling motion and let it spin to the floor. She had a certain amount of grace, Komaso decided. Fate had not been completely unkind to her.

"Would you like something cool to drink? Some pomegranate juice?"

"Sure."

Tove smiled, opened a wooden chest, and filled two glasses with ice that had been finely shaved. She poured ruby-colored juice over, handed Komaso his. He took a sip and tasted alcohol.

"You're wincing. Don't you like it?"

"What else is in here besides the juice?"

"Just something to make you relax. It won't hurt you."

"I'd rather have water."

"Oh, very well." She filled another glass with water from the drip pans and gave it to him, watching as he drank it down.

"You're a strong-minded boy. Usually, I have no patience with strong-minded boys." She sipped her drink, lowered the glass, and tipped it in the direction of his groin. "There's where I want a man to be strong."

"I'm strong enough," Komaso said, not quite knowing why he did.

"Ha! Where did you learn to be so forthright?"

"It's not something you learn."

"Out of the mouths of babes and men," Tove said, curling into a pillow. "Do you know, when I was a child I had a nurse who fancied herself a soothsayer. She talked on and on about a new age coming. We grew potatoes on our estate, and

we were always having worms infest the crop. How our nurse
divined things was to take a potato that had been bored
into—oh, she'd have to find a certain kind of flower on the
plant, and then dig it up at night when the moon was full or
something. Then she'd sleep with it, and hold it in her hands
when she got up. After that she cut it into thin sections until
she found the tracks the worms had eaten through. Every
time, she'd find signs of a new kind of man, new kinds of
women, the end of the old ways."

"Did you believe her?"

"I never cared much one way or the other. I had lots of
nannies. Mother burned that one, I think, for stealing an
earring or something." Tove put down her glass and patted
the pillow next to hers. "Why don't you sit down?"

"That's okay."

"I'm *offering* you something, stupid boy! Here, take that
filthy shirt off and let me show you how nice I can be."

"I don't see what that has to do with my shirt."

"I'm warning you—"

"In fact, maybe it's time you knew something."

"By Psyche's purse, I'm not interested in anything you've
got to say! Either shut up and do what I tell you, or I'll shove
your dead carcass onto the side of the tracks!" Tove yanked
her dagger from its thigh-sheath, holding it point up, expecting that the mere sight of it would make him wilt.

Komaso kicked it out of her hand. Tove hissed, dove at his
legs, but Komaso caught her wrists and bent them back so
that she had to look up at him.

"You think I'm just some orphan, some foundling that you
can do with what you please?" He shook her arms. "Haven't
you realized yet that I'm not what I seem to be? That I *know*
you?"

"H-how could you know me? You don't come from Jelavay.
I've never seen you on my estate!"

"I saw you *christened*! I put the oil on that narrow little
forehead of yours with my own thumb! I came there because
your mother asked me to, because we'd been in convent
together!"

"Convent? You're Sun-struck! My mother's been dead
almost twenty years!"

"Maybe you wish you hadn't sent your Bachelors away, eh, Tove? Well, it's Fate that you were so greedy to stuff me inside you, just as it was Fate that we met on this train. But there's no fighting it. I needed help to get back to my sisters—yes, my sisters!—and you're going to be the one to give it to me. You're going to protect me and care for me until we get to Almheraz."

"But you're nothing but a boy!"

"I am a boy in form only! Look at me, damn you! I am the Arcopatrinas!"

Wild-eyed, Tove tried pulling away. "Help me, Goddess," she wailed. "Strike him dead for his blasphemy. Make his soul wander until the earth rots beneath it, until all is dark and cold and Rho returns to take terrible vengeance on those who desecrate your name!"

Komaso slapped her.

"Shut up! Save your curses for people who deserve them and listen to me. I was killed at my house on the river by Warden Sheeme. She used one of her birds to take my soul. I think she intended to trap it, but something went wrong. I was released, but stunned, and I did not have enough strength to pass through Heaven's gate. Because of that I could not be reborn in the usual way. You've heard the rumors! The sisters have not been able to find the rebirth. They can't because they're looking for a girl child, and what they're looking for is me! I regained consciousness in this body. I know what it knows, can do what it can do, but I am the Arcopatrinas all the same, and must convince the sisters to accept me. That way, we can gain revenge for the crimes committed against us by Cyre of Panault. Then, once that's done, we shall free my soul from this cursed, male prison, so that I can be reborn! That's the only way to correct the imbalances this foul King has caused. The only way! Say you'll help me!"

"I-I don't know what to believe. I've got to think—"

"This is nothing you think about, you stupid cow! This is an act of faith. Look at this place! The world would be better off without your stupidity, your selfishness. You're part of the reason men like the King think they've got to seize power for themselves, establish new orders! Believe me, or by the Goddess, it will be *your* carcass the buzzards feed on along the side of these tracks! Open your soul, if you still can! *Look at me!*"

Tove looked. She started to cry. "What do you want?" she moaned.

"For now, I want some food."

"Yes."

"Yes, what?"

"Yes . . . my . . . my Lady."

Komaso smiled. "Good. One thing more." He released her wrist, so that she could wipe the tears from the sides of her face.

"Anything!"

"Those blocks of ice. Have your Bachelors chop them up when we stop again. Everyone on this train's to have some!"

NINETEEN

"LADY? A moment, please?"

Princess Careev saw Magister Eccles at the top of the stairway, his white robes dazzling, caught in a shaft of light from the arched windows above the landing. She asked her attendants to stop a moment, and he trotted up to join them, moving his long, lithe body with easy grace.

"Magister," she said, ignoring the way her Vestals tensed. "I'd hoped to see you today."

Eccles bowed. "May we walk a little?"

"I'm on my way to see the Queen. . . . But, yes." Careev looked at her attendants. "Tell them I'll be along soon." The Vestals hesitated, curtsied, and left, giving the Magister a sidelong glance as they did.

"They don't have much use for me, I'm afraid," Eccles said with a slight smile.

"They were being rude, weren't they? I'm sorry."

"You mustn't take responsibility for the rivalry between

Vestals and Templemen. It·was here long before you were born, and I daresay will go on after we're both interred.''

Careev said, "I'll have a word with them. And I am very glad to see you. What happened· with that stranger? Poppa seemed so upset, and I've been worried about it all morning.''

"You needn't worry about the King, Lady.'' They began to walk together, the priest being careful to remain a half-step behind her. "I've just left a meeting he conducted with the civil authorities of the city. The subject was the state of preparedness for the upcoming Festival, and I assure you, your father proceeded with his usual combination of force and, shall we say, rough charm? He had his way with them, in all respects that mattered.''

"Oh. So nothing happened then!''

" 'Nothing' is perhaps not quite true.'' Eccles bowed as a pair of Virgins passed them. Somehow their gowns seemed whiter than his.

"The stranger,'' he said in a lowered voice when they were gone, "was a schell with a name. He called himself Sportus, and claimed to have been sent by your aunt. He asked to be alone with the King, and the King agreed. Some minutes later, the King emerged alone, very much agitated, and, curiously, without his clothes.''

"What did the schell want?''

"I'm afraid your father refused to tell me. He did say, however, that the schell transformed himself from a man into a woman in front of his eyes as a kind of demonstration.''

"Is that possible?''

"The Warden Sheeme has considerable power at her command. Even so, form is a fundamental property of existence in this world. To change form at will requires the ability to persuade Heaven to change. It would be a considerable accomplishment for your aunt to do so, even with the help of the Dark Goddess.''

"But why should Poppa say that she had?''

"It's possible this schell was able to impose a powerful delusion upon the King. Which is why I wanted to speak to you now. When you left with your sister, Lady, did she give any sign that she might know anything about the stranger?''

"No, I don't think so. Though she did seem intrigued.''

"In what way?"

"Well. . . . The way she gets sometimes, when she's interested in a boy. There's a look on her face; her eyes get, oh, shiny, and her mouth changes. She almost looks like a different person!"

"I see. Beyond that, did she say anything about your father at all?"

Careev stopped. "Magister, you must know that there are things between Poppa and Maud that I know nothing about. They don't want me to know!" She blinked, fighting tears. "I learned a long time ago not to ask about them."

"I know it's difficult—"

"Do you, Magister? He seems to like you well enough. You have his confidence!"

Eccles waited, stroking the forks of his beard. "Do not think," he said after a moment, "that your father doesn't love you."

"Why not? You see how he treats me! Maud and I both gave him baskets. She didn't spend five minutes making hers, and joked about it the whole time, while I tried as hard as I could to make mine perfect, something he would like. He didn't even look at it! Didn't even care. . . ."

"Sometimes," Eccles said softly, "people react to things they see in others that they don't like about themselves."

"But I'm nothing like my father!"

"Ah, but you are. The King is a man of action. Yet, I believe that the reason he insists upon it is that, inside, he's a dreamer, like you. He would rather dream things than carry them out. In you, Lady, he sees a person who can afford to dream. He, on the other hand, sees dreaming as a liability. If he indulges in dreams—no matter how much he may want to—his enemies will catch him unaware, and destroy him. He therefore envies and resents you, for being able to do what he cannot."

"I don't know whether I can believe that, Magister."

He smiled. "Then believe you have your father's love—no matter how it might seem at times."

Careev wiped her eyes. "What will Mother think, seeing me like this?"

"That she has an excellent daughter who will one day become a great Queen."

Careev laughed. "You do know how to flatter someone."

"I am a courtier, as well as a priest," Eccles said with a bow. "But you shouldn't keep your mother waiting. Tell me: where is your sister now?"

"She said something about going for a ride in the Grove."

"Then perhaps I can still catch her. In the meantime, if you hear anything at all about this schell, please come see me. Better yet, come see me, even if you do not hear anything. It is always a great pleasure to talk with you, Lady Careev. Please greet the Queen for me."

Careev found herself thinking of Eccles as she entered her mother's apartments. He really was a charming man, and sincerely seemed to like her. She wondered if her own eyes got wider when she talked to him, and whether her mouth changed the way Maud's did. There was a tall mirror in the foyer, and she stopped in front of it to see. As far as she could tell, her lips were as they always were, pale and a little chapped.

Maybe it was something you had to practice.

She found Queen Gormayne sitting behind a desk that had slender, carved dolphins for legs. She was wearing her spectacles and, as usual, pouring over a prayer-scroll and so did not look up when Careev entered the room. Careev curtsied anyway.

"Hello, Mother."

"Is it time already, dear?"

"I'm a little late, I think."

The Queen motioned to one of the Vestals. "They'll bring in a nice lunch," she said. "Oh, and it's getting awfully stuffy in here. Would you mind opening a window?"

"Yes, Mother."

Careev went over to one, unlatched the shutters and swung them open. Beyond the terrace wall she could see a stretch of the Tumulos, with a white paddle-wheeler churning the water, headed downstream for Baraqu perhaps, and the Crescent Sea. How lovely it would be, she sighed, to be on board that boat right now!

The Queen's Vestal returned with a tray of covered dishes.

Gormayne removed her glasses, rolled up the scroll, and nodded for the servant to put it down in front of her. Then she lifted one of the covers.

"Some nice fish today."

"I'm really not very hungry, Mother."

"Oh. What's that you're holding then?"

"I made you an Adon's garden. And one for Poppa, too, just like it."

"Bring it here."

Careev put it down next to the tray, watched as her mother smoothed the wet sand with her palm.

"You've planted it already," she said. "Did you say a prayer when you did?"

"No," Careev said, embarrassed to admit it.

"Well, that's not really right. Say it for us now, please."

Careev swallowed, and recited the prayer Nana had taught her when she was hardly old enough to walk:

> "Sunblessed Adon
> Lord of Light
> Born and Dead by
> Lover's Spite.
>
> Bless the Hands
> That touched these Seeds
> Bless our Thoughts
> Bless our Deeds."

Saying it made her feel like a little girl again. The elation she had felt leaving Magister Eccles had vanished.

"It's good you still remember," the Queen said with a smile. "Are you sure you won't eat?"

"Yes."

"Then read to us from the scroll."

Careev picked it up from the desk. The parchment was soft as butter, churned by the devout hand of the Queen.

"What would you like me to read?"

"Someday, when I've breathed the Power into you, you'll have to play the Bride at the Festival. Why don't you read the Passion?"

"Yes, Mother." She found the end of the scroll, where the faded, hand-lettered text began. Gormayne was picking all the bones out of her piece of fish. When she had finished—after bending close to make certain none were left—she cut it into tiny pieces with a knife and fork.

"In the Beginning," Careev read, trying not to let the desolation she suddenly felt overwhelm her. "In the Beginning was Darkness and Repose: Great Mother Rho, who is the Beginning and end of all things." Was this how it was everywhere, with all parents, and all children?

"Through formless Eternity she slept. Then came the Bright Arrow, Kronnos. Father Kronnos pierced Mother Rho deeply with his mighty Arrow of Light, rending the Darkness. And She conceived.

"Out of the repose of Darkness came the three Great Children: Psyche, bright and quick like her father; Perse, somber and dark like her mother. And between them, Lord Adon, whose face was so beautiful that anyone who looked upon it fell in love with him.

"So it was with the daughters of Rho. Both Psyche and Perse, coveted Adon. Each Goddess wanted life, and wanted to fill the universe with children of their radiant brother. Each said to herself that she would have him, and so by strength or guile strove to capture his heart. Because of their struggle, the Universe quivered, and all was chaos."

Careev stopped. She thought of the look on Maud's face when Sportus had come into the weight room.

"Is there something wrong, Careev?" the Queen asked. She wrapped her napkin around a finger, dipped it into her water glass, and wet her forehead.

"No."

"I thought the worst of this weather was over. That whatever was displeasing Heaven had been corrected." She looked up at her daughter. "What do you think?"

"Maybe it's just a hot day. I mean, couldn't it be?"

"Please keep reading."

"Their struggle tore the Universe from pole to pole until at last their mother could stand it no longer. 'I shall divide the world into darkness and light,' she told them, 'with each year likewise divided between them. Psyche shall have dominion in the World of Light, Perse in that of Darkness. And Adon shall go to each of you in turn.'

"And so it was. The day, the seasons, and the year were all divided: darkness from light, air from water, the heavens from the firmament, body from soul. When it was light, Adon could only see Psyche's beautiful face; when darkness reigned, he had eyes only for Perse's somber magnificence.

"But as it happened, when the world was dark, and Psyche banished to her realm in the bright moonlit sky, she grew lonely. 'He really loves me more,' she told herself. 'He's his father's child, after all! Why must I long for him half the year, when the Fates have decreed that he must always be mine?' So thinking, Psyche traveled deep into the earth, where she found the twisted Giant, Alamos, at work before his heavy forge.

" 'Build me a fire,' Psyche said to the Giant. 'I want a fire such as has never been seen, fire enough to drive this cursed Darkness away so that my Adon can return to me!'

"Alamos stopped his pounding, for he was secretly in love with Psyche himself, and eager to please her. 'I fain would do so,' he said to her. 'Yet what will I use for fuel? I only have enough coal to feed my forge.'

" 'Look around you, Alamos,' Psyche replied. 'The earth is fuel for our purpose. Burn it, and remember: anything that can be done, shall be.' So saying, Psyche smiled her fairest smile and kissed the Giant with great passion, driving the doubts from Alamos's mind.'

" 'I shall do it!' the Giant declared. He took his bellows, gave them a mighty squeeze, and watched as flames roared out of the top of the forge and set the very rocks of the earth aflame. Harder and harder the Giant squeezed the bellows. Higher and higher leapt the flames. Psyche took her place in the sky and soon the earth burned brightly enough to illumine her. Enamored by her radiant beauty, Adon forsook Perse and went to her sister.

" 'I love you,' he said, 'for you have given your world over to make me see you. But where shall we go to consummate our union, when all the earth is aflame?'

"Psyche kissed him, and replied that she knew a place the fire could not touch. Thus she took him to a deep grotto that was shaded by the intertwined branches of mighty trees, cooled by the fall of an icy river, which tumbled like diamonds and sapphires between columns of rocks that seemed to hold up the sky. This grotto was protected from the fire by steep, knife-edged cliffs. Beneath them they found a bed of morning glories, where Adon took Psyche into his arms.

"Meanwhile," Careev went on, "the sky glowed with fire, and the people of the earth huddled on the peaks of mountains or swam until exhausted in the rapidly shrinking seas in order to avoid the flames. Desperately, they prayed to Perse for darkness and the quenching of all fire. Their entreaties gave the Dark goddess strength. She held her hands over the earth, blew gently, and blew again. Rain began to fall, softly at first, then, as the winds swirled and skies darkened, in torrents that quenched the fire and flooded all the land. Swiftly, the waters rose, until the mountains that protected Psyche's grotto were breached by the torrent.

"Now the flood roared into the grotto where the lovers lay, filling it as easily as a wash basin. Psyche, who was quick as light, escaped easily. Adon tried to follow her, but caught his sandal strap on a branch. The waters swirled over his head; when they receded, the Lord of Light was drowned.

"How great was Psyche's sorrow, how terrible her wrath when she found him! Rising up, she pointed a trembling finger at the people of earth. 'You asked for light and I gave it,' she cried in a terrible voice. 'Yet, you did not trust me, and you prayed to have the light extinguished. Now it has truly gone out, and it is you who shall pay to get it back again. Because it was wood that trapped my poor Adon, wood shall you burn to get your light! Because it was water that covered his head and stole his life away, water you shall find scarce, and it will be bitter and taste of salt when you do find it! And finally—finally!—because you have shown yourselves to be fickle, and of two minds, I shall divide you body from soul, soul from body. The needs of the one shall be the harm of the other; you shall spend all of your days unsatisfied, searching for your other self in order that you may be completed, but that satisfaction will never come to you in this life. No! Death shall be your solace, and your deliverance.

And always, though you worship Adon, you will never find him!' "

Gormayne coughed loudly, reached for her water glass, and quickly drained it. Fearing her mother had choked on a fishbone, Careev took a step toward her. Gormayne waved her away.

"We're all right. Read me the part where she prays for her mother to bring Adon back to life."

Careev hesitated. Something about the way her mother was sitting—stiff and bent forward, as if she could not get comfortable—bothered her. But then the Queen seemed to relax, and took another bite of fish. Careev started to read again:

"Then, looking toward the heavens, Psyche prayed to Great Rho. Mother! He was your son! Restore him to life so that those who love him may feel his tender touches, and bask in the warmth of his brotherly gaze! Rho heard her daughter's prayer, and reached down with her Dark Hand, and touched the cold, gray lips of the dead Lord.

"And he became Light.

"Yet Perse still desired him. 'Had not Psyche started the Great Fire in the first place?' she thought, 'and yet, she has gone unpunished. She thinks she's won, but we shall see!' With that, she unpinned the dark folds of her gown, rose to the heavens with it spread in her arms, and covered Adon's face. Then, wrapping him in her Veil, she took Adon back into the underworld. And there—" Careev paused. The room seemed to have gotten hot. "There, greedy to gaze upon his divine face, she parted the veil until she could see his eye. . ."

Careev smelled something burning; *burning hair,* she thought as her mother's tray crashed to the floor. A plate wheeled across the room, spinning to a stop in front of the open window; then, the Queen, face black-red, eyes wide and terrified, pushing her chair away from the desk with both feet, still pushing when her back hit the wall. Grimacing with pain, she clutched her stomach with one arm, pointed at something behind Careev with the other.

"Mother!"

"No . . . don't move! *He's* . . . here!"

"Who?"

"Can't you see him? He's looking at me! Calling . . . calling my name. Adon! Lord, forgive me, my . . . sins!"

Careev threw down the scroll and went to her, trying to hug her close, but her mother's body was stiff, almost in rictus. There was no question she was seeing something, from the way she trembled. Spit foamed the corners of her mouth.

"Vestals!" Careev shouted, but no one came.

"Beautiful . . . horrible . . . What Perse saw, when she lifted . . . Veil . . . from his . . . Ohhhh! I can feel his flame. I can feel his flame—"

"Vestals!"

The Queen's body wrenched itself from the chair, twisted up and out of Careev's grasp. The desk tipped, fell forward with a sharp crack of splintering wood. Gormayne landed on top, limp now and draped over the wreckage. The doors opened; Bachelors with drawn swords halted in confusion, unsure of what had been done to the Queen, and what they ought to do with Careev. Gormayne's attendants followed, and Careev spoke to them.

"You! Get the physician. You others, help me get her into bed!" She knelt down by her mother and gently turned her over.

"What's wrong, Lady?" one of the attendants asked.

"I'm not sure. She's had a vision, a seizure—I don't know. Be careful now—"

Gormayne's eyes fluttered as they lifted her up. "It's all right, Mother," Careev whispered when they got her into bed. She brushed the hair back from her damp forehead.

"Careev . . ."

"Shhhh."

"Have them . . . take me to Queen's Island."

Careev straightened. "Mother, no!"

"Queen's Island . . . Time . . . your time. Ohhh."

She groaned and lost consciousness again. Moments later, Avra, the physician, arrived. Taking command of the situation, she quickly questioned Careev about what had happened, and ordered the apartment cleared. Careev watched Avra check the Queen's pulse. She seemed to be breathing a little better.

"Can I help?"

"Bring a dish of water and some cloths."

Careev did.

"Thank you. I can watch her now, Lady," Avra said, wringing out a cloth and laying it on the Queen's forehead.

"I want to stay."

The physician shook her head. "It's got to be as quiet as possible. Souls sometimes take flight just because they're frightened by all the commotion following an accident like this."

"But this wasn't an accident. She was seeing things—"

"Later," Avra whispered gently. "I've got to watch the Queen now. Get some rest, and collect your own thoughts. When the crisis is over—"

"But what if—"

"There's only so much we can do about Fate, Lady. Please." Avra guided her to the door and closed it firmly behind her. In the outer office, Bachelors had already cleaned up the mess. They had put the Queen's desk right again. One of the dolphin legs was split, but otherwise everything was as it had been when Careev had arrived.

Thoughts spun in her head. *What if the Queen is really seriously ill?* Queens went to the Island to die, after all; surely Gormanye would not have asked to be taken there if she did not have some presentiment of death. If she did die, and soon, what would her youngest daughter do?

She did not want to be Queen.

And what about the King? His office ended the instant the breath of Power was passed from the old Queen to the new. If it happened now, when Cyre was still engaged fighting off the Vestal challenge to his authority, wouldn't he assume that his daughter was another enemy, a worse threat to him than the Vestals?

I have no one to protect me, she thought.

Then Careev saw something that stopped all thought. She could only stare, heart pounding, at the woven basket that sat on the top of the desk, next to the prayer-scroll. The basket was bursting with bright-green stalks of barley and wheat, some bending with the weight of full heads of ripening grain. In the center was a three-foot stalk of corn, its tassels open and dusting the basket and the desktop with yellow pollen.

It was the garden she had planted for her mother this morning. Maybe her mother *had* seen a vision of Adon, who had caused the garden to grow as a sign of His presence. Surely that was it!

She had witnessed a miracle. She told herself over and over again as she stroked the corn tassel.

Then why, if she had seen a miracle, was she so full of doubt?

TWENTY

"ROONNEE!"

Princess Maud yelled for the kennel mistress and paced the dusty yard in front of the Citadel kennels. Wolves were being exercised and groomed by schells who used their brushes with long, even strokes, to which the animals submitted stoically. Other schells hosed out cages, worked on carriages and sedans, or soaped down saddles and rigging. Flies were everywhere, and there was no getting around the smell of a kennel being turned inside out.

Maud yelled again. Finally, the wizened little kennel mistress, who had once been Grandmother Cleilla's favorite rider at Baraqu racecourse, stomped out from inside.

"Didn't you know I've been waiting out here?" Maud demanded.

"I had one or two other things pressing before I could attend to you." Ronnee said, adding sweetly: "Your highness."

"Maud flicked her crop shoulder to shoulder. "I'd like to ride now. Bring out Mint."

"The Princess Royal's Mint?"

"Yes, the Princess Royal's Mint! Careev gave me permission."

"That may be, but I've got a responsibility for the beast. We just finished combing her out."

"If I have to come back down here with my sister, you'll have two of us angry instead of one! Mint's the one I want. Now will you bring her or not?"

"My Lady's wish," Ronnee said, bowing so low that her spiky hair almost touched the ground. She disappeared back into the barn. Maud paced. Why did she have so much energy today, when it would have been so much better just to sleep?

A few minutes later, Ronnee led Careev's wolf out into the yard. Mint looked magnificent, her black-tipped, auburn fur gleaming in the noontime light of the Eye. Her long, silky ears poked through a golden visor that protected her from the sun, and she wore a blanket in the Gormayne colors of blue and gold beneath a small parade saddle. When she saw Maud, her front legs stiffened, but she was enough of a lady to keep her growling low.

"She's had her run this morning," Ronnee said, "so mind where you take her. You there! Help the Princess up!"

Ronnee took the reins while a schell gave Maud a boost into the stirrup. He was not a bad-looking schell, she thought, glancing down at his hard-muscled body. It glistened with sweat. What a shame she couldn't bring him along!

Starting off, Maud realized that Mint was stiff. She leaned forward, taking strips of dried fish from the pocket of her coat.

"There, now, Mint girl! I know you love these. They're the same ones little sister gives you."

Mint glanced back, then ate the fish, shaking herself when she was done. This seemed to mollify Ronnee, who curtsied politely and went back to her work without bothering with more warnings. Maud started Mint slowly, letting her warm up, gradually increasing their pace along the path that swung behind the temples to the northern edge of the Citadel Rock. There the main path joined the switchback road down to the city. To the right, through the marquis, was a fainter trail that seemed to lead straight over a cliff. It ran alongside a set of

stairs that descended into a deep gorge between the Citadel
and the Tablelands to the north. The trail actually traversed
the steep slope, zig-zagging to the bottom, where a spring-fed
creek ran through a densely wooded grotto said to be the very
place where Adon drowned in the flood unleashed by his
jealous sister.

At the edge of the trail Mint hesitated, and Maud did too.
The narrow path demanded the utmost concentration from a
rider, and an agile and willing mount. Her saddle was wrong,
and Maud wasn't sure Mint would respond to her direction.
But it was not a good idea to wait too long before doing
something like this. Maud flicked Mint's haunches with the
crop, pulled on the reins, and started her down.

The trail was very steep, and so narrow in places that the
wolf's shoulders brushed the canyon wall as it stepped down.
Maude kept her moving all the time, standing in the stirrups
and anticipating how the wolf would take the trail. Mint
shortened her stride as they dropped into the shadows, but
Maud never stopped leaning forward or guiding the wolf with
pressed-in knees. Grudgingly, Mint accepted the fact that
Maud knew how to ride her and relaxed.

They entered a grove of trees, olive and slender poplars
first, and then twisted pines whose boughs slapped at their
faces. Maud was breathing hard, the hood of her sun-cloak
blown back so that she could feel the dense, cool air of the
grotto pushing through her hair.

Abruptly, the trail leveled out. Mint dropped to a trot
across a meadow carpeted with thick grass and beds of red,
yellow, and green flowers. Far above, Maud could see the
dazzling white facade of Psyche's House, and part of the
porch of the Temple of the Sun, both shimmering as the Veil,
in its unsteady late-summer aspect, shifted and pulsed around
the Eye.

"That was wonderful!" Maud cried. "Gods you're a mar-
velous beast!"

Mint was limping.

Maud reached down to touch her neck; the wolf growled
and nipped her wrist.

"Damn!" she yelped, whipping the crop across the wolf's

ears. There was blood on her wrist, and she sucked at it.
"You know you liked that ride as much as I did."

As she peered at the wound, something flashed in the
corner of her eye. She looked around, but saw nothing.
Feeling a little hurt by what the wolf had done, she hopped
down, and threw the packet of dried fish onto the ground.

"Limp around, for all I care. But you'd better be ready to
go up when I am!"

Mint ignored her, nosing the package.

Maud turned and followed the creek across the meadow to
where it entered a dark grove shaded by manzanita, crabapple,
and pomegranate trees. Pausing beneath one, she twisted one
of the still-green fruits free of its thorny stem. They were very
big this year. In another four or five weeks, the seeds inside
would be tart-sweet and red as rubies.

Maud walked inside the grove to a smooth slab of rock that
hung over the water. The Queen had taken her here when she
was a little girl, telling her the story of how Adon had
drowned because of catching his sandal strap on one of these
trees. There was a bed of morning glories on the other bank
of the creek, and a little up the slope, where the trees grew,
were other slabs of stone set into the ground. Some had
tumbled, or broken up, but there were enough standing—each
one drilled with a hole—to mark this place as sacred. Centuries ago, when the Old Believers were strong, this place had
been the holiest spot in all the Realm.

Maud took a silver flask from her pocket, opened it, and
took a long drink of fortified wine. She thought about the Old
Believers dancing around huge bonfires during their Festival.
How they would dance and drink until they could speak to the
Goddess, and then, as the fires burned down, reenact the
marriage of Adon and Perse. There were no priests or Vestals
then. Men and women danced closer and closer on the soft
grass, and soon the dancers embraced each other, until the
whole grotto became a temple of passion, and the sound of
their combined ecstasy was heard all the way to Baraqu!

How she would have liked to have seen that! People wildly
fucking, yelling in unspeakable tongues, levitating and spinning together like rolling pins in the air!

She took another drink and touched herself. How she wished

she had brought that schell with her! She closed her eyes, touched herself again.

"What are you thinking about, Lady?"

Maud gasped and pulled her hands out from under her cloak. A dark-haired man stepped out of the trees and onto the rock. His dark eyes were blank, but there was something about his face—perhaps a hint of a smile on his lips—that made Maud blush . . . even as she realized that this was not a man at all, but a schell: the schell with a name that had come to see the King in the training room!

He stood over her and his eyes came to life. Maud felt small, almost paralyzed. He could swoop down like a hawk and carry her away. . . .

The gaze went blank again. Maud recovered and said angrily, "You've got no business wandering around on your own. Go back to where you belong!"

Sportus did not move.

"Are you deaf? I'm giving you an order."

"I have other orders."

"Like following me?"

"I am to speak to you privately. This seemed to be a good opportunity."

"How did you get here? There's only one trail down here, and you weren't on it."

"I waited here for you."

"Really? And how long would you have waited if I had decided to ride some other trail?"

Sportus said, "I knew you would come."

He sat next to her. "This place is special to the one who made me. She said you liked to come here."

"Aunt Sheeme, you mean?"

"Yes."

"You came to talk to me for her? The way you did to my father?"

Sportus said nothing.

"She sent you because she's afraid of him. Isn't that right?"

"The Warden is not afraid. But she has much to accomplish in a little time. I . . . assist her."

"What does she want?"

"Your help."

"*My* help. Why should I help my aunt? She hates my father. I'd never help her!"

"You did once," Sportus said.

"You don't know anything about it!" Maud snapped, drawing her dagger. Sportus glanced at it, eyes blank once again. "You forget your place. I'm a Princess of the Realm. You're something my aunt grew in a bubbling pot! Stand up, schell!"

Slowly, Sportus got to his feet. He stood with his arms at his sides as Maud stuck the point of her dagger into his gut.

"If you know everything, you'll know that Auntie tried to make me kill a schell that day. I ordered it to put his hands over his head. He did it. He would have stood still while I gutted him, because his life meant nothing! I want you to put your hands over your head, just like he did, because your life means the same! Go on. Do as you're told."

Sportus raised his arms—then slapped the dagger out of her hand. He pulled her close, put his mouth on hers, and kissed her.

Emotion slapped her down like an ocean breaker, sent her tumbling through turbulent sea foam like a rag doll. She opened her mouth, kissing him back, warmth and weakness spreading through her until she had to hold onto him, nothing else being solid, nothing else real.

He pushed her away. His eyes were burning now.

"We've learned a lesson, you and I. We've learned what you really think is important in this world. Not family. Not the Realm. Not power. It's ecstasy that's important to you. That's why you come here, isn't it?" Maud tried to look away, but Sportus put his hands on her face, forced her to look at him. "Isn't that right, my Lady? You want to speak to the Goddess, don't you?"

Trembling, Maud nodded her head.

Sportus kissed her again; she was lost, utterly swept away, until she realized he was speaking to her again.

"The King thinks he can cheat us. He's got plans for you, but he's never asked what you wanted, has he?"

"No."

"Good." Sportus smiled, stroking her hair. Maud reached

to kiss him again, but he stepped away. "I'll send a message
to you tonight. You'll speak to the Goddess then!"

Sportus turned and walked back across the rock into the
trees. There, it seemed to Maud that he become shadow. She
heard no footsteps, no rustling leaves or breaking twigs. And
when she called his name—so loudly that it echoed back and
forth across the gorge—the valley seemed cold, forlorn, empty.
Maud trembled and tried to get a grip on her feelings. She
took a drink of wine and told herself that what had just
happened was some kind of spell. It couldn't have been real.
A single kiss from a schell: how could that be enough to
make her think of betraying her father?

And yet, Poppa was ready to betray her.

No. It was all a lie. A dream or something. It was time to
return to the Citadel, take the wolf back to the stables, have
dinner with Poppa, and the Queen. She found Mint drinking
at the creek. She still showed a bit of a limp when Maud
mounted her, but seemed willing, when Maud turned her,
to tackle the trail home.

Tonight. It would be the easiest thing in the world not to go
to Wharvesunder. She would simply go to bed and sleep, and
if the tension became too great, there was always one of the
schells ready to do whatever she told it to.

Maud told herself these things, and started Mint up the trail
knowing they were lies, knowing that tonight was already an
eternity away.

TWENTY-ONE

THE ALMHERAZ RAIL STATION was a consecrated Temple of the Sun, managed and staffed by Templemen. It boasted an altar, altar-screen, and a system of mirrors that directed an image of the sun from the heliotrope in the Red Courtyard down onto a round mosaic laid into the southern wall, above the track ends. The tiles showed the dark-clad Rho kneeling to bestow her life-giving breath upon her drowned son. During the autumnal equinox, at the height of the Festival, the image of the Eye was cast where Adon's face ought to have been, completing the soot-stained portrait.

Mirrors were necessary because the station was the only Sun-temple that was underground.

It was an enormous vaulted space dug out of the silt and hacked through bedrock. Aboveground, only a line of brick wells and venting stacks gave any indication of what was below. Each well protected a skylight that threw golden beams across the main tracks and platforms, and the chuffing engines and wagons that discharged pilgrims from every corner of the Realm. The station echoed with their voices, mingled with the screech of metal wheels on tracks, the blasts of train whistles, the chugging of driver pistons. Whole families of pilgrims disembarked from the wagons dragging their possessions in impossible-looking bundles held together with wires or rope. Some craned their necks to see above the crowds, looking for people who had come to meet them. Others stopped to speak to red-cloaked Templemen, who gave directions first, then sold blessings. Vestals were also out in force. There was a haze of eye-stinging smoke and cinders, the smell of burning oil, and then the shock of the heat when you walked up the long ramps out into the burning noontime Eye.

Marten the Traveler had been sleeping as the train pulled into the station, and now, only half awake, he was carried along in the crush of passengers leaving his wagon until, like a stick in a stream, he reached a relatively calm pool and could turn around slowly to get his bearings. It felt strange to be somewhere without his rig and his wolf. And now that he had finally reached Almheraz, he realized again how much he missed Komaso.

Gods, why was he so weak? He didn't ''need'' Komaso, any more than he needed a gold comb for his beard or honey mead to drink. Children and family were something that gentry collected, like cattle, or plates in the pantry.

Yet, there was no denying that everything had changed for him the moment he heard the boy call his name at Semele Market. In an instant, his life had been shattered by the dull pain of wanting something that he could not have. Why had Fate given the boy to him, only to take him away? Surely it had to be a test. For the rest of his life to be worth anything at all, Marten knew he would have to try to find Komaso—even if Komaso were lost in the Realm's biggest city, during the Realm's holiest Feast.

The crowd leaving the station thinned, and a new crew of Templemen came to replace the one that had brought Marten's train to Almheraz. An engineer swung his big lantern as he walked past Marten, followed by his crew. The old man hurried after and stopped him.

''Pardon me,'' he said politely.

"Shove off!"

"The train that came in before this one," Marten persisted. "Where would the crew be?"

"Where we're heading now," the engineer said. "You're welcome to come along, if you've money to drink with!"

Marten felt the weight of his full purse tug on the belt of his cloak. He nodded.

"All right then! We're dry as dust!"

That said, the engineer swung his lamp and led his crew and Marten out into the Agora. Normally, during midday both shoppers and stall-keepers took shelter from the Eye. During Festival week, however, people forgot about the sun and went about cloakless, as if daring Adon to show his power. Shoving through this bold crowd, Marten and the trainmen reached a canvas marquee that shaded the door to the underground tavern. Here it was also crowded, full of smoke and the din of midday drinkers.

"See him?" the engineer asked Marten. "The man who's black as the insides of Perse's purse, sittin' on benches enough for three grown men? That'll be Baltus, drowning himself in a bowl of bock beer!"

The crowd was getting to Marten, but he managed to grab a seat at the table with the big man. Swigging from his tankard, the engineer barely gave him a glance.

"I understand you're the engineer of the train that left Semele evenin' before last," Marten said.

"Who wants to know?"

Marten stopped one of the schells who roamed the tavern with a tray of glasses and skins of various liquors slung around his neck. He ordered brandies, got out his purse, leaving it on the table after he paid.

"My name's Marten. I'm a traveler, out of the Steppes, and looking for a boy who was on your train."

Baltus tossed back his brandy. "Ye've wasted the price of a drink, pilgrim. A boy on my train! Ye could guess the number of boys on that train better than I can!"

Marten pushed a glass toward him. "Maybe, but this boy was different. For one thing, he was traveling alone. For another, he didn't have any money. Your conductor would have told you if he'd put anyone off the train for not paying, wouldn't he?"

"Nobody got put off the train." Baltus mumbled. He drank the second glass of brandy. "But a boy with no money—I might be able to tell you something about that, for another taste."

True to his word, Baltus sat silently until Marten was able to catch another schell. He ordered three glasses this time, doling out the first.

"Well, there was a boy all right. He insulted a fine Lady when we stopped to tank up, and then tried to steal her purse! I left it to the Lady to say what to do with him, and she decided to put him to work stoking the boiler, which he did, 'til my engine broke. We was helpless, but this kid, and don't ask me how, finds out what's wrong and then hammers a bent piece of steel straight—something I never seen anyone but a Templeman do!"

Marten sat up. "This kid," he said. "What did he look like?"

"I don't know . . . tall, I guess. Kind of moon-faced, and like I said, he had a smart tongue to the Lady I told you about. Gods only know why she didn't gut him where he stood!"

"Did he . . . say who he was?"

Baltus eyed the brandies. "Are you warming your hands with those?"

"No. Here."

"To your health, then, pilgrim!" the engineer said, and drank it down. "Ahh! It was Koko, Komo, something like that."

"Komaso?"

"That sounds like it."

"Do you know what happened to him?"

"Lady took a likin' to him, had him ride the rest of the trip in her wagon. Saw 'em go off together, too, lucky for him, what with Vestals arresting anyone that don't got money or a place to stay here for the holidays."

"All right. This Lady— Who is she?"

"The Lady was Tove, an' her name rhymes with love," Baltus sang, embellishing the line with a tremendous, liquid-sounding belch. "Ask one of the bitches in white where she is. She's thick with 'em. Got a whole crew of Vestals! 'Fact, I heard this boy say he's one, too!" He laughed, shaking his head. "Stupid shit!"

Marten stood up, tied his purse to his belt. "Thank you," he said, keeping his temper. The engineer grunted, and went back to his beer. Marten went back up to the market and found a stall tended by a pair of sisters in white.

"G'day, Ladies. I wonder if you'd help me—"

"That we can do." The Vestal held up a patch of black cloth that was fastened to a silk ribbon. "You need a scapular to bring the blessings of the Goddess upon you, to soothe and ease your worldly pain."

"Thank you, thank both of you, but what I want, really, is to know whether you have heard of the Lady Tove, from Jelavay."

The sisters looked at each other.

"You're not wearing a scapular. That could be very bad luck here in Almheraz this week."

"All right, all right!" Marten fumbled to open his purse and took out some coppers. How he hated money! Everybody who wanted some seemed to be able to smell it on him here.

"May Psyche protect you," the Vestal said, slipping the scapular over his head. "Now, you were saying?"

"Do you know where Tove, who is a high-born Lady from Jelavay, might be staying?"

"What you need, is a guidebook to the city. There is a map of all the streets in it, and a list of approved lodgings and inns and such."

"Does approved mean you own them?"

"That is an aggressive remark from an old man looking for assistance, wouldn't you agree, Sister?"

"For someone without a guidebook, yes."

Marten sighed. "How much for a guidebook?"'

"One gives what one feels one can," said the younger Vestal in a melodious tone.

"Would four coppers satisfy you?"

"The question, old man, is whether the giving of four coppers would satisfy you."

"Ten then! Would ten make you happy?" Marten waited. Finally the Vestal scooped the money up and handed him a scroll.

"There are villas on the rock above the Agora where high-born Ladies stay for the Feast. She might be there."

"But you don't know for certain?"

The Vestals smiled. "Nothing is certain. Perhaps you need to reflect upon what is real, and what is illusion in this world. We have a book of meditation, very soothing and edifying to those who practice its devotion. The Goddess will take your sex into account when she considers your prayers, and will reward you accordingly."

"Pardon me, Sister," her companion said, "but from the look of him, he'd profit more by drinking a jug of our red wine."

"For which one gives what one feels one can?" Marten asked.

"You're a clever old man!"

"Sisters, I'm afraid you'd have my lifeless body on your hands if I drank any now. But when I do need some wine—and there'll come a time soon when I do, my Ladies—I'll be certain to return to this very place to buy it."

"Psyche willing," the older Vestal said, glancing at the other woman. "Fare thee well!"

The streets above the Agora were narrow and twisting, packed with sagging, half-timbered houses. This was the oldest part of the city, and it appeared to have grown on the Rock the way mold does on a corner of a cheese. Marten consulted the Vestal guidebook several times, but all he could find in it was a map showing the location of Vestal winesellers all through the city, and a "prayer for lost pilgrims" printed on the end of the scroll.

Still, Marten continued uphill until he reached a stone stairway shaded by palm fronds and scented by the blossoms of hanging clusters of jasmine and fuschia. After ascending a considerable distance, the stairway made a turn into a polished brass gate guarded by some Bachelors who had a long time to watch Marten as he trudged toward them. Marten did not have much love for Bachelors. They, in turn, did not seem at all pleased to see him.

"We were taking bets," their leader said by way of greeting. Marten hung his head, trying to catch his breath. "What?"

"I lost ten coppers. I bet you'd have a stroke before you got here. Well, now you're here, what do you want?"

"I'm seeking a high-born Lady from Jelavay. Her name's Tove, and I'm given to understand she has a villa further up the hill."

"She expecting you?"

"Not exactly. You see, actually, it's my son I'm looking for. I think she might have him with her—or at least be able to tell me where he is."

The Bachelor nodded with a knowing expression on his ruddy face. "Think that makes you something special? We get fathers here all the time looking for their kids. High-borns are dragging them up faster than they can make 'em!"

"Do you know about a woman from Jelavay?"

"That depends."

"On what?"

"On whether you've got a pass or not. There's a gate here, old man. Keeps the riff-raff out. Keeps *you* out, if you don't got a pass."

Marten shrugged. "Where could I get one?"

The Bachelors laughed.

"Look, I just want my boy." He hesitated. "I can pay. . . ." He lifted his purse so that the Bachelor could see it.

"You trying to bribe me?"

"You asked for a pass," Marten said. "Here. I'll take a few coppers out for lodgings and food and you can have the rest."

"The rest? What about my sworn duty to protect these Ladies? The sisters don't take kindly to those that like to break their vows for money."

"Can I at least send up a message?"

"No."

"Surely you understand what it's like to be a father—" Marten began. The Bachelor's face clouded. Of course he could never know what it was like. He was a Bachelor. The Order took both manhood and a life of service in exchange for the comforts of the barracks and regular meals.

"Lord Adon keep you," Marten said, turning away.

"You're on a list!" the Bachelor yelled after him. "Don't come around here again!"

Wearily, Marten trudged down the stairs back toward the Agora. When he reached the cobbled streets of the Old Town, he realized that something was making him feel uneasy. He looked behind him quickly. Did someone just duck into a doorway? Marten turned a corner and slipped onto a doorway himself, waiting. People walked past, but no one particularly threatening-looking.

I'm just too damn tired, he thought, starting off again. He turned another corner, realized he'd reached a dead-end and started back.

The Bachelor he had talked to at the gate, and another one in a cowl and sunglasses who Marten didn't recognize blocked the way out of the alley. Both drew their daggers.

"Old man!" the red-head said with a smile. "You forgot something."

Marten's heart sank as he pulled his own knife from its leg-sheath. All his life he'd had to fight like this. He was good at it. You had to be to travel, and live for very long. But today, of all days! Today he knew he didn't feel the things you needed to feel in order to fight and win. He was tired, confused. His fierce pride about who he was and where he wanted to go was missing. Marten could not fight in this city the way he could on the road. But he was not going to lie down, either. There still was Komaso to think about.

"You left your post." Marten said matter-of-factly. "Aren't you worried about mobs of irate fathers pouring through that gate?"

"Hand over the goods, old man."

"So. You prefer assault to bribery, do you?" Marten unfastened the purse and held it out. "Come here and take it from me."

The Bachelors walked toward the old man casually, not expecting much trouble in spite of the knife. Marten waited until they had almost reached him. Then, with a yell, he swung the purse, hitting the man with the dark glasses in the forehead. As he staggered back, Marten burst forward, slashing with his knife.

The remaining Bachelor swore in pain and missed when he tried to grab Marten, but the traveler caught his heel on a loose cobblestone. He fell forward, and by the time he scrambled to his feet again, his attackers were on him.

"You cut me!" the red-head rasped. "How'm I gonna explain this to the watch captain?"

"That's your look-out. Take his money."

"You know, maybe it's time he found out what it feels like to be a Bachelor! Hold him!"

The red-head tested the edge of his knife with his thumb. Blood from his wound soaked into the arm of his cloak, but he had forgotten all about that. He ripped Marten's shirt open, cut the drawstring of the old man's trousers with the tip of the dagger. Marten twisted and kicked, but the other man had his arms pinned. He was too strong, Marten realized, steeling himself for the moment when the pain would come. . . .

Suddenly, the red-head's eyes got very wide. He tore at his shoulder as though someone had dumped a hot coal on it; at the same time, the grip of the other Bachelor suddenly wavered and broke. Marten sagged back against the wall, watching confusedly as the soldiers came together and separated like puppets being made to dance, directed by someone who had come into the alley behind them. Their heads crashed together. Struggling now, flailing arms and legs, the Bachelors ran out of the alley. One of them still managed to scoop up Marten's purse on the way out.

"Thanks, stranger," Marten gasped, then fell silent.

The man who had helped him had no eyes, no nose, no ears. Only a round, red-lipped mouth through which the tufts of a yellow tongue protruded slightly. It was a seer. And not just any seer, Marten realized. He could see shiny, newly healed burn scars where the skin of its legs showed through its tattered cloak.

This was the creature that had stolen Komaso away from him.

TWENTY-TWO

"BLAST YOU!" Marten yelled. "What do you want?"

The seer stood with its legs slightly spread, clasping its long-fingered hands together. It seemed relaxed, waiting for something, Marten thought.

"A jinx, that's what you are. Someone's laid a curse on me and you're it!" Marten moved forward. The seer's tongue flicked out, and then it stepped sideways to block his way.

"You'd better move. You saw what I did to those other two!"

The seer bent down, picked up Martin's dagger, and held it out, hilt first. After a moment's hesitation, the old man took it from him.

"Maybe you want to make it up to me. Well, I guess you got the kid loose once, and me out of trouble twice. But why'd you take him in the first place? And what'd you do to him? He never talked before you laid those spongy hands of yours on 'im."

The seer made a snuffling noise and held its hands, palms out, in front of its chest.

"You're offering me something? Well, no thanks!"

The seer dropped its hands. Sadly, Marten thought.

"Those boys, you know, took my goods. Why didn't you save my goods? This town's a hard place to bed in with no coppers—and me without tools, or a place to bed down. I should never have come without my rig, but I was dead anxious to get my kid back. And that's your fault, damn you!" Marten was pacing. "What am I doing, talking to you. You can't help me. Leave me alone, so I can figure out what to do!"

The seer grunted, bent and picked something up—a cloak and glasses it had pulled off one of the Bachelors. It slipped the cloak on, and tried to fit the glasses, but without a nose to rest on, the glasses kept slipping off.

"Oh, what are you doing?" Marten growled, snatching the glasses away. Marten untied the cowl string from his cloak and tied the bow-ends together with the string. He cut off a short piece of thong with his dagger making a harness for the glasses with the thong passing through the bridge and up between the bows.

"What the hell," he said, putting the glasses onto the seer's head. When he pulled the seer's cowl up, covering the thongs, he had to admit that the creature looked more or less human. He'd seen uglier than this in the course of his travels.

"Satisfied?"

Now the seer let him out of the alley. Marten turned onto the street that lead down to the Agora. The creature followed him. It kept right on following him through the marketplace and right on down to the river where the breeze off the water offered some relief from the heat.

Marten walked out onto a pier and sat down on wearily on a piling. There, he filled his pipe and watched the crew of a river steamer—stevedores and some schells—struggle with a netload of cargo dangling from the end of a crane. Something was wrong with either the line or the windlass, so that no amount of tugging by the crew, or cursing by their captain, a skinny man who leapt excitedly from the deck of his boat to the quay and back again like a rat springing from one side of his cage to the other, could budge it.

The same old story, Marten thought. People using machines by rote without having any idea of how they actually worked. He got up, strolled over to the the the boat. Immediately, he realized that the tackle lines were not threaded properly inside their pulleys.

"Damn you all!" the captain screamed. "Cut the net open and load those boxes by hand."

"That'll take all night!" one of the stevedores complained.

"Well, how the hell else are we getting this cargo on board?"

"You might try rerigging your tackle," Marten said, loudly enough for the captain to hear.

The little man hopped off the gunwale. "Is that so? And just what the hell do you know about it?"

"Enough to tell you that unless you thread your cable through all the pulleys in that block, your winch won't have power enough to hoist that load."

"Worked fine before."

"You've never tried to lift this much before, have you?"

"How the hell should I know? I'm not a bloody scale!"

"Save your curses, Captain. I'll be glad to rig it up for you. All's I need is a wrench, and five minutes."

Just then, one of the schells growled. In an instant, all of them were milling around angrily while the stevedores tried to quiet them.

"What's wrong with those damn things?"

"Something's spookin' 'em, cap'n," one of the stevedores replied, shooting Marten a suspicious glance.

"It's me all right," Marten said to him. "I'm your mother's ghost."

"Don't you talk about my mother—"

"Back off!" the captain shouted, stepping between Marten and the other man. "Take the schells below and get 'em something to drink. Workin' with you all day's what's got 'em half-daft. I'll take care of the old man."

Reluctantly, the stevedore herded the schells aboard. When they were gone, the captain produced a rusty spanner and gave it to Marten. Quickly, the traveler loosened the cargo hook, ran more cable out from the winch drum and threaded it through the block pulleys. After resecuring the hook, Marten attached the cargo net and waved for the captain to try the winch. When he started it the cargo lifted easily off the pier and swung around over the deck.

"Well, I'll be damned," the captain said, lowering the load into the hold. "You've got more sense than the rest of my crew put together. Thank you!"

Marten nodded. He felt a pang of regret. Normally, this would have been the time to bargain for something in exchange for his services.

"It might help you to make a little drawing of how that block's set up," Marten said. "Good day!"

"Wait!" The captain hopped off the steamer to catch up with him. "What's your hurry? Come on up to my cabin, and we'll have a quick draught, and maybe talk a bit."

"Ah, well, talk's not what I need right now."

"Here, here! I wanted to do things civil-like, but if you're set on leaving, I might as well have out with it. How about signing on with me? You seem to know rigging well enough, and I'm maybe thinking you could be useful with the steam engines as well. Know anything about steam?"

Marten just smiled.

"Then, by Perse's black cave, I want you!"

"Captain, don't think I don't appreciating it, but the fact is, I'm here looking for somebody. I can't work for you and look at the same time, can I? Now, you're a quick-brained man, and your blood's running hot about what I can do for you. Why don't you forget about it? You got your cargo aboard. Just go on as if I never came along and you'll be content. You'll see."

"If it's a bargain you want. . . ."

"Captain, if I wanted to bargain, you'd be dancing to my tune right now. As I said, good day to you!"

As Marten turned to go, a party of Bachelors led by a Vestal officer came onto the quay. They began boarding the other boats tied there, poking bundles with their daggers and questioning anyone they found aboard.

"Look at that," the captain growled. "Third time in two days."

"What do they want?"

"Vagrants. They've been hauling them out of Almheraz by the wagonload."

"You know, Captain, maybe I will have that drink you offered me."

The captain grinned. "That's more like it. Come aboard, man!"

But it was too late. The Vestals already spotted Marten.

"Stay where you are, old man!" the Vestal commander shouted. Marten wondered whether the Bachelors would go into the water after him if he swam for it.

Their commander stepped up to Marten, looked him in the eye, took out a notepad and a pencil. "You live in this town, old man?"

"I've been trying my best, Lady," Marten replied truthfully.

"Address?"

Marten tried to remember a street name from his guide-book, but none came to him. How could his luck possibly be any worse? But the captain piped up:

"Address? Why his address is right here of course!"

"And who are you?"

"Shipmaster Thoms, which I'm sure you'll recall, since you were here yesterday, and the day before. This man's my engineer. You'll have to excuse him if he seems slow, but he's below all the time with the pistons knockin' around him, and it's made him a bit deaf."

The Vestal flipped through the pages of her notebook. "I listed all your crew, and I don't remember—"

"Gods, my Lady, we went through this yesterday! Do you really want to roust the whole crew, and check your books, when there's plenty of other likelier-looking men waiting to be arrested on some of these other piers? My good Lady, this man's been with me five months. And look at him. Even if he was a vagrant, how much work do you think you could get out of that wasted, dried-up body? He'd never earn what you fed him, and believe me, I know. Just between you and me, I think he's got a tapeworm!"

"Spare me the details," the Vestal said, closing her book. "Let's go."

When the Bachelors had left the pier, Thoms slapped his thigh. "Go screw yourselves! If you could!"

"Thanks, Captain," Marten said.

"Just a minute. You think I spoke up for you just so you could go your merry way? You're my engineer now—unless, if you'd prefer I called that bunch back here and told 'em I don't know you from the moon's backside."

"No," Marten sighed. "But I can't just ship out and leave. Not without finding who I'm looking for."

"This ain't a cruise ship. We leave tomorrow noon, hit Baraqu tomorrow evening, and back with another bloody load of pilgrims by next day noon. We'll be twelve hours loading then—that's when you can do your looking. I mean, what else can you do, friend? Here's food and a place to sleep in return for a little work. This way, you keep the bitches off your back. It's easy. You've got something I need, I got something you need. You can understand that, can't you?"

"More than you know, Captain."

"How about it, then?"

Marten considered. Not knowing where the boy was gnawed at him every minute. But now Fate was pointing him in another direction. Perhaps it was best not to fight it.

Have some faith, old man, Marten told himself. *This was meant to be.*

"You've got yourself a new crewman, Captain," Marten said.

TWENTY-THREE

NOT FAR AWAY, a dark-haired, broad-shouldered man walked out of the waterfront park and headed for the last pier of the harbor. It was the longest pier, broad and sagging, but there were no barges or boats tied alongside.

At the head of this pier there was a gate covered with nailed-on circles of sheet tin. Each of them bore a painted representation of the sun's Eye, some half-eclipsed by slashes of black. Each was marked with the cypher of the family who had placed it there. These were ancient families, the oldest in the Realm; the ancestors of some of them had lived in the heights on top of Citadel Rock before there were temples or a palace. Now they lived in the shadows beneath a rotting pier.

The gate guarded Almheraz's sole enclave of Old Believers: Wharvesunder.

Most citizens of Almheraz were convinced that the Wharvesunder folk did nothing but practice profane and orgiastic rites, for which a constant supply of bodies—and sometimes souls—was required. Periodically, demands were made to the Mayor that Wharvesunder be razed and its people sent east to live in the Preserve with the rest of the Old Believers.

These campaigns never got very far.

For one thing, the enclave was under the protection of the Warden, who was always either the elder sister of the Queen, or her first cousin, and therefore a power in her own right. For another, the fishing industry of Almheraz—and therefore of the whole central region of the Realm—was completely dependent on the labor of the Guild of Net-Tyers, which, by royal and heavenly sanction belonged to the denizens of the shadows beneath the pier.

Of course, Wharvesunder folk came into the city all the time. They dressed like anyone else, conducted their business and returned home without attracting attention. But for a citizen, entering the shadows-world of the Old Believers was dangerous. The instant a stranger passed through the wooden gates, all of Wharvesunder seemed to know about it. A visitor might be allowed to come below. Or be turned back. Or dumped into the river with her throat slit.

The person with the dark hair was not worried.

He pushed open the gate with both hands, *hitting* it open, striding through with heavy boots pounding the boardwalk. He stopped to look around, watching a yellow, pennant-bedecked barge as it rounded the bend at Point Draco. Then his face clouded, and for an instant everything on and below the pier seemed to freeze into silence. The man with dark hair took advantage of that moment to lower himself to the deck, swing his legs over the edge, wrap his feet around a piling and shinny down to one of the rope bridges that crisscrossed the bottom of the piers like the webs of a demented spider. There, the man waited for his eyes to adjust to the shadows.

Ribbons of light darted off the wavetops and outlined the forms of basketlike huts suspended from the bottom of the pier. The river slapped against the pilings, echoing against the mossy boards above the catwalks. People laughed and shouted, children cried, cooking pots clattered, their contents filling the air with spicy aromas that flavored the fishy smell of the river at low tide. The quick, dark children darted along the catwalks. Through it all came the mingled sounds of hundreds of tinny prayer-bells whose clappers were attached to bobbers and rang with the rise and fall of the waves.

The stranger got his bearings and crawled toward the middle of the pier, where the rope catwalk intersected with a good-sized square of planking that was provided with some low tables and chairs, the whole area illumined by blue lamps that attracted swarms of moths and river flies. Stooping to avoid hitting his head, the stranger crossed this floor and entered the Inn of the Blue Lamp.

The inn was a tidy place that smelled of incense and chouris tea. As soon as the stranger sat down, the proprietress burst through the beaded curtain that separated the guest rooms in back from her own living quarters. This woman, whose name was Tory, seemed designed for a life along the catwalks: short, thin, with impossibly large hands and spindly fingers that twisted together whenever she was agitated.

She was twisting them now.

"There you are!" she said sharply.

The stranger turned his head toward her, not looking at her exactly. His eyes were too blank for that. "You've changed," he said flatly. "A week ago you were very pleased to see me. Even during The Feast."

"That was last week. Now I've got an empty inn—and I'm turning folks away—Folks that'd be buying my food and drink."

"I paid more than normal trade would bring. Don't go on to me about normal trade. You don't know anything about it. Oh, you put on airs and show me you can think and talk as well as any man, but don't you ever forget that I know what you are. You wouldn't be here now if your mistress the Warden wasn't my third cousin! See this?" Tory held up a finger. "That's Perse's blood running through these veins. You can't say the same. Your kind don't even have blood, for all I know."

"I believe I want some food," Sportus said.

"What do you want?"

"Raw chicken for my Lady's hawk. Fresh fruit for me, if you have some."

Sportus smiled at her. His eyes came to life and he showed his teeth, and when he did, Tory stopped wringing her hands.

She opened her mouth a little, a flush spreading across her forehead and down onto her cheeks. She recovered only when Sportus stopped smiling.

"Wait in your room, then. I'll call you when you can come get it."

Sometimes it was comforting to take orders. He was a schell after all. He went to his room at the rear of the inn. There, behind a striped blanket that served as a door was a small space just big enough for a narrow bunk and a small table. Between them stood a perch where a young, hooded hawk slept, her braided leash dangling down and almost touching the blankets on the bed. The bird shifted on its perch when Sportus came in. He ignored it. The hawk, for her part, seemed to hold Sportus in contempt, deigning to notice him only when he offered her strips of meat, which she snatched quickly from his fingers as though his touch tainted the food.

Sportus sat down. He seldom slept. Instead, he caught bursts of rest during which he entered an intense, trancelike state. He sat that way, eyes open but unfocused, until the sound of voice brought him to. The voice was whiny, out of breath, and Sportus knew that it belonged to Marko, the teenaged son of the innkeeper.

"Sorry, I was late, Mum. But there was a big commotion in town. Something about the Queen."

Sportus visualized the yellow barge, and the yellow, blue and gold colors on its masts and rigging.

"—People were saying she's gone. They've taken her to Queen's Island."

"Well, you should have come back. You know I don't like to be alone when he's here—"

"No, Mum."

"No, Mum! Finish cutting this chicken for me. My ankle's been giving me trouble all day. I'm getting too old for this life, Marky. And too old for the likes of him!"

The Queen was ill. It was true! Sportus could feel it, the way the barge had churned through the water, sparks shooting out the stacks. He could replay that memory so that it was like a vibration in his bones.

He knelt down, got out a wooden box from under the bed, and set it on the table. He fumbled a little with the straps. He was annoyed by that, and stopped a moment until he felt calmer. Then he opened the box.

The inside was lined with plush, and on one side there was a compartment in which rested a polished silver brazier about as wide as the span of his hand, and a tripod whose legs were held together by a fine chain. There were also compartments for three glass-stoppered bottles, and three measuring spoons.

He smiled to himself as he set up the tripod and fit the brazier on it. He then took one of the spoons and a bottle filled with amber liquid, and measured out some of it into the brazier. He did the same thing with a second bottle and spoon, mixing them until the liquid turned green and gave off a sharp smell like vinegar. The third bottle contained something heavy and silvery that rolled around in the spoon like mercury, but which melted instantly when Sportus poured it in to the brazier.

The brazier sizzled, and sent up a slowly expanding plume of heavy smoke that gathered itself and twisted into a blue cloud that hung in the middle of the room. Sparks fizzed inside the cloud, which seemed to separate into light and shadow, gradually clarifying into an image of an overgrown thicket of trees.

Sportus watched a moment. Branches stirred around the breeze. Slowly he spread his hands, cupping them beneath the brazier, tilting it gently so that the bubbling liquid inside did not swirl and break up the image. The trees in it shifted; Sportus tilted the brazier some more until he caught the image of Sheeme standing in the shade of a thicket, rubbing her shoulder with her free arm as though she'd suddenly felt a chill.

Now Sportus moved quickly. There was one phial left in the box, and he got it out. It was pencil-thin and filled with thick oil that was blacker than ink. Sportus unstoppered it and let a single drop fall into the brazier pan.

The result was spectacular. First the liquid in the pan boiled up violently into a deep purple foam that hissed and steamed like lava flowing into seawater. The brazier began to rattle on the tabletop—indeed, the table and the whole room shook so hard that Sportus had to hold onto it to keep his balance. The new burst of smoke now obscured the image of the Warden, and as Sportus held on and waited for it to clear, the innkeeper Tory, white-faced and barely able to keep her own feet, stuck her head through the door.

"What by Alamos' damned forge are you doing? Stop that!"

"Get out." Sportus replied through clenched teeth, not looking back.

"Out of my own house!" Something screeched. It was hard to tell if it was Tory or the hawk, who now hopped side to side on her perch.

"If you do not leave," Sportus said calmly. "I'll burn this house down. And I'll make sure you burn with it. You and that fat son of yours!"

Tory wilted and staggered away to the front of the inn, certain she had a one-way ticket to limbo. Meanwhile, Sportus waved his hand at the smoke, clearing some away so that he could see the Warden.

Sheeme was in the middle of a struggle of her own. She stiffened, lurching about; Sportus could hear her gasping, a tiny sound, like a voice coming through the wall from another room. Then the smoke evaporated, and Sheeme's anima stood alone in the center of the brazier.

"My Lady," Sportus said, softly. "Can you hear me?"

Sheeme nodded.

"Something's happened. The situation may have changed." Sportus hesitated. The anima on the brazier flickered, and when it did, Sheeme winced in obvious pain.

Finally, he said, "I met the King today. He intends to cheat you. Also, by chance, I followed the Princess Maud when she went riding in the Grove. She seemed most attracted to me, and readily agreed to meet me later. Everything is going as you planned."

"Why are you calling me?"

Sportus almost sounded embarrassed. "I called because I need guidance. It takes time to become an addict of hawk venom. The Queen's dying. Wouldn't it be simpler to use her attraction to me to bring her to you?"

Sheeme winced again. "You'll never bring her to me. Why pretend you will?"

Sportus looked at her. The image was flickering now like

the last embers of a fire, and the Warden Sheeme looked ill.
It would be an easy thing for him to simply turn his back on
her and wait. Then he would truly be free to do as he pleased.

"Look at me." Sheeme said. "I'm telling you to do
something."

"I hear."

"How pleased the Gods must have been to see their children grow up as headstrong as they were. They wanted love,
Sportus, and for that their children had to be able to choose
them. I, on the other hand, want obedience. It's not at all the
same thing, is it?"

"No."

"Tip the brazier."

Sportus obeyed. A black wafer, hard and shiny as obsidian
and smelling faintly of burnt sugar, slid onto the table, spun
on its edge like a coin. When it was still, Sheeme's anima
vanished. Sportus sat down on the bed. After a time, he heard
someone knocking on the wall behind him. It was Marko,
with the food.

"I had to bring this for Mum," Marko said nervously.
"She's not feeling very well right now." He set the tray
down quickly, intent on hasty retreat.

"I want you to deliver a message for me," he said, without
looking at the boy. He took pen and paper out of his trunk
and wrote something down in neat, even lettering. "Bring
this to the Vestal who guards the elevator below the palace.
She'll know what to do with it."

"All right. I'll just tell Mum and go."

"No." Sportus caught his arm. "Go quietly. You'll be
back before she knows you're gone."

"Y-yes, sir!"

Sportus gave the boy credit. He was able to slip away
without alarming his mother. And the mother had done
well, too, giving a larger portion of raw chicken than ever
before, and fresh fruit, rather than fruit fit for the trash
can. Sportus reached for an apple, hesitated, then picked
up a strip of raw chicken breast instead, put it into his
mouth.

The taste stirred something inside him. Having smelled the
meat, the hawk ruffled its feathers and pecked at the ties of its

hood. Sportus held some chicken in front of her. The hawk extended her neck, trying to find it.

Sportus closed his hand around the back of her head. A quick twist, and the bird dropped from its perch and swung by its feet for a time, back and forth at the end of its leash.

There would be no more venom.

Sportus was on his own.

TWENTY-FOUR

ON THE FRONT of the King's desk in his office was a mechanical model of the universe. Turning a key on the base sent three little globes—one yellow, one green, and one silver—spinning around in time to tinkly music that also came from the base. Careev had always loved this model. Now, waiting for her father with Maud, both girls sitting in the low chairs in front of his desk, she was tempted to wind it up. It was as if the music could banish the future that intruded now with shocking force and speed.

She glanced over at Maud, who picked at the split ends of her hair. God, it was hard not to hate her sometimes! The door opened and the King came in.

He looked stiff in a red satin tunic crossed with a gold sash, and he was wearing boots—new boots, from the way he walked in them. He had a leather folder under his arm that he tossed onto the desk before he sat down.

"Thank you for coming, ladies," he said. Maud looked

up. Careev noticed the Adon's garden Maud had made for him sitting on a table in front of the windows.

"Because of the emergency, the Templemen received permission from our Vestal friends to connect a telegraph link to Queen's Island. Your mother got there a half-hour ago. According to her physician, she's still unconscious, but no worse. The physician is burning some of the Queen's blood, and hopes to make a diagnosis shortly." He puffed on his cigarette, coughed, looked at the cigarette disgustedly, and stabbed it into his ashtray.

"Will she be all right?" Careev asked.

"How the hell should I know?"

Careev flushed.

"Sorry. I'm just. . . . Nobody's ever ready for this stuff. I'm sorry."

"It's all right, Poppa."

"I've called a meeting of the Realm Council for eight o'clock. I'd like both of you to be there, for obvious reasons. It's possible I may not be King much longer, but as long as I am, and as long as your mother is still alive, I intend to use all my power to keep order. I'm going to have to rule and reign. That means things are going to be more formal around here. Every procedure that's to be followed by law or by tradition is going to be observed. I'd like to have the cooperation of both you girls."

"Sure, Poppa."

"Stop playing with your hair, and sit up! I'm serious."

Maud leaned forward in her chair, but did not let go of her hair. The King sighed.

"We don't know yet what's wrong with your mother. But you both saw that dark-haired schell that your aunt sent here. The thing can change shape, or seems to anyway, and if that's true, it could be anywhere in this palace. If you've had the thought that anybody you might have seen or talked to today was strange, I want to know."

"Strange compared to what?"

"Maud—"

"I'm sorry, Poppa. It's just that I'm not quite sure what you mean."

"I mean that schell—Sportus, he called himself—could still be here! Just think about it.'"

"I don't have to think about it. I haven't seen anybody like that."

The King gave her a hard look. He then leaned back in his chair, swiveling toward Careev.

"You were with your mother. Tell me what happened."

"Father, you don't think that I—"

Cyre lighted a fresh cigarette.

"Just tell me."

"I-I went to see her, to bring her one of the gardens I'd made. She was having lunch, some fish I think—"

"Did you eat any?"

"I wasn't hungry."

"Then what?"

"She asked me if I would read to her from her scrolls. Because it was the Festival and everything, she wanted to hear the Passion. So I was reading, and then all of a sudden, she sat up and pointed to the wall behind me, and said she could see the Lord, that he was coming for her. Then . . . I don't know, she just started shaking, having a fit. I didn't know what to do, so I called the Vestals, and then the physicians came." Tears pooled in Careev's eyes, and her voice cracked. "She really did see him, I think."

"Who?"

"The Lord. She was smiling. And the garden I made her. . ."

"Yes?"

Careev took a deep breath. She had thrown the garden over the wall, and in spite of her desire to tell the truth, she was too ashamed to tell what she had done or explain why.

"Never mind."

Cyre nodded. "And what about you, Maud? Where were you when all this was going on?"

"I took Mint and went out for a ride in the Grove."

"Alone? That wasn't very bright."

"That's the only way to be sometimes, Poppa."

"Oh, you little shit," Cyre said. "Let's go to this damn meeting and get it over with. You got any more smart comments?"

"Nope."

"How about you, Careev? Here, wipe your eyes. They're gonna be looking at you in there. I want you to stand up for yourself, be strong. That goes for you, too, Maud. Somebody is trying to destroy this family. We're going to show them that we won't let that happen. The Gormayne family rules Almheraz, and that's not going to change, no matter who the Queen is. Come on."

The Realm Council chambers were inside a pergola at the very top of the palace. Since it was seldom used, and baked by the sun much of the year, the room was stale-smelling. A pair of schells worked cranks that turned overhead fans, stirring dust around the room. Queen's Guards stood stoically at attention between the windows, resisting the impulse to sneeze.

The King was seated at one end of the oval conference table. Next to him were Magister Eccles, the two Princesses, Lady Tambar, who was Mayor of Almheraz, and noblewomen representing estates from the Steppes, the Northern and Southern Cordillera, the Tablelands, and Baraqu on the coast. This last Lady, who was called Baxhage, was dressed exotically in a tunic made of wired-together seashells that rattled like dice when she moved. The final chair, at the opposite end of the table from the King, belonged to the Arcopatrinas, or her representative. It was empty. The King poured himself a glass of water from the pitcher in front of him, sipped it, and then stood up.

"Apparently, the Order of Vestals are unable to send a representative to this meeting, so we might as well begin now. Thank you all for coming on such short notice and interrupting your holiday. We particularly appreciate the presence of Lady Tove of Jelavay, who just arrived by rail this afternoon, and must certainly be tired."

"Oh, we've been keeping ourselves amused, sir," Tove replied with a mysterious smile.

"Good. I'll come right to the point, Ladies. I'm sure you all know, either directly or through rumor, that the Queen was taken ill this noon. Contrary to what you might have heard, she is not dead. She requested that we take her to Queen's Island, and we have done that. Presently, she's under the care of Physician Avra, and resting comfortably. However, she is incapacitated. In her absence, and until she can resume her duties, she has directed that the agreement regarding temporary transfer of power, which was signed on our wedding day and approved by this council take effect. Under its terms, I continue to rule as King, and assume the office of Queen's Regent, giving me full power to reign as her proxy. The Magister has brought along copies of this document for you to review. I would appreciate it now if the Council would reaffirm its consent this evening. I think all of you would agree that the Realm needs at least a show of unity from the powers of the land, and you can see from the terms of the agreement that it in no way threatens the constitution of the government, nor the transfer of power to the Queen's heir in the event, Adon forbid, of her death. This is not a pleasant task for me. But it's necessary. We all remember the situation that faced us before the rains came—''

"Yes, King Cyre! Please tell us about that!"

Now Matron Rarei, looking pale and thin, but determined, limped into the chambers with the help of a crutch.

"Matron!"

"I wouldn't have missed this for anything, my King. Keep going. Tell us about the 'situation'!"

Cyre blanched. A moment ago he had been in complete control of the meeting. Now the focus had shifted to the other side of the table. Rarei sitting there looking so frail, yet holding her crutch like a scepter!

"If you insist, Matron. It's pretty common knowledge that elements of your Vestal troops were out of control during the summer. Some were openly rebellious. Revolutionaries sanctioned by you!"

"It's you who fancies himself a revolutionary."

"And why not? Can anyone here at this table tell me their lands were free of this Vestal scourge? Their properties seized, their men dragged away into slavery for trumped up offenses against the White Goddess? All this perpetrated by troops sworn to loyalty to the Queen. They ignored her orders as they disregarded mine, or any of yours! Why, they even went to my home town—to land directly under my protection, and seized the farm that belonged to my mother. This woman led the raid herself!''

With an effort, Rarei stood. "Let's not exclude you from the class of murderers, King! Who gave the order that finished the Arcopatrinas? Who conceived that it was her soul as well as her life that was to be taken?''

"Warden Sheeme was responsible for that. We're looking for her.''

"As are we! In the meantime, it is no coincidence that the rebirth of our Mistress has not yet shown herself. Murderer and soul-stealer—"

Eccles jumped up to prevent the King from lunging at Rarei.

"Majesty! Lady! We are not in a position now to launch an inquiry into these terrible crimes. Surely you can see that.''

"Who knows what she sees?" Cyre growled.

"Everyone here," Eccles went on, guiding the King back to his place, "has the good of the Realm at heart. There can be no argument about that.''

"Of course not," Lady Tove put in brightly. "And as for the Arcopatrinas, why, I may just have him at my villa right this moment.''

Cyre pushed Eccles off. "What the hell are you talking about?''

"Well, of course, it can't be the Arcopatrinas, but I met this boy on the train from Semele. The most disrespectful, presumptuous, blasphemous boy I'd ever encountered in my life. He kept saying he was the Arcopatrinas. I almost had him gutted for it, but he does seem to know a lot. In fact, he's kept a whole house full of guests absolutely stunned all day long telling what he supposedly knows about life inside the White Temple. It's absolutely amazing. I certainly can't explain it.''

Rarei stared at her for some time, her hatred of the King momentarily forgotten. At last she said, "I would appreciate it if you could arrange for me to see this boy.''

"I'd be thrilled, Matron Rarei! I intended to send you a note about him, but I wasn't sure how you were feeling.''

There was a lull. Eccles seized it. "Please, Majesty, if you could continue with the business at hand.''

Staring incredulously at Tove the whole time, Cyre described how the Princess Royal would stand in for the Queen at the Marriage Ceremony the night after next. The people, he said, were to be told as little about the Queen's condition as possible, other than that she was resting at Queen's Island. As he was assuring everyone that nothing would happen except that which was ordained by Heaven, a messenger entered the chamber, bowed quickly, and handed a scroll to Maud. She read it, shoved it into the pocket of her tunic, and then, when the King finished speaking, asked to have the floor.

"Pop—I mean, Father. It's really very stuffy in here, and what with being worried about the Queen, I'm just about ready to faint. Would you all please excuse me?"

"All right," Cyre said, scowling. When she had made her bows and left, the Mayor began a report on how wine sales were to be restricted during the late hours on Festival nights to avoid any breakdown in law and order. The Council meeting ended without further incident. The King adjourned the meeting and left quickly, avoiding the Matron, who left in the company of nobles. Now only Careev and Eccles remained. Careev was crying softly to herself. Eccles touched her shoulder.

"Courage, Lady. You knew this would happen one day."

"I don't want to be Queen! I'm not made for it. Can't I resign? Give it to Maud? She's like Poppa, she's strong and doesn't care what people think about her."

"I know you have that strength too, Lady." Gently, he turned her head so she could see him. "And you're not alone."

"What do you know about it?"

Eccles hesitated. "Perhaps, if you went to the Island, saw your mother."

She shook her head. "No. I hate it there."

"But you will have to go eventually," Eccles persisted. "I could go with you, do what I can to help. More than you know."

Careev sighed, getting up. "I'm very tired, Magister. I think I understand you, but I don't want to think about it now. I just want to sleep."

"Of course."

"Good night, then."

"One moment, Lady?"

Careev looked back. She seemed to have aged during the course of the evening.

"Your sister got a message earlier, just before she left. Would you have any idea what it was about?"

"You'll have to ask her," Career said coldly. "Good night."

TWENTY-FIVE

LADY TOVE WALKED OUT of the palace feeling light-headed and exhausted. The meeting of the Realm Council had certainly been disagreeable, what with the King showing off and Matron Rarei backing down from him just when their argument was heating up. And those boring reports about the city of Almheraz, as if anyone other than the Mayor really cared! What she wanted now more than anything was a hot bath, and a night in bed with the boy, if he was willing.

At the top of the steps, Tove stopped and frowned. There was a white carriage down in the courtyard, but no sign of her own sedan.

"Honestly!" Tove said to one of her attendants. "Find out where that driver is!"

The door of the white carriage opened. Tove's breath caught when she saw who was inside.

"Matron Rarei!" Tove exclaimed. "Have you been waiting here long? You didn't by chance see my sedan here?"

"I told your driver to go home, Lady Tove," Rarei said. "I hope you don't mind, but I'm very interested in meeting that boy you mentioned. I thought perhaps we could ride to your villa together."

"Of course, Matron. I'd be honored," Tove stammered, silently cursing her bad luck. Why did she have to open her mouth? Fate wasn't about to let her keep the boy, if she insisted on advertising.

"It's really not necessary for you to do this," Tove said when the carriage got underway. "He's lying, of course."

"Oh, but what an intriguing lie! A boy, claiming to be the rebirth of the Arcopatrinas. That's certainly novel."

The brakes of the carriage squealed as it started down the long grade along the face of Citadel Rock.

"It was silly of me. He's just a crazy boy. In fact, he stole money from one of my maids on the train. That's how I met him. And I had him arrested and put to work on the engine, but then we broke down. Somehow, that boy put a piece of metal into the furnace on the engine so they turned white hot, and he hammered it straight."

"He used a forge," Rarei said, thinking of Alamos, and how his forge had set the world on fire.

"All I know is that he fixed the train, if that's what you mean. Anyway, I thought he deserved some kind of reward for that. I decided to take him in. That's when he started this nonsense about being the Arcopatrinas. If I had been at home when I heard this, I would have had him gutted right off for blasphemy, but sometimes being on a journey makes a person, I don't know, more tolerant. And it's strange to admit, Matron, but when I talk to him, he sometimes almost has me convinced that he really *is* the rebirth. Something about his eyes, I suppose, the way they change all the time."

"He seems to have made quite an impression on you then."

"A little," Tove said, blushing.

"Maybe it was a good thing he kept his claims so modest. He might have said he was Father Kronnos, and then where would you be?"

Struck by lightning, Tove thought. *And happy about it!*

•   •   •

When they reached the house, Tove helped Rarei outside, but the Matron insisted on using her crutch to make her way into Tove's villa. Tove's villa was not grand; it did, however, have a fine garden, and a view of the whole city. Inside, they found things in an uproar. Tove's housemaid and several Bachelors were sweeping up broken pottery and glass, and collecting sticks of smashed chairs. Cushions had been ripped apart, the feathers still floating around the room.

"Gods, what happened here?" Tove wailed with such anguish that Rarei was forced to bite her lip to keep from smiling.

"It's that boy!" the maid replied. "He insulted your guests, and then, when somebody said he ought to be hanged, he got a knife from the kitchen and drove everyone out. I didn't know what to do. He threatened to kill himself if we came near him, and then he started smashing everything, and said he'd tear the whole place down if we didn't take him to see Matron Rarei at the White Temple. I was afraid he *would* kill himself, ma'am—oh, the look he had in his eye!"

"Can't I leave the house for five minutes? Look at this! By Psyche's holy lantern, how stupid can you be!"

"Never mind," Rarei said to the maid. "The Matron has come to see him."

"Oh, my Lady! I'm so sorry!"

"Shh," Rarei said. "Where is he?"

"There," the maid said, pointing at a door.

"I'll handle this, Matron!" Tove declared. She pounded the door with her fists. "You! Boy! Open this door right now!"

"Forget it!"

"You're in serious trouble, boy!"

"I've done my answering already. I'm through talking to those overfed cows you call guests!"

Rarei pointed to the door with her crutch.

"Break it down," she ordered.

"With pleasure, Lady," said one of the Bachelors.

"Wait a minute! Who'll pay for it?"

"The Order will. Break it down, please."

The Bachelor smashed the door with his shoulder hard

enough to shake the whole house, and it gave way so quickly that it simply seemed to vanish. Rarei hobbled over it with her crutch. The others followed, keeping their distance.

Komaso was sitting on the bed, knife raised. Slowly, he let his arm drop.

"I know you," Rarei said. The shock of recognition was powerful, and she had to grip the doorframe to keep from falling over. It couldn't be!—and yet, there was no mistaking the sandy hair, nor the big, jade-green eyes.

This was the boy she had tried and executed in Panault.

"And I know you," the boy replied. He started to laugh.

"Leave us alone." Rarei said.

"But Matron, that knife—"

"Here," Komaso said, sliding it across the floor past Rarei's feet. The door was still hanging on its bottom hinge, and as Rarei struggled to move it out of the way, she tried to sort her thoughts. It had been four weeks from the time the boy was drowned in Panault and the night the Arcopatrinas was killed. There could not have been much of a body left to reanimate, after two weeks under water. Not to mention the problem of the boy's own unshriven soul, forlorn and trapped on earth near the place of the body's death, which would surely have fought the Arcopatrinas's soul for possession of it.

"I want you to listen to me," Komaso said. "Try to see through what's in front of your eyes to the truth. Even now, everything that happened to me isn't clear. My soul was trapped. I got weaker, until something captured me and brought me to this body."

"How? How did you escape?"

"What do you mean?"

"I mean you were thrown into the water chained to a piece of granite!"

Komaso looked startled. "I've been waiting for this moment. You don't know how I've been longing to see you again, and now. . . . Now I'm remembering things this body knows. I remember carrying that rock! And it was you that condemned me to die that way, on the orders of the Arcopatrinas. Hah! my very own orders, and now I can remember suffering the consequences!" The boy shuddered. "It was not pleasant for me. For him. There was no way for him to answer any of your questions. 'Cut the King's stock down, pull it out root and all!' That's what I said to do, wasn't it?"

Rarei said nothing. Komaso cocked his head.

"I'll tell what happened. An old man saw what was happening from the other side of the pond. He dove in with a pair of bolt cutters and freed me."

"What old man?"

"Marten was his name. A traveler. He took wonderful care of me. Taught me things. . . . But then. . . . It was dark and storming out and something came into the camp, took hold of me! Oh, Rarei, it was worse than even passing through to the afterlife! It was a seer, Rarei! A wonderful, terrible creature! It held my soul in its hands the way you or I would hold a baby bird that had fallen out of a nest, and it fed my soul to this body! I woke up raving, out of control on the road to Semele. I didn't care what I had become, all I cared about was that I had a voice. Someone reported me to a Vestal patrol. I was going to be burned for blasphemy!

"They put me in stocks in the public square at Semele. I resigned myself to dying, however horribly—because at least I'd have a chance of being born again. And then I saw the old man again. . . .

"He'd found me somehow, because he was in love with the boy we tried to kill. Something changed inside me when I saw him . . . oh, I fought it. I pretended I was insane, like I did tonight. I spat in his face just to get him away from me, just so I wouldn't have to think the thoughts that were inside me. This body wants to change what I am, and I couldn't let that happen, so I denounced him and almost got him arrested.

"But he came back that night. He distracted the guards and opened the wagon, set me free. I still couldn't face him and so I ran and hid myself in the crowd waiting for the train here. I got aboard, and ran afoul of Tove on the way. She took a liking to me, so I went along with it. I thought it was the best way to get back to the Citadel. I had to let you know I was alive! There's work to be done, and we've got to do it together."

"You expect me to believe all this?"

"Why not? The whole structure of the Order is based on the rebirth of my soul. Who can say that the Goddess did not choose to use that seer as Her instrument? The destiny of the Order is at stake here. Surely you can't deny that!"

"And surely you can't expect me to present a teenaged boy to the Order as the reincarnation of the Arcopatrinas! For all I know you're a ghost, a vampire."

"Don't fight it, Rarei."

"I need proof. Some kind of sign that I can give to the women who are searching for the rebirth!"

"Very well." Komaso went over to a desk and started writing on a slip of paper. Finished, he folded it in half, and in half again. "Here. Has my testament been opened yet?"

"Of course not. We were waiting—"

"You're waiting for something you'll never find! Go to the Temple, Rarei, and open that scroll. See if points two, three and four match what I've just written here. Rarei, you must do this! The King is ready to move against the matriarchy. He has power and ability that we can't ignore—"

"Don't lecture me!"

"We've been given a great gift, Rarei, and we must not squander it. This body, this boy, is more than a mere kinsman of the King, more than his cousin. *This boy is the King's son!* Think of it, Rarei! Fate has given our Order the means of the King's destruction through the son he hoped to crown King one day himself. I can feel him in me! With your help, I can control him, make him ours!"

Rarei shook her head. "It's too much . . ."

"Damn you, I didn't lose my life to come back and see you hesitate! Go to the Temple and open my will. Then, one way or another, make up your mind."

Rarei nodded. "Will you wait here?"

"Yes, but my patience is not infinite. You are facing a test, Matron. Do not fail us now!"

Head spinning, Rarei left Tove's villa and returned to the Citadel. Inside the White Temple, she painfully descended two flights of stairs to the basement repository, where the wills of important nobles of the Realm were stored until they could be read and executed following the interment of the mummy of the deceased.

The walls of the repository were divided into thousands of pigeonholes, each holding a scroll tagged with a ribbon and a wax seal. The Order of Vestals was charged with the security of these documents, and in the middle of the room was the index cabinet guarded by the leathery mummy of Lena, Fifth Arcopatrinas of the Order and the builder of the repository. The mummy's eye sockets had been filled with blue glass that shimmered in the dim light and seemed to follow Rarei's limping progress around the room. The mummy made her uncomfortable; Rarei was glad that she knew where the Arcopatrinas's will was, and did not have to use the index.

She had to climb a ladder to reach it. Exhausted, she nearly fell, but managed to retrieve the green-sealed scroll. At the long table next to the index cabinet, she cut the ribbon with her dagger, spread the scroll, and then unfolded the paper the boy had given her.

Article two read:

"The lands pertaining to my estate at Colchis shall be divided equally between the Trustees of the Order and the family of my kinswoman, Mara of Panault. Should Mara of Panault become incapacitated, or predecease me, the gift will pass in its entirety to the Trustees of the Order."

The boy had written it out word for word. Even the handwriting was the same.

Rarei put her face in her hands and tried to clear her mind. The soul of the Acropatrinas in the body of the King's son. If such a person had been made by Heaven's will, what purpose could he have? To rule? To set the Realm on a Vestal course? To support the Gormanye heir if the Queen should die? Hours ago, Rarei's mission had seemed so simple. To defeat the King. Now, to have to beat Cyre and then convince the Order and the Realm of the legitimacy of this strange and awful rebirth!

With all her heart, Rarei prayed to the Goddess. She relaxed a little then, and waited. After a time, an idea came to her. She thought about it, and when she did, she realized that she knew what she had to do.

Slowly, she resealed the scroll, climbed the ladder again, put it back. She must get some rest. Then she would do as Psyche surely had instructed her.

TWENTY-SIX

IT WAS LOW TIDE and barges listed in the mud in Almheraz harbor. A steam packet churned slowly upstream, giving a forlorn blast of its whistle when it passed an anchored ship; overhead the yellow beam from the light at Point Draco swept across, seemingly making a hissing sound as it did, like a broom pushed through fine sand.

Hugging the shore, a small poling-punt pushed by two schells headed for the easterly pier of Wharvesunder. The punt carried a passenger who wore a dark cloak and sat very still.

A little behind it, a dory driven by a puttering steam engine held its position against the current. Its occupants watched the slow progress of the pole-boat.

Meanwhile, in Wharvesunder, at the Inn of the Blue Light, innkeeper Tory drained a cup of rice whiskey and screwed her courage up to go back and have a look inside the room where the schell Sportus was. Things had been quiet for almost two hours after the horrible shaking and howling. The creature hadn't stirred, she was sure. She remembered how he had looked, holding onto the table with that brazier burning like the sun itself in front of him. *Maybe he's poisoned himself,* she thought hopefully. Or maybe, Perse willing, he'd burned himself up. White light, after all, was anathema to Old Believers, and Sportus had filled the room with white light.

A pile of ashes, that's what I want to see, Tory thought, putting her cup down and walking cautiously to the back of the inn. *Please, Perse, by your love for Adon. . . .*

She pulled the curtain aside, peeked in and covered her mouth with her hand.

Dangling from its perch was the young hawk the creature had brought from the Preserve with him. Tory had been honored to have the hawk in her house. The only reason she had allowed Sportus to stay was because of it, and now it was dead, neck broken, from the look of it. Outrage rose in her. If only the Warden could see this!

Then she noticed Sportus stretched out on the bed. His eyes were closed and he did not seem to be breathing. Tory stepped into the room, knelt down. Slowly, she put her hand out in front of his face.

His eyes opened.

Gasping, she tried to back out, but he seized her wrist and held her where she was.

"Where's your boy?" he said.

"N-not here! Let go!"

"You have trouble minding your own business. You promised me when I came that you did not bother about the private business of your guests."

"You're no guest of mine!" Tory hissed. "There's something wrong with you. Look what you did to that poor bird! You're the devil's own, that's what you are. I don't believe you have anything to do with the Warden. She'd put a dagger in you, just like you deserve!"

Sportus showed his teeth. "Why do you keep staring over there? Ah, it's your great regard for hawks, is it?"

"They're the noblest things on this poor earth! The only things that are pure and undefiled. That's why they live so long. You wouldn't know about that, though, being a schell, and a rogue schell at that! Let me go! I'll see your mistress finds all about you!''

Sportus got up from the bed and pulled the innkeeper over to the dead hawk's perch. "I can't afford to have any more of your meddling here tonight. Let's have a taste of this bird you admire so much!''

With his free hand, Sportus took the hawk by the tail, and used his thumb and forefinger to work the stinger out of its sheath. The barb at the end of it was now exposed: bone-white, curved, and sharp as a needle. Quickly, Sportus released Tory's wrist and caught her by the hair. One pull tipped her head back. He brought the stinger close to her mouth, tightening his grip on her hair. Her mouth opened in pain. When it did he squeezed the base of the barb, and a thin stream of milky liquid squirted over her tongue. Tory gagged; Sportus squeezed the barb again.

"I didn't have a chance to milk her these three days. You can have as much as you want.''

"Stop. . . . It . . . it burns.''

"Not for long. Swallow it.''

She shook her head. Sportus let go of the hawk and clamped her mouth shut in the crook of his arm, pinching her nostrils shut as he did until she was forced to obey. He let her go then. She sat down on the floor and shuddered, blinking her eyes.

"You're going to float away now,'' Sportus said. "Your soul is free to go wherever it wants. Go lie in Adon's arms. Feel his heavenly caresses.''

Tory's mouth opened. Venom dribbled down her chin. Sportus took her by the arms and dragged her into the next room. She was breathing very slowly when he left her.

He went back to his room and put on the green quilted tunic and soft boots of a forester. With his knife, he cut the hawk's leash, then opened the shutters and dropped the body into the water. There was a mirror in the room and he looked at himself in it, running his hands through his hair. He grimaced, baring his teeth, rubbing them with his finger. When he was satisfied that they were clean, he straightened the room and went to the front of the inn to wait.

• • •

"Tie up here."

The punt drifted alongside a piling outlined in faint blue light. Maud knew the inn. As a child, she had often slipped away from the palace and come to Wharvesunder to fish, and sometimes, her Aunt Sheeme would meet her there. They would have something to eat at the Blue Light while Sheeme questioned her about goings-on at the palace. Always, the conversation would gradually move to the King. What was he doing? Was he happy? Did he ever talk about the Warden of the Queen's Preserve?

Maud knew then that Sheeme was banished, and felt it was her fault because of what had happened to the baby. Her aunt never let Maud forget that—or failed to remind her that someday she would come to the Preserve to live with her.

Now she was coming back to meet someone else. "Blue Light Inn—Sportus" was all the message had said, but she read it over and over in the boat, by the light of the poling schell's lamp. Each time she finished, she closed her eyes and remembered exactly what it felt like kissing him. She could replay the chill he'd given her over and over, like a voice on one of the recording machines Eccles kept at the Temple of the Sun.

Her heart was pounding as the schell tied the boat up.

"Wait for me here."

Then she climbed the spikes up the piling and onto the deck of the inn. Everything was as she remembered it. The tables were empty, though, and the inn itself looked dark and deserted. She drew her dagger and went inside.

Sportus stepped out of the shadows. "I knew you'd come," he said softly. "I've been wanting very much to see you again."

"Where's my aunt?" Maud showed him the dagger. Sportus looked at it. His eyes, which had been sparkling, now looked like a pair of buttons. He turned his head jerkily, then smiled.

"May I offer you . . . some refreshments?" His voice was disappointing, so dull and schell-like that Maud wondered if this really was the same creature who had thrilled her so much.

"Refreshments?"

"Yes. Anything you like. Ale, fruit. Anything."

"All right, I'll have some wine."

"Please . . . sit down." Maud put the dagger back into its sheath and sat down on the divan. Sportus went out, returning a moment later carrying a wine bottle and a single glass on a tray. He poured the wine into the glass, bowed, presenting it to her.

"You do that very well, Sportus."

"I was the Warden's valet for several years. While I was learning."

Maud sipped her wine. It was resiny, the kind of wine Sheeme liked.

"Learning is not something a schell is supposed to be able to do."

"I was made to do things schells are not able to do."

"And you were not made to be modest."

"Modesty, my Lady, is a virtue no one is made for. Not even humans."

"Well put. And I'm glad to see that my aunt did not forget to build some charm into you as well."

Sportus nodded.

"Is she well?"

"Who?"

"My aunt, of course!"

"Yes."

"I'm very disappointed that she's not here. Where is she?"

"If I told you, I'd be endangering you both. She did ask me to say that she sends her love."

"Is that what you were doing in the grove this afternoon?"

The schell showed no emotion. "She wants you to know that it is time to begin your training. She wants you to give your consent, and come to the Preserve after the Festival, as soon as arrangements can be made."

"That's not possible."

"What is possible is that you can become Queen. You need only give your consent to be initiated into the ways of Perse, and you will be. It is only right that an Old Believer should rule in Almheraz!"

"Stop. You don't believe a word of what you're saying."

"You're wrong. I can believe anything I want."

Maud was silent a moment. Then: "What do you expect

me to do? Get up and leave with you right now, this minute? Just because you say so? You can't expect that. I haven't even seen my aunt for a year." Maud shook her head. "You tell her I can't do anything right now. My mother's sick. My little sister needs my help."

Sportus's eyes came to life. "I know what you really care about." He moved to block the door as Maud jumped up. Catching her in his arms, he forced her to look him in the eye. "You want to speak to the Goddess. I can help you. . . ."

He kissed her; she tried to push away but that only made her feel his strength more. She closed her eyes, breath catching, feeling herself let go.

There was a noise behind them. She looked and saw a plump young boy staring in obvious fear.

"What's going on," he said. "Where's Mum?"

Sportus growled and swung his arm. The boy's head snapped back. He arched away from the schell, crashed into a table off on the darkened deck. After that, everything was still.

"You've killed him!" Maud cried.

"Admit that makes me even more attractive! You're feeling the fear of death—put it to work for you! Isn't it just like the fear of pleasure you feel, just before you let go? Why don't we see!"

Sportus grabbed the front of her tunic and tore it open. He pushed her down to the floor and pinned her with his body, then opened his trousers and forced himself inside her. Waves of pain and pleasure battered her. She was breathless, shrinking . . .

"Look at me!" Sportus rasped, driving deeper. Maud tried to keep her eyes closed but they opened and she could see his face, dark, and angry and somehow beautiful.

"You'll do what I say."

"N-n—"

"You'll do what I say! Tell me."

She tried to nod her head.

"Say it!"

"Yes!" Her arms stopped pushing against him, closed around him instead.

"And you're mine to do with as I please. Say it!"

"Oh, Gods, yes, yes!" Now she was pulling him close. "We'll rule together. We were made for each other!"

"Yes!" Head back, triumphantly. "Yes, oh God, yes, yes, yes!" Tears in her eyes, on her face, rolling down her neck. She would do what he said. She loved him. She loved him!

The schell had been waiting at the end of the pier for a long time, resting in the dormant half-sleep that was a schell's natural condition when it was not being used. When the two figures climbed down the piling further in, the schell sat up and watched as the Princess stepped into her boat. The other one leaned down, hanging from the pier, and kissed the Princess for a long time.

Though the night was warm, the schell felt a deep chill that troubled its dim, rudimentary emotions. He fumbled with the valves getting the launch started again, and nearly put the fire out adding more coal to the boiler.

Had the schell been a man, he might have said that seeing the figure on the piling had put the fear of death into him.

As it was, he did something a schell never did.

He hurried back toward the Citadel.

TWENTY-SEVEN

THE BED was too soft. The sheets were too smooth. The room was too cool, and the wind chimes outside the bedroom window clanged like cowbells. *Useless to try to sleep*, Komaso thought as he got up.

Maybe it was the clothes Tove had given him: satin trousers, red tunic embroidered with gold wire on the collar and cuffs, black slippers. They felt all wrong. Rooting around the floor—Komaso found the clothes he'd worn from the north bundled up in the corner. Tove had ordered them burned, but in the confusion tonight her Bachelors had forgotten about it. The clothes were rough, filthy; why, then, did they feel so good on him? It was hard to understand. Wasn't he used to fine things? In all the lives he had lived as Arcopatrinas, had he not been pampered, carried around, fed the daintiest food?

He picked up the satin trousers; then, seized with an idea, he wadded up the bedsheets and stuffed them inside the legs. He did the same to the tunic with a comforter. Leaving a blanket, he arranged them on the bed and covered them up, so that in the dim light it looked as though someone were sleeping. Komaso stood back to inspect his work, and felt safer. Let them think he was asleep, he thought.

He paced around the room, thinking of Rarei. He knew Rarei believe him. She had not been willing to say so, and Komaso was sure she was going to open that will and see for herself, but she believed him all right. Why did he feel so uneasy about it, then? Wasn't making Rarei believe him supposed to be the difficult part? Why did he feel so confused then, so trapped?

Maybe it was those other memories, he thought. That trial the boy had gone through in Panault. He could *remember* it as if it had really happened to him: It was a hazy memory of darkness and cold, and wanting to breathe, strong enough to make him shudder when he thought of it. *But it has nothing to do with me!* he thought as he angrily paced the room. *That boy doesn't exist any more. It doesn't matter who he was. Even if he was the King's son, he died the moment my soul entered his body!*

What was happening to him now was the opposite of what always happened when his soul was reborn. When he was a baby, there hadn't been any memories to compete with the consciousness of his former incarnations. Eventually those memories did come back, until, if he lived to be an old Matriarch, he had the whole picture. Then he could see the chain of lives stretching inward like the reflections in a pair of mirrors.

Gods, he needed to think. If he could only get away, see some of the places he'd lived in before he died, pray to the Goddess in her Temple. . . .

Komaso went to the door and listened. The house was quiet. Carefully, he pulled it open and saw the Bachelor who had been ordered to guard him asleep on the divan. Komaso tiptoed around him and went outside.

There were torches lighting the garden in the front of the house. Komaso yanked one from its stand and walked down the lane a little, turning so he could see the dark bulk of Citadel Rock blocking the stars. The glow at the top came from the palace, and the Temples. Now he smiled. One of the things he remembered was a way up the Rock. There was a path he had played on when he was a little girl. . . .

Holding his torch up, he started along the lane, peering past each house for signs of the path. A few doors down he reached a pair of twisted pine trees that looked familiar, and he stopped. The path up to the Citadel ran straight between them.

Once through the trees, Komaso picked his way through the boulders and maquis. It felt good to be out in the night air, good to be able to climb with such strength and control. How long had it been since the Arcopatrinas had even been able to take a brisk walk? She had been fat and lazy, he thought. Worse, she hadn't even cared.

The path got steeper, and with bad footing on gravel and loose stones, Komaso was tempted to get rid of the torch. But he knew that once he reached the base of the Citadel wall he would be looking for a small breach that was undoubtedly overgrown, or possibly even repaired. He did not trust himself to find it without the torch; the glow from the stars, and from the Temples and the city below, where scattered bonfires twinkled, wasn't enough. He lifted the torch, got his breath back, and kept on climbing until the path turned sharply at the base of the Citadel wall.

The wall seemed enormous, stretching into the distance beyond the reach of his torchlight. Slowly—because losing his footing now would been mean a fall halfway back to the houses he'd started from—Komaso followed the base of the wall toward the eastern corner, stopping every few feet to push away brush or loose stone that might cover the hole he was looking for. Just when he was beginning to think that he might never find it, he spotted a crack spidering down that gradually widening to a point where some tree branches were grew. Komaso lifted one, looked into a tunnel through the brick just wide enough for him to crawl through. He jammed the torch into the dirt and wriggled through. It was damp and mossy—the sides having been worn smooth by water over hundreds of years—and also curiously warm. Big, heavy things take a long time to heat, he remembered Marten telling him. And they hold onto heat a long time.

He stopped, took a deep breath. He would not think about the old man. The old man did not exist anymore!

Cool air again. He was free from the waist up and could smell spice. The smell of the Red Courtyard, the incense clinging to the tapestries inside the Temple. Here was sandalwood and fine cooking, and rare breezes above the stench of Tumulos mud. He was excited now, scrambling to his feet inside the wall, as he had been as a girl hanging on for dear life to that tree branch outside. He wiped the dirt off his hands and had a look.

There it was. The palace with its red columns, patched, whitewashed walls, sets of double doors opening out onto the balconies on the upper floors, and to the terrace and gardens just up the slope from him. Higher still, scallops of pale yellow light outlined the pillars of the Arcade, while at the very top, the windows of the Realm Council chambers were bright as the flame of an oil lamp. Their light spilled to the edges of the pink-tile roof, where Komaso could see weeds growing in the gutters.

That was appropriate, Komaso thought, licking his lips. Things thriving where they did not belong lived inside the palace as well. There was Cyre the usurper, who wished to reshape the Realm to his fantasy of masculine superiority; Gormayne, whose mind had been lost to Heaven and whose soul would soon follow.

Then there were the daughters. Where did they sleep? Komaso wondered. Where was the older one who had her father's fire and will, who'd looked the Arcopatrinas defiantly in the eye each time they'd met. And the youngest, the one named Careev. She looked like her father, but hardly spoke, and never looked back at the Arcopatrinas without blushing and turning her face away. She was a mouse who would soon be Queen.

She won't last long, Komaso thought, smiling to himself. He was thinking like the Arcopatrinas again. Seeing the palace had brought everything back. Now he wanted to go to the White Temple, enter the sanctuary, and pray to the Goddess on his own throne. Let the sisters try to keep him out!

Komaso vaulted the wall and walked along the terrace toward the north side of the palace. Suddenly, he heard

voices, saw torchlight reflected along the tiles ahead of him.
Queen's Guards! He did not want to be discovered here, but
now the gardens sloped too far away from the wall for him to
jump safely. He looked around. There was a pair of doors
behind him. He tried them. They opened, and he stepped
inside, pushing them closed again with a soft, almost imper-
ceptible click.

Someone's bedroom. There was a plain narrow bed on the
other side of the room with a dresser, and, closer to him, a
dressing table. The space was much too large for such simple
stuff, Komaso thought. Why, there wasn't even a rug on the
floor. He went to the dressing table. There was an ivory
comb, a basket of hairpins, pots of eye paint and lip rouge
that looked dusty and unused. Propped against the mirror was
a diviner's box. The mud inside the glass had dried up and
cracked, obliterating the patterns made by the worms that had
once lived in it. What fortune, Komaso wondered, had prompted
the owner of this box to stop watering it? He picked it up,
looking for traces of burrows. He'd learned to read them
when he was a little girl, and had kept a fresh box of worms
all her last life for a hobby.

The frame came apart in his hands, glass shattering on the
floor.

"Who's there?" someone had been sleeping in the bed; she
switched on a lamp. (*Electric lamps in the palace now,*
Komaso thought with a mixture of amazement and disgust.)
Komaso came forward as the girl reached for the rope that
would signal her attendants.

"Wait!" he said, realizing who she was. "I don't mean
any harm, Lady."

Careev looked him up and down. With her hand still on the
rope, she said, "Lift your arms."

Komaso obeyed.

"Now turn around. Very slowly, please."

Again, he did as he was told, but stopped with his back to
her. He thought about running out through those doors, hesitating only because the guards would still be out on the
terrace. He felt weak-kneed. Seeing the Princess had made
him that way, he was certain.

She's my sister, he thought.

"Face me and tell me honestly whether you have weapons or not."

He turned.

"I'm unarmed, Lady, and as I said, I'm not going to hurt you."

"What are you doing here then? How did you get in?"

"Through those doors." Komaso couldn't take his eyes off her. She was really quite lovely in her own way. "I'm a visitor to the Citadel, Lady, and got lost. The guards scared me, so I tried the door."

"And why should the guards frighten you?"

"If you didn't know where you were, and they didn't know you—wouldn't you be frightened?"

Careev smiled. "Truth, they frighten me a little now."

"Then we have something in common."

"You're a strange boy! What's your name?"

"That's not important."

"No? Well, do you know who I am?"

"Everyone in Almheraz knows the Princess Royal," Komaso said with a bow.

"You don't have to be so nervous. You're safe. Nobody comes in here without my permission."

"I did."

"Well," Careev laughed. "Nobody but you, then. Would you mind sitting with me awhile? I really wasn't sleeping very well, and since it seems that Fate's brought us together, why not take advantage of it."

"As you wish, Lady," Komaso said in a thin voice. He was half panicked, half fascinated by her.

"There's a chair in the corner. You can pull it close to the bed if you like."

She's frightened too! It was as if she really believed he did mean to kill her and was tempting Fate, welcoming it.

"It's very strange," she went on when Komaso sat down. "I was dreaming about my sister just now. Actually, I was looking into a mirror—I mean I remember walking in front of a mirror, because I'd just put on a cloak and wanted to straighten it—but when I looked, it was Maud in the glass and not me. Her face, her body. The strange thing was, I was convinced that she was just trying to play a joke on me. So I moved my right arm, and so did she; I made a fist and hopped up and down, and so did she. No matter what I did, she did it too, until I finally had to believe that it *was* my reflection. I shouted at it! I didn't want her in the room. Then all that glass broke, and you were there when I woke up. What was that noise, anyway?''

''Your worm-box, Lady. I guess it came apart when I picked it up. I'm sorry . . .''

Careev's voice turned somber. ''Don't be. I don't want to know anything about the future.''

''Really. You're an unusual person to believe that.''

''Well, I am an unusual person. I'm the only person in Almheraz who will become a Queen.'' She rubbed her hands together slowly. ''You don't seem very impressed.''

''I'm just listening, Lady—''

''Perhaps you'd like to hear my story? The tragedy of being born to do things, to be something that you don't want to do or be?''

''We're all like that, though, Lady. If you believe that everything we do here's been done in Heaven already. But, if you don't mind me asking, what's there about being Queen that makes you feel such despair?''

''Because I can't choose! Because I can't go out into the world like you can, and find out what I want to do. I can't choose a husband and get married and raise a family and take pride in how they grow up, and help them. I can't go down to the Agora and buy a melon! Fate's played a cruel trick on me. It's given me a gift I can't possibly appreciate. . . .''

A tear rolled down her cheek. Komaso reached out and touched it, feeling a chill as he did. This was his sister! He found himself wanting to protect her, to help her all he could.

''There are other gifts,'' he said softly, gazing at her eyes. They were the color of pearls.

''Tell me about them.''

''I. . . .'' He stopped. This was not why he had come to the Citadel. The boy, who could do nothing but mimic other people, was taking hold of his soul!

''I've got to go.''

''Wait! Please don't leave me yet. I don't even know your name.''

"Komaso," he said, pushing the doors open. He felt sick.

"I want to see you again," she cried. "Will you come back? We can meet here tomorrow night—"

"No!" He slammed the doors and ran back across the terrace to the garden. He prayed to Psyche as he ran: *Why do you test me this way, Lady? What do you want from me!* Branches scraped his face; he crawled under the acacia tree, through the mossy tunnel and out onto the top of the Rock. He scrambled down the path, avalanches of loose stones following him as he ran toward Tove's villa.

There, at least, he was back among sisters. He must get word to Rarei, tell her of his dangerous state of mind, ask for advice. Perhaps he ought to be killed so he could be properly reborn, but that wasn't the kind of decision a person could make for himself. His soul was part of Pscyhe. You couldn't just kill the body it was in without making sure that the Goddess wanted it that way.

He stopped. His eyes teared; he saw smoke coming up in a thick cloud that glowed dull red, sparks swirling 'round it like fireflies. One of the villas was burning.

Slowing his pace, he emerged from the end of the trail and stood in the shadow of the pine tree. There were Vestals and Bachelors watching the fire. Nobody did anything to help put it out.

Komaso joined the crowd. The roof of the villa collapsed, sending up a huge column of sparks. A moment later, a detachment of Bachelors pushed through and reported to a Vestal mounted on wolfback.

"We've been all along these streets, Lady," the Bachelor squad leader said. "Nothing."

"Where would he have gone? Tove must have known something."

"I wrung her neck myself, Lady. She was beggin' for her life. If she knew anything at all, she would have said so."

"What about the rest of the staff? And the guests?"

"Rounded them all up. Anybody who ever heard of him is dead. All we have to do is find him. He couldn't have known anything was up. Probably, he'll come right back here sooner or later."

"Ring the whole neighborhood, then. The Matron wants

him dead, and there's a hundred crowns for the Bachelor that finds him!'' She wheeled her wolf around, and rode off.

Komaso pulled the hood of his cloak up. No one in the crowd, nor any of the Bachelors, noticed him. Stunned, he stared at the fire and tried to absorb what had happened.

Rarei wanted him dead. And the Goddess had contrived to protect him.

The Bachelor squad leader was giving orders to his men, pointing out checkpoints on a map of the Rock. Komaso slipped out of the fringes of the crowd and headed down to the gates that separated the villas from the rest of the city.

When he found it unmanned, he breathed a silent prayer of thanks, and started toward the Rock.

TWENTY-EIGHT

"I'M SORRY TO WAKE YOU, Lady Careev, but the King is here." He was Marywynn, since Nana's death, her lady-in-waiting.

"Poppa? What's he want?"

"He didn't say." Marywynn offered her a basin with a warm moist towel in it. Careev sat up and applied it to her face.

"He didn't say. Should I tell him you won't see him?" she asked.

"No. Bring me some tea. I'll see him."

Looking disappointed, the Vestal went off. A moment later, the King came in. His tunic was wrinkled, his eyes red, and his complexion was pale and doughy-looking.

"Good morning, Lady," he mumbled. It was the first time he had ever called her Lady.

"Good morning, Poppa."

He sighed and looked around the room. "You don't happen to have an ashtray?"

"I can get one for you."

"No, no, that's okay. I smoke too damn much anyway." He pulled a chair close to Careev's bed, turning it so when he sat down he rested his forearms on top of the chair back.

"You look like you didn't get too much sleep," he went on. "Sorry to have to wake you up."

Marywynn returned with tea and toast on a tray. She put it on the nightstand, shot the King a suspicious glance before curtseying and leaving.

"They love me here," Cyre said with a faint smile. "How about a cup of that tea?"

Careev poured him one. The King held the cup under his chin, so that the steam curled up through his beard. He took a sip, wrinkling his nose.

"Thanks. Truth is, I haven't slept much myself. Things . . . things aren't very good with your mother. I just got word from the telegraph. She's asked us to come to Queen's Island."

Careev closed her eyes.

"Yeah. That's about the way I feel, too." He sipped his tea. "Anyway, I've got the barque all fired up. We can leave just as soon as you're ready."

"You want me to go with you?"

"I thought it would be nice. We've got some things to discuss."

"Is Maud coming?"

"Eccles said he'd take care of her. I think they're going to take that flying contraption of his."

"Oh."

"Something wrong with that?"

"No. I just thought you'd prefer to have her along."

Cyre frowned, and gulped the rest of his tea. "I think maybe I will have that cigarette," he said, lighting one and flicking the ash into the cup.

"Eccles insisted on taking Maud," he said. "I wasn't in any mood to argue with him, or find out why. She ran off last night, and I'm thinking he probably had her followed. I'll find out what's up soon enough."

"Don't you care?"

"What the hell kind of question is that? Of course I care. But right now, it's you and me."

"Right now," Careev repeated.

"Don't be snippy. We're not talking about who gets to ride on the back of Poppa's wolf now. There hasn't been a transfer of power with a still-living King around for a long time. We have to figure out what we're going to do, and what we're going to tell people, and we've got those damn Vestals to keep in line. That's not going to be easy, either. I heard those crazy bitches even torched a villa down on the Rock last night."

"Crazy bitches? Poppa, did it ever occur to you that I might not think about them that way?"

"Look—"

"Do you really feel we've got to work together? Now that the Realm has business for both of us? Gods, Poppa, I'm nineteen years old, and I can remember every time you've ever been kind to me. I can tell you what time of day it was, and what I had for breakfast, and how the sky looked and how hot it was outside! I can remember what you were wearing. I can remember every single thing you said, every single word! And I'd sit there between times and remember over and over again, and make myself be thrilled, as if you treated me that way every single day. And that was almost enough, almost! But what is too much now is for you to come here and tell me who I am, and who you are, and what we're supposed to mean to each other! Gods, Poppa, last night a boy came into my room from the terrace. Just some stranger, lost on the grounds and afraid of running into the guards, and he came in here and we talked, and we had more between us in one half hour than you and I have ever had! So don't tell me who I am. You don't have the right!"

"Have your say," Cyre growled, grinding his cigarette into the teacup. "I probably deserve it. But that doesn't change anything. We both still have a job to do."

"I don't care."

The King stood up. "I could have sent a schell to do this. I should have sent a goddamn schell. Are you coming with me or not?"

"I'll go to the Island, but not with you."

"How the hell else are you going to get there?"

"I don't know. Take a steamer. Hire a boat."

"The doctor says there isn't much time."

"I don't care! I need to think. And this might be the last chance I have to be alone. You go on, Father. I'll get there. When I do, we'll discuss what's to happen after. . . . If Mother gets worse."

Cyre nodded. He had his arms folded and he was looking at Careev as if he was trying to take her all in for the first time.

"You probably won't believe this," he said finally, "but I really do care for her. And she was a great Queen before she lost the baby. Even after that, she could still get things done—she'd come back and know where she was and what needed her attention. I never forgot that, Careev."

Careev bit her lip. She did not want her father to see her cry. He lingered, waiting for her to soften, but she held on, and he finally turned to go.

"Don't take too long," he said.

"When you go to Baraqu to visit your parents, how do you get there?" Careev said to Marywynn.

"Riverboat, Lady. There's one that leaves every day right at noon."'

"Good. Pack some things. We'll go to Queen's Island on that boat."

"Oh, Lady, that's not for you! It's not seemly. There's a rough crowd that isn't used to dealing with royals."

"They won't have to." Careev opened her closet and found a rough-spun sun-cloak. She dressed quickly in a white tunic piped in blue and gold, and pulled the rough cloak over that. Marywynn returned carrying a small leather satchel— and dressed in her best whites.

"That's liable to get dirty where we're going, Mary."

"I don't care. Somebody's got to uphold the honor of this house."

"Well, you'd better change out of those sandals and into some shoes at least. We're going for a little hike."

"Ah, Lady," Marywynn said in a stricken voice. "What did the King tell you that's made you want to run away?"

"Mary, I swear you sound more like my poor old Nana every day! Change your shoes!"

Marywynn grumbled, but did as she was told. Careev took the satchel, and went outside across the terrace and into the garden to the twisted acacia, stopping so her maid could catch up.

"Through here there's a path that leads down to the city," Careev said. "Just follow me, and step carefully once we're outside the wall."

They crawled through the tunnel; Careev pulled Marywynn outside and helped her brush the dirt off her cloak, then started down the path. It was steep, but not as steep as Careev remembered, and soon they reached the ring of trees just above the gate that led into the villa quarter.

"There, Mary, that wasn't so bad, was it?"

Careev glanced back, and saw her maid wide-eyed, pointing to something in the bushes.

"Something's in there, Lady!"

"Silly, it's just the wind stirring the branches."

"The wind don't stir branches like that!"

"Don't be—" Careev began, then gasped as someone scrambled from the brush. It was a boy, dressed in torn clothes and waving a dagger.

"Back off," he warned. "It'll cost you dear to come any closer to me!"

"Oh, Lady, I knew we shouldn't have done this!"

"Shh! I . . . I think I know him." Slowly, she pulled her cowl away from her face. "Komaso?"

The boy picked up a rock.

"Komaso, don't you remember me? Last night, in the palace? I hid you from the guards."

"And now you're searching for me."

Careev blushed. "Of course I'm not searching for you. I'm on my way down to the harbor."

He glanced warily at Marywynn. "And what about this Vestal?"

"I'm her lady-in-waiting!" Marywynn piped up boldly. "And you'd best speak of my Order with more respect!"

The boy started laughing too hard, almost like a scream. The sound of it shocked Careev. Surely Komaso had lost his reason! Then, abruptly, he stopped. Standing tall, he looked at the two women.

"If you only knew how much respect I really do have for the Order of Vestals. Or the amount of respect they have for me! So much respect, in fact, that they burned down the house I was staying in."

Careev remembered what the King had said about the Vestals burning a villa.

"They were trying to kill you?"

"Still are. I daresay your Matron would generously reward anyone who told her where I was."

"I don't like the way he's staring at me, Lady!"

"Shhh! Komaso, I think perhaps you weren't telling me the whole truth!"

"Last night I didn't know the whole truth."

"Well, put that dagger away!"

Reluctantly, Komaso slid it back into its thigh-sheath. "They've scoured the rock looking for me," he said. "I suppose I should thank the Goddess you're not a squad of Bachelors. Anyway, they've got the gates blocked off."

"But why? What did you do that makes them spend so much effort to find you?"

"I'm a blasphemer, that's why. Rarei happens to be particularly interested in how I've blasphemed."

"Surely it can't be that serious!" Careev said, wondering how the boy could know Rarei.

"Oh, but it is. You see, the Matron believes in my blasphemy. She gives full credence to all my claims! Or those that she knows about. Perhaps you'd care to hear them all, and decide for yourself!"

"Not now," Careev said. "My mother's very ill. We're trying to catch the noon steamer to Queen's Island."

"Take me with you! At least help me get through the gate and into the city."

"But how?"

Komaso's manner changed. He tossed the rock away and smiled coyly.

"*I* could be your maid," he said.

"No man ever wears this cloak." Marywynn exclaimed. "This is a Vestal habit!"

"I'm more Vestal than you'll ever be."

"He's mad, Lady!"

"Maybe. But we're going to help him. Take off your cloak, Mary."

"But it's blasphemy!"

"And he's already been condemned for it, hasn't he? Let Heaven judge him for whatever crimes he's committed; I intend to help him."

"I suppose that means take off my cloak," Marywynne grumbled. "Very well! I've got a clear conscience about it!" She took the cloak off, folding it carefully, and when Komaso reached for it, she snatched it back against her chest.

"This is for the Princess and not for you. Boy!" she added, frowning when Komaso laughed scornfully at the insult.

"Boy. You wouldn't know a boy if he came and bit your little Vestal ass!"

"*Lady!*"

"Never mind, Mary. Just put these on." She gave the maid Komaso's rags; shuddering, Marywynn slipped them on. "To think," she wailed when she'd tied up the cowl. "A Queen's maid, forced to look like this—"

Komaso was not so quick to change his clothes. He held Marywynn's cloak out in front of him and simply stared at it.

"This is a Novice's cloak," he said. "I haven't worn one like this for a long time."

"What's he talking about, Lady? Long time since he wore one."

"I'm not sure, Mary. Komaso, we've got to get to the harbor before noon—"

Komaso pulled the cloak on and fit his cowl. He walked hunching his shoulders and taking small steps. His head was erect; his movements smooth and effortless, so that he appeared to float over the rocky path. Finally, he pronounced himself ready and went ahead into the trees. It was pleasant in the shade. Careev found herself wanting to linger there, and stopped once to drink from a small clear pool of a spring. Komaso urged her on. He'd got his courage up and now was the time to move. Finally they reached the gate, which was open and apparently unguarded. Through it was a lane that wound down into the Agora. They followed it around a tight switch-back and there found the way blocked by Bachelors who were boiling a pot of tea in the shade of a makeshift canvas awning.

"Look at this, boys," their captain said, slapping a bat-tered sun-hat on his head and stepping out into the road.

"Good day, Ladies," he said.

"Good day." Careev replied.

"You're not from the neighborhood, are you."

"Not exactly."

"We've got orders to check everyone who comes through here. Take down your hoods for a moment, if you please."

"Very well. Mary?"

"Yes, Lady!" Marywynn looked uncertainly at her mis-tress as Careev pulled her own cowl back.

"You, too," the bachelor said to Komaso.

"Wait," Careev said. "She's just taken her vows. That means she's not to show herself to the Eye for two months."

"I've got orders, Lady."

"And perhaps you haven't taken a good look at me, either. You might do well to look again."

"Yeah? And what am I supposed to see?"

"Alamos's forge," one of the others exclaimed. "Ain't she the Princess Royal?"

"What the hell would the Princess Royal be doing walking around here?"

Careev drew her dagger. "Collecting disrespectful tongues. They look very nice dangling from my belt."

"Now, look, Lady, we didn't hear anything about the Princess coming around here this morning. This area's sealed off. I start letting people through, they'll take my whole head!"

"Nevertheless, we are going through. Care to stop us?"

"Let me see her face, and I'll stand aside."

"I won't allow her to break her vows on your account. What's your name?"

"Petro, Lady," the Bachelor said uncertainly.

"I'm giving you one last chance, Petro. Will you let us through?"

"You do look like the Princess," Petro said. "Though I've never seen her up this close."

"Aw, every woman's a Princess far as you're concerned," one of the other guards said.

"Shut up!" The Bachelor rubbed his jaw. "Hell. Go on. And pray remember my name, if you are who you say!"

"Psyche will bless you," Komaso whispered to him, as they passed.

TWENTY-NINE

THEY WALKED IN silence the rest of the way down to the river. Careev was feeling the heat. The market and waterfront, meanwhile, were as crowded as she had ever seen them. In two days, the Festival would officially begin with the Wedding of Adon and Psyche. The pilgrims milling around so anxiously now would jam the Grove and crane their necks to see the torch applied to Adon's effigy. Now it was certain that Careev would set the Sun-god aflame, and all these people who bumped by her now without wasting a second glance would be sending their most fervent prayers for health and happiness and good Fate to her. As if she could do anything about them!

"There's the steamer, Lady," Marywynn said when they reached the third pier. "It looks like they're almost ready to go."

Indeed, schells were busy stowing lines and drawing in the booms of the cargo cranes. There were not many passengers, but there was a heavy load of cargo on deck, and the steamer lay low in the water. Up on top of a stack of crates, a skinny man bellowed orders.

"Excuse me," Careev said, shading her eyes with her hand. "Are you the captain?"

"Depends on who's asking, Lady. Tie off them lines, blast you!"

"Well, I'd like to book passage for myself, and my maid." She looked at Komaso. "And you? I'll gladly pay your passage to Baraqu. You'd be safer there."

Komaso's face fell. "Can't you protect me here, sister?"

"Here. You speak to the Lady with respect!" Marywynn snapped.

"And you kick at me again, I'll slap you so hard your ears will ring for a week!"

The captain hopped down to the deck. "Ladies in white— and squabbling too! It's too bad we're booked up. Come back tomorrow. I'll be glad to listen to you then!"

"But I really must get to Queen's Island this afternoon."

"Queen's Island, is it? And just what business would you be having there?"

"Thanks anyway," Komaso said to Careev suddenly, "but my business is here in the city."

"Wait! Don't go—"

"We'll meet again, I'm sure, Lady Careev! Good-bye!" Komaso waved and started off. The Captain's expression, meanwhile, changed from annoyance to complete horror.

"Lady *Careev*? By Adon's sandal strap, it is you! But you can't just come up and ask for passage like anybody else! We weren't informed. There's no cabin—"

"The deck will do," Careev said absently, staring after Komaso, who was gliding through the crowd at the foot of the dock looking every inch a Vestal. He was wearing a black scapular around his neck, she realized, wondering where he could have got it, then reaching for her own and not finding it. A thief, too, and an excellent one!

"The deck!" the captain was exclaiming in the meantime. The deck's not seemly. You there!" he called to one of his crew, a stocky, old man with a white beard. "Marten! We've got the Princess Royal with us today."

Marten came over wiping his hands with an oily rag. "That boiler of your's in sad shape, Captain."

"Never mind that! Go clean out my cabin. Take anything, uh, that's not fit for a Princess, and stow it below."

"All right."

"All right! Is that any way to respond to an order?"

"I'm not a sailor, Captain. You'll just have to get by with my best." He bowed to Careev. "As for you, Lady, I'll only say that you've brightened my day considerably."

"Argh, will you just get going!" When Marten had gone, the captain stammered, "It's hard finding a crew that knows how to work and has manners too."

"And who can be trusted to shift whatever contraband you've got stowed, Captain!"

"Exactly! I mean no! I mean—"

"Never mind, Captain. We appreciate your making room for us."

Cleaning the cabin took only a few minutes. Careev and her maid were shown aboard; then the schells cast off and the barge got underway with three blasts of her whistle and a tremendous, deck-rattling surge of power from the engines. The boat seemed reluctant to leave the harbor—the paddlewheels churned the water and her hull creaked and popped. But when she found the river current she leapt ahead, rounding Point Draco and leaving the bluffs of Almheraz behind as she headed for the sea. Above and ahead of them, the Eye floated over the broad expanse of the Tumulos, shining dully like old brass plate behind a wispy curtain of Veil. In another day or two, the Realm would see the naked Sun. It was the time of year when Fate was suspended, and all things were possible.

The captain's cabin overlooked the foredeck. Careev threw open the windows, taking in the smell of the river and the cool breeze that blew in, seemingly in defiance of the Sun. On deck, some of the passengers removed their sun-cloaks. Wine-bags appeared. Careev could hear the rattle of dice, and smell meat and vegetables being grilled on skewers by enterprising vendors who had set up braziers in the bow. Watching them work, she felt the sway of the boat as it moved across the currents, and sighed deeply.

"Is something wrong, Lady?" Marywynn asked.

"No. I just envy them a little, that's all."

Marywynn was struggling to get out of Komaso's cloak. Careev helped get it over her head. "Thank you, Lady," she puffed. "You might envy them, as you say. But who knows how many go to bed at night dreaming of living in a palace!"

"Nobody's ever satisfied, are they?"

"I'd be satisfied, if I'd gotten my cloak back."

Careev smiled, and leaned against the window sill with her elbows. "My sister and I went fishing near that point once. We snuck away, came down the same path we traveled today, and when we got to the river, there was a little motorboat and a couple of schells to run it. Maud had arranged the whole thing."

"When was this, Miss?"

"I suppose I was ten or eleven."

"You must have given your poor Nana a scare. I know I'd be vexed."

"But that's the whole point. Anybody else in Almheraz can go fishing without vexing someone. We wanted to be like that. Just disappear, and that's what we did. We went out, had the schells drop anchor underneath a tree that hung over the bank, and we just sat and let our lines drift, and talked about how we were never going back to the palace. It was so wonderful. . . .

"Then, later on, when the tide dropped, we took off our shoes and walked around in the mud. Maud found some divining worms. She scooped one up with a stick and made me hold out my hand. I didn't want to do it, of course—who would! But she told me if I didn't I had no right to pretend to be Queen of anything. So I closed by eyes and held out my hand, and she put the worm into it. I could feel it squirm and push with its nose, as if my hand was made out of mud, you know? Then I opened by eyes and saw the most amazing thing! It was turning colors, one two three, just like that, from brown to white to red and yellow and back again, and there were birds screeching over us, as though they could see what was happening and were calling the other birds to come watch! It kept on until finally the worm twisted off the edge of my hand and disappeared into the mud.

"I looked at her and said, 'What can this mean?' At first she just said that the worm had been trying to blend with its surroundings, so the birds wouldn't be able to see it. But then she told me, no, it must be an omen.

"My eyes got big and I asked, 'What kind of omen?' Maud said, 'You're going to crawl and change colors the rest of your life!' And then she pushed me down in the mud. We were wrestling around in it—we looked like a couple of burrowers ourselves, until some schells came."

"The King had sent them. Oh, he was furious all right, though he didn't speak a word about it to me. It was Maud he was angry at, because she could have got lost or hurt. Me, he didn't care about, I guess. Anyway, after that, he sent Maud up to the Winter Palace for three whole months. When she came back she was . . . different."

"How, Lady?"

"It's hard to explain. I was only ten, after all. But she seemed older. She didn't want to talk about the things we used to like to talk about anymore. It made me sad all the time, wondering what had happened to her up there. Oh, it's such an awful place, that Winter Palace. No girl should ever have to live in a Winter Palace!"

Careev felt silent. Below, the captain had come on deck and was giving orders to his crew. He wanted some sail to take advantage of land breezes that were rising in the afternoon. Some schells moved forward to unlash them, but then balked.

"What the hell's wrong?" the captain shouted. "Get on those stays!"

Now all hell broke loose on deck. The schells scattered, knocking over braziers, one even leaping into the water. Passengers screamed. Careev leaned through the open window, and saw what looked like a Bachelor bucking around on his hands and knees like a ram crazed by sheepsbane. The poor lunatic howled and thrashed about, tangling himself in the sail lines while passengers clawed each other trying to get out of his way.

"Lady! What is it?"

"Somebody's gone crazy, I think."

Just then someone hammered at the door. Marywynn rushed

to open it, and there stood the captain, wringing his cap in his hands, an expression of absolute horror on his face.

"A calamity, Lady, that's what it is! There was a seer inside one of my sails. None of my men will go near it, and you've seen what it does to the schells. You've got to help us. I'd tackle it myself, but I'm just married, Lady. My wife's old mother'd have me gutted if she knew I'd touched a seer!"

"A seer?" Careev felt a flash of excitement. "Just what do you expect me to do about it?"

The captain flashed a miserable grin. "Beggin' your pardon, Lady, but it's certainly Fate you're on board today. Heaven would never have put a seer on this boat without a way of taking care of it."

"Taking care of it," Careev repeated.

The captain twisted his hat again. "Lady, you're Princess Royal. Now, that creature's been punished for sins of a past life, and it's got to wander the earth without a soul until it can steal one. But you, being of royal blood, and reputedly a virgin, too, if I can be so bold, you're under Psyche's protection! The monster can't steal your soul. Heaven would never allow such an abomination! Please come down, Lady, if only to help calm my passengers!"

"Very well."

"Lady!"

"Hush, Mary. Do you have any beer, Captain?"

"Beer?"

"Not very long ago, I saw one of the creatures in the Agora. A crowd had attacked its owner, and was trying to burn the poor thing inside its cage. Anyway, when it was all over, somebody gave the seer a bottle of beer. It was in a lot of pain—its legs had been burned—but the beer seemed to calm it down almost at once. Please fetch some, and I'll meet you on deck."

"You won't!" Mary said as the captain ran down the stairway.

"Yes I will, and you're going to watch," Careev said, grabbing her hand.

By the time they reached the deck, a couple of young men had improvised torches out of lengths of tarred rope and, swinging them madly over their heads, had cornered the seer in the prow of the steamer. In spite of having no eyes to see or nose to smell the flames with, the seer seemed to be able to sense what was happening and bawled like a calf, waving its arms in front of its face. The noise gave the attackers courage. They moved in, while the other passengers urged them on.

"Knock it in!"

"Yeah! Water burns it just as bad as fire!"

It was becoming a cruel sport; nobody cared about souls now. Letting go of Marywynn's hand, Careev shouldered her way through the crowd and snatched the rope-torch away from one of the attackers.

"Hey! What do you think you're doin'?"

Careev looked him in the eye.

"Shut up."

"You got no right to talk to me that way. I'm risking my soul to save these good folks."

"You're not torturing it anymore."

"Who says so?" The man yanked his torch back; the crowd closed in, forming a circle that kept Careev away from the seer and its tormentors. She felt like a child lost in the marketplace, powerless and without an idea of what to do next. Then, suddenly, somebody took her by the elbow and pushed her forward again. It was the old man who had helped get the captain's cabin ready.

"Listen to me, all of you!" he yelled, "Listen to me!" The crowd quieted, and he went on. "You think you're saving your souls doing this, but let me ask you what price you're saving it at when you show such disrespect for the Lady who tomorrow, or the next day, will be Queen of Almheraz! Here, pull down your hood, Lady, and show them who you are!"

Careev did, turning so the passengers could see her face. There was a shocked hush; everyone seemed frozen, and even the seer craned its neck a little, as though it wanted a better look at her.

"Gods, Lady, I had no idea—" stammered the man who had pushed her.

"Throw that torch over the side. You too!" Careev made

her voice sound as forceful as she could. The torches went over the side, just as the captain arrived with the bottle of beer she had asked for.

"Lady! You were supposed to wait for me!"

"There wasn't time. Here." She took the bottle from him and stepped closer to the seer, who had its arm wrapped around the forward rail. Sensing her, it lifted its narrow, bald head, parted its suckerlike lips and stuck out its yellow, tufted tongue. It held out its free hand, which trembled slightly. *That could be my hand, or anyone's*, Careev thought as she slowly extended the beer bottle, put it into its hand.

Their fingers touched.

A few of the passengers gasped, but for Careev it was like the time before in the Agora. The seer's skin was dry, and cooler than hers, and gentle. She felt light-headed, but nothing like she imagined she'd feel if her soul was being wrenched loose.

The seer trembled again. How much it looked like the one she had wished on at the market! *I should make another wish*, Careev thought as she gently cupped her hand behind the seer's head and put the bottle to its lips. *I should wish for mother to get well. I should wish that I'll never have to be Queen.*

The seer sighed with unmistakeable pleasure and began to drink the beer.

"There!" Careev said. "It hasn't harmed me, has it?"

"That's because you're royal," someone yelled back. "It'd be a different story with one of us!"

"That's right!" The crowd of passengers pressed in. Careev could see the captain frowning. "As long as it sits here we're in danger, whether the thing's swilling beer or not!"

Now it was the old man who spoke up, waving his arms and shouting, "No! I can vouch for the thing. I've seen it before—more than once. It's got something on its mind. But I don't think it means any harm to anyone on this ship."

"Just a minute," the captain said, shoving his way forward. "This creature's yours?"

"I didn't say that."

"You said you'd seen it! Where?"

"At Semele. And near the town of Panault." Marten hesitated. "The fact is, I think it followed me here from the Steppes."

"And you smuggled it aboard! That's what all the commotion with my schells was yesterday. They knew! They hate a seer, and they could smell it. Gods, I knew there was something funny about you. That thing's going over the side—and you with it!"

"No!" Careev said.

"Lady, the man's bad luck. He's jinxed us by bringing this thing on board my boat. I'm sorry, but I'm master of my vessel, and I won't have 'em here. Besides, he looks like he can swim. As for that thing, I don't care if it can swim or not."

"And what about you, Captain? Can *you* swim?"

Hearing some of the passengers laugh, Careev went on. "I'm sorry, but the old man is under my protection. And so is the seer! I'll take them both to my cabin so you won't have to look at them, and you can let all of us off at Queen's Island. Will that be satisfactory, Captain?"

"I've got to sleep in that cabin!"

Careev leaned close to him and said in a half-whisper, "You have a license to operate this steamer, don't you? I've got an excellent memory, Captain. And I will soon have some influence over the decisions of the Almheraz harbormaster. . . ."

"Oh, very well, Lady!"

Careev went to the seer again. It had finished the beer and stood rocking from foot to foot, making soft hooting sounds. *It's a little tipsy!* Careev thought to herself. She took its hand again, gave the bottle back to the captain, who stared at it in horror and then flung it overboard. "Come along, sir," she said to Marten. "You'll ride with me." She started for the ladder. Marywynn had already scurried to the top, and stared at the seer as though it were Death itself. Fleeing inside, she squeezed into the far corner of the cabin and watched warily as Careev and the old man guided the seer into a chair.

"I'd ask the captain for another bottle of beer," Careev said. "But I'm not sure he could stand it!"

"Never mind," Marten said, unbuttoning his cloak and unslinging a wine-bag from his shoulder. "It likes this well enough. Here. You remember how to do it, don't you?"

The seer felt the bag, squeezing it a little so that some wine squirted out. It snuffled like a wolf, and stuck out its tongue; then it tilted its head back and started drinking, the wine shooting out in a stream that the seer managed to get into its mouth without spilling a drop.

"Ooh, Lady, how can you bear to be near it?" Marywynn wailed. "It's enough to freeze my soul just looking at it!"

The seer belched. It put down the wine-bag on the deck, shifted in the chair, and seemed to relax, head nodding.

"I believe it's asleep!" Careev exclaimed.

"Can't hold its liquor at all," Marten said with a chuckle. "Well, then, Lady, you should have some as well. I believe I'd be treading water right now if not for you." He picked up the wine-bag and drank, offered some to Careev, who shook her head. He looked over at Marywynn.

"And what about you, eh? You look as though you could use a drink."

"I don't drink with strangers. Or sorcerers!"

"Sorcerer? Me?" Marten went over to her, cupping both hands over her ears for a moment. "What makes you think I'm a sorcerer?" Marten smiled, stuck out his tongue. One of Marywynn's earrings was on it. He put it into the palm of his hand, turned it over—and showed two earrings. Marywynn gasped, and touched her ears.

"You see, Lady!"

"Mary, I think this man is what's known as a sleight-of-hand artist."

Marten bowed. "I'm a traveler, truth be told, my Ladies. But I'm not above using a trick or two to amuse a skeptical crowd. Fast fingers have saved my hide more than once. But I'm impolite. My name's Marten, Lady. I hail from the Steppes, and travel the roads all through the northern reaches of your Realm!"

"It's not mine yet, Marten, and, our Lady willing, it will not be mine for a long time."

"Oh, I'm sorry. I don't mean to make mention of your mother's illness. But then, when I had my breakfast this morning I did not imagine I'd be riding with a Princess—and the likes of that seer!"

"But you said it followed you."

"That it did, Lady. It's the cause of my misery and the reason I'm in Almheraz now." He paused, as the seer snored loudly. It had slumped in the chair, and its cloak, which was unbuttoned on the bottom, fell away from its legs. Careev looked at them.

"Those scars on its legs. Do you know how it got them?"

"No, Lady, but life can be hard for a seer. The burns were fresh when I first saw it, though."

"Then I think I know this seer too. You remember, Mary. The day we got caught in the riot in the market?"

"I can't think about it now without shuddering, Lady."

"I tried to help the seer, but it ended up saving me," she said. "And it touched me. I had always heard that a seer would steal your soul if it touched you, unless you made a wish. And so that's what I did. I made one. I said it out loud, and it seemed to hear. I remember its tongue came out, and got bigger, and bright red like a flower at the end. Then the seer just seemed to vanish. If it could do that, I thought, then why had it let itself be caught by a mob and burned? Because it certainly would have been burned if Maud and I hadn't . . ." Her voice trailed.

"And how long ago was this, Miss?"

"Two months."

Marten nodded. "It's possible then. We first ran into it a month ago, on the road out of Panault."

"We?"

"My boy and I. See, Lady, I was traveling through Panault during the worst of the drought. People were not quite in their right minds, I think. I saw the Matron Rarei lead a jury of Panault women down to the banks of a quarry pool. They had a boy with them who'd they'd chained to a stone. He was condemned, and they threw him in, wanting to drown him so his soul would wander without being shriven! I couldn't stand that, Lady, and so I dove in without them seeing me and managed to get him out in time.

"He was a strange boy! Couldn't speak, didn't seem to hear—sort of like that seer, in a way, though he was very pretty to look at. But he could copy things. I'd show him something once, like that trick with your maid's ear-bobs, and he could do it. I took a fancy to him. He seemed to have no brains, and yet there was something there . . . I could tell he knew me, and that he . . .'' Marten wiped a tear out of the corner of his eye. "Well, he seemed happy, that's all. We were getting along. He helped do my work. Then the rains came and people started coming out of their houses again, feeling hope. I had all the business I needed. You get used to being alone, Miss. Maybe you don't know, living in a palace with your family and servants all around all the time, but it's something you get used to.''

"I know,'' Careev said.

"Well, it's fine, when you're used to it. But then something happens to change things, and you're not alone anymore. You're going along and you realize all of a sudden that being alone is not something you want. You get to where you can't *imagine* being alone again. That's what happened to me. We were camped out one night, having our tea by the fire—me and my wolf, and the boy—when the creature appeared at the edge of the camp, staring—or looking with that tongue it's got—at my boy.

"My wolf chased it off—I thought—then a storm come up. I was busy tying things down, trying to keep my wagon from blowing away. It wasn't until I secured everything that I realized my boy was gone.''

Marten pulled a rag from his sleeve and blew his nose. "When the storm let up I spent two days looking for him. My wolf come back but there was no sign of the creature or my boy. I told myself it was Fate, that the Lord had given me a taste of what it was like to be happy, and that I ought to be grateful for that and just go on. And I almost managed to do that, Lady! But then I went to Semele, which was mobbed with pilgrims catching the train to Almheraz for the Feast. I was in the market square. Some Vestals were bringing some prisoners to put in the stocks, and there he was! My boy! Only he had changed, Lady, he could speak! He saw me and used the name I had given him, only his manner was horrible. He ridiculed me in front of the crowd, and almost got me arrested to boot.'' Marten shook his head. "Oh, Komaso—''

"What? What did you call him?''

"Komaso. It was my uncle's name, you see, something of a famous name among travelers—''

"I know him!" Careev exclaimed.

"Please, Miss, don't toy with me. You couldn't possibly know him."

"But I do! He came to the palace the night before last, telling me the Vestals were after him. I didn't really believe it, but then last night, they burned down a house on the Rock, the place he was staying at! It was for blasphemy, he said."

"That's him! See, he was condemned to burn in Semele and they were holding him, but then the seer appeared again, and helped me get him loose. He wouldn't stay with me, though. Said something about finding Matron Rarei, taking his rightful place as head of the Order. Miss, I came to Almheraz to find him—in fact, I tried to go to that very house, I think, but your Bachelors kept me off. Do you know where he is? Please, you've got to tell me!"

"He came down to the quay with me," Careev said. "He was disguised as a Vestal. Did you see him?"

Marten groaned, grabbing his hair with his fists. "This all's been played for somebody's amusement, Lady!" he exclaimed.

Now Careev's eyes got big. "But wait," she said. "You said that you found the boy in Panault. That Rarei had put him to trial and tried drowning him?"

"That's right."

"Are you sure about that? Sure of the town, and of her?"

"What reason do I have to lie to you, Lady? It was Rarei all right, riding a wolf big as this boat!"

"That's my wish!" Careev exclaimed. "Don't you see, Mary? Poppa said at the meeting that the Vestals had come and killed one of his kinsmen at his house, and that Rarei had conducted the trial in Panault! *That kinsman was his son*, don't you see? My brother! In fact he called me sister when we said good-bye. I wished for my family to be together, and the seer understood, and made it happen."

"But what would the King be doing, keeping a boy in Panault all these years?"

"I don't think he knew. I don't think anyone knew but Nana Mara—and somehow, the Vestals made her tell that she was caring for the King's son! That's why she killed herself. Because she must have told the Vestals about him!"

"That may be," Marten said. "But where is he now?"

"Still in the city. He told me he had to get through to Rarei . . . that he wanted his rightful place back."

"Then I've got to go return to Almheraz. Just once more. If I can see him just once, talk to him, I'll be happy. I'll be able to go on."

"I have a feeling that any protection I might be able to give you and the seer will evaporate the instant the boat leaves the Island." Careev thought a moment. "No. That seer seems to have brought us together. I don't believe that it's acting at random, either. There's a purpose in what it's doing. Maybe you should stay with me."

"Lady!" Marywynn protested. "There's no men allowed on the Island."

"He can stay on Father's boat. Anyway, I need somebody to help me care for this creature, until we can figure out what it wants, and how we can help."

"I don't know, Lady. I appreciate your wanting to help, but with the Vestals looking for the boy . . ."

"I, too, have Vestals under my command—or Mother does. I'll give orders that the boy is not to be harmed until the Queen can talk to him herself. He is looking for the Matron, and Rarei is looking for him. He'll be found. And if he is my brother, the King must know too. Oh, Marten! You've got to accept that Fate's brought us together, now, during the Feast, when my mother. . . ." She bit her lip. "Just say you'll stay and help mind the creature. At least for the next day or two, until we know what we are. Whether I'm to be Queen now, or later."

Marten stroked his beard. "You don't know me," he said. "How can you trust me so easily?"

"If I'm to be Queen, and live, I've got to learn to trust those who ought to be trusted. You've got a kindly face, Marten. And you're good with your hands. That's a sign of honesty, I think. Believe me, if I could bring the boy to you now, I would. As it is, we both want the same thing. Say you'll help?"

"What about this Lady? She looks as if she wishes I'd disappear!"

"This Lady," Careev said, going over to Marywynn and

giving her a hug, "who is nineteen going on ninety, is a dear, sweet thing who'd never dream of doing anything that might possibly hurt me. She knows I can trust you—though she's doing everything she can to hide it!"

"Oh, we all should have stayed in bed this morning!" Marywynn wailed.

"But we didn't. Marten?"

"Well. . . . I suppose I could have worse protection than yours, Lady Careev. If it's a seer-keeper I'm meant for, than that's what I'm to be. I'll stay!"

THIRTY

TWO HOURS LATER they were deep into the Delta, with the boat floating higher as the river grew brackish close to the Crescent Sea. Though the Eye had not yet set, the half moon rose back above the Tablelands, adding an orange cast to the pale violet glow of the sun spreading across the waves of the main channel of the river. Ahead, with the sun hanging above, was a dark headland with a glint of gold hugging the water, like a pendant on a necklace. The land was Queen's Island, the pendant, the golden barque of King Crye, which was tied up in the Island harbor.

The riverboat captain didn't waste his time with signal flares or blasts from the horn, instead steaming straight into the harbor to tie up next to the barque. Passengers watched fearfully—some of them making signs to ward off the Eye—as Careev and Marten brought the seer ashore, Careev holding its hand, Marten following to make sure the creature didn't bolt. The captain bid Careev farewell, and gave her a bottle of beer.

"Just to show you, Lady, there's no hard feelings. Maybe you will forget about me, if you're inclined to!"

"Captain, I sincerely doubt that I'll ever forget you!" Careev said. "But here's for your trouble."

She gave him a gold crown. He bit it, waved, then jumped up to the helm and sounded a horn blast that rattled the trees on shore. Then the smokestacks belched fire, the wheels churned, and the boat caught the current and headed out to sea again.

"You'll have to stay on the docks, or on this boardwalk, Marten," Careev said. "I'll get someone from Father's staff to help you with a place to sleep."

"And what about him—I mean, it?"

The seer stood quietly with its cloak on and hood up. Marten straightened its sunglasses; if you didn't know what it was, there was no way to tell it from a regular, if slightly strange looking, citizen.

"We'll say its your poor old father," Careev said.

"And may he forgive you for saying so."

Just then, Magister Eccles waved from the gangway of the barque and came over. He was dressed in a yellow cloak, as though ready to officiate at an interment, and wore a veiled headdress embroidered with a representation of the Eye. His gait betrayed weariness, but he seemed glad to see Careev, and bowed to her courteously.

"I was about to send word to fetch you, Lady Careev," he said. "My compliments for successfully arranging your own transportation. I trust the journey was refreshing."

"It was interesting. How's Mother?"

"There's been no change. She seems to be waiting."

"For what? To die, you mean?" She spoke heatedly, and the Magister's eyebrows rose in surprise. He then looked at Marten, and at the seer, pausing to take in the creature and then turning back expectantly toward Careev.

"This is the traveler Marten," Careev said, "and his father. I met them aboard the boat. It seems they were in Panault at the time the Vestals seized Poppa's land. I wanted a chance to speak to him about it, and thought perhaps Father would want to as well. Do you think you could arrange for a cabin in the barque, while we're all here?"

"Of course."

"Hard to believe," Marten piped up. "The Queen's Island. Lord!"

"Why, yes," Eccles said, as Careev suppressed a smile. Marten must be a quick judge of people, to have realized so quickly that the best way to have the Magister discount him as a threat was to pretend to be simple.

"And who're you?"

"This is the High Priest of the Sun, Marten."

"So it is! Sorry, your Excellency, but I didn't recognize you. Must be the hat!"

"My Lady, if I could have a word with you, privately."

"I need to see Mother—"

"It will only take a moment."

Marten smiled. "Go ahead, your Majesties. Don't mind us!"

Eccles took Careev's elbow and led her a little down the boardwalk.

"I must apologize to you, Lady, for I sense that you're not entirely pleased with me at the moment. Perhaps you sensed this morning that I was not entirely telling the truth about your sister. In point of fact, she only returned to the palace an hour ago, and in a most distressing condition. She was wildly drunk, and entirely uncooperative. I questioned her about where she'd gone last evening, and she refused to answer me."

"But do you know where she went?"

"No, Lady. My schells were unable to keep up with her." He lowered his voice. "I'm hoping, Lady, that when she recovers a little, you'll talk to her. We need to know where she's gone and who she's been seeing."

"Why, Magister?" Careev said. "What do you suspect?"

"Suspicion is not my thought at the moment, Lady. I am merely concerned."

"That's all?"

Eccles looked flustered. "She disappeared for seven hours, and it would not be wise to allow her to indulge whatever whim it is that led to her disappearing—"

"I'm not sure I trust you, Magister."

Eccles said nothing. Careev could see his jaw tightening

and realized that at the moment she found him extremely irritating. *I'm not a child anymore*, she thought, *and yet he still treats me like one, lying to me.*

"Sorry, Magister. Of course I'll talk to Maud, as soon as I can."

"Thank you, Lady."

"And how is the King?"

"He wants to see you again."

"He'll have to wait."

"There are important matters that have to be discussed with him, and soon."

"Look. My mother's dying, and I'm supposed to go in and take her last breath! The whole idea sickens me, Magister, but right now, it's all I can think about. I'll see Poppa as soon as I can. Tell him I'm here, and that he is still the King. Tell him that, in case he's worried!"

Eccles bowed. "As you wish, Lady."

They were standing close together; all at once, Eccles took her hands in his and kissed them. It was an act of submission, but there was arrogance in it too, as if the Magister thought the gesture sealed something between them. Careev clasped her hands together.

"Marten, please take care of your father. Magister, I'll be down again soon."

Queen's Island was a truncated volcanic cone, and the house where Queen Gormayne had come to die was tucked inside the center of the collapsed vent. The house was surrounded by rings of lush foilage, nourished by the rich soil, and fed by two hot and two cold springs. Because of the influence of these sources—the cold springs coming from an underground river flowing from the Northern Cordillera, the hot pushing straight up through the still-warm chimney of the volcano, the vegetation in these rings changed drastically the closer one came to the center of the Island. Heading for the house, Careev passed beneath stands of bamboo, then under the boughs of pines and birches. She usually preferred these cooler places; today, she shivered in them.

Finally, she reached the moat that guarded the open well leading into the house, which was carved in a spiral down

along the ancient vent, safe from the degenerative effects of
the Eye. Globes of red and blue glass were strung along the
foot bridge over the water. The moat itself was overgrown
with the reeds Careev and Maud had kept trimmed as children, when they had woven baskets and mats to pass the long
summer days. Careev stopped in the middle of the bridge to
pull one. She had never liked coming to Queen's Island, and
dreaded what she had to do.

The ramp into the house began just across the bridge. She
started down, past Vestals who stood like statues against the
outer wall, holding staffs topped with fans of green feathers.
Between them, streams of water fell from spouts driven into
the moat, splashing into a pool at the bottom of the central
well. The streams had at one time driven tiny prayer-wheels
at the edge of this pool; now some of the spouts were
clogged, and Careev heard no sound of bells. She glanced up.
Amber clouds floated across the opening, a moveable ceiling
that added to her sense of unease.

"Lady, I'll see about your rooms," Marywynn said. Her
eyes darted nervously from Careev to the other Vestals. Everything seemed frozen; dust sparkled in the shaft of light
shining through the well, and it did not move either. Then
Avra, the Queen's physician, hurried up the ramp.

"Oh, Lady, it's good you've come. She's been asking for
you. And her illness . . ." The physician shook her head.

"Lady?"

"Go on, Mary. Get some rest."

The physician waited for Marywynn to walk away. "She's
been in and out all day. I thought the illness might carry her
away, but she hung on somehow. I think her desire to see you
was enough to keep her here."

"I'm sure you've done all you could," Careev said, squeezing her hand.

"Of *course* she has."

Maud's voice seemed to drift from the shadows like smoke.
She padded over barefoot, silver goblet in her hand, her hair
unpinned and tumbling down to her hips. Her skin was pale
and shiny-looking; her lips were swollen, the lower lip cracked
and bleeding a little.

"Tell her all you've done, Avra," Maud said. "Tell her

how you burned Mother's blood in a pan and drew out the figures on a piece of parchment, and looked up the shapes in your book while she cried out for water!"

Avra appealed to Careev. "I did it because I didn't know what else to do. Her condition . . . I've never seen the like of it before! She's feverish, but her temperature is below normal. Her chest is congested, and yet she's hyperventilating. No one in Almheraz would know what's wrong with her—"

"It's all right, Avra. I trust you. You have the confidence of the whole family."

"And you! My dear little sister." Maud laughed. "So very nice! A model of mercy! How I love my dear little sister!" Maud sauntered to Careev and kissed her on the mouth, forcing her tongue inside. There was something sharp and musky about her smell. Careev shuddered as Maud drew back.

"Pardon me, but I have to wash the taste of Queen from my mouth." She drank from her goblet and spat on the floor. Alarmed, the physician quickly stepped between them.

"All right," Careev said evenly. "I can see how distraught the Princess is."

"Distraught!" Maud laughed harshly. "Why should I be distraught? You're the one that ought to be distraught. In fact, I'm surprised you've come at all."

"Why shouldn't I have come?" Careev's voice was not as strong as she wanted it to be.

"Do I have to spell it out for you? We're done. Mother, Father, you—" she drank again. "—me. We're all done. We don't have the power anymore. The Queen lies there dying and this idiot—" she swung her goblet toward the physician "—does nothing but brew tea! Others are waiting. Now it's too late for us. When you go down to take her last breath, Mother will have nothing left to give you."

With that, Maud flung her cup over the rail. The sound of it crashing against the stones at the bottom of the well made Careev flinch.

"She's a quack! A quack who pretends she can help when there isn't any hope. And you, little sister, standing here when you ought be taking a pillow, and putting it over Mother's face. That's how it was done in the old days!"

"That's barbarism."

"That's right. *Bar*barism. Leave the *bar*barism to your enemies. You're too nice, aren't you? Too merciful. You'll make a wonderful Queen . . . for as long as you'll last!"

"Maud—"

"You accident! You go down there and take what's left for all the good it'll do. Go on! Go on!" Laughing madly, she turned and walked away, gathering the shadows until she disappeared, with the last echoes of her laughter fading into the depths of the well.

"My Lady," Avra stammered, "I'm so sorry! She was drunk when the Magister brought her. He asked me to give her something to make her sleep if I could, and I slipped something into her drink. But the mixture had the opposite effect. She's been raving, threatening to gut me. I. . . ."

"It's not your fault," Careev reassured her, in spite of the queasiness she felt at the top of her stomach. Something had happened to Maud. There had always been some bitterness in her, but this! It was as though something had turned her sister inside out. *This is too much*, she thought. She took a deep breath, touched Avra's shoulder.

"Let's go see the Queen."

"Lady?"

"Yes?"

"Try not to be shocked when you see her. She's . . . very changed."

Careev nodded and went with Avra down the ramp deep into the house, past the kitchens, and the quarters for the Vestals and servants, past ancient shrines where greasy candles illumined stone slabs, each drilled with a hole to represent the Sun's Eye. The air grew colder and heavy with moisture; Careev hurried past the rooms she and Maud had used during the summer visits of their childhood.

"Are you all right, Lady?"

"I'm remembering something. Maud and I used to lie awake late at night when we stayed here, and she'd tell me the volcano wasn't really dead." Careev smiled. "Gods, that used to scare me! I felt, oh, I don't know, *squeezed* with all that rock over my head, and that white-hot lava pushing up underneath the floor. I used to imagine I could see the floor-tiles bulging, about to burst!''

The Queen's apartments were at the bottom of the well, just beyond the prayer pool. Green scum floated in the water; the few water wheels that were left tilted in their frames. Maud's goblet was wedged in the vanes of one of them, water from the moat hitting its side and spilling onto the floor.

It was not a good omen.

Avra excused herself, went into the Queen's apartment, and emerged a moment later.

''I told her you were here. I think she understood me.''

''Thank you.''

The Queen's Vestals eyed Careev impassively as she walked in; the room smelled of medicine, and boiled chouris leaves. Above the sickbed, a mural of dolphins—identical to the one in the Queen's room of the Palace—leapt above an endless parade of curled waves. The bed itself looked empty.

When Careev came closer to it, she saw her mother.

The Queen seemed so small, and in spite of Avra's warning, Careev feel a deep, disheartening chill take hold of her. Gormayne's hair, once full and lustrous, was nothing more than a few strands the color and texture of spiders' webs. Her smooth, healthy skin was deeply wrinkled, and had taken the color of old porcelain. And this horrible change had taken only days!

Gormayne stirred.

''Mother?''

Careev leaned close enough to have a taste of the Queen's breath, as she would at the last moment, taking the power from her mouth. In truth, she felt none of the power of a Queen there; instead, she felt *suction*, as though the Queen were stealing Careev's life away. She felt dizzy and weak, and backed away.

The Queen's eyes opened. Avra brought a stool over to the bedside and Careev sat down.

''Is it you, Daughter?''

''Don't speak, Mother. Rest. There's no need for words.''

With great effort, Gormayne smiled. ''I was in the most beautiful place. The Grove below the Citadel. Do you know it? There was a young woman there, lying in a bed of morning glories who was waiting for someone. She had the most peaceful expression on her face! And then *he* came. Like Adon, though not bright, but dark instead. When he came, the light in the place . . . *went* to him, as though he was drawing it in. It . . . was your sister, I think, Carry. All wrapped around him and rising up, starting to spin, crying out. . . .''

Gormayne sighed and licked her lips.

"Here, Mother. Have something to drink." Careev helped prop her head, and tilted a water glass to the Queen's mouth. Water dribbled down her chin at first, and then the Queen began to drink a little.

"Thank you."

"Shhhhh. . . .''

Gormayne smiled. "How is your father?"

Careev looked at Avra, who nodded.

"I think he's all right. I haven't seen him yet. We . . . we sort of had a fight."

"You didn't start it."

"No."

"I never did, either," she said. He was so handsome. And clever, and strong-minded, for a man." She coughed. "My sister loved him too, did you know that?"

"I think so."

"He knew how to make me anxious. Make me wait, until I wanted him so much I'd do anything for him. Even let him . . . go ahead and try to change everything. I wanted to see if he could do it. He wanted to use me to do it!"

She coughed again. Avra came over with a steaming pot of chouris leaves and fanned the fumes over her face. She grimaced, breathing them in and then turning abruptly away.

"He wanted a son to succeed him. To establish his own line!"

"Mother—"

"Oh, that was a special child. The first time I felt him stir inside me, I knew how special he was. I think . . . no, I know, they were giving me something, a drug, something that made my soul split in two, one half to me, one half to my little boy, because I never loved anything the way I loved that baby. I wanted him to be King one day! I didn't care that he

was a boy. He could have ruled in your place, Careev, but
then. . . ."

She groaned and drew her knees up. Her eyes flickered.

"Avra!"

"Your sister! My sister! Your sister . . . took my life
away. Took my love . . . my love. . . . Down . . . in the
Grove, under the . . . trees. She was there with him, they
were wrapped around each other, floating, his arms around
her, taking in the light. Taking. . . ."

Her eyes opened again. "You won't rule long," she said in
a strong voice, as though they were talking over breakfast.

"I don't want to rule. Let me abdicate! Let me give it to
Poppa, or Maud, or whoever wants it!"

In answer, her hand closed around Careev's wrist with
terrible, trembling strength. Then, like a fishing line snapping, the strength vanished.

"Mother?"

She seemed to shrink before Careev's eyes, was sinking
into the bed, sighing with the passage of her traveling soul.

"*Mother!*"

There was no answer; only a gasp from the shadows behind, and the physician moving forward in horror.

"My Lady! Her Breath!"

Stunned, Careev forced herself closer. Her mother's eyes
were open, unseeing. She trembled and made herself put her
lips on the lips of her mother. There was a stir of breath.
Careev drew it in and held it, the way her mother had taught
her long ago.

It was dry and cold, and there was no power in it at all.

THIRTY-ONE

EVERYTHING IN THE DEATH ROOM was still, as if the corpse had a hold on the life there. The air seemed almost solid, like glass. Avra gently pulled the Princess away from the bed, and opened a box atop the bedside table. She fit a pair of candles into a hole in the lid and lighted them. Then, wetting a cotton ball with oil from a bottle, she annointed Gormayne's eyes, her forehead, and her lips.

"May the Goddess prepare a place for you in Heaven, and may she guide your weary soul into the arms of the Lord," she said. She crossed the Queen's arms over her stomach, arranged the pillows, found a brush on the vanity and stroked it through the brittle gray hair. All the while Careev watched her, fascinated by the physician's movements the way a baby is fascinated by the movement of dappled sunlight stirred by the branches of a shady tree, or a cat is fascinated by fish swimming in a tank: not comprehending, neither threatened nor attracted, but simply watching.

Finally, Avra smoothed the sheets over Gormayne's body,

blew out the candles, and took a spool of silver wire out of the box.

"I'm very sorry, Lady," she said softly. Careev tried to smile. "But we should leave now, and seal the door, before her soul regains the use of its will."

"Yes." Careev pulled some of the wire off the spool, wrapping it around her finger. The mural above the bed had gone dark. She whispered, "Good-bye, Mother," as she followed Avra out and then let the physician close the double doors behind them.

"Can I help you?" Avra asked, eyeing the spool.

"I'll do it." Four times she wrapped the wire around the door handles, crossing over in a figure 8 so that the seal resembled the symbol for Eternity. Twisting the ends together, Careev bent the excess length back and forth until it parted. Now the Queen's soul, wandering dazed about the Island until the shriving rituals were attended to, would not be able to enter the apartment and reanimate its former body. Careev felt a small comfort having sealed the doors. She did not want to think about the possibility of her mother becoming a zombie, and suffering the zombie's fate of death by fire.

"There," Careev said, giving Avra the spool back.

"I'm going to call the embalmer." Avra hesitated slightly. "He'll be here tomorrow morning, early."

Careev nodded.

"I know how difficult this is, Lady. My own mother died very young. I was the last-born daughter, too. I know it doesn't compare to what you've just gone through. . . ."

"I'll be all right," Careev said, taking her hand and squeezing it.

"What I mean is, I can give you something to help you sleep."

"I don't think so."

Avra smiled wanly. "It's such a helpless feeling. . . ."

"You did your best. Now you'd better get some rest yourself. I want to find my sister and tell her."

"Very well . . . my Queen!"

"Not yet, Avra. Go now. And have somebody send word to Father down in his boat, please. Say that I'll come see him tomorrow, after the embalmer's done his work."

Avra curtsied and went off. Careev stared at the door for a time, then shook herself, and started up the ramp until she found a Vestal.

"Which room did the Princess Maud take?"

"There," the Vestal answered, pointing to a doorway up and on the opposite side of the well. Careev walked to it, and found the door ajar. There were no sentries about, but the lights were on. She went inside and found Maud face down on the bed, snoring loudly.

"Stupid . . ." Careev whispered. She took Maud's shoes off, pulled the blankets back, and got her underneath. There were red blotches on her sister's neck. Maud mumbled something. Careev turned off the lights, went out and asked one of the Vestals to please check on the Princess every hour or so, in case she had drunk enough to make her ill.

The first flashes of light and muffled booms came from outside. *Fireworks*, Careev thought. *Father's schells must be setting them off now.* There would be more fireworks in Almheraz, and in all the cities of the Realm tonight, as soon as news spread of the Queen's death. Another soul passed on to Heaven. Another pathway of Fate, followed to the end.

When she closed the door to Maud's room, Careev found Marywynn waiting for her outside. She was crying; Careev began to realize that she was going to have to comfort people who had made themselves distraught trying to comfort her. Her rooms were ready, however; Careev lead her maid to them, then bid her firmly good night. Then she filled a basin with warm water, washed, and slipped out of her clothes and into a bed. The sheets were musty and damp. No one had slept here for a long time.

The fireworks rattled the walls. *It sounds like the end of the world*, she thought. Had the night of the Fall sounded this way? Was the last vision of the ancient world one of bursting red and green lights, and the peal of thunder rolling into the distance across the sun-blasted plains?

Waking the next morning, she felt dull surprise at having slept. She dressed in the yellow mourning gown Marywynn had brought from the city. She drank tea, and carefully buttered and spread jam over the toast her maid had brought in. When she finished, she put on a blue and gold cloak and went down the stone stairs to the quay, where the breeze was tangy with the smells of salt and burnt gunpowder and the cardboard barrels of spent rockets floated between the slips.

The curved-prow embalmer's boat bobbed alongside its mooring. Maud waited next to it with her hand on the gunwale; alongside her was the embalmer, a skinny, owl-eyed man whom Careev had often seen at funerals in Almheraz. His skin was dark and leathery from long years of handling the potions and chemicals of his trade. She had always thought he resembled one of the mummies he was so expert at preparing.

"Condolences, Lady Careev," the embalmer said with a bow. He kept glancing at Maud, who was cloakless and dressed in the old style of mourning: fringed skirt and a laced bodice that pushed her breasts tightly together.

"Are you ready?" Maud asked, without acknowledging Careev.

"Yes, of course I'm ready. If you'd care to come aboard."

Maud looked better than she had the day before, but her eyes were hard and bitter. She bumped Careev with her elbow as they came up the ramp.

"Hope you've had your breakfast, Sister."

"Are you feeling all right?"

"Am I drunk, you mean?"

"No, that's not what I mean."

"Let's get on with it."

"Maud—"

"That little man is waiting."

The embalmer took them down into his spotless hold, where Gormayne's draped remains lay on a huge stone table that had channels on the edges that drained into a jar on the deck. More jars were secured to the bulkheads by leather straps. There were also several racks of polished metal tools: blades, hooks, syringes, trouchees, forceps. As soon as both sisters were in the hold, the embalmer signaled a young boy, who wore the brown mantel of an apprentice, to open a new barrel of sparkling natron, carbonate pickling salts gathered along the sun-scorched tidelands of the Crescent Sea.

The embalmer sniffed loudly, pulled the blanket from the Queen's body, and pressed her flesh with his thumb. The apprentice handed out cloth masks; Careev tied hers on. Maud let hers drop to the deck.

"Please stand back a little," the little man said. "I need some leverage here." With that, he took a chisel and hammer from the apprentice, put the blade between Gormayne's eyes, and with a single, expert hammer-blow broke open the small bones of the corpse's nose. The apprentice moved in with forceps; his master inserted a long hook into one of the Queen's nostrils, twisted his wrist, and yanked. Out came a shiny gray mass that was streaked with blood: the brain, which he promptly deposited into a pan. The apprentice washed it immediately, then plunged it into a jar of preservative. After the thirty days of shriving, when Gormayne's soul was to be released from Limbo, her brain would be burned in expiation for sins of the mind.

Maud's eyes shone, taking it all in. Careev wondered what was she thinking, watching her mother's brain being stirred in a pot like part of a casserole. Certainly not that one day this very thing would be done to her.

The embalmer cleared his throat. Careev realized that it was expected that she approve each gruesome step of the process. He really did seem to take pride in what he was doing.

"Well done," she managed to say, through her mask. Maud snorted loudly. He ignored her and spoke to the apprentice.

"Bring in the shriver."

In a few moments, one of the apprentices returned with a young schell dressed head to toe in the yellow color of mourning. The embalmer gave the schell a curved knife from his tray.

"Make the incision here," he said, drawing a line with his finger across Gormayne's belly to mark the place. The schell followed his instructions perfectly; when it was through, it stood there, silent and beautiful. The embalmer took the knife from him and handed it to Careev.

He waited. Careev looked at the schell's eyes. They were like the eyes of a newborn baby.

"I can't," she said.

"It's not difficult," the embalmer insisted with a frown.

"Drive the knife right here, between the second and third rib." He put his finger on the place to show her where.

"I'm not going to kill it," Careev said, more emphatically this time.

"Sometimes, the close quarters here on the boat are difficult. Perhaps you'd rather kill the schell on deck. For everyone to witness."

"Send the schell away."

Now the embalmer was exasperated. "Surely I don't have to explain to you that the sins of your mother's body must be shriven. This schell opened her body, and took those sins into itself. If you don't kill him, your mother's being will never regenerate. She'll be an anima. A soul without a body!"

"I'm not going to kill it."

"My Lady, you must think of your poor mother's soul!"

"In that case, here!" Careev cried, breaking the knife over her knee and running up the ramp and onto the quay. She pulled up and tried to catch her breath. Her heart was pounding. She knew that she was expected to kill the schell. Anyone who could afford to waste a schell was always shriven that way, but she simply couldn't do it.

From behind her: "You little fool—"

Careev did not turn. "There was no point killing it."

"No point except that you were afraid to do it. Why didn't you ask me? It would have been fun!"

"Shut up!"

"Don't tell me you think you're going to be a *nice* Queen. That would be something. A nice Queen. I don't think we've ever had one of those before—"

Careev whirled around hand out. Maud smirked.

"Nice Queens don't slap their sisters."

"I can't kill it."

"Why not?"

"Don't you see? Killing that schell is the end of Mother once and for all. I was there when she died, Maud. I took that last breath, and there was nothing in it. I couldn't feel anything! She was just too weak, but I couldn't help thinking that she wanted to help me somehow. I just want to wait a day or two. We can have it killed then."

"All right." Maud yawned. "What do I care?"

"I need your help too!"

"Really? Well that's too bad. You've got your throne, and I've got my bed. That's where I'm going."

"Maud! Maud, listen to me. Momma said something about seeing you with someone, someone with dark hair, someone who meant both of us harm. You know who I'm talking about. I knew you were with him last night—Eccles tried to keep it from me, but I knew anyway. Don't you see? He's making you give up. If you were thinking right, you'd want to help me. I'll give you the throne, if that's what you want!"

For a moment, she thought she had gotten through to her. Maud's silvery eyes softened, but then grew hard again.

"Keep it," she said coldly, pushing her aside. She climbed the stairway up over the rim of the caldera, pausing at the top just long enough to glance down at her. Then she disappeared.

"I'm sorry about your mother, Lady."

It was the old man, Marten. He sat on the edge of the dock, smoking a pipe and dangling his legs into the water. The seer, still disguised in its sunglasses and cloak, sat next to him, swinging its legs too. It annoyed her to see them look so relaxed.

"Thanks."

"Never had one myself."

"You're lucky."

Marten nodded and puffed on the pipe. Careev said, "Did they take care of you last night?"

"Wouldn't call it that, exactly. Oh, they got a bunk for me and for this thing, except that it disappeared about five minutes after we came aboard. Good thing, too. All those schells on that boat were ready to riot. Things were in an uproar anyway. First they had everybody taking things down from the walls, rolling up the rugs, and striking all the flags and banners. They got done with that and then started shooting rockets off. Couple of their firing tubes got jammed, so I helped clean 'em out, and wound up doing more rockets until they ran out. Went down to my bunk about three in the morning. Had my eyes shut, just about to drop off, when there was a bloody commotion on the deck above mine. Somebody crashing around, all this bellowing. I didn't know what to make of it. Got up, and the Magister grabbed me and said if I didn't get back below he'd have me gutted. I told him sorry, but it was a little hard to sleep with all that noise, and he said something about my being an unwelcome guest, that I was only there because of you. That was enough for me, Lady. I rolled up the blankets from the bed and went out here to sleep. When I woke up, our friend was back, sleeping right next to me quiet as you please!''

Marten tapped the pipe out against the edge of the dock. ''There's something about being on an island that doesn't agree with me. I wish I was back in the city, so I could look for my boy.''

''I'd like to find him too,'' Careev said.

''Did you see the King?''

Marten shook his head.

''Technically, Father stopped being King the moment she died. That's why they've taken everything down on his boat.''

''They're not too happy, that's sure.''

Careev nodded. ''I've got to see my father now. Can you be patient a little longer and stay with the seer? I can arrange transport back to Almheraz later today, I think. We just need a Templeman to take you instead of a schell.''

''That's a wise idea, Lady. It's so strange, the effect this creature has on the schells. It's like they were made to hate it. Maybe it's lucky it's got no eyes or ears. It's got to be a horrible fate, being born a thing that everything else in creation hates. Assuming it's born, that is!''

''I wish I knew what it wanted,'' Careev said, going over and putting her hand lightly on top of the seer's head. Her hands tingled; suddenly, she felt herself being rushed away to another time and place. Suddenly, she was a little girl again, hiding beneath a table because she had snapped a nib off the King's favorite pen. His voice was thunderous and harsh as he called for her, and she was so frightened, she thought her heart would burst. He came in, passed close to her hiding place. She saw his powerful legs, his sandaled feet. He would crush her. . . . And then the vision burst, like a bubble.

''Hey, now, Lady, that's not wise!'' Marten had got up and pulled her free. She shuddered.

''I-I saw something.''

''You went stiff as a statue's what you did.''

"It made me see something. Maybe that's how it talks. Maybe it can tell me something about my brother—"

Marten frowned. "Lady, I'm sorry, but I'm not about to let you touch this beast again. You don't know what it wants. Maybe it doesn't know. You best get on with your business. I'll worry about the seer."

Careev smiled. "And why should you care whether I touch it or not?"

"Because I've decided I've taken a liking to you, Miss. For gentry, you're not bad. In fact, if it's anything to you, you've got my pledge of loyalty!" He bowed, sweeping the pipe out of his mouth.

"Thank you, traveler." Her voice quavered.

"It's Fate, that's all, and that's something only a fool argues with. Now go on, see your father!"

Careev started off. She had only taken a few steps before she realized that the seer was following her. Marten hopped up and stepped between them, but he was hesitant to touch it, and finally Careev shook her head.

"Let me try something." She took the creature by its shoulders. "You stay," she said slowly. "No go."

The seer stuck its tongue out, and rocked from foot to foot.

"What do you think, Marten?"

"I've had this problem before. I think it's going to come with you no matter what. We could tie it up somehow. . . ."

"No. If it wants to come, there must be a reason. All right, since it won't stay with you, you'll have to come with it. Let's go!"

THIRTY-TWO

THE KING'S BARQUE had been stripped of most of its gold pennants and sunburst sails; all that remained was the red-bar ensign of the Panault family hanging limply on the mainmast. On deck, Careev could see some of Cyre's Templemen, similarly stripped of their old finery; they tensed visibly when Careev came on board, and some of the schells growled softly when the seer appeared.

"Look at that." Marten whispered. "It makes me wonder. A schell isn't supposed to be capable of violence on its own."

They went to the fantail cabin, which the King used as a receiving room. Careev felt nervous going in; seeing how bare the cabin was did not make her feel any better. Cyre's sun-crested King's throne had been replaced by a plain chair of new wood. All the allegorical tapestries depicting the union of the sun with the world through the divine Adon were gone. Without these and other trappings of kingly authority, the barque was in truth a shabby vessel. Her paint was peeling in spots and tears of rust spread red talluses from her rivets.

The seer sat down in the wooden throne, gripping the armrests with his fists.

"Looks like it was born to rule, don't it, Lady?"

The cabin door opened and a Templeman looked in; a few moments later, Eccles appeared, out of breath and flustered.

"My Lady! I thought you would be coming alone."

"These are friends you've met before." Careev said. "Marten the Traveler, and . . . his father."

"Yes, of course. They spent the night here." He hid his suspicion well, Careev thought, knowing it was there all the same. Eccles turned suddenly, extended his hand to the seer. The creature took it, but its tongue darted out at it did, and the priest jumped back as though he had grabbed a white-hot poker.

"A seer," he said, staring at his palm with fascination. She could see Marten suppress a smile. "And a well-trained one at that. Where did you get it?"

"Actually, it belongs to Marten. It seems to be fond of me, however. We met on the boat, as I said, and it's quite attached to me. I'm sorry you're shocked."

Eccles closed his hand. "As I recall, I saved you from a seer once."

"It's harmless, Magister."

Eccles stroked the forks of his beard. "If I can be so bold, do you intend to have this creature with you . . . permanently?"

"Maybe."

"Lady, I would advise you to seriously consider—"

"What are you so worried about?"

"It is a wild thing, Lady. It neither thinks nor acts as we do."

"Pardon me, Excellency," Marten said, "but I think you could say the same thing just about anybody."

"Marten—"

"Sorry, Lady."

"Now, Magister," she continued, turning away so as not to see him smile, "I don't want you to worry about the seer.

It got aboard the steamer I took here, and I prevented the passengers from throwing it overboard. The traveler's its keeper, more or less. As soon as we can leave the Island and find a place to release it safely, we'll be rid of it. Until then, you'll just have to get used to it being around, if that's what it wants. As you said, it's a wild creature. I haven't the faintest idea how to get it to do anything.''

"Of course, Lady."

"Good. Now, would you tell Father I'm here? I'm sure he's anxious to discuss his status with me."

"He is, of course, very upset about your mother. I should add my condolences, too, Lady. It is a great loss for anyone to have to bear."

"Thank you."

"I shall only be a moment."

Eccles went out and then came back. "He's resting, Lady. Your mother's death was a terrible blow. A difficult thing to lose one's wife, to be secure one moment, attached to a center that nourishes, brings warmth, makes life possible— and then, to be cut free. Adrift, lost . . ." His voice trailed. "Perhaps it is not possible for a woman to understand."

"We have business."

"I am perfectly willing to convey your wishes to him, when he wakes up."

"All right. Please write this down."

Eccles bowed. "Of course." He took a stylus and a pad from his tunic pocket, and sat down cross-legged on the deck.

"I wish to name Father Regent for the period of mourning. He's obviously equipped to govern as I am not, and I intend to make the transition as painless for the people and for my family as possible."

Eccle's narrow face betrayed no surprise. "That goes beyond the Agreement of Succession, Lady. In spite of your altruistic reasoning, it is quite generous to your father."

"My generosity has conditions. Father will continue to enjoy all perquisites and authority due a King. In return, he will pledge to do two things."

"Those are?" Eccles jotted something down on the pad.

"First, he must renounce his family. It's really only a

formality, since no Panault matriarch survives. There are some distant cousins, I believe.''

"Three."

"They can carry on the line as well as he. At any rate, if he agrees, I shall formally adopt him into the Gormaynes.''

Eccles merely looked up from his writing. The seer made a soft buzzing sound and shifted on the throne.

"The second condition is that the King will sign an instrument to the following effect: That, should anything happen to me during the period of mourning, he pledges to submit to the same fate. If I lose my eye, he loses his; my life, his life.''

"There are accidents, Lady, and illness."

"Yes. And their circumstance and effect will be duplicated as is practically and medically possible.''

"I shall inform him," Eccles said.

"Will you advise against such an agreement?''

"There's little I can advise him about presently, Lady. However—''

"Yes?"

"I think you are wrong to fear the King."

"He wants to go on ruling, doesn't he?"

"I won't deny that."

"And I have no quarrel with his going on. So long as he understands that he's the end of his line. There'll be no more attempts to overthrow the Gormaynes. I am Queen of Almheraz now, and head of my family. If he's willing to accept that, I shall be happy to have his help.''

"You fear for your life too much, I think." Eccles said, putting the pad away. "Life can be like a beautiful flower, Lady. Held too tightly, it is crushed into nothing. However, I shall have an instrument prepared. Whether or not he'll sign it, well," he smiled, "who can say."

"Tell him I want him to sign it."

Eccles said, "May I speak to you a moment alone?"

"You can speak freely."

"Very well. This is personal, but as you've given me no choice. . . . Lady, I fail to comprehend why your manner toward me has changed so drastically of late. Have I done

something to offend you? Because, if I have, I assure you it
was done by accident and not by design. You know how I
have always held you in high esteem. In fact, it has always
been my wish that our friendship might some day develop
into something deeper. . . ."

"In other words, you'd like to be King yourself!"

"My feelings in this regard have nothing to do with earthly
power, or with the trappings of office or political necessity. I
am a man. My feelings are those of a man."

His earnestness surprised her, coming as it did from a man
who had always kept himself under control. There was emotion in his voice; a week or two ago, if he had said this to her,
she would have gladly pledged herself to him. She looked
into his eyes, searching for something beyond their cool gaze,
and as she did, her unease grew. Whatever had changed in
her had also changed their relationship forever. Careev realized that she just did not believe him—and also that it would
be dangerous to tell him so. She took his hands.

"This isn't the time, Magister," she said gently. "We're
all on edge. Later, when things have settled, we'll talk. For
now, please tell Father what I've said, and ask him for my
sake to consider agreeing to my conditions."

Eccles stiffened. "Of course, Lady. You see, I, too, am
not quite myself." He bowed. "Now, if you will excuse me,
I've some matters to attend to."

When he had gone, Careev turned to Marten. "Well,
traveler. What do you think?"

The old man looked startled. "*Me*, Miss? I don't know
anything about royal business."

"You trade, don't you?"

"I did until I came to Almheraz."

"Well, then, if you were to trade with him, what would
you think?"

"I'd make sure I was standing between him and my goods
when the deal was struck."

"Yes. And do you know, Marten, that was always the
thing about him. I always felt I could trust him. He was one
of the few people I grew up with that I thought really cared
about me, and now . . ." She reached for the seer's arm

suddenly, and pulled it to its feet. "Something's very wrong here. Marten, I want you to go to the embalmer and tell him we'll ride back to Almheraz with him as soon as he can leave. Tell him no one else is to know—if anyone asks why he's leaving so soon, he's to make an excuse. The Festival or something."

"All right, Miss."

"I'm going back to the house to get Marywynn. You and the seer meet me on the boat."

"What about the King, Miss? Don't you think you ought to tell him where you're going?"

"My father and the Magister have always been very close. No. The King will just have to wait."

"Yes, Miss. I'll be waiting for you."

The traveler went off. Careev had hoped the seer would follow, but the creature only snuffled loudly and stepped close to her. When she moved, it moved. Careev sighed.

"What is it you want from me?"

The seer's tongue came out, red-tipped bristles standing on end.

"Very well, come along if you must, though I don't know what we'll do about that schell the embalmer wanted me to kill." If the schell went crazy, she thought, she might have to kill it after all.

They left the barque and climbed the steps together, Careev feeling the heat. Only a few wisps remained of the Veil today, and the Eye burned small and bright, like a point of candlelight focused through a magnifying glass onto a piece of paper. Tonight the Festival would begin, she thought. Tomorrow she would have to play Adon's bride, and marry his effigy. Tonight that effigy would be burned, and bonfires lighted all over the Realm to commemorate the great fire that lighted the way for the Goddess and consumed the earth at the same time. *To see something, you have to destroy it,* she thought. *For me to understand myself, I have to destroy what I am and become something else, something I no longer understand. . . .*

Over the rim of the Island, Careev and the seer passed through the first ring of tropical forest. The air was steamy and she was very thirsty, but the pools were all sulfurous, marked by lumpy yellow columns of crystallized minerals and guarded by humming clouds of insects. Careev passed through the ring quickly. It was a relief when the trees abruptly changed and the air cleared further in. She spotted a spring that was a little off the path, and stopped suddenly to have a drink.

The seer crashed into her from behind; they fell into the mud tangled arm and leg. It was too much. She kicked at the creature and called it every name she could think of and stormed off along the path toward the house trying not to hear the disgusting noises the creature made behind her. When she finally stopped, the seer did too, craning its neck.

"Oh, I've had enough of you!"

The seer grunted.

"Go back down to the boat!"

It did not move.

There was an apple tree above the path that had a few withered apples hanging from its branches. Careev picked one. She glanced at the seer, and had an idea. Rearing back, she threw the apple down the path as far as she could.

The creature grunted excitedly and crashed off after the sound. She watched it go, and decided that she could not afford to waste any more time with it. If Marten was absolutely unable to control it, she would have it killed as painlessly as possible as soon as they got back to Almheraz.

She was feeling hungry, and picked another apple to eat. The spring continued nearby. She knelt down, drank the icy water, splashed some on her face. As she stood again, there came a rustling noise from the brush to her left. She thought that the seer couldn't possibly have circled back so quickly.

Fire tightened around her throat. *Steel wire*, she thought, clawing at her neck. Her vision constricted to a tiny point of light, and she began to feel detached from her pain. Her soul was ripping free of its body, she thought, and that point of light was her doorway to escape. The garotte tightened. *It's not so hard to die*, she thought as her body grew slack and her hands fell away from her neck.

Sounds kept her there: shrieks of fury, and the rattling wings of birds startled into flight by the noise. She opened her eyes and saw the seer struggling with someone. They had their hands around each other's necks. Then the seer seemed to dig in with its fingers, and its opponent stiffened, and finally sighed. Careev realized that the assassin was not a man, but a schell. The same young, blue-eyed schell she had declined to kill aboard the embalmer's launch.

She tried to stand. The seer chirped, and let the dead schell drop to the ground. *Mother . . . shriven at last* was her last thought as she fainted into the seer's arms.

THIRTY-THREE

FESTIVAL DAY.

The gates to the Citadel were opened at dawn, and a huge stream of pilgrims filed up the road to the top of the Rock to gather in the Red Courtyard for the Queen's blessing, to enter the main hall of the Palace to sign the Visitor's Ledger and to eat skewers of fresh fruit provided by the royal family; to worship at the Temple of the Sun, or walk around the White Temple; to contemplate the Black Stone between them; to breath the rare atmosphere high above the city. The walk to the Citadel was normally a festive one, but today, the crowd moved uneasily.

It knew, although no formal announcement had been made, that Queen Gormayne had died last night. It wanted to hear the new Queen say so, and see her on the balcony. It wanted to greet Careev and wish her well, to see her clasp hands with the Arcopatrinas and with the High Priest of the Sun. It wished for these things knowing it might not have any of them. The Arcopatrinas was also dead, and her rebirth had still not been found. As for Careev, and the Magister, rumors abounded as to their whereabouts. Some said the two had run away together, or been taken bodily into Heaven by the soul of the dead Queen. Some said that it was Maud who would appear, and declare herself ruler of Almheraz; the King, others insisted, had killed them all, and would appear himself, having taken the offices and titles of the persons he had slain.

There were those who whispered that the Dark Sister had finally triumphed, and that she would manifest herself on the balcony with Adon, who would declare his undying devotion to her and open a new age, in which the Goddess's mysteries would be revealed, and her magic made commonplace. New ages of darkness, new ages of gold were predicted. The food served in the palace hall was criticized. All was unsettled. The crowd wanted form and had none.

The Bachelors and Vestals and Templemen whose job it was to protect the sanctity of the temples and the security of the palace felt the unease of the crowd and some of them wished their duty lay elsewhere. A few of them slipped out of uniform and joined the crowd, preferring the certainty numbers provided, putting the responsibility for their decision to Fate.

The crowd had a life of its own and its own mind, existing independently of its parts, giving back illusions of immortality and anonymous power in return for the cooperation of those parts.

Komaso felt that power as he walked up the road. He felt it when he reached the courtyard and joined the procession around the White Temple.

He had spent the night walking the streets of the Old Town, avoiding Vestal patrols, finally catching some sleep just before dawn beneath a pile of straw in a stables at the end of a narrow alley. There, scarcely able to sleep because of how the straw itched, he had troubled dreams of flying out of the alley and to the palace bedroom of the Princess Careev. Somehow, he could not stop thinking about her. There was a bond between them that should not exist, but did. He cared about her; he wanted to know what she thought and how she felt. He wanted to help her as much as he wanted to help himself.

But the Order of Vestals was dedicated to the overthrow of the royal line; the royal line required the fealty of the Order of Vestals, just as his soul required the body descended from the royal line. There was no resolving the conflict, at least by any way he could think of. It was in the hands of Fate.

But he had to act. He had to follow through with his plan, find Rarei, convince her that killing him was not necessarily in the interests of the Order. In spite of what he was, Komaso was no different from any other man or woman. He wanted —no, needed—to live, as long and as fully as he could.

Psyche's Temple was draped in white fabric. None of the entrances were marked, so that a stranger—or a man—wanting to get inside would have to pull away the draping to see where they were. Bachelors were posted around the top of the stepped pedestal to prevent anyone from doing so, but Komaso, who had lived in this building so many lifetimes, knew exactly where he should go. On the north side of the building was a service door at the end of a ramp, and the Bachelors there looked particularly glassy-eyed. Komaso pulled up his hood—he was still wearing the Vestal cloak belonging to Careev's maid—and left the line of pilgrims.

"Lady, get back down there," one of the guards challenged. "Please."

"Somebody's sick. They're about to faint."

"Where?"

"Right—oh no, she must have fallen already. You've got to help her."

"We can't leave our post, Lady."

"What if she's trampled to death? Do you want that on your conscience?"

"No." The guard looked at his partner. "Maybe you'd better go down."

"You'd better both go down. She must weigh at least 300 pounds!"

"How can somebody who weighs 300 pounds be trampled?"

"I don't know. You'd better see."

The Bachelors nodded and went down the ramp to investigate. Komaso slipped beneath the drapes, and went through the door.

We need to recruit better Bachelors, he thought as he went into the temple. *The ones we've got stink!*

It was warm inside, and the air smelled of dust and stale incense. The corridors were narrow, high-ceilinged, the walls stained with centuries of candle soot. Komaso knew the turns and twists of these halls. His own feet had helped wear smooth channels into the stone floor. He found the back staircase that led down to the lower levels, where the hospice and living quarters were. Rarei must be there. She was still weak, and would never have agreed to convalesce at a convent, or on one of the vineyard estates, so long as the Order was without a living Arcopatrinas.

Downstairs, the light was better, and there were plenty of guards standing with lances along the corridors. Rarei's rooms were at the end of the hall; nobody challenged him as he approached.

His hand was turning the knob of her door before the guards grabbed him.

"No one's allowed in without an appointment, sister—"

His hood fell back. If he had been a red ant dropped atop a nest of black ones, the discovery could not have caused more or an uproar.

"—a man!"

"—gut him!"

"—blasphemer—"

They were on him in a swarm, pulling his hood over his head, pummeling him—

"*Stop—*"

It was quiet.

"Get him up."

He was yanked to his feet like a doll, and saw Rarei leaning on a crutch in the doorway.

"Matron, every second he's here is an offense to the Goddess. We must kill him now!"

Rarei managed an ironic smile. "The Goddess may make an exception."

"There can be no exception. No male may enter this Temple and live!"

Rarei drew her dagger. "Are you saying I don't know the rules of this Order?"

"No, of course—"

"If you'd been more vigilant, he would never have gotten this far. As it is, he's come to see me. I'll decide what's to be done with him, and when. Is that understood?"

"Yes, Matron!"

"Go back to your posts. Komaso, please come in."

No deference, Komaso thought. *She's treating me exactly as what I seem to be.* He walked past her into the apartment. When he was Arcopatrinas, he had always been slightly suspicious of the Spartan arrangements here: plain wooden table, batted-cotton mat on the floor, a shrine consisting of a vase of dried flowers and a pair of candles opposite the bed. It was plain enough to have been an affectation, and he always wondered whether Rarei had a real bed in a sumptuous villa somewhere down on the Rock.

"Take a chair," Rarei said, hobbling in with the crutch. "I'll lie down again, if you don't mind."

Komaso sat down. Rarei was gaunt, but getting her strength back. She looked at him for a long moment, trying to gauge him.

"I had hoped you were dead."

"I have a way of coming back."

"So we've seen." Rarei dropped the crutch and lowered herself to the mattress. "You understand that I acted against my feelings? That I had to try to kill you?"

"You made a mistake. Everybody does. What we ought to do now is forget about it and go on. I'm willing, if you are."

"It's not that easy. Put yourself in my place, Komaso. Our Order has a long tradition. How can I tell the Order that the new Arcopatrinas is a man? I can't. And I can't let you go, either. You've got the soul of the head of the Order inside you. It's my duty to get it back somehow. You see that, don't you? We believe in the rebirth of that soul. We have to. If we don't, we don't deserve to exist as an Order. The Goddess would destroy us, as surely as the King would."

"So. I should let myself be killed."

"For the good of the Order, you should, yes."

"Is that what you would do?"

"I don't know what I would do."

"Well, that's fine, except for one thing, Matron. I want to live. Having this body has changed my soul. I think we could live with that change, if you would only think about it."

"I have thought about it. I've spent two days praying, waiting for an answer. In the end, I did what I thought was right. You haven't changed my mind at all."

Komaso pulled out his knife. "I've got one of these, too. You can call your guards back, but you'll be dead before they get here. And whether or not they kill me, I've got one advantage you don't. I'll be reborn. You'll, well, who knows? The Goddess may not appreciate how you've interfered with her intentions. She may have a sorry Fate in store for your soul."

"It's a stalemate, then," Rarei said.

"And the Order suffers. We've got a new Queen. We should be able to take advantage of her, before she gets her legs under her."

"That's an unfortunate choice of words."

"Sorry." Komaso thought for a moment. "There might be one person who can help us."

"Who?"

"The Warden of the Queen's Preserve. She's made a science out of stealing souls. She tried to steal mine, in fact. Perhaps she knows a way of moving me into a body the Order can deal with."

"Assuming I agree to consult her before doing anything else, there is still one problem. She's vanished. The Order's done everything it could to find her, and there's no trace."

"I know a way."

Rarei looked skeptical.

"Still thinking of me as a boy, aren't you? Didn't reading my will convince you I was telling the truth? Doesn't the fact that I'm standing here now in this Temple mean anything at all?"

"All right."

"You'll have to follow me through the tunnel to the Black Stone. Can you handle that?"

In answering, Rarei used her crutch to pull herself up. "I can handle it."

"A capable woman," Komaso said. "I always knew it."

Along the east wall of the lowest subbasement of the Temple was the entrance to the tunnel. Komaso waited patiently for Rarei to negotiate the last set of stairs. The Matron was out of breath, but game; together they forced the door open.

The tunnel was dark, dripping with water. The walls were fuzzed with pale green moss that looked phosphorescent by torchlight. Rarei held her crutch in one hand and her dagger in the other, gripping both as though they were her only connection to her world.

"This was dug when the Queens first banished the Old Believers" Komaso said. "It was here before either of the Temples were built. Up ahead is a chamber, right underneath the Black Stone. . . ."

A few yards further, the tunnel made a turn, and opened up into a dark space that looked as if it had been dug out by hand. Rarei could see what looked like finger gouges in the stone and she shuddered. There was a smell in this place, something acrid and sweet, like blood burned on an altar.

"This was a place for ecstasy," Komaso said, eyes glittering in the torchlight. "The Believers came here to speak to Perse in her own language. They were not so civilized in those days, Matron! Sometimes, the worship ended with everyone torn limb from limb. Think about it, Rarei. Who was the last to go? Who tore *herself* apart?"

Searching the walls, he found a sagging wooden box set into a niche. "They kept things here that they needed for their arts," he said. "Supplies, potions." He pulled the box out a little and opened the top. "Old Believers still come and replenish the supplies. Hold the torch, please."

As Rarei watched, Komaso set up a brazier on tripod legs, into which he poured drops from three different bottles. Smoke filled the room suddenly; when it cleared, she could see the anima of a white-haired woman standing in the brass.

It was not quite solid—Rarei could see the torch flame shine through the middle of its body when Komaso circled around it—but it breathed and moved its head and looked around the chamber.

"It's Sheeme," Rarei whispered.

"That's right!" Komaso said gleefully. "You remember Rarei, don't you? And surely you'll remember me—or rather, both of me. Souls in a jar have a way of winding up in the wrong hands—or bodies!"

"You're . . . my nephew," the anima said. "And . . . something else. Another soul. . . ."

"The one you wanted to kill! And isn't it justice that I now have your soul in my hands, to do with as I please."

The anima closed its eyes, and the image faded a little. When it spoke, the voice was weary, dead-sounding.

"What . . . what do you want? Why have you called me?"

"We need your help. Where are you now?"

"Somewhere . . . in the Preserve. I'm not sure where, exactly. It's a prison, though. I'm imprisoned here, guarded . . . by schells who are loyal to one of their own kind. A shape-changer. A rogue. Sportus . . . is his name."

The anima smiled wanly. "I created him. Made him in my image . . . all too well. All too well. He's got plans of his own, now. You'll meet him . . . soon enough. He's a new kind of thing. He doesn't care about Dark Gods and Bright Gods, or acting out what's been written in Heaven. Nothing's been written in Heaven for him. Heaven couldn't conceive of such a thing as Sportus!"

Sheeme coughed. "He ordered my schells to keep me here. They won't give me anything to eat, and only just enough water to keep me around to slowly starve to death. It's my punishment . . . I suppose."

"What about your birds?"

"Don't . . . know. Fantil escaped. The rest . . ." There were tears in her eyes.

"We want to help you," Komaso said.

"We can send enough Vestals to free you—" Again, the anima laughed. "There are fifteen thousand young schells here. The King wanted to make an army of them, but they're Sportus's now. They don't fear for their lives the way we do."

Now it was Rarei who spoke. "You were very cruel with me not so long ago, Warden. You made me crawl for my life, and I did, and every inch of the way I vowed to myself that somehow, I'd make you crawl for yours. But I can see now you wouldn't crawl. You've given up. You don't have the will left to fight for your own life!''

"What for? To help my enemies prosper?"

"To help yourself! Tell us where you are."

"No."

"Tip the brazier," Rarei said. "She deserves her Fate."

"Wait—" Komaso cried.

"Look at her!"

The anima had fallen to its knees. Its mouth was open and its head tilted back and it moaned. "Gone," the anima said. "Gone! my love—"

The brazier turned over and bounced across the floor. The anima had disappeared. As the smoke cleared, Rarei backed toward the door. She tightened the grip on her dagger, watching the torch. When she could see Komaso, she spoke.

"She can't help us."

"I'll call her again. I did it once."

"No. The only way is the way it's always been. The old Arcopatrinas has to die so the new one can live. You know that. You know what you are, and you know what has to be done. The pain is a small thing."

"You expect me to stand here and let you gut me."

"It's your Fate."

"No! Here's yours—"

Jabbing the torch at her, Komaso lunged around Rarei and got past her. He heard her crutch fall to the floor and the Matron's curses as he ran through the dark tunnel back to the Temple basement. He pulled his hood up when he got there, and managed to get outside without attracting the attention of any more sentries. It was a relief to get back into the crowd of pilgrims. He stopped, took a breath, tried to get calm, but there was no fighting it; he was escaping, and as long as he lived as Komaso there would be no going back. He wanted it that way, and there was something else he wanted, too.

He wanted to see his sister again.

THIRTY-FOUR

EVEN BEFORE SHE AWAKENED, Princess Maud felt the pressure of his hands on the inside of her thighs. She stirred in her bed, yawned, turned over. Her head hurt as she opened her eyes, and at first, because the light was so dim, she thought she had been dreaming.

She recognized Sportus, and gasped.

"Get out!"

The schell laughed softly.

"Get out, before I call the guard!"

Sportus had still not moved his hands. "I don't really belong anywhere, do I? And as for the guards . . ." His fingers found her pubic hair and twisted just enough for her to cry out. "I think we can count on having as much privacy as we need."

He bent and kissed her, and she found herself kissing him back. She reached for him. He stood up.

"So much for resolutions," he said. Maud turned over.

"Leave me alone!"

"But you don't want me to leave you alone, do you? You're thinking about last night, even while you tell yourself it was all a mistake, something that will never happen again." He let go of her hair, smoothing it with the back of his hand. "That's the thing about the human mind that never ceases to fascinate me. The ability you have—especially you women—to hold two conflicting thoughts. Here's a third thought for you. You're getting up."

"No."

He yanked the covers off the bed. "Oh yes you are. You're cleaning yourself up so that you look something like what you're supposed to be, *Princess*. There's going to be a wedding tonight in the Grove. You remember the Grove, don't you? There's going to be a wedding, and you're going to be the bride."

Blood pounded in Maud's head. "Bride? But that's Mother's—I mean Careev. She's to do it."

Sportus went to the vanity and filled the basin with water from the pitcher there. He also turned the lights up, so that Maud could see his face in her mirror. He soaked a cloth in the water, wrung it out, looked up so that their eyes met, and smiled. His eyes were anything but blank.

"I'm afraid there's some bad news, Lady Maud. Or shall I say, Princess Royal. Your sister seems to have vanished." Sportus pulled her out of bed and led her to the vanity, putting the cloth on her face. She managed to squirm away.

"Vanished? What are you talking about?"

"She's not on the Island. Oh, they've looked everywhere. A few of the sentries claimed to have heard a commotion in the woods just after your sister left the embalmer's this morning. You remember this morning, don't you?"

"Yes!" Maud answered miserably.

"They found a dead schell just off the path. He'd been strangled, and *he* had a wire in his hands, as though he'd been strangling someone else. Somebody said that it was wearing the embalmer's colors . . . that she hadn't killed it in the usual way after the Queen's body was opened. At any rate, she's gone. Whether she's really dead, or whether she left the schell to throw people off the truth doesn't really matter. I'm taking you to Almheraz."

"Why you? Where are my maids? Where's the physician?"

"I sent all of them away. You don't need them anymore. You've got me."

He gave her a towel. She buried her face in it.

"There. I do that as well as a maid, don't I? And there are other things I do so much better than a maid could ever think of doing."

"I've had enough of this—"

Sportus slapped her, hard enough to send her sprawling back atop the bed. "We haven't even begun. Get dressed." He got a gown from the closet and a cloak and stockings and shoes and threw them on top of her, then stood with his arms folded across his chest while she sobbed and put them on. By the time she was ready, she had recovered a little. She faced him, and stood as tall as she could.

"We'll never get back to Almheraz in time."

"We'll be back at the Citadel in fifteen minutes," Sportus said, opening the door. "After you, my Lady. . . ."

Maud's joints ached, and her stomach felt queasy, but the walk out of the house soon made her forget these complaints. They passed Vestal guards, servants, and her own attendants, all of whom bowed in deference to her. But those who were sworn to protect the sanctity of Queen's Island with their lives, if necessary, paid no attention to the rogue schell. Once, he even pushed someone from the kitchen staff out of the way; she stumbled, but did not react as though the person who had pushed her existed. She shook herself and looked at her feet, as though she had caught her heel on the edge of a loose stone. Sportus, for his part, walked with grim determination, mouth set, concentrating. He took her over the moat, into a clearing in the first ring of forest. In it sat the Magister's flying machine.

"Get in," he said, voice flat and schell-like.

Maud climbed aboard. Sportus pulled the top down and started the motors, checking the control settings expertly.

"How do you know how to fly this thing?" Maud asked.

"I am the only person in Almheraz capable of doing so, my Lady." He looked over at Maud. Something about his face was wrong. . . .

"Eccles!" she exclaimed. "You look just like him! How—"

"I know what he knew," Sportus replied. His face returned to their normal, black-eyed state, and he grimaced, as if the demonstration had cost him something.

"Knew? He's—"

"I killed him the day I came to see your father." Sportus revved the engines, pulled on a handle, and the machine lifted off the ground, swinging away from the Island and up over the river. "Though perhaps killed is the wrong word. Absorbed might be more descriptive. Lady.

"He was an interesting man, and he had plans. I carried some of them out as he intended. He planned to poison your mother, for instance, and I did it as he would have, in the manner of someone from Baraqu, who would know what fish are not to be eaten in certain seasons of the year. I also know that he was very attracted to you, even though he was practical enough to want to marry your sister. Perhaps we'll play that game, before this is all over. The Sun-priest will marry the Queen!"

Maud lunged for the control handle and yanked it toward her; the flyer yawed violently, diving toward the water. She resigned herself to death, telling herself that perhaps it would make up for what she had done to her family. Then she felt his arm pinning her against the back of her seat, too far away to hold the control bar. The feel of him was like cold water poured through her, and she knew she did not want to die. She was weak, worthless. . . .

He regained control. "The only question was when," Sportus said. "You knew we were high enough so that we probably wouldn't crash."

"Poppa will stop you," she said.

Sportus laughed. He looked over at her and laughed even louder, the sound of his laughter drowning out the engines.

"What are you laughing about?"

"Poppa! We don't have to worry about Poppa."

"You didn't kill him. Tell me you didn't kill him!"

"It was not even an interesting struggle. He bellowed like a bull, as though he could pay for his life with his voice."

Now the bluffs of Almheraz were in sight; the Citadel looked like a block of white butter set atop a nest of ants. *Pilgrims*, Maud thought. *Come to see the Queen. Come to see.* . . . She felt flushed and confused, she wanted to kill him for what he'd done, and yet she knew that if she could never see him again she herself would die.

She cried softly as Sportus began to bring the Magister's flying machine down. She belonged to him, and there was nothing she or anybody else could do about it. The creature was outside Fate. No one in Almheraz could help her now.

Back at Queen's Island, the servants were in an uproar. The royal family was gone, and nobody knew where, or how they had left. It was as though everyone had come home to find thieves had broken in. There was outrage over what had happened, and frustration at not being able to guess who the thieves were, or when they had come.

Avra, the physician, eventually established control, dispatching Vestal guards to the docks to search the King's barque. She issued orders for parties to comb the forest, and telegraphed Almheraz to inform both the Sun Temple and the Vestals about what had happened.

When the telegraph failed to respond, Avra dispatched messengers in two separate boats. The guards, meanwhile, returned to report that the barque seemed deserted. One of the cabins was locked. The rest had been abandoned. There was food on the table in the mess, and half-cups of wine and water. The locked cabin presented a problem for the physician; she had no authority to order it opened by force, and so posted sentries around the barque in case anyone emerged.

In the meantime, in the midst of the confusion, no one noticed a speck high in the afternoon sky. It hung above the Island, moving in tiny circles as the naked Eye reached the horizon and sank into the mouth of the Tumulos.

Inside the locked cabin, the body of Cyre of Panault jerked as though someone had applied an electric current to it. Heels drummed the deck, and the great chest heaved once, twice, three times, until at last a long sigh came from the King's mouth.

Cyre sat up. He twisted his head from side to side. He held out his stubby arms and looked at his hands, opening and closing them stiffly. He coughed loudly and spat mucus onto the deck. Then, slowly, and with great effort, he got to his feet.

"So," he said in a pinched, squeaky voice. "So this is what it's like, you old shit."

He adjusted the voice to a more normal timbre. "You old shit." Cleared his throat, lowering it another notch. "You old shit. Who's got a . . ." Waiting, suddenly dizzy. "Who's got a cigarette?"

He pulled himself to his feet, walked to a chair, and sat down heavily.

"Shit," he repeated, breathing hard.

This was not going to be easy. He stood up, unlocked the door, and went up to the main deck of his boat.

THIRTY-FIVE

IT WAS LATE AFTERNOON, and the curved prow of the embalmer's boat cut against the current as it worked back toward Almheraz. There was little other traffic on the river. Tonight was Wedding Night, the first night of the Festival of the Sun. Even in normal times, people took their places early for a holy day; now, rumors of death had chilled the Realm, and everything seemed to have stopped. Everyone waited, listening for news of who would be Queen, thinking of death, and how it could come to anyone at any time.

Down in the hold of the embalmer's boat, Marten felt that chill. He watched the little man go about his work—he was packing natron around the body of the former Queen inside a curing box—and envied him. The embalmer never gave death a second thought. Death was his business.

On the marble table, the daughter of the Queen turned her head and sighed softly. Marten had been holding her hand; now he jumped up, took the cloth from her forehead, wrung it out in a basin of water and carefully refolded and put it back.

"Won't do any good," the embalmer said. He drove a spigot into the bottom of the curing box to drain off the fluids the salt would draw out.

"What do you know about it?" Marten snapped, annoyed at the embalmer's certainty. "You're not a physician. You've never cured anybody."

"Oh, but I have!" The embalmer chuckled at his joke. "And my patients always recover—or at least they will, when the Lord returns to the world." He looked over at Careev. "Besides, I can tell a few things from the way she's breathing. If it was just being choked, she'd be awake by now. No. I'd be willing to bet, if I could get a look at that wire she was strangled with, that it was poisoned, too. She'll get no better, if it's true."

"If you know it's poison . . ."

"Why don't I do something? Like you said, traveler: I'm not a physician. I reckon I'll be working on her soon enough! Might be before we get back. Oof! Would you mind helping me with this top?"

Marten grabbed an end of the weighted board that nested inside the curing box and pressed down on the body inside. He felt sick and helpless because someone else he felt drawn to, in love with even after knowing her so short a time, was being taken from him. It was too much, Marten thought, looking at the cruel red line cutting across the smooth skin of her throat. *Just too much. . . .*

The embalmer wiped his hands with a rag. "She should have gutted the schell, like she was supposed to. It was too presumptuous. Goddess didn't like it, I'm sure—"

He stopped as the seer came down into the hold. The sunglasses were askew on the creature's face, and blood and dirt were streaked across the front of its cloak. The embalmer made a choking sound and grabbed a curved knife from his tool rack.

"I told you I wouldn't have that thing aboard my boat!"

"I didn't see it come aboard. It disappeared after we brought the Princess down here."

"I don't care! Get if off now!" He was hopping up and down. The effect of such agitation on his wizened little body would have been humorous in other circumstances. As it was, Marten put himself between them.

"I already told you, I can't control what it does."

"Then I'll control it. Out of my way, traveler!"

Marten could see that the embalmer was good with a knife. Then again, the people he practiced on never moved. Marten stepped in quickly, catching the little man's wrist, pulling it down sharply across his knees. He had to do it again before the embalmer let go, but when he did Marten twisted the embalmer's arm behind his back and pinned him.

"You can believe what you want, but I've seen enough of that thing to know it doesn't mean to harm anyone. In fact, it's loyal to the Lady there. I don't know why, but it wants to protect her, and if it wants to be down here with her, then we'll let it stand here quietly and do what it wants to do. You got that, embalmer?"

"Y-yes!"

"Good." Marten let him go and picked up the knife, watching as the seer put its hands on Careev's neck and whimpered softly. Its tongue came out. The tufts were yellow, the color of mourning.

She dreamed of the embalmer standing over her with his knife, ready to make the incision that would release the sins of her body and then pack the cavity with salt. She didn't have that many sins of the body yet, and that salt would burn like passion. Better than passion. Salt would make it last.

She heard bells. Prayer-bells, from the bottom of the well of the house in Queen's Island. Bells missing. Bells sounding for her. She wanted to fix them, felt herself getting up from her bed. When she put her foot on the floor, however, it was hot; she drew back and watched the floor bulge, and finally burst with lava the color of pomegranate jelly. . . . She looked back at the embalmer to tell him, but his face had changed. It was thick, bearded. It was the face of her father the King.

"They're boiling that damn tea in here," he said. "That chouris tea your mother always liked to drink."

"It's not very good, is it." Careev said.

"It's god damned awful." The King smiled. "Well. After all this, we finally agree on something."

She felt tears welling in her eyes, and he saw them and shook his head. "That's not the way. You wanted me to love you and it didn't work out. Crying won't change that. It just didn't work out. Doesn't mean there was anything wrong with you. You were a sweet kid, in fact. Smart. Good with people. And you're starting to find out how strong you are, too. That's good. Makes me proud now, but that doesn't mean there's a law that says parents have to love all their kids equally or as well. God, I wish I could smoke."

"Don't you have any cigarettes?"

"They don't let you smoke here."

Careev smiled.

"That's better. You're my daughter. You've got things to do. It's not time for you to go out yet, no matter how much it hurts to stay. You can't run from it."

"And what about you?"

The King shook his head sadly. "I tried to do too much at once. Wanted to change the whole world and do it alone, so it would get done right. I'm not sure what they think is worse. . . . But don't make the same mistake I did. Don't try to do everything alone. You've got someone here who wants to help you. And you've got me. For a while, at least. Here." He held out his hand. "It doesn't change what happened between us, but it's a start. Let me help you, daughter. Let me help . . ."

She felt his hand, but mist gathered around him, and he changed. The face of the King became a flower with a red stem and tufted yellow stamens.

Above the slab, the seer tilted its head back and screamed.

"By Adon's Holy Eye," the embalmer wailed, "it'll kill us all!" He lunged for the tool rack again, but Marten snatched him by the collar.

"Look at that," he whispered. The seer's scream faded; it trembled as it held on to the Princess, then, as Marten and the embalmer watched, a red line appeared on its neck, very faint at first, but then turning angry and vivid. It let go of Careev and sat down hard on the floor.

Careev groaned and tried to get up.

"Lady! Wait! Don't move—" Marten rushed to her side,

gently pushing her back against her pillows. The mark on her neck was gone.

"Marten?"

"Yes, Lady."

"You shouldn't be. . . . I mean, I was walking through the . . ." She looked around. "This is the embalmer's boat!"

"That's right, Lady," the embalmer said. "And it's time somebody informed him of that fact!"

"But I. . . ." She felt her neck. "Someone tried to kill me. Your schell!"

"It's all right," Marten said, squeezing her hand. "We're off the Island, on our way back to Almheraz."

"My father's dead."

"Shhh. Lie down and rest."

"No, no, he's dead. I saw him! He told me. . . ." Her eyes grew wide. "Where's Maud?"

"That I can't say, Lady."

"*I* can," the embalmer put in. "One of my apprentices said he saw her leave the Island with the High Priest, in that machine of his. The one that flies."

"Why would they leave?"

"I don't know, Lady."

"We've got to get back. How much longer?"

"Another hour, maybe," the embalmer said.

"See if you can go any faster!"

"This is an embalmer's boat, Lady. They didn't have speed in mind when they built her!"

"I'll see what I can coax out of her, Lady," Marten said. "In the meantime, try to lie easy. You're safe here. We'll get to where it's not so safe soon enough!"

Up on the Citadel, the crowd in the Red Courtyard was beginning to thin out. The palace had been closed at noon when Gormayne's blue and gold banners were lowered to half-staff above the portico, and Cyre's gold and red colors stripped. Since the Festival would open at dusk down in the Grove, most pilgrims took advantage of the early closing to go there and settle in choice spots close to the altar where the Queen—whoever was Queen now—would become the Bride of Adon, and set the stage for the tragedy of his Death a few days later at the height of the Feast.

Flying Eccle's machine, Sportus circled the Rock, banking so that he could look at the crowd streaming down the steps into the gorge. He had not spoken for a long time, and Maud saw then that his expression had gone vacant. *It costs him something to maintain his will,* she thought, just as it cost him something to transform himself. Perhaps the power he had over her was the same way.

She stared at him as he turned the flyer and tried to hate him. He was a rogue schell, nothing more! But his face was so beautiful! There was something hard and direct and elemental about those black eyes and strong jaw. He was pure. And he was alone.

I want to transform him, she thought. *I want to make him into something I can control. . . .*

They swept over the grove, almost brushing the treetops, and Sportus's face came to life again. When it did, Maud felt a rush of elation, almost as strong as the fear she felt seeing the branches reaching for the machine.

"Look at them," he said. "So many, and they all add up to nothing. No wonder the Gods hate you so!"

He brought the flyer up and around, climbing over the wall and pulling back on the stick until the craft settled gently on the rear terrace of the palace.

"We're going to take them tonight," Sportus said, as the sound of the engines died down. "Tonight will be the beginning of a new age. The Gods won't hide behind the Veil anymore. They'll be right here, within easy reach!"

He kissed her, and Maud knew all her resolutions meant nothing. She wanted him now, and moaned, asking for it, reaching down to feel the heat between his legs. But his body felt cold. Maud opened her eyes, and saw that she had been kissing the Magister.

"*Damn you*—" She swung at him, but he put up his hand and fended her off as though she were nothing but a child.

"It's when I want it," he said in Eccle's voice. "My *Lady*. Right now, we've got things to do. The palace and the Temple are in an uproar, I'm certain. You must get ready for the ceremony. I've got to assure my Templemen that all is well. I'll call for you when I'm finished.''

"But we have guests here. What do I tell them if they ask about Careev?"

"Tell them anything you like.'' Sportus smiled. "You are Queen of Almheraz now!''

The body of the King of Almheraz moved slowly along the boardwalk between the golden barque and a dock guarded by a squad of Vestals. There was a speedboat tied to the end of that slip that could reach the capital in an hour and a half, and the soul that was directing this body intended to take it.

Every step was torture. Sheeme's ordeal in the Preserve had weakened the resources of her soul, considerable as they had been. The King was also not in the best shape. Years of smoking had taken its toll. His death at the hands of Sportus the evening before this had not helped either. Her soul was animating the body, and could take no nourishment from it at all. It would only be a matter of time, she reckoned, before her energy was exhausted completely.

She intended to stop Sportus before it was.

Moving his legs, keeping his body straight, he approached the Vestals at the dock. The body was not breathing, and she had to inflate its chest to have the air to speak.

"I'll have that boat,'' she said, realizing that his voice did not sound at all imposing from inside. *Maybe he never knew how he sounded*, she thought. That was a sad thought.

The woman looked her up and down, pure insolence in her eyes.

"You'll have nothing,'' she said. "You're just a man. Get the hell out of here.''

"I'll have that boat,'' Sheeme repeated, wondering how far they would go with her. Only his physical size, she thought, and the fact that he might have a weapon with him, would make them cautious.

"Why don't you swim?'' the Vestal shot back. Sheeme felt a moment of panic. If this body went into the water, she did not think she would be able to save it—nor did she have strength left to transfer her soul to someone else. Moving like an automaton, she backed the body away. Then, from the corner of her eye she noticed Fantil circling the forest above. She filled the lungs again, pursed the lips, and with the last of her strength, managed to give three sharp whistles.

The great hawk, her yellow feathers gleaming in the last of the day's light, looped around and dove down toward them at terrific speed, casting a shadow on the speedboat that grew bigger and bigger until she spread her wings and tail—the sound of it was like a door opening out into a winter storm— slowed, and lighted on the King's shoulder. The weight of her almost knocked the body off the dock, but Sheeme managed to steady it.

The Vestal stared at the hawk, open-mouthed and completely astonished.

"You call hawks," she stammered.

"Better than that. They *come* when I call."

She made the King's body reach up to stroke Fantil's ruff of soft neck feathers, then whisper: "You know me. I need your help, if you'll give it."

Fantil shrieked.

"You've got to feed me, the way you feed your young. I am like a child to you now. You know me. Feed me, the way you fed Yundai!"

Fantil shifted on the King's shoulder. Sheeme felt her tense, and heard the whip of the stinger now behind his back. Suddenly, the hawk spread her wings, lifting into the air to circle over the river, rising with a keening call that sent shivers even through the dead spine of the King. Then, at the apex of her flight, she tucked them in close, shot down, and hit the Vestal in the back. She grunted loudly, wind knocked out of her. Before she could move, Fantil drove her stinger deep into her side; sensing the urgency Sheeme felt, the hawk did not wait, or hood her prey. She drilled into the Vestal's skull, put her tongue in, and drew out the woman's soul.

Sheeme made the King kneel. "Here," she said weakly. "Please."

Fantil turned, walked off the Vestal's back and over to the King. There she hesitated just long enough for Sheeme to feel a moment of panic. Then she lifted her head, put her bill against the King's lips, and thrust her tongue inside.

The feeding did not take long. When it was over, Sheeme

felt the King's heart beating. He stood, cradled the exhausted hawk in his arms, and put it gently into the boat. It would take her some hours to recover, and another five or six to regenerate her venom. She would use it then to feed herself; Sheeme had to hope that she would not need the hawk to help subdue Sportus.

The King of Almheraz cast off the lines, started the steam motor and sped away, the boat throwing a rooster tail of white water behind it.

Vestal attendants worked on Maud as if they were draping a statue. They strapped her into pads that were stiffened with whalebones, and fit a mask onto her shoulders that was suspended a fraction of an inch from her skull by strong silk webbing. The appliances made her look like a giantess. They were also insufferably hot, and Maud finally had to halt her dressers in order to step outside the costume for some air.

They had been working frantically, she realized, because of how uncertain they were. And Maud had seen them obey her orders instantly. People were more likely to obey orders when they were confused or afraid. That would be a good thing to remember, when she was Queen.

When she was Queen. She looked out over the city and felt a little sick. Crowds of pilgrims still walked up the Citadel road, and across the courtyard to the stairs down to the Grove, their feet stirring up a dust that rose in a haze over the city, and over a river that looked flat and lifeless as the blade of an old iron sword. Where had Careev gone? she wondered. She thought about what her sister would do, and tried to suppress the doubts she had that Sportus might not be telling the truth. Truth meant nothing to him, no more than the life of a young Princess.

The Realm deserves better, she thought, but there was nothing she could do about that now. . . .

She looked at the mask she would wear for the ceremony. It was white enamel over beaten copper, with huge, fig-shaped eyes outlined with red and black lines drawn to points at the corners. The grim mouth was also done in the same colors. Maud did not care much for that mask. Once, when she was five or six, the King got drunk and put it on,

sneaking into the playroom where she and Careev had just
finished a wall they had spent all morning building out of
blocks. Cyre had been wearing the mask when he'd burst into
the playroom with a great, blood-curdling scream, waggling
his tongue through the mouth hole and bulling into the wall,
thrashing his thick legs around until not a block was left
standing.

Careev had cried for two hours, and Nana had finally given
her a drink of some paregoric and rocked her until she fell
asleep. Maud blamed Careev for the whole thing, somehow—
maybe it was the crying that had got to her, or maybe it was
because then she thought Poppa could do no wrong. Thinking
about it now, looking at the mask, she began to feel sorry for
her sister, for how their father had always treated her.

One of her dressers came out to the terrace. "Excuse me,
Lady," she said, "but Matron Rarei is here." Rarei, in the
guise of Rho, was to officiate at the marriage ceremony. She
walked in with her crutch, looking pale and almost too tired
to move in her heavy dark robes.

"So it's to be you," she began.

"That's right."

"What about your sister?"

Maud whirled to face her. "Haven't you heard? She's run
away!"

"Then the ceremony's got to be cancelled."

"Why?"

"Because the Queen is dead. And her daughter is missing.
Possibly murdered."

"Oh, really! And since when has the Order been worried
about murder?"

"This is a solemn occasion, Lady Maud. We risk disaster
by profaning it any further."

"Don't tell me what's profane. Oh, I know all about you!
You killed my brother. Didn't you!" When Rarei said nothing, Maud shook her head. "You'll go on all right. The
Sun-God and the Bright Goddess are getting married tonight
before the people of Almheraz, and there's not a damn thing
you can do about it. I'm Queen now, Matron. You either do
your duty, or I'll see every last piece of property you own

burned and plowed under and salted so that nothing will ever grow on it again!!''

"The High Priest is ready, Lady," one of the Vestals said.

"Thank you. Are *you* ready, Matron?"

Rarei said nothing.

"Yes, or no?"

Reluctantly, the Matron nodded her head.

"Good. Then we'll ride down together."

THIRTY-SIX

IN ALL HIS LIVES, Komaso could never remember seeing so many people in Adon's Grove before. The entire length of the canyon was filled, as were the hillsides; pilgrims hung from trees, or perched precariously on rocks. They stood in the streams, pressed together, sat on shoulders for a better look at the flower-bedecked altar stand, lighted by torches set around it, and by the beams of searchlamps trained from the northern wall of the palace, and from the roofs of both temples.

The crowd was an organism. It was galvanized by shared impulses jumping from soul to soul, impulses that short-circuited the faculties that normally allowed each individual in the crowd to survive alone. The organism was an anxious one. It arched and writhed its body and cried out hungrily for nourishment, for the thing that justified its existence and gave it life.

Komaso, having taken refuge in the crowd, nevertheless resisted the impulse to join it. He had used it to escape his

Vestal pursuers in the Red Courtyard; now he observed it, half fascinated, half horrified.

He was very hungry. He had not eaten since the night at Tove's villa, and he stared at an enterprising vendor near him who was selling skewers of fish and griddlecakes from a stand along the avenue that twin ranks of Vestals and Bachelors had somehow managed to keep clear in the middle of the throng. He had no money, of course, and at first he tried not to think about it. Finally the smell of grilling fish was too much. He looked around, saw a woman holding a bag on her shoulder. The clasp of her bag was open. Komaso moved close to her, and his hand slipping into the purse was like smoke curling into a chimney. When it came out, there were coins in it.

Komaso pushed through the crowd and bought his food. He wrapped the fish with the griddlecake, pulled the skewer out, and started to eat. After a while, he realized that people were watching him; confused, he looked down and saw that he had absently been doing finger rolls with the coin he had left. In and out, between and around, just the way the old man had taught him!

What's he doing now? Komaso thought, missing him, and feeling surprised. He held out his hand in a plane flat to the ground and worked the coin until trumpets sounded and the Vestals holding the corridor open pressed back against the crowd.

Acolytes appeared holding candles; these were followed by Vestal Virgins who tended Psyche's House, and were allowed outside once on the Wedding Night to act as bridesmaids to the Bright Goddess. Tossing flower petals from wicker baskets, they led Bachelor bearers who carried Magister Eccles on a litter. The Magister looked very dour, and blessed the crowd impatiently. Finally, preceded by trumpeters, came the Queen. Komaso's heart beat faster, and he considered throwing himself at her feet and begging for her protection.

But he did not. In spite of the fact that she was wearing a bulky gown and a huge mask, there was something wrong about the way she moved. He was puzzled a moment until he realized that it was not Careev inside the costume, but her sister, Maud. The crowd was too dull to notice the difference.

It roared to her as she climbed the steps to the marriage altar. And when she turned and raised her arms to acknowledge it, it curled back on itself like a slug under a stream of salt.

From the back of the stage came Matron Rarei, wearing a dark mask and moving slowly with her crutch. Magister Eccles climbed down from his litter and stood in front of the altar. He was radiant in his white gown; when he raised his arms, the crowd fell silent.

Faintly, Komaso heard the sound of a horn all the way from the river. *Something is terribly wrong,* he thought. People were hardly moving. He felt the paralysis himself, but fought it, and perhaps because he was not part of the crowd, he was able to move through it, closer to the altar to where he could see better. When he did, he realized the Magister had changed. He was shorter, and more heavily built, and there was something frightening in the eyes behind the mask he wore.

It was almost dark now. Lightning flashed from the northeast. As Komaso watched, Adon said something to Rho, pointing to a spot in front of the altar. Rarei moved there, turned, and began to speak:

> Children!
> I did not want you.
> I was surprised as I lay in beautiful
> Sleep and found I had a womb.
> You were stolen from me.
> I would devour you if I could,
> For I want to sleep.
>
> But you live
> You are part of me;
> You cannot survive alone, and
> I cannot see you fall and die.
>
> Therefore you must have each
> other.
> Swallow each other whole if
> you must.
> Having one, ever wanting another

He is the key to eternal life
She is the gate to darkness and rest
She is the portal to a cold and amber Sun.

Your heart beats only because another
longs to hear it beating
Heed that sound!
I will not heed it.
I have no heart.
I only want to Sleep.

Adon stepped forward. He spoke in a voice that seemed soft, yet filled the gorge and echoed off the heights. "I come before you now and I will take my bride," he said. "But before I do, you will know me for what I am."

He took off his mask and the crowd saw that it was not the High Priest of the Sun.

"I am Sportus," he shouted. "And henceforth it is I who rule in Almheraz!"

The crowd began to cheer. Komaso turned to the man next to him and shook him. "What's the matter with you? What are you yelling for?" But the man could see only what was on the stage. This was sorcery, Komaso thought, pushing closer as Sportus yanked the mask off Maud and draped her over the altar. *He's going to have her there*, Komaso thought, dreading what would happen. Thunder clapped again, more loudly, and jagged streaks of lightning split the air over the Rock. The crowd began to move forward, as if it wanted to have the Princess too, through Sportus. And then—

A girl, and an old man, and someone tall in glasses and a cowl ran up the stairs to the altar.

"Hear me!" the girl yelled, waving her arms. *Princess Careev!* Komaso was fighting his way closer now, as Careev yelled again.

"This is no man! This is a schell, a rogue schell who has nothing in his heart for you but hatred! He has killed my mother, and my father, and the High Priest, and he tried to kill me as well! Listen to me! You must not accept this schell—"

Sportus pushed her down. The bearded man who had come

with her tried to hit him, but the schell simply slapped him off the platform with the back of his hand. He landed almost at Komaso's feet. When he looked up, their eyes met.

"*Boy!* By God, it's you!"

"Show her what you think of her mother—" Sportus shouted.

A huge roar of derision.

"—and her father—"

Another roar.

"—and her precious priest! Wife, stand up here!" Sportus took Maud's hand and yanked her from the altar. "If you are to be my Queen, you must act like one. And here—" he pushed at Careev with his foot "—here lies the one obstacle to your rule with me. This is a holy night, and requires a sacrifice." He drew a dagger from a leg sheath. "Take this. Take this, my love, and kill her."

As the crowd screamed its approval, somehow Marten and Komaso managed to climb the stairs together. Sportus saw them and snarled. Komaso pulled his knife, but the schell knocked it out of his hand.

"This is very touching. The whole royal family here together. Well, my Queen, it seems you've got more work to do. What do we do?" His voice rose. "Do we kill them all?"

A chant rose: "*Kill them, kill them,*" and the crowd moved in time to it, shaking the walls of the palace itself with the force of its voice. Schells came from the sides of the platform and dragged Komaso and Marten back into the crowd, while Sportus pushed Careev toward the altar. She tried to struggle, but didn't have the strength. It broke Komaso's heart to see the tears in her eyes.

She's giving up, he thought, realizing now how much he wanted her not to give up.

Then King Cyre pulled himself up on the stage.

Sportus turned, and his dark face went pale. The King and the schell stared at each other.

"I killed you!" Sportus snarled. "This can't be!"

"Believe your eyes, Sportus."

"You're not Cyre." Sportus smiled mockingly. "Cyre's *body*. But not Cyre. . . ." He stepped up to the King, pushed him with one hand. Cyre's body staggered back, and almost fell from the dais. "Not Cyre at all. I wonder who it is then?" The schell's hands closed around Cyre's throat. "My old mistress perhaps. Is that who it is?"

Cyre's body dropped to his knees. His eyelids fluttered. *He doesn't have any strength,* Komaso realized. Then, suddenly, a cry pierced the heavy silence in the grove, a yellow ball of fury hurtled from above, exploding on Sportus' shoulder in a swirl of feathers. *A hawk!* Komaso realized. The great bird's stinger lashed out, plunging again and again into the small of the schell's back. *Yes,* Komaso thought, remembering how Fantil's sting had felt. But something was wrong, the venom wasn't working. Sportus smiled. He reached back, closing his fist around the bird's head. Fantil shrieked and beat her wings on Sportus' back; the King struggled to his knees and tried to pull the hawk away, but Sportus hurled him aside as easily as a child. Cyre's body hit the front of the altar, and was still.

"*Father*—" Komaso tried to move forward but the crowd had closed in. He stared at the King, and heard himself screaming his father's name again and again. Cyre *was* his father, and now his father was dead, killed by this imposter on the altar, the dark-haired man profaning the memory of Adon. *Goddess,* Komaso prayed, *take your vengeance. Take it now!*

And then the seer came. Calmly, it walked across the dais, reached out and took the schell by the wrist. Sportus looked back as the seer's fingers closed tighter and tighter; he grit his teeth, and then screamed, the cords in his neck standing out, until gradually, his grip on the hawk's head loosened. The bird rose above the altar, shrieking and circling to the left. The seer seemed to watch it for a moment before lifting its arm, forcing Sportus to his feet, holding him up, holding both their arms out to the darkening sky. Komaso saw the seer's yellow tongue flicking out to touch the side of Sportus' contorted face. Later, he would remember seeing, for the briefest instant, a ball of brilliant blue light enclose the heads of both seer and schell. For now, he was blinded by a tremendous fire-bolt that fell like a shaft of white-hot steel from the heavens, followed by thunder that seemed powerful enough to shatter the world.

His ears rang painfully. Then he blinked his eyes, vision

returning. The seer and the schell had vanished, leaving Careev, Maud and the Matron Rarei—her dark mask gone now—alone on the dais. Slowly, Careev got to her feet. Komaso realized then that someone was clinging to his arm. He looked and saw Marten.

"I found you, boy!" he said. "Took some time, but I found you."

The crowd began to recover. Stunned silence gave way to cries: "Give us a sign! and "Where is the Queen?" Maud sat up on the altar and looked around. Careev looked back at her sister, nodded, and stepped forward.

"People of Almheraz," she cried. "Your Queen is here!"

THIRTY-SEVEN

CAREEV LOOKED OUT over the city of Almheraz from the terrace outside the Queen's apartments. There were few bonfires burning this night; the mood of the city, like the mood in the palace, was subdued. Maud sat at the round table under the arbor and smoked a cigarette. Behind her, Komaso and Marten sat together on a bench. Rarei stood next to them, leaning on her crutch.

"Sportus killed Aunt Sheeme," Maud was saying. "He called her anima out and trapped it."

"Why?" Careev's questions had been cold, direct and quick.

"Because she was the only one left who could control him. Strong as he was, she was always a threat to him, and when he realized that he wanted power for himself, he waited for the right opportunity, and took her soul. She was getting old. She never expected he could turn on her."

"Did you help him?"

Maud blew smoke. "I don't know. I suppose I did. She

. . . gave him something, some kind of spell. . . . When I
was around him, I just. . . ."

"Just what? Forgot your family? Forgot your duty?"

Maud said miserably, "I don't know!"

"Did you know he wanted to kill me? Or that he killed
Poppa? Or the Magister? Or the Queen? Answer me!"

Marten stepped between them. "Lady," he said gently to
Careev. "I don't think the Princess meant you any harm."

"What do you know about it, old man," Maud snapped.
"Who is he, anyway? What's he doing here?"

"His name is Marten, and I owe my life to him," Careev
said. "As does our brother."

"We don't have a brother."

"Yes, you do," Komaso said. Rarei's expression looked
pained for a moment, but she said nothing.

"I should have you gutted," Careev said to Maud. "That's
how they did things in the old days. Isn't that what you said
to me?"

"Do what you like."

"Damn you, Maud! Don't you understand anything? Don't
you realize how much I love you? I need you, Maud. We're
being forced to change things. We have our family together.
Stop fighting it. I've stopped. So has Komaso. Just let go.
Please. Please. . . ."

Maud looked up. There were tears in her eyes. "But I've
let you down. I'm no good to you—"

"You have Poppa in you. We need that. We need you."

Maud began to cry. Careev went to her and held her.

Marten watched a moment, and said, "Well, that leaves
me. I've got my goods up in Semele. It's time I got back on
the road."

"No," Careev said. "I want you to stay."

"Lady, I'm a traveler. Life with the gentry's not for me."

"Or me, either," Komaso said.

"What are you talking about, boy? Your place's here, with
your sisters. You've got your duty, same as me. No, I've got
a wolf up there waiting for me."

"Bring him here. Please, Marten. Just for a little while,
until Mother and Poppa are interred, and we get our feet
under us again." She blushed. "Sorry, Matron."

Rarei lifted her crutch. "No offense taken, Lady."

"If I come, I'll come by road, the way a traveler should."

"And I'll go with you." Komaso said.

Marten shook his head.

"You know that's what you want, old man. Now who's fighting Fate?"

Marten smiled, and said nothing.

"Very well," Careev said. "You can go—but with an escort. Rarei, will you arrange it?"

"Yes, Lady."

"Good." Careev brushed her sister's hair, and turned to the city again. "We have something new," she said. "Something our mothers and fathers never had."

"What's that?" Marten asked.

"Heaven's let us go. We've got a future."

"Well, then, let's make the most of it. Come on, boy, let's get ready!"

Rarei said, "Come with me and I'll arrange some transport."

They went out, and Careev and Maud were alone. Firstborn and lastborn daughters of the King and Queen. Maud took out a cigarette, offered one to Careev.

Careev looked at it a moment, then shrugged, put it in her mouth, and let her sister light it for her.

Book Four of the Apprentice Adept Series
by
New York Times Bestselling Author

PIERS ANTHONY

OUT OF PHAZE

*Welcome to the astonishing parallel
worlds of Phaze and Proton. Where magic
and science maintain an uneasy truce. Where an
accidental mind-switch plunges an apprentice
wizard from Phaze into the mind-boggling
technology of Proton. And where a robot named
Mach is, in turn, swept away to a world
of bizarre and terrifying wonders:
the dazzling world of Phaze...*

___ OUT OF PHAZE   0-441-64465-1/$3.95

MORE SCIENCE FICTION ADVENTURE!